I0572827

Blue Waters

Paige Marie

Copyright © Paige Marie 2025

No part of this publication may be reproduced, distributed or transmitted in any form or by any means without the permission of the publisher, except as permitted by U.S. copyright law.

This is a work of fiction. The story, names, characters, and events portrayed are fictitious. No identification with actual persons (living or dead), places, and products is intended.

Book Cover by Lena Yang

979-8-9994440-0-4

Author's note

See the back of the book for a content warning.

One

Izzy
My dog is trying to kill me.

It makes no sense. I'm Jason's provider. He needs me. How will he get head scratches or overpriced bacon treats without me? Shouldn't something in his DNA warn him not to plot against the very person he depends upon for survival?

Self-preservation has apparently taken a backseat in Jason's furry little head. At least that's how it appears as I study the shreds of pale blue fabric scattered about the living room. While I was getting ready for work, Jason took it upon himself to turn my older sister's expensive throw pillows into chew toys. Tufts of cotton litter the carpet, the remnants of his misdeed. The culprit himself is curled up on the couch, yawning lazily. He seems unconcerned, despite having signed and delivered my death notice.

"Goddamn fucking shit." Curses fly off my tongue in rapid succession. Churchgoers would clutch their pearls and pray for my salvation if they could hear me. I probably could use their prayers, seeing as I'm about to die.

Goodbye, world. It was nice knowing you.

It might be over for me, but that doesn't mean I'm going down without a fight. Quickly, I drop to my knees and begin scooping up slobbery bits of fabric. *It's not that bad*, I tell myself. But who am I kidding? Delia's pillows are unsalvageable. They look like they went through a woodchipper. She's going to freak out when she sees this.

Especially since it's not the first time Jason has taken liberties with her belongings.

Last week, he ate a pair of Delia's socks. And the week before that, he tore up her day planner. I don't know how Delia is going to react to my dog's latest rampage, but I have a feeling it's going to end with my head on a spike.

It took months to convince Delia to let me adopt a dog. My sister is not an animal person. She laughed the first time I brought up the idea.

"As long as it's not staying here," she said, assuming I was only joking.

To be fair, I've been living rent-free at Delia's place for six months. She had every right to say no. But that didn't stop me from begging. And I can be quite persistent. Eventually, Delia relented…with the caveat that my dog couldn't become a nuisance. It seemed like a simple request, but I underestimated Jason, my little troublemaker.

The people at the animal shelter warned me he was a handful. As someone who's been called a handful plenty of times in her life, the comment struck a chord in me. *I guess we can be handfuls together*, I thought as I patted the sweet-looking black lab on the head. I figured we could be teammates. Partners in crime. Jason, however, had other ideas. In the two months since I adopted him, he seems to have made it his life's mission to make me break my promise to Delia.

I glare at the couch. "If you're trying to get us thrown out, you're doing an excellent job," I mutter. I tell myself not to give him any bacon treats tonight, but it's an empty promise, and I know it. I'm a terrible, enabling dog owner. When Jason hits me with those big dark eyes, I crumble faster than a sandcastle.

Still, I'm mad at him. I didn't need this today. It's only seven-thirty, and I'm already having a rough morning. I slept through my alarm, so I had to get dressed in a rush. I threw on the first clothing items I could find: a pink sweater dress with a grease stain on the left boob and a pair of yellow tights. Initially, I thought the outfit was fun and colorful, but I'm starting to feel like a bottle of Pepto Bismol. It's too late to do anything about it, though. I guess there are worse things than looking like nausea medication.

My lateness also meant I didn't have time to style my hair, which wouldn't be an issue if I hadn't made the regrettable decision to cut bangs last summer. In my defense, I was going through a personal crisis. And I firmly believe there should be laws that prohibit hairdressers from giving ill-advised haircuts to people who are clearly not in their right mind.

I'm rocking a serious case of bed head, so I hope we don't have any important clients coming into the office. The last thing I want them wondering is who is the disheveled woman at the reception desk sporting last night's hair?

As I grab another piece of wet fabric off the floor, I hear the telltale click of the front door being unlocked. Delia's home. *Shit.* With no time to waste, I shove the remains of her throw pillows under the couch.

I pull myself off the floor just as she waltzes into the kitchen. She's dressed in workout clothes, and her dark hair is pulled back in a sleek ponytail. She must be getting back from her morning run.

That's right. My sister runs. For fun.

I hate her sometimes, too.

Delia is two years older than me and about a million times more put together. She's the human equivalent of a day planner. Sleek. Precise. Organized. Growing up in her shadow wasn't easy. While Delia was earning perfect grades and charming her teachers, I was constantly being called to the principal's office for talking during class.

It was impossible not to compare myself to her when I was younger. I still do sometimes. We might not be kids anymore, but our dynamic hasn't changed. Delia has a thriving career in marketing and a boyfriend who adores her. Me? I was fired from my graphic design job earlier this year. And my last relationship ended in a dumpster fire.

Delia's life is flourishing in all the ways mine is not, but I don't resent her for it. If anyone deserves happiness, it's Delia. She's always looking out for me. Any time I need her help, she's there with a to-do list in hand. Though it's highly likely she won't be so generous once she realizes my dog brutalized her pillows.

"Hey, Iz," Delia says as she grabs a glass from the cabinet, filling it with water from the fridge dispenser. She frowns when she notices Jason sprawled on the couch. "What did I tell you about him being on the furniture?"

"That he's welcome to it because he's such a good boy?"

Delia frowns. "That I'll find him a new home if his owner can't remember a few basic rules." She doesn't seem amused.

I snap my fingers, signaling Jason to get down from the couch. He looks somewhat annoyed as he jumps onto the carpet. "I'm sorry, boy," I say, giving him a gentle pat on the head. Jason may be part demon, but I love him anyway. Delia does too, though she pretends otherwise. "The mean lady says you can't be on the furniture."

Delia scowls over the rim of her water glass. "The mean lady *was* going to take him for a walk during her lunch break, but maybe she'll do laundry instead."

"Did I say mean lady? Because I meant to say nice, generous lady." I flash a smile at Delia as I make my way into the kitchen, Jason following at my heels.

Delia appears unimpressed by my antics. "I talked to Mom last night," she says.

"So that's what all that screaming was about," I say as I sidle up to the counter. "And here I thought you were testing an at-home waxing kit."

Delia rolls her eyes. "She told me you haven't been answering her calls. She wanted me to ask you to call her back."

I snag my ceramic travel mug off the counter, then head over to the coffeepot. "I didn't know you were moonlighting as a carrier pigeon," I reply as I fill my mug to the brim. The scent of fresh coffee floods my nostrils. "Can you do me a favor and ask Morgan what she wants for Christmas? I have no good ideas. I'm this close to getting her tube socks."

"She probably wouldn't mind that." Ugh. It's true. Our younger sister, Morgan, is a ball of sunshine. She can make the most out of any bad situation. Not only would she find a use for a crappy gift like tube socks—she'd also be grateful for it.

"So, what's your deal with Mom?" Delia asks. "Did you two get into a fight?"

Taking a sip of coffee, I shake my head. Getting into my issues with Mom is the last thing I want to do right now. It's not even eight o'clock yet, and my hands smell like dog slobber. I'm just trying to make it out the door in one piece.

Delia arches a brow. "She said she called you three times last week. If you aren't mad at her, then why haven't you been picking up?"

"I have a very active social life, Delia."

"When I asked if you were free last Friday night, you asked if I was kidding."

I'll admit, I haven't had the most exciting social calendar since I moved to Seaview. The small town on the coast of Massachusetts offers plenty of charm, but all my friends are back in New York City. Aside from Delia and her boyfriend, I don't know many people here. My social life consists of binge-watching TV shows and taking walks with Jason.

Delia folds her forearms against her chest. "Look," she says in a serious tone, "I'm not trying to tell you what to do, but Mom is getting worried. She asks how you're doing every time we're on the phone. I always say you're doing great, but you not returning her calls is giving her other ideas. She thinks something's wrong, Iz."

"I'm gonna call her," I insist.

"Well, can you do it sooner rather than later?" Delia asks. "She's gonna be here on Christmas Eve. I don't want things to be awkward." That's right. Delia is hosting a Christmas Eve party. It's her first holiday gathering since she and Tanner got together. His mom is coming, too.

I know Delia wants it to be perfect. She's been stressing over the party for weeks. We spent almost forty minutes at the grocery store the other day while she debated between homemade or store-bought eggnog.

I'm not going to screw up Delia's party. It means too much to her. If me talking to Mom beforehand will help settle the waters, then so be it. Truthfully, I've put Mom off for long enough. I usually get back to her within a couple of days.

"I'll do it tonight," I assure her. "Now, can we focus on the more pressing issue here? Morgan's present. What did you get her?" Unlike me, Delia has had her Christmas shopping done for weeks.

"I'm not telling you."

"Why not?" I gasp, pretending to be offended.

"Because I'm not letting you steal my idea. It took me weeks to come up with it."

"I wouldn't steal it, per se. I'd use it for inspiration."

"Well, find your inspiration elsewhere. You're not getting any from me."

"Fine," I reply. "But when our family is torn apart because Morgan hates me for getting her a terrible present, you'll be the one to blame."

Delia appears to be on the verge of a sarcastic response, but then her gaze shifts over my shoulder. It takes me a second to realize she's looking at the living room. Confusion mars her features. "Izzy, where are my throw pillows?" she asks.

Oh, shit. She noticed.

The blood drains from my face immediately. What should I do? Feign ignorance? Delia can't prove anything without a confession, right?

I blink at her. "What throw pillows?"

"The ones that were on the couch before I left for my run."

"Huh. I don't seem to remember those."

Her eyes narrow into slits. If looks could kill, I would be a pile of ashes. "Izzy, what did you do with them?" Her tone is sharp, unforgiving. I don't know whether I ought to keep denying it or beg for mercy.

Luckily, I'm bailed out by the crunch of tires in the driveway.

"Do you hear that?" I ask, tilting my head. Before Delia can reply, I scamper over to the front windows. A truck pulling up the driveway, headlights slashing through the dark morning sky. *Thank you, universe. I owe you one.*

"Tanner's here." I turn back to face Delia. She's fuming. "Well, I should probably get going," I announce. "I wouldn't want to keep him waiting." I keep my voice casual, but in my head, I'm doing cartwheels on a mountaintop. Tanner's timing is impeccable. He has no idea, but he just saved his girlfriend from a lifetime prison sentence.

Right away, I'm on the move. Running back to the kitchen, I screw the lid on my coffee mug and jam my feet into a pair of waterproof boots. Then I head to the foyer, grabbing my thick nylon coat off the rack next to the door.

Jason, meanwhile, is whining at my ankles, desperate for attention. He knows my routine and demands to be acknowledged before I leave for the day. I lean down, giving him a quick peck on the head before I wrap my palm around the handle to the front door.

When I glance back, Delia's standing in the kitchen doorway, looking pissed. "We're not done talking about this," she says sternly. But I can't hear her. My brain is already out the door, free from the tension and stress.

"Bye, Del!" I exclaim as I step outside. "Have a nice day!"

Two

Izzy

I expected working at a construction company to be full of chaos.

When I took this job, I imagined myself surrounded by a constant stream of noise: hammers pounding, drills whizzing, loud, bearded workers barking orders at each other from across the room.

The reality couldn't be more different.

The offices of Ryan & Son Construction are nestled in a quaint brick building in downtown Seaview. The small, two-story office only sees a handful of employees every day. Though Tanner has about two dozen employees, most of them are out on job sites, not sitting behind desks. He mainly uses the office space for client meetings.

My desk sits in the lobby. It's a fairly basic setup, complete with a comfortable swivel chair and a large desktop monitor. Shortly after I started, I stuck a glass candy dish filled with peanut butter cups on the counter, along with a note that says "take one." It wasn't to be nice. I get restless if I don't talk to anyone for more than a couple of hours. Having candy on my desk entices people to come see me. And when they do, they're forced to make conversation with me.

Basically, I'm a praying mantis that traps people into social interaction.

I've been the office manager at Ryan & Son since July. Delia hooked me up with the job. Her boyfriend, Tanner, owns the company. He needed someone to help with work around the office, and I needed a steady paycheck. It was a mutually beneficial arrangement.

It's not a bad gig. Tanner is a good boss, and the work itself isn't hard. I spend most of my time mailing invoices, scheduling client meetings, and talking on the phone with suppliers. Tanner even lets me organize office events, which can be fun. The karaoke night I put together last month still has people raving. And I'm certain the boozy hot chocolate bar I'm arranging for the holiday party will be a hit.

Still, work can get dull. My old graphic design job required me to use my creative muscles, but this position is much more formulaic. *Send this. Call them. Organize that.* I rarely get the opportunity to do anything that sparks my creativity.

The phone rings, jarring me from my thoughts. I answer using the most professional voice I can manage.

"Ryan & Son Construction. How may I help you?"

"Izzy, is that you?"

"Mom?"

"It *is* you!" she exclaims. "I've been trying to get a hold of you forever!"

I pull the phone slightly away from my ear. Does she have to shout like she's in a wind tunnel? "Is something wrong?" I ask.

"As a matter of fact, yes," Mom says. "You haven't been returning my calls."

I roll my eyes. "I meant, is there a family emergency?"

"Oh, no. Everything's fine."

While I'm relieved to hear there's no immediate crisis, it doesn't stop the panic from settling in. There's a reason I haven't been picking up Mom's calls. I wanted to be the one to call her. Her calling me means she gets to be on the offensive. And she never calls without a reason. I need to be alert. If I show any signs of weakness, Mom will strike faster than a fighter jet on the unsuspecting enemy.

Comparing a phone call with my mother to warfare might be a tad dramatic, but our conversations have been known to get ugly. I'm the Family Disappointment. Mom always finds something about me to criticize. I'm too loud. Too opinionated. I lack seriousness and direction. I'm twenty-five years old, but I haven't actually grown up. And if I don't make serious life changes soon, I'm setting myself up for a bleak future.

I've heard it all. Luckily, we live several hours apart, so I don't have to deal with her all the time. And if I'm honest, being the screwup isn't that bad. Mom might not have a lot of faith in me, but I never fall short of her expectations. In a strange way, her anticipation of my failures sets me up for success. You can't let someone down if they have already decided you're incapable. It's like being an overgrown toddler.

It helps if you have a sense of humor. With Mom, I like to play little games. When we're on the phone, I count the number of times she follows a scathing insult by telling me she's only saying this because she cares. I also time the length of the awkward pauses. She was speechless for almost two full minutes after I told her I got fired last spring. I haven't been able to beat that time yet, but I'm sure I'll find new ways to baffle her with my ineptitude.

"Did you call for any particular reason or just to chat?" I ask.

"I have a reason," she replies. "Is now a good time? I assumed you weren't too busy."

There it is. Mom's first attack. Brutal, cutting, and effective. I have to hand it to her—no one can deliver a subtle insult quite like my mother. She knows just how to hit you without leaving a mark.

"Now is fine," I tell her.

"I want to congratulate you on your work anniversary."

"My *what*?"

"It's the sixteenth, isn't it? You've been at Ryan & Son for exactly five months."

I glance at the date on the hot pink calendar on my desk. It looks like she's right. "Huh. I guess I have."

"It's amazing how quickly time flies, isn't it?"

"Oh, yeah. It's been a real whirlwind."

"I mean it, Izzy," she insists. "You should be proud of yourself. Delia says Tanner has been impressed by your work ethic."

Make no mistake. It might sound like Mom is praising me, but there's a layer of shock in her voice that quashes any real sense of pride. She thinks she's happy for me, but what really pleases her is that her disappointment of a daughter has managed to hold down a job for almost half a year.

Mom likes things orderly. When I was unemployed, she flooded my email inbox with dozens of job applications on a daily basis. *This could be a good fit for you*, she wrote alongside a posting for an administrative assistant position at a car dealership. Never mind that I have bachelor's degrees in graphic design and drawing.

She was thrilled when I got the job with Tanner. Now that I'm employed again, I'm no longer a concern to her. Everything is back in a neat, orderly fashion. And Mom is determined to keep it that way.

The problem is, I agreed to work for Tanner's company on an indefinite but *temporary* basis. I'm still planning to go back to the graphic design world, eventually. I need a job that fulfills me creatively. Staying at Ryan & Son forever would bore me to death. I can't imagine sending invoices every day for the rest of my life.

Mom doesn't get it. She thinks Ryan & Son is my best path forward. I know she only wants me to do well, but it's my life. My decision. I've told her a dozen times that I don't want to be an office manager, but she never listens. She needs to respect my choices instead of constantly trying to talk me out of them.

"I'm glad it's going well," she adds. "It seems like a great fit for you."

"I mean, it's nice for now," I say. "But I'm not staying here forever."

Mom sighs. "I don't know, hon. A decent job is hard to come by. Who knows if you'd be able to find something else as good as this?"

"Are you saying you don't think anyone else will hire me?" It's not the worst insult I've ever received from Mom, but her lack of confidence in my ability to get another job still stings. Would it kill her to believe in me a little?

"I just think it's important to be realistic about your expectations," she says. "Finding a good job is hard for anyone."

"Especially for someone as incompetent as me, right?"

"Don't be like that, Izzy. I'm only saying this because I care about you."

I rub my temple with my free hand. There's no point in fighting with her. Mom has been making the same argument for months. Nothing I say is going to change her mind. I should hang up the phone before this gets any nastier.

"Mom, I've gotta go," I say, gazing around the empty lobby. "I have stuff to do."

"Oh, all right," she says, surprised by my abruptness. I don't know why. Does anyone want to argue with their mom on the phone at work? "Well, have a great rest of your day. Call me back when you have time."

"Thanks. Will do."

I end the call and set the phone on the desk before releasing a frustrated sigh.

That is why I avoid talking to my mother.

***

"Ready to get out of here, Izzy?"

Tanner's voice startles me. I didn't hear him come into the lobby. When I look up from my computer screen, however, he's standing in front of my desk in his usual baseball cap and jeans. Unless he's meeting with clients, Tanner dresses casually. He doesn't enforce any workplace dress code. I've gotten away with wearing sweatpants to the office on a few chilly mornings. I sit behind a desk all day. No one sees me from the waist down.

I nod. "All set," I reply as I close out of my browser. I wrapped up my work for the day about an hour ago, so I've been playing a video game to pass the time. It's called *Galactic Rush*. It's based on the popular sci-fi series with the same name.

I've never been a huge fan of video games, but I stumbled upon *Galactic Rush* one afternoon, and I've been hooked ever since. My avatar is a purple alien named Hela. She has color-changing hair and can shoot fire out of her eyes. I haven't read the game's instructions too carefully, but I think I'm supposed to be trying to save the universe. Unfortunately for the residents of the *Galactic Rush* universe, I'm a self-interested player. Rather than complete quests, I fly around in my spaceship and steal coins from other players.

Tanner caught me at the worst possible time. Hela just stumbled upon the fuming wreckage of a spaceship on the remote desert planet of Lovia. I was going to scour the mess for coins. I'm so close to having enough to buy a rocket launcher

15

for Hela's ship, but it looks like I'll have to wait till I get home to search the wreckage.

I power down the computer. Hopefully, Tanner didn't catch me playing video games on company time. Though I made sure all my work was finished before I pulled up the *Galactic Rush* game, I don't think it would be a great look.

Of course, I'm not at any real risk of being fired. One perk of working for your sister's boyfriend is job security. Unless I burn this place to the ground, I'm fairly certain my position is safe.

"So, what did you do to piss off Delia?" Tanner asks as I collect my purse and empty coffee mug. Dread curls in the pit of my stomach. I almost forgot about Jason's massacre of Delia's throw pillows. I'm guessing she found what remained of them by now. I bet I'm in for an earful when I get home.

"It wasn't me—it was Jason," I argue. I'm not proud of myself for throwing my dog under the bus, but what choice do I have? "He chewed up her throw pillows."

Tanner frowns. "You mean the silk ones?"

Oh, shit. Delia's boyfriend is the type of guy who wouldn't know the difference between body wash and shower gel. He wouldn't know Delia's throw pillows are made of silk unless she talked about them. And she would only talk about them if they were really important to her.

I can't contain my surprise. "You know about those?"

He bobs his head. "Delia got them at some fancy furniture store last time we were in Boston," he says.

Dammit, Jason. Why couldn't he have ruined a dish towel instead?

"Well, it looks like you'll be in the market for a new office manager soon," I say as I rise up from my desk chair. I walk over to grab my coat off the rack by the door. "Delia's gonna skin me alive."

"You'll be fine," Tanner says. "She likes having you around. For some reason."

"I'm going to ignore the offensive part of that comment."

After I slip on my coat, Tanner and I head out the door. Cold air pierces my skin as I step outside. I shiver quietly as I wait for Tanner to lock up the building. Once he's finally done, he pockets his keys, and the two of us start toward the near empty parking lot.

"You pissed off my girlfriend the same day we have dinner reservations," he says, mild annoyance flaring in his green eyes. "I'm not exactly thrilled with you."

"You and Delia are going out tonight?" Perhaps I'm not dead. If anyone can convince Delia to go easy on me, it's Tanner. "Are you taking her somewhere nice? Did you get her flowers? You know, I saw some great ones at the grocery store the other day. We can pick them up on the way home."

Tanner laughs. "I'm not getting involved. It's your mess— you clean it up."

"I'll keep that in mind the next time she's mad at you."

"Go ahead. Unlike you, I know how to make it up to her."

Tanner unlocks his truck, and I jump into the passenger seat. He climbs into the driver's side and starts the engine. Warm air pulses out of the vents. I hold my chilly fingertips in front of the one closest to me.

"You know what would really put Delia in a good mood?" I say casually as Tanner backs out of the parking lot, snow crunching under the truck's tires. "You asking her to move in."

When Tanner scowls at me, his eyes are downright venomous. "Wow. It's true what they say about couples turning into each other. You've got Delia's murder eyes down," I tell him.

"You know I can fire you, right?"

I scoff at his empty threat. "Oh, please. You should be thanking me. I'm only telling you what you want to hear, boss man."

Anyone with the slightest sense of awareness could tell Tanner wants Delia to move in with him. He's been dropping hints for ages, constantly suggesting she leave more stuff at his place. Last month, he bought a freaking treadmill so Delia would have somewhere to run in the crappy weather.

I know Delia would be on board. She loves Tanner. She moved from Boston to Seaview for him. What complicates things is my living situation. If Delia moves in with Tanner, she'll have no reason to keep her house, leaving me with no place to live, a fact I'm certain has crossed both their minds.

I was worried I might be holding them back, which is why I told Tanner point-blank he should ask her to move in. I want Delia to be happy. She's found something good with him. As much as I appreciate her letting me live with her, I don't want to be the obstacle stopping her from getting what she really wants.

"What have I told you about staying out of my business?" Tanner asks.

"No need to get defensive," I reply. "I know facing your fears is scary, Tanner. Do you need me to do it for you? I don't know if Delia would appreciate me inviting her to move into your place, but I'll tell her you tried to be brave."

"You're fired."

I grin, thrilled to have annoyed him. "Don't be like that. We're practically family now."

He groans. Probably because he knows it's the truth.

The Forrest sisters are a package deal.

Three

Izzy

"I think you missed a turn there," I say as Tanner zips past the entrance to Delia's neighborhood. I've lived in Seaview for less than a year, but it's a small town. Learning my way around didn't take long. After all, I spent the past six years living in New York City. The first week of my freshman year of college, I successfully navigated me and my drunk friends from a party in Hoboken back to our dorms in Brooklyn. Direction comes naturally to me.

"We've gotta make a quick stop first," Tanner replies. He hits his blinker at the next intersection, taking a left turn down a quiet, snow-lined road. "I promised Jacob I'd drop by to get measurements for his new porch. It should only be a few minutes."

I blow a piece of dark hair out of my face. Damn bangs. "And here I thought you decided to be merciful and pick up those flowers for Delia."

"It's your funeral, not mine."

I watch silently out the window for several minutes. Seaview is a beach town. In the summer, sunburnt tourists flood the streets like bees on honey, but winter Seaview has a sleepy energy. The roads are almost empty, and many shops are closed or only open for limited hours. It's as if the town has gone into hibernation mode.

After a few minutes, Tanner pulls into the driveway of a charming blue house with white trim and a square porch. He gives me an odd look as I unfasten my seatbelt.

"You're going inside?" he asks, surprised.

I shrug. "Someone has to keep Jacob company." It beats sitting in the truck while Tanner takes measurements.

"Don't terrorize him," Tanner says.

I roll my eyes. "No promises."

Both of us climb out of the truck. Tanner heads around the side of the house, tape measure in hand. I follow the stepping stones to the front door and press the small black bell. A ring echoes through the house. I shift on my heels as I listen for movement inside.

Within seconds, Jacob opens the door. His long limbs take up most of the doorway. He's wearing a pair of black chinos and a white button-down with the top button undone, showing off a small triangle of skin. A few strands of thick, dark hair fall over his forehead.

Jacob is good looking. He has a strong jaw, straight brows, and warm brown eyes framed by black glasses. He reminds me of a professor I had a crush on in undergrad. I used to show up early for Dr. Stewart's fundamentals of graphic design class just so I could get a spot at the front of the lecture hall. It was textbook teenage desperation.

I look up at Jacob from beneath my eyelashes. "I hear someone has been causing trouble," I say in an overly sultry voice. "I'm afraid I'm gonna need to come inside and ask you a few questions. I hope you can handle the heat."

His mouth twitches. "Is that supposed to be your stripper voice, Forrest?"

"I don't know, officer. You tell me."

"Hang on. *I'm* the officer?" He shakes his head as if totally lost. "You're gonna have to break this down for me. The narrative is very unclear."

"The only thing unclear is why you haven't let me inside yet. It's freezing, Jacob. I'm, like, ten seconds from turning into a human popsicle."

Chuckling quietly, Jacob moves out of the doorway and motions for me to come inside. I step into a small beige foyer that smells vaguely of citrus. The space is simple and clean, lit by bronze wall sconces. It's exactly what I would expect for someone like Jacob.

I don't actually know him that well. He's Tanner's best friend, so we've hung out a few times at parties and social outings. On the surface, Jacob and I don't appear to have much in common. He's quiet and observant. I'm loud and love getting under people's skin. Yet I've found him to be an easy person to talk to.

Despite his calm personality, Jacob isn't afraid to joke with me. Some people find my brand of humor off-putting, but he responds with friendliness and amusement. We make good conversation, but I wouldn't call us friends. I have no idea what Jacob is like outside of our brief interactions. Who knows? He could be a totally different person in his day-to-day life. Maybe he collects cat hair or leaves piles of dirty dishes in the sink for weeks.

"What are you doing here, Forrest?" he asks. I slip off my coat, and Jacob takes it from me, placing it on a hanger in the nearby closet.

"Tanner's out back getting measurements for your new porch," I reply, smoothing out the wrinkles in my dress. "I didn't feel like waiting in the truck."

He nods in understanding. "I see. So you're here to be entertained."

"My plan was to seduce you. You ruined it by insulting my well-crafted narrative."

"I apologize. I didn't realize you spent so much time working on it."

"It's too late," I tell him, sighing. "The damage is done. My ego is destroyed. My hopes and dreams are shattered."

"Would a drink make up for shattering your hopes and dreams?"

I tap my chin, pretending to think seriously about it. "It's a start."

Jacob motions for me to follow him, and we head through the doorway at the back of the foyer. It leads to a tidy kitchen with sandy-brown cabinets. The floor is spotless, and the granite countertops gleam under the overhead light. No dirty dishes anywhere.

Jacob opens the doors to the stainless steel refrigerator. "What'll it be?" he asks, glancing at me over his shoulder. "I have beer, Pepsi. There might be a can of iced tea in the back, but I think I've had that since I graduated college."

"Pepsi's good," I reply. "I wouldn't waste the iced tea. It might be worth something by now." Jacob is only five years older than me, but I can't resist the opportunity to tease him.

He takes the dig in stride. "You're right," he says. "Maybe I can use the money to hire someone to help you with your seduction skills."

"Watch it, old man. I'm still fragile."

I take a seat on a stool at the counter. Jacob snags two cans of Pepsi from the lower shelf and then shuts the fridge. He sets the cans on the counter and cracks them open, handing me one before settling onto the stool beside me.

Taking a sip of my soda, I give Jacob an assessing look. He dressed nicely, but he doesn't look like he just got back from a day at the office.

"You look fancy," I tell him. "Where are you going tonight? Is there a model train convention in town?"

Jacob lifts a brow. "Model trains? That's a low blow, Forrest. Even for you."

"Allow me to rephrase. Where are you going tonight, Jacob? I'm making no assumptions about whether it involves model trains."

He drums his fingers on the edge of the counter. "Who says I'm going anywhere?"

My eyes drop to his feet. "Your shoes. Unless you're the type of person who wears them around the house. If that's the case, I should probably get out of here, seeing as you're probably on some sort of FBI watchlist."

He drinks his soda, then sets it on the counter. "I have a date tonight," he says finally.

Interesting. I could do the polite thing and leave it at that. It doesn't seem like he's interested in having a conversation about it. Unfortunately for Jacob, I'm nosy and have self-control issues. Of course, I'm going to press him for details.

"Who's the lucky woman?"

"Her name's Marina. She's a dental hygienist from South Port."

"Is this your first date with Marina?"

"It is."

"How did the two of you meet?"

"True Connections." Jacob cringes as if the concept of using a dating app mortifies him. I'm not sure why. *Everyone* uses them. Myself included. Though I can't say any of my experiences have proven fruitful. The last time I went out with a guy I met on True Connections, he brought his pet fish and asked if I could take care of it for a week while he was out of town. When I told him no, he spent the rest of the date acting silent and moody. I had to feign a work-related emergency to get out of there.

"So, what's your exit strategy?"

Jacob frowns. "Exit strategy?"

"You know, in case Marina thinks the Earth is flat or enjoys torturing small animals," I say. "How are you gonna get out of there if things go south?"

"I don't think that's gonna be an issue," he says. "Marina and I have been talking for several days. I think I'd know by now if she was the female Hannibal Lecter."

"You can never be too careful. Letting your guard down is like sending a Bat Signal to the universe, inviting it to fuck with you."

"It's nice to get such a level-headed perspective."

"I'm just giving you a friendly warning. Everything seems fine until your date tells you he hopes the kids get your big, beautiful eyes."

Jacob looks horrified. "Please tell me that didn't actually happen."

"Never ask questions you don't want to know the answers to."

He shakes his head, disturbed. "What is wrong with people?"

"Men, Jacob. Not people."

"I guess that's fair."

"Still, there are plenty of unpleasant women out there," I tell him. "If you need an exit strategy, you could always use mine. Pretend to have an allergic reaction to something you ordered. Don't overdo it, though. If you play it up too much, you'll spend the rest of the night with your date in the ER."

Jacob shakes his head, a smile forming at the edges of his mouth. "That is a solid idea, Forrest," he says. "Got any other first date advice for me?"

I pluck the tab on my soda can as I consider my response. "Don't order anything with too much garlic."

He rolls his eyes. "Obviously. I'm not a barbarian."

"And don't be too touchy-feely. You don't want Marina feeling smothered."

"I wasn't planning on accosting her."

"Well, you don't want to make her feel like she's contagious either," I say. "A light touch here and there is good if she's open to it. A hand on her lower back as you walk her to the door. Your thumb brushing the inside of her wrist while she's talking."

A dip forms between Jacob's brows. "You want me to *stroke* her wrist?"

I wrinkle my nose. "Never use the word 'stroke' in reference to your date again."

"It was *your* suggestion."

"What I suggested was a sweet, romantic gesture. Stroke was never used."

"It's a synonym for brush."

"Well, pick a less creepy one. Sweep and caress were right there."

"You think *caress* is less creepy than *stroke*?" he asks, baffled.

Okay, he might have a point. "It has a romantic connotation," I argue weakly. I might be on the losing side here, but I'm not going down easily, dammit.

"I'm sure serial killers who caress the hair of their decapitated victims would agree with you," Jacob replies, amusement twinkling in his eyes.

A knock at the back door pauses our conversation. Tanner stands on the other side of the sliding glass. He glides the door open and steps into the kitchen, snowflakes coating the top of his light-brown hair. He looks at Jacob and nods in greeting.

"Everything's good to go for the porch," Tanner says, slipping his tape measure into the pocket of his jeans. "I'll place an order tomorrow for the materials."

"He means *I'll* place an order tomorrow," I clarify. Purchasing supplies is a big part of my job. In my five months at Ryan & Son, I've learned more than I ever expected to know about lumber. "You better be nice to me, Jacob, or you might wind up with a lime green porch."

"Joke's on you, Forrest," Jacob replies. "Tacky is just what I was going for."

Tanner's eyes flash my way. "You ready to go, Izzy?"

I bob my head, then drain the rest of my soda. Hopping down from the bar stool, I toss the empty can in the recycle bin and follow Tanner and Jacob to the foyer.

"The porch won't take that long," Tanner tells Jacob. "We're wrapping up a couple of projects right now, but my crew should be able to get started after the holidays."

"Sounds great," Jacob says.

"We still on for Seaview Tavern on Thursday?"

"Works for me."

Jacob opens the closet and pulls out my coat. He hands it over, and I slide my arms into the puffy sleeves.

I turn to face him. "Thanks for the drink," I say. "For the record, I still think I make a convincing stripper."

Jacob smiles slightly. "Your material needs work. That and your delivery."

I match his smile with my own. "Good luck on your date tonight," I tell him. "Fingers crossed she doesn't have the kids' names picked out before dinner arrives."

Tanner glances between Jacob and me, seemingly confused. "It feels like I missed something weird," he says.

"Don't worry about it," I reply, giving him a patronizing pat on the shoulder. I open the front door and step outside before he gets a chance to say anything else.

Four

Jacob

Oh, this is bad.

Our drinks haven't even shown up, and I'm already calling tonight a bust.

Across the table, Marina fiddles with her necklace, staring blankly at the white tablecloth. Her shoulders are stiffer than plywood. After a second, she glances up and gives me a tight smile that screams, "this blows."

I tug at my shirt collar, discomfort washing over me. Normally, I don't struggle with small talk. I've been on plenty of first dates over the past year. Even when they're not going well, I'm usually able to keep the conversation flowing. This date, however, has been an unfortunate exception. Marina and I can't seem to find a rhythm.

We chose to get dinner at a little Italian place halfway between Seaview and South Port. Neither of us expected the place to be busy on a weeknight, so we didn't make reservations. That decision became an obvious mistake the minute I pulled into the parking lot. Apparently, this place does a half-price spaghetti night on Tuesdays, and it's wildly popular. When Marina and I walked inside, there wasn't even an open spot at the bar.

We had to wait twenty minutes for a table. We stood in the crowded lobby, trying to get to know each other over the sounds of the rattling heater and the toddler wailing on the bench by the door. I thought things would improve once we were seated, but I was wrong. If anything, they've only

gotten worse. Without distractions surrounding us, it's
become more apparent that Marina and I can't string more
than a few sentences together.

"So, what's it like being a dental hygienist?" I ask. I want
to take the question back as soon as it leaves my mouth.
Work? Seriously? Could I ask about anything more boring?
Still, I had to say something. We'd been sitting in silence for
a few minutes. I couldn't take another second of it.

"It's all right," Marina says, tucking a piece of blonde hair
behind her ear. "It gets kind of repetitive, but the hours are
consistent." She twists her necklace again. "What about you?
What's it like being an actuary?"

I really shouldn't have mentioned work. The only thing
duller than Marina's job is mine.

"Nothing exciting," I tell her. "But it pays the bills, I
guess."

Marina nods politely. We stare at each other for several
seconds before shifting our eyes in different directions.
Conversation hums steadily at the tables around us. I can't
imagine how we must look from the outside. It feels like
we're middle schoolers on our first date ever, awkward and
unsure what to do next.

This is my fault. Everyone knows you should do drinks on
a first date, not dinner. If it goes well, you order a second
round and keep the momentum going, but if it turns
disastrous, you finish your beer and claim to have an early
morning. Committing to an entire dinner before you know if
you have chemistry with someone is a gamble, but I was so
certain Marina and I would hit it off.

We've been messaging on True Connections for days.
Both of us like books (her, historical fiction, me, sci-fi),
dogs, and Italian food. We grew up in small towns in

Massachusetts. We're close with our families, and we're both looking for long-term relationships. On the surface, those similarities may seem shallow, but it felt like we had enough in common to guarantee a decent first date.

I was wrong. And I should've known better. If the past year of my life has taught me anything, it's that nothing involving dating is simple.

I turn thirty in two weeks. I've been single for the better part of my twenties, but it hasn't been by choice. Casual dating has never appealed to me. I'm the type who wants to commit to someone. Build a future with them. I always expected it to happen naturally. That the right woman was just around the corner, and I had to be patient.

Except the right woman hasn't come along. I'm still single. And the closer I get to thirty, the more I'm feeling the pressure. Not from my parents or extended family. From myself. I've always pictured myself settling down. By thirty, I thought I would be engaged…if not already married. It never occurred to me that I might not meet someone. And as I've watched everyone around me pair up and ride off into the sunset, it's forced me to realize that I'm nowhere close to finding that myself.

Reality struck like a freight train on my twenty-ninth birthday last year. I was at a New Year's Eve party, surrounded by couples, when it hit me that I'd probably still be single going into my thirties. If I wanted things to change, I needed to do something drastic. I vowed to spend the last year of my twenties doing everything possible to meet the right woman.

I created profiles on various dating apps. Asked friends to set me up. Took any opportunity I could find to go on dates. Being proactive about my dating life felt like the best way to improve my chances. Yet it hasn't gone as well as I imagined.

Over the last year, I've gone on nearly two dozen first dates, but there haven't been many seconds. Things have either fizzled out, or the woman suddenly stopped responding to messages. Two promising dates with a freelance writer last spring turned sour after she revealed she was moving to Colorado and only looking for a way to pass the time.

Meeting someone can't be this difficult for everyone, can it? A lot of people get married. Have all of them crossed over this horrible minefield of self-doubt and disappointment?

People say you should enjoy dating in your twenties, but I'm tired of the bad dates and stilted conversation. I'm ready to enter the next phase of my life. Marriage. Commitment. I've always considered it to be a realistic goal, but the way things have been going lately has me reconsidering.

Looking across the table, I force a smile at Marina. Both of us know this isn't going to work out, but we can't admit that. At least now the pressure is off. Marina and I might not have a future together, but that means nothing that happens tonight is of consequence. Surely I can fumble my way through another hour of low-stakes conversation.

"So, have you—"

"I can't—"

We share an awkward laugh as we trip over each other's words. I don't understand why simple conversation seems to be so difficult for the two of us. We sound as stale and lifeless as a pair of robots practicing human interaction for the first time.

Luckily, our pathetic attempt at conversing is cut off by the arrival of our server. The young guy sets two wine glasses on the table, apologizing for the delay.

"It's about time," Marina says tersely. "I thought I was gonna have to go behind the bar and pour this for myself." She pays the server no more than a quick glance before picking up her wineglass and swallowing the first sip.

I stare at her, stunned. I'll admit, it took a while for our drinks to get here, but the restaurant is packed. Our server can't be more than twenty-two, and he looks tired and frazzled. Is giving him a verbal lashing really necessary?

The server, seemingly uncomfortable, offers another apology. I give him a sympathetic smile, hoping it communicates my disapproval of Marina's rudeness. He takes our entrée orders before dashing off to the next table, leaving me with a visibly annoyed Marina.

"I can't believe so many people like this place," she says, shaking her head in disappointment. "The service is awful."

Mortification sweeps over me. Ending this date early felt rude, but that was before Marina snapped at the server. I've never lied to get out of a bad date before, but I don't feel so bad about the idea right now, especially knowing that kid is probably going to spit in our spaghetti.

Without giving it much thought, I cover my mouth with a fist and cough. "Excuse me," I say, grabbing a drink of ice water. I set the glass back on the table, then cough again.

Marina frowns. "Are you all right?"

"I don't know," I reply, shifting from side to side in my chair. "My throat feels itchy all of a sudden. It's like I'm having an allergic reaction or something." Yup. Those words did, in fact, just leave my mouth. Apparently, I'm using Izzy Forrest's exit strategy.

"An allergic reaction?" Marina repeats, sounding confused.

"It, um, must've been the bread," I say, gesturing toward the small wire basket at the center of the table. "It looks like there are sesame seeds in the rolls. I didn't notice them before. I have an allergy." Holy shit. I cannot believe I'm actually doing this. My face feels as if it's on fire, my skin hot and clammy.

"You're having an allergic reaction? To bread?" Marina appears less than impressed, sitting back in her chair with her arms folded over her chest. My story sounds totally made up, and I'm not a good liar. I'm sure the truth is evident on my face. But at this point, I've already committed to it. There's no going back now.

"It seems so," I say. "Listen, I hate to do this, but I should get going. If I don't take Benadryl in the next fifteen minutes, my eyes are gonna swell shut." Clumsily, I step up from my chair, causing the silverware on the table to rattle. I grab a few bills out of my wallet, placing them on the table. "Enjoy your dinner on me. It was great meeting you." I don't bother suggesting we reschedule. Both of us know that isn't going to happen.

Marina looks like she wants to feed me to a pack of wolves. "You too," she says through gritted teeth. "I hope you feel better." Ha. If anything, it sounds like she's rooting for my allergic reaction to take a turn for the worse.

***

"Well, you're back early."

Mom is sitting in her favorite recliner when I walk in the living room, wrapped in a thick blanket. She's clutching a set of knitting needles, a ball of purple yarn resting in her lap. She smiles, the skin around her brown eyes crinkling softly.

Lulu is resting by Mom's feet. Her head shoots up when I step through the doorway. She rises and scurries over to me, tail wagging and nails clicking on the hardwood. Bending to pet her, I glance at Mom.

"How was she?" I ask. Lulu is only two, and she has a lot of energy. I don't like leaving her alone for long stretches of time, especially when I've been at work all day, so I usually drop her off at my parents' place when I know I'm going to be out for a while.

Fortunately, my mom loves Lulu. When I adopted her a few years ago, Mom debated getting a dog so Lulu would have a friend. Dad got her to reconsider by reminding her of the negative aspects of dog ownership: the constant barking, shoes being chewed up, muddy paw prints on the carpet. Ultimately, Mom decided she was better off as a dog grandparent than an owner.

"Perfect as usual," Mom replies. I'm not surprised to receive a glowing report. Lulu is a boxer mix with a sweet temperament. Occasionally, she'll chew up a paper towel, but she's almost always well-behaved.

"Out of curiosity, how do you think she'd react if I put her in a sweater?" Mom asks.

I raise a brow. "Is that what you're knitting?"

She folds her lips. The half-knitted project in her lap looks about the size of a dog sweater. I doubt Lulu would mind Mom putting it on her, but I decided to give her a hard time, anyway. "I leave Lulu here for a couple of hours, and you're making her clothing. Maybe you shouldn't retire, Mom. You've already got too much time on your hands."

My mom looks affronted. "You don't need to worry about my mental state." She's planning to retire in about a year and a half, so she's been taking up all sorts of hobbies to keep herself busy. She's already tried painting and crocheting. Knitting is her latest venture. I hope this one sticks. Mom gives me a lot of her handmade creations. It's easier to store hats and scarves than large canvases.

"I'm guessing the date didn't go well," she says.

My hand freezes on Lulu's back. I've always been close to my parents. I'm an only child. Growing up, they gave me a good mix of guidance and support while still allowing me to be independent. Still, that doesn't mean I share the details of my dating life with them.

"How did you know about that?" I ask.

"Tanner told me," Mom says, sporting a cat-like grin. Of course he did. My oldest friend knows how to hold a grudge. I ticked him off last year when I accidentally told his mom about his girlfriend, Delia, before they officially started going out. I bet he's been plotting his revenge since then.

"Wasn't that nice of him?" I mutter, reminding myself to give him hell when we meet up for beers later this week. At least his relationship with Delia was going somewhere. Now I have to tell Mom all about my failed first date.

"What happened?" she asks.

I run a palm over Lulu's coarse fur. I don't want to get into the specifics, so I keep my response vague. "We just had different priorities." One of mine is trying not to make servers hate themselves. "I'm sorry to disappoint."

"What are you apologizing to me for?"

"Well, I figure you want grandchildren at some point."

Mom laughs. "There's nothing to be sorry for. Soon enough, you'll meet the right woman, and she'll make you forget all about the bad dates." Her words sound like they came straight from a book of clichés, but I know she means them.

A door clicks somewhere behind me.

"It sounds like I'm missing all the action," Dad says. I turn to see him emerging from his home office. He's an English professor at a local college, so he's usually holed up in there, working on his latest paper. He looks like he just finished a long writing session, his glasses askew and his clothes rumpled. In typical Sam Howell fashion, he's wearing a blue robe and a pair of plaid pajama pants.

"You're just in time, honey," Mom says as he walks up behind her recliner. "Jake was about to tell me about his date."

Humor dances in Dad's eyes. "Is that right? Well, let's hear it, Jake." He reaches over the back of the recliner to rest his hands on Mom's shoulders. "Who is she? Where did you take her? When are you going to introduce us?"

I shake my head at my parents. "Your lack of respect for boundaries is deeply unsettling."

Mom scoffs. "Can you believe this?" she says, glancing over her shoulder to exchange a look with Dad. "We're getting grief for being involved parents."

"The nerve on this kid is something else," Dad says. "Where did we go wrong with him?"

"Don't blame me. His deficiencies are on you."

Dad clutches his chest as though physically wounded. "Thirty-six years of marriage, and you're ready to throw me under the bus like that?"

"You knew what you were getting into when you married me."

My parents smile at each other like they're speaking their own language. They've been together long enough that they just might be.

Mom and Dad started dating when they were in ninth grade. Their first date was at Seaview High School's annual fall carnival. Mom was still in braces, and Dad's body spray was so potent it stunk up the entire gymnasium (or so Mom alleges). They had to hitch a ride with my grandparents since neither of them had a driver's license yet.

They've been together since then. For some, being in a relationship for so long might lead to resentment, but Mom and Dad have nothing but genuine love for each other. I consider myself lucky for it. A lot of kids grow up watching their parents' marriages fall apart, but my childhood couldn't have been more different. I wasn't afraid of catching my parents arguing when I walked into a room unannounced. They were always dancing or sharing a laugh.

Mom and Dad taught me what a healthy marriage looks like. A stable partnership between people who deeply care about each other. I know how fortunate I was to see that. To *still* see it, even though I'm almost thirty and haven't lived under their roof in years.

Still, part of me worries my parents might've warped my expectations when it comes to relationships. Their love is rare. It's not the sort of thing you find every day. I've always wanted something similar for myself. And I've spent most of my life believing it was only a matter of time before I found it.

With the way my dating life has been going, I'm beginning to wonder if that's a realistic goal. I haven't given up yet, but I can't deny the sliver of doubt taking shape.

Have I been chasing the impossible this entire time?

Five

Izzy

"*Fuck* me."

I bury my head in my hands, resisting the urge to scream. I feel like a child on the verge of a tantrum. I haven't thrown a good one since I was seven or eight, but I used to be quite the nightmare. Mom called me her Tasmanian devil.

"What is it?" Cynthia asks, a note of amusement in her voice. Apparently, watching me have a mental breakdown over FaceTime is funny to her.

"Delia sent me the link for those throw pillows Jason destroyed," I say. "They're a hundred dollars apiece." I knew the pillows would be expensive. My older sister has always had a taste for the finer things, so I braced myself for a hefty price tag, but I never thought they would cost as much as a car payment.

Cynthia's eyes widen. "You're kidding."

"Nope." I check the listing on my phone again just to be sure, but the number is still there, taunting me. "They're plain blue pillows, Cynthia. There's *nothing* special about them. I could make them myself using shit from the craft store."

"Do you think Delia would notice if you bought cheaper ones somewhere else?"

I can't help but laugh. "She probably has the thread count memorized." *I* might not spot the difference, but Delia would weed out a pair of counterfeits in a second. Besides, I'd feel guilty. Part of our agreement when I adopted Jason was that I would replace anything of hers that he destroyed. Granted, I thought he would wreck socks, not overpriced decorations, but fair is fair.

Though I fully intend on holding up my end of the bargain, I can't be bothered with it right now. Powering off my phone, I toss it to the other side of the bed. It lands with a soft thud on the plush comforter, disturbing Jason, who's curled up by my feet.

Delia might not approve of letting pets on furniture, but she doesn't know what happens in the confines of my bedroom.

It's a little after seven, and I'm tucked in bed with my back against the headboard and a warm laptop resting on the tops of my thighs. On screen, my best friend, Cynthia, sits at the kitchen table in her (formerly, *our*) apartment. The refrigerator behind her is adorned in more tacky magnets than a souvenir shop. Cynthia has been collecting magnets for as long as I've known her. She has everything from the Statue of Liberty flipping the bird (courtesy of me) to a three-dimensional coconut tree that plays "Escape (The Piña Colada Song)" when you press the palm fronds.

It's strange not seeing Cynthia and her quirky magnet collection every day anymore. Before I moved to Seaview, we'd been living together since we were eighteen. We got paired up as roommates our freshman year at Kells College and have been inseparable ever since. Cynthia has seen me through a lot of bad decisions, most of which involved tequila and douchey frat boys. I love her to pieces, and I miss her constantly.

"Let's talk about something else so I don't have to think about all the money I'm about to blow on pillows," I say, hoping a change of subject will brighten my mood. "How'd it go with Ken? Weren't you two supposed to meet up the other day?" One of our old friends from Kells recently moved back to the city and has been asking Cynthia to catch up.

"Don't get me started on that," Cynthia says, shuddering as if reliving a bad dream. "It was a mess. We spent almost five hours in the ER."

"Oh, my god. Why?"

"Ken fell in Central Park," she explains. "Well, he didn't just fall—he *faceplanted*. God, you should've seen the blood, Iz. We tried getting napkins from the grumpy guy at the pretzel stand, but he wouldn't give us any unless we bought something, and he only accepted cash. I had to dig through my purse for change while Ken stood there, bleeding out."

"Oh, shit. I take it you two had plenty of time to catch up."

She nods. "We exhausted pretty much all conversation by hour three. Ken told me I could leave, but I felt guilty abandoning him in the ER. He doesn't have any family here. And he hasn't been back in New York for long, so he doesn't know a lot of people."

I picture poor Cynthia slumped over in a chair in a crowded ER with a bloody Ken sitting beside her. "Why didn't you tell me about this sooner?" I ask. "Didn't you meet up with Ken, like, three days ago?" This is the sort of misfortune that Cynthia and I would normally update each other about in the moment. I'm surprised my phone wasn't blowing up with texts and pictures of Ken's mangled face.

"These are the adventures you miss when you abruptly move out of state." Her tone is playful, but it has an edge. Cynthia took it hard when I left New York. We went from spending every day together to talking for a few minutes on FaceTime now and then.

It wasn't supposed to happen like this. I only intended to stay with Delia for a few weeks. But once I settled in here, I realized how much I needed a change of scenery.

In Cynthia's eyes, it seems I randomly abandoned my entire life in New York, including our seven years of friendship. There's a lot she doesn't know. A mess of thoughts and feelings tangled up in my head. I want to be honest with her, but I haven't found the words yet. It's hard to have tough conversations over the phone.

"Are you ever gonna visit, or am I only gonna see you over a grainy camera for the rest of my life?" Cynthia asks.

I let out a sigh. "I want to. Believe me. But I don't think asking Delia to look after Jason for me is such a good idea right now." Hashing everything out in person would be amazing, but who knows what Jason might destroy in my absence? I literally can't afford it.

Cynthia saws her bottom lip. "Then maybe I should come to you."

"Seriously?"

"Yeah. I mean, why not? I've been dying to see the place that dragged you away from New York." Excitement over the possibility blooms in my chest. It's been *months* since Cynthia and I have had a proper reunion. The last time I saw her was when I went back to New York to move the rest of my things, and that was tense and awkward. Having her here would make it so much easier to talk to her. I want to explain myself. Give context behind my sudden departure. It would be much more comfortable to do that without a screen between us.

"I need a drink."

A deep voice rings out on Cynthia's end, followed by a door slam. Heavy footsteps bound across the hardwood, and

Dominic enters the picture, unaware that Cynthia is on a call. His back faces the camera as he rummages through the contents of the refrigerator. Seconds later, he turns around and cracks open a silver can of beer.

Cynthia's eyes flicker to him. "Hey, Dom. I take it the shoot didn't go so well."

He takes a swig of beer before he replies. "It was horrible. It was an engagement shoot, and the couple wouldn't stop fighting. The guy showed up late, and his fiancée was pissed. We were there for almost two hours, and I didn't get one decent shot."

Frowning, Dominic sets his beer on the counter. He looks tired, strands of blond hair sticking up in the back of his head. And I have to bite my tongue to keep myself from smiling like the Grinch when he decides to steal Christmas.

It's wrong to enjoy another person's misery, isn't it? I shouldn't be delighted that Dominic had a shitty night, but there's no denying the pleasurable warmth coasting through my body. Maybe that makes me petty, but I don't mind. Spending time around your horrible ex-boyfriend will do that to you.

As he goes to take another sip of his beer, Dominic looks at the laptop screen. "Oh, hey, Izzy," he says nonchalantly, as if I didn't just hear his little tantrum.

"Hi, Dom," I chirp back. I've had a lot of practice being cordial with him. Acting like I don't despise basically comes as second nature to me. "I'm sorry to hear about your night. What a bummer." My tone sounds genuine, but I hope he knows I don't mean a word.

Dominic is Cynthia's cousin. He slipped into our friend group a couple of years ago when he moved to New York. I didn't think much of him, other than that he was nice and occasionally funny, but everything changed last fall when he confessed he was in love with me.

The confession shocked me. Generally, I consider myself to be perceptive, but I had no idea about Dominic's feelings. I'd never looked at him as anything more than a friend.

But things at my old job were getting bad, and I hadn't been in a serious relationship since college. I felt directionless. Confused. And here was someone claiming to *love* me. Of course, I took it as a sign from the universe. Being with Dominic was going to help me find my way again. I was sure of it.

And, oh, how wrong I was.

Dominic glances at his beer can. "You know, Cynth, I could use something stronger than this. Wanna hit Minnie's? I think it's still happy hour."

Uncertainty flashes in Cynthia's eyes. "Oh, I don't know. Izzy and I just started talking."

"Can't you talk later? Happy hour is only for another thirty minutes. I'm sure Izzy will understand." I grit my teeth, annoyed by Dominic's obvious attempt to get me off the phone, but I refuse to give him the reaction that he wants.

Sometimes, it's hard to believe I actually dated him. We started going out shortly after Dominic's love confession. At first, things were good. We already spent a lot of time together since he was part of our friend group, so it was easy to develop feelings.

The problem? Being in a relationship with someone means you see all of them, not just the pretty parts you put on display. And as Dominic and I got to know each other better, I realized he loved certain aspects of my personality, not all of me.

He liked dating me in theory. I was an interesting idea to him. An amusing character to have on his arm at parties. And I think he expected our relationship to be an extension of our friendship. Light and easy and fun. We certainly had our moments, but you can't have the good without the bad.

I tried opening up to him about my struggles at work. How unmotivated I felt. The way I kept missing deadlines and turning in lackluster projects because I simply couldn't concentrate. Something wasn't right, and I didn't know what to do. Dominic didn't want to hear it, though. He expected me to be Fun Izzy all the time. If I was in a bad mood and didn't feel like joking or going out, he treated me like a stranger.

Tension between us simmered for months. Our relationship clearly wasn't working, but neither of us wanted to be the one to end it. We reached our breaking point after I got fired. When I told Dominic, he went off on me, calling me selfish and irresponsible and accusing me of sabotaging our relationship. *I don't know why you want to be miserable all the time, Izzy, but I'm so over your shit.*

I knew we couldn't keep pretending after that, so I ended things right before I left for Seaview. Dominic acted surprised, but he had to know it was coming. He asked if we could keep the truth of our breakup from Cynthia and the rest of our friends. He said he didn't want to make things uncomfortable or ruin the dynamic of the group.

It seemed like the mature decision. Cynthia loved having Dominic around, and I knew our breakup would change things. So I agreed to tell her that we split up because we realized we were better off as friends. I didn't think it would be a big deal, but I underestimated how hard it was to be around Dominic post-breakup.

I was hurt. I wanted nothing to do with him. Yet he was at my apartment nearly every night, eating dinners I cooked and laughing on the couch with Cynthia. It didn't take long for resentment to build. So when I saw an opportunity to get out of New York, I jumped on it.

"You should go," I say, putting on my fakest smile. "We can talk later."

Cynthia frowns. "Are you sure?"

"Of course. Happy hour waits for no one."

She looks like she wants to say more, but she doesn't. So we end the call with a promise to talk more about her making a trip to Seaview.

After Cynthia hangs up, I stare at my empty laptop screen, feeling defeated. I can't deny that I played a huge role in my current predicament. I honestly believed hiding the truth was best for everyone. But I can see now that the decision made things worse. I'm being cagey and distant, and Cynthia doesn't know why.

The worst part is that it's all working out for Dominic. His relationship with Cynthia has stayed the same, even though he's the one at fault here. Our breakup makes *him* look bad, not me. He disregarded my feelings during some of my most vulnerable moments. Made me feel like I wasn't allowed to be anything more than a good time.

I wonder if Dominic knew that. Maybe that's why he wanted the secrecy. To protect himself from his own horrible behavior. He guilted me into it. He knew I wouldn't be able to say no when he brought up how our breakup would devastate our friends.

Next time, I won't be so naïve. When Cynthia comes to visit, I'm going to tell her *everything*. She's going to know the kind of person he is.

Hopefully, the truth will bridge the emotional distance that's been growing between us since the day I left New York.

Six

Jacob

Apparently, my suffering is hilarious.

Tanner can barely contain his laughter as I finish telling him about my awful date with Marina. He tries to hide it behind his half-empty beer glass, but he's less convincing than an actor in a cheesy TV movie.

"An allergic reaction?" he says, shaking his head as if he just can't believe anyone would make up such a ridiculous excuse. "Christ, Jake. Why couldn't you tell her your dog was sick or your niece was in the ER?"

"I don't have a niece," I remind him. Lying about Lulu's health is out of the question. I'm not a superstitious person, but I can't give the universe *another* reason to screw with me. My dating life is torturous enough.

Tanner barks out a laugh. "Your imaginary niece needing a few stitches is more believable than you having a life-threatening allergic reaction to bread, dickhead." He removes his baseball cap, setting it on the wooden bar top.

His words are brutal, but not untrue. If there's one thing Tanner is, it's honest to a fault. I've known him since we were kids. Our moms grew up in Seaview, and they've been friends for ages. Both of them used to call Tanner the ultimate humbler. He wasn't afraid to admit when he didn't like something. He got grounded for three weeks in second grade after he told our choir teacher that she sounded like a dying bird. He's gotten less abrasive with age, but he saves his directness for those who know him best.

Still, I don't need Tanner's brand of honesty to realize that
I messed up the other night on my date with Marina. I
could've said *anything* to get out of the rest of that dinner.
Why did I have to choose the worst excuse imaginable?

I take a sip of my IPA, the bitter flavor lingering on my
tongue. I'm sitting beside Tanner at the mostly empty bar at
Seaview Tavern on Thursday night. A basketball game is
playing on the flatscreen in front of us, and laughter booms
from the group of women seated at the corner booth. Tanner
and I pop in here once or twice a month. The place isn't
fancy, but the beer selection is good, and the bartenders
know us by name.

"I can't believe you actually went on a date worse than the
one with the Puker," Tanner says, clapping me on the
shoulder. Last summer, I went to a baseball game with a
friend of a coworker. Halfway through the third inning, she
got horribly sick. I had to hold her hair back while she threw
up in the bushes outside the stadium.

I wince at the memory. "I don't know if I'd call it worse."
That incident gave me a taste aversion to soft pretzels. I can't
look at one without my stomach churning.

"Well, at least you made it through that date," Tanner
argues. I flip him off, even though he's got a point. Ditching
Marina wasn't my finest moment.

I've tried not to let the past year of failed dates get to me,
but every bad experience makes it more difficult. It was easy
at the beginning, when each date felt like a new possibility.
Would *this* be the night I met the right woman? Would I
finally put an end to my crappy dating streak? Hope kept me
going. But the bad dates have piled up quickly. I'm starting
to see things in a less optimistic light.

Dating was supposed to be a means to an end. Instead, it feels like an endless loop. I'm a hamster on a wheel, running to nowhere. And I don't know how much longer I can keep it up. I know I have to get back out there, but given how badly things went with Marina, the thought seems as appealing as ripping the hairs from my head with tweezers.

"I blame Izzy Forrest," I say, letting out a heavy sigh. I set my beer glass on the bar top. "She put the allergic reaction idea in my head right before my date."

"Well, there's your first problem," Tanner replies. "Why would you take advice from Izzy? You know she once suggested Ryan & Son do a shirtless calendar as a way to make extra revenue, right? Her advice is terrible."

Tanner might have a point there, too. That night, Izzy talked to me in a stripper voice and debated me about the creepiness of the word "stroke." I should've known not to take anything she said seriously.

"I'm telling Delia you said that." It'll be my retribution for Tanner telling Mom about my date with Marina.

"The hell you are," he says. "I like my balls exactly where they are."

I chuckle under my breath. Delia has really done a number on him. Before he met her, my oldest friend didn't care about relationships. Now, he's openly admitting that his girlfriend has him by the balls.

"Have you thought about taking it easy on the dating stuff for a while?" Tanner asks. "Going on as many bad dates as you have would make anyone depressed." It would, and it has. Unfortunately, slowing down isn't an option.

I'm twenty-nine. I want to be married with kids by the time I'm in my late thirties. Taking a break from dating isn't possible, especially when I've been trying for a year, and I have nothing to show for it but a string of bad dates.

"Taking it easy won't help anything." If anything, it will only make me *more* aware of how single I am.

"Well, I think you're overthinking it," he says. "You're gonna meet someone. It just takes time." It's hard to believe *Tanner* of all people is giving me relationship advice. Before Delia, he had zero interest in dating. He was too focused on work. Said he didn't have time for a girlfriend. I never imagined he would settle down before me.

Don't get me wrong—I'm thrilled he found someone. Delia's great. Tanner has been a lot happier since they started going out. But I'd be lying if I said I wasn't a bit envious. All I want is a good, solid relationship. I've done everything I can to make it happen, and my effort hasn't gotten me anywhere. Tanner, on the other hand, wasn't even looking for something when Delia waltzed into his life. Where is the logic in that?

I stare at the bottom of my glass. "I'm thirty and single. There's not much to overthink."

"You're freaking yourself out for nothing. There's no time limit."

"I mean, I'd like to be able to run around with my kids."

Tanner balks at my concern. "*That's* what you're worried about?" He shakes his head in disapproval. "Jesus Christ. You're twenty-nine, Jake. You're not on your way to the retirement home yet." Maybe it's a little premature to panic about kids, but it's hard to be rational when I'm not any closer to settling down now than I was a year ago.

"No, but I might be turning into Luke Daniels." Otherwise known as a walking HR violation. Luke is a forty-three-year-old single guy who works in my office. He drives a Ford

Mustang with a vanity license plate and complains about people being too sensitive for his jokes. He's always razzing the married guys in the office, claiming he doesn't understand why anyone would want to be tied to one woman for the rest of their lives, but it's obvious he's deflecting. His wife left him a couple years back, and the divorce was messy.

"Except you're not a douchebag," Tanner says.

"I don't know." I pinch the bridge of my nose. "Maybe I'm doing something wrong." After so many failures, it might be time to admit the problem is me.

Tanner frowns. "Don't do that shit. That's Maggie talking."

"Not this again." As if things couldn't get any bleaker, Tanner had to bring up my ex-girlfriend. "It's been seven years, Tanner. I think I'm over it by now." Especially since Maggie cheated on me. Multiple times. But I don't feel like prodding at old wounds.

"All I'm saying is that shit sticks with you," he replies. "I wouldn't be surprised if Maggie still had her claws in you in one way or another."

"You're only saying that because you can't stand her." Tanner's dislike of Maggie goes back to our early years. The three of us grew up on the same block, so we hung out a lot in the summer. Once, when we were in high school, Maggie stole a few beers from her dad's fridge, and we drank them in her basement. When he later found the empty cans, Maggie put the blame on Tanner and me. We were only kids, but Tanner never quite forgave her. He said she had no sense of loyalty (and, no, the humor isn't lost on me).

"That's true," Tanner says, unashamed. "Can you imagine what your life would've looked like had you married her? You'd be raising a bunch of hellions."

"The kids would've gotten my genes, too."

"Your genes would've been no match for Maggie's demon spawn."

I chuckle softly. I wish I could blame all my problems on Maggie, but she isn't the one screwing up these dates. Either I'm choosing to go out with the wrong women, or there's something I'm doing to make the right ones steer clear of me.

I'm not aware of any major personal flaws, aside from the fact that I'm not particularly interesting. I work a dull office job. Live in the small town I was raised in. Prefer quiet nights at home over going out. But I didn't think those were bad things, especially since I'm looking to settle down. Safe and boring is good. Stable. Isn't it?

Or maybe it's holding me back. What if my dates aren't interested in me *because* I'm safe and boring? Is my personality pushing them away? If so, I don't know how I'm supposed to fix it. It's not like I can dissect myself and throw away the parts that aren't compelling. But if it *is* the reason for my perpetual singleness, then I'm going to have to figure out something.

I won't get in the way of my own future.

***

Izzy

"Do these look right to you?" Delia asks, holding up a long strand of twinkling lights. "They were supposed to be soft white. They look like floodlights to me." Uncertainty ripples across her face as she examines the bulbs like a diligent inspector.

"They look fine," I tell her as I unroll a spool of silver garland. Delia asked me to measure forty feet, which is exactly how much we need for the tree, but I was too lazy to hunt down a tape measure, so I'm ballparking it. We could have twelve feet or sixty feet—I'm not very good with measurements. Fortunately, Delia is too preoccupied with the lights to notice.

"You're sure?" she asks, seemingly unconvinced. "You're not just saying that because you think it's what I want to hear, right? Because I'd rather you be honest. I don't want the house to be lit up like a football stadium."

Only Delia would have this much to say about basic white lights. I admire her attention to detail, even if it's a pain in the ass. "Delia, when have you ever had problems with me not being honest?" At Thanksgiving dinner, I once told our great aunt that her stuffing tasted like sweaty gym socks. I was only eight, and Aunt Dorothy had forced me to take a serving even after I said I didn't want it, but still. I've never shied away from the truth. Except with the Dominic thing. But Delia doesn't know about that.

She sighs. "You're right. I'm overdoing it, aren't I?"

"Well, yeah. But overdoing it is sort of your personality."

We've been getting ready to decorate the Christmas tree for almost an hour. Delia, Tanner, and I went to the tree farm last night to pick it out. We got a good one. It's a full tree with thick, proportional branches and dark-green needles. It's tall and wide without being too big for Delia's small foyer. We left the tree alone overnight to let the branches settle. Today when I got home from work, Delia was already lugging boxes of ornaments out of the attic. Tanner helped us for a while, but Delia eventually kicked him out, claiming he didn't have an artistic eye.

Delia rolls her eyes. She pushes the sleeves of her black sweater up to her elbows, then motions toward the tree. "Ready to help me string these lights?" she asks.

"Not really." I'm quite comfortable in my spot on the floor, Jason pressed up against my side like a personal space heater. "But I *will* help you since I'm just that considerate." Tossing the garland on the ground, I rise to my feet, dusting my palms on the back of my leggings.

Delia barks a laugh. "If you were really considerate, you would keep that dog away from me," she says, scowling at Jason. He's blissfully unaware of Delia's rage, his fluffy tail thumping against the tile. "I still haven't forgiven him for what he did to my pillows."

"But he paid for his crimes," I remind her. More accurately, I paid. A lot. A pair of new throw pillows is en route to Delia. I sent her the tracking information this morning.

"That doesn't mean I have to forgive him," she says stubbornly. Of course, Jason chooses that moment to get up and wander over to her, brushing up against her leg. Delia pats him on the head, clearly resisting a smile. Not forgiven, my ass.

Delia gathers the lights into a ball, then connects them to the outlet at the base of the tree. We take our positions on either side of the tree and start passing the ball of lights back and forth, wrapping it around the sides. I breathe in the sweet scent of fresh pine needles.

"I'm sorry about all of this, Iz," Delia says, gesturing around the room, which is packed with cardboard boxes. "I know I'm being annoying. But this is the first party I've hosted since the move. Plus, Mom is meeting Tanner's mom for the first time. I want it to go well."

"You have nothing to worry about," I insist. "Mom and Ellen are both middle-aged women from Massachusetts. Talk about golden retrievers or the new serving platter you bought at Marshalls, and they'll be on a roll."

She nods. "I know I'm probably overthinking it. Mom loves Tanner, and she knows how happy I am in Seaview. I guess there's a part of me that still thinks she isn't thrilled about us living in Grandma Aggie's old place. You know she never got over the stuff with Dad. Not that I blame her."

If there's one thing Mom and I can agree on, it's that Grandma Aggie was the worst. My paternal grandmother got into a huge fight with my dad years ago after he asked her to move into my family's place in Boston. He was worried about her being alone in Seaview, two hours away from family. In response, Grandma Aggie cut us off completely. We didn't hear from her for twenty years, even after Dad passed away.

When Grandma Aggie died last spring, my sisters and I were shocked to find out she'd left us her house. Delia ended up coming to Seaview to scope out the place, which is how she met Tanner. Grandma Aggie wrote a letter to me and my sisters. I'm sure it contains a bullshit apology. I haven't actually read it, and I don't intend to. While I'm happy to be in Seaview, it doesn't mean I forgive Grandma Aggie for her years of unkindness toward my family. Her death doesn't change the way she lived her life.

"I doubt Mom is even thinking about that," I reply. "This place looks nothing like it did when it was Grandma Aggie's." Delia has done a ton of work since she moved in, updating old appliances and refurbishing the wood floors. It almost looks like a new house. "I mean that in the most positive way possible." Grandma Aggie's house was a garbage dump when we found it.

Delia smiles. "Thanks."

"Don't mention it. You know I love to stick it to Grandma Aggie."

"So, how are you feeling about seeing Mom?" Delia asks, her tone going serious. "Are things okay between you two? She didn't mention you when she called me last night, so I'm assuming you talked."

I fiddle with the light strand, my stomach sloshing like the inside of a washing machine. I haven't told Delia about my awkward phone call with Mom the other day. I don't know how much (or little) I should share. Venting about Mom's lack of faith in me would probably feel good, but Delia is already fretting over this Christmas party. The last thing I want to do is add to her stress.

"We're fine," I say. "You know how it is with me and Mom. We argue. I disappoint her. The sun sets. The world turns."

"You're not a disappointment to her, Izzy."

"You're right. I think I've disappointed her so many times over the years that she's actually become indifferent toward me."

"I know she's hard on you," Delia says. "I'm not saying this is an excuse, but I think she's only like that because she wants what's best for you. Or what *she* thinks is best." I've never doubted that Mom wants the best for me. The problem is, her concept of what's best and what I want to do with my life are two different things.

"I'm tired of having to justify myself to her. Every time we're on the phone, it feels like an interrogation," I say.

"It might help if you talked to her about what happened at your last job," Delia says. My shoulders stiffen automatically. "I know that's probably not what you want to do, but you haven't said much. Not knowing the truth has been killing her."

Everyone seems to think my getting fired was the result of something big and dramatic. A blowup with my boss. A conniving coworker sabotaging me on a project. However, that couldn't be further from reality.

It happened slowly. I started working at the design firm right after college, eager to put my artistic background to use. For a while, I thrived. I worked long hours. Came up with solid ideas. My boss loved me. Three months into my tenure at the firm, he said it was only a matter of time before I would be promoted.

Things changed last fall, shortly after I celebrated my two-year anniversary at work. It was like the creativity had been sapped from my body. I lost focus. Had a tough time coming up with ideas. I started handing in projects late. Missing meetings. After a few months, my boss sat me down and asked if something was wrong, but I couldn't explain myself. How do you tell someone that you suddenly have no interest in something that used to matter to you? That your sense of motivation just up and disappeared?

I received multiple warnings about my performance not meeting expectations. I tried to pull myself out of this rut, but nothing worked. I was careless. Sloppy. In March, a displeased client told my boss I sent him a brochure past deadline with *several* typos. It was the final nail in my metaphorical coffin.

More than a year after I fell into this slump, I'm still not sure what happened. My family has asked for details, but I haven't offered many. It's hard to open up about something when you don't fully understand it yourself. I know I want to get back into the design space at some point, but I'm terrified of the same thing happening again. What if I'm just as uninspired at another firm as I was in New York? What if I fail for a second time?

I suppose there's a part of me that fears Mom is right about me. That I'm hopeless and directionless and that I'm setting myself up for failure. I used to deflect her criticisms, letting them roll off my back like raindrops. But lately, it's been harder to tune her out. Mom's voice sounds a lot like the one in my head.

"If you don't want to talk to Mom about this stuff, you can always talk to me," Delia says. "I'm happy to be your sounding board."

"Thanks, Del." I don't know if I'll ever be ready to talk about it, but it's nice to know she has my back. "I'll keep that in mind."

A few minutes later, we finish wrapping the lights around the tree. Delia sticks the plug in the wall socket, and we take a step back to observe it in all its shining glory. With a smile playing on the edges of my lips, I turn to face Delia.

"You know, now that I'm looking at it, maybe it does look like a football stadium."

Glaring, Delia grabs a handful of tinsel and tosses it at me. "Not. Funny."

Seven

On Christmas Eve, I decide to be a coward.

While Delia's busy arranging pinecone centerpieces and vacuuming the spotless carpet for the hundredth time, I head out to do some last-minute shopping. The nearest shopping center is absolutely jammed, but I find a spot for my powder blue Beetle in the back of the lot. I spend hours drifting in and out of stores, barely looking at anything as I inch through the crowded aisles. A frazzled-looking woman nearly bowls me over with her overflowing cart at T.J. Maxx. She apologizes profusely before zipping away.

Subjecting myself to the Christmas Eve rush when I've already finished my shopping may seem like self-inflicted torture, but it's better than being at home when Mom arrives. We haven't spoken since our phone call. I'm still annoyed at her for trying to control me.

I don't want to fight with Mom all the time, but she makes that impossible when she's constantly belittling me and undermining my decisions. I wish I could talk to Delia or Morgan about it, but they wouldn't understand.

My sisters have always been perfect. They got good grades in school. Made smart choices. Our mom never had to worry about them disappointing her. They were her golden children, walking around with imaginary halos on their heads.

I was a much different story. Teen angst may have skipped Delia and Morgan, but it hit me hard. Growing up, I had a penchant for trouble. I talked back. Snuck out. Made reckless choices that spiked my parents' blood pressure. Simply put, I was a mess, and Mom was always trying to clean me up.

We fought. A *lot*. Most of it was my fault. I was an asshole back then. And Mom's constant criticism only made me want to act out more. But I've grown up since then. I'm not a kid anymore. I don't steal bottles of vodka from my parents' liquor cabinet or drop lit joints in the grass at the park and accidentally set it on fire (again, *asshole*).

I went to college. Got focused. I haven't deliberately done anything reckless in years, but Mom still sees me as that screwup kid. She always thinks I'm self-sabotaging, and it makes me feel like I'm incapable of doing anything right.

Delia and Morgan don't know what it's like to be on the receiving end of Mom's critical side. Trying to explain it to them would be like trying to describe a color without using its name. It's best for everyone if I keep these feelings to myself. There's no reason for me to stir up trouble between Mom and my sisters.

I wind up staying out till six-thirty, a full hour after Delia's party started. I know I've pushed my luck when I check my phone to find new messages from Delia. *Everyone's here. Where are you???* As much as I'd like to ignore her texts, I know that isn't an option. I promised her I would be back in time. Plus, Morgan's in town. I haven't seen my younger sister in months. I can't ditch this party when it would hurt both of them.

Begrudgingly, I retreat to my car, then make the short drive back to Delia's place. A few cars are sitting in the driveway when I pull up—Morgan's SUV, Jacob's sedan, and an unfamiliar silver Civic. I assume the latter belongs to either Tanner's mom or Jacob's parents. Delia mentioned Jacob's family would be joining us tonight. Apparently, they're close with Tanner's family, and they usually spend Christmas Eve together.

After I park along the curb, I head up the driveway, entering through the front door. Delia did an impressive job decorating. A twinkling Christmas tree sits in the foyer, adorned with tiny bows and red and gold bulbs (no crappy handmade ornaments for Delia Forrest). Sparkly garland is wrapped around the railing, and a tasteful wreath is hanging over the entryway to the kitchen. The house even smells like sugar cookies, which I know must be the work of a scented candle. For all her talents, Delia can't bake to save her life.

I follow the sounds of chatter and Christmas music into the house. Standing in the kitchen, I notice a group gathered in the living room. Delia's on the couch in straight-leg jeans and a sleek red blouse. She appears to be in conversation with Tanner's mom. Her boyfriend is sitting beside her, his arm draped over her shoulder.

On the other side of the room, Jacob's mom, Brenda, stands beside a tall man with graying black hair and glasses. He must be Jacob's dad. The resemblance is uncanny. He has the same lanky build and straight brows.

Jacob's parents are talking to Mom. My heartbeat quickens when my eyes land on her. Her back is turned to me, but I recognize her slight frame and short gray-brown hair. Nerves slosh around my stomach. The mature thing to do would be to put on a smile and walk over and say hello.

Naturally, I do the opposite.

Instead of making my presence known, I head to the other side of the kitchen. I'm hoping to have a minute alone to calm myself down, but I find Jacob crouched on the floor behind the counter. He's petting Jason. My dog lies on his back, his tongue lolling out the side of his mouth, and his tail thumping against the hardwood. The sight brings a small smile to my lips, despite my anxiety. Jason looks absolutely pathetic.

"He's never gonna leave you alone now," I say. "That dog is a stage-five clinger."

Jacob looks up, his brown eyes locking with mine. "He can't be as bad as Lulu."

"Lulu?" I repeat.

"My dog," he explains. "She's relentless."

I lean my hip against the counter. I had no clue Jacob had a dog, but we don't know each other that well. There's probably a lot I don't know about him.

"I didn't realize you were here," Jacob says.

"I just got back. Delia has been on a warpath all afternoon, trying to get things ready. I figured it was best to get out of her hair for a while."

Giving Jason one last pet, Jacob stands to his full height. The move draws my attention to his appearance. He's wearing a royal blue sweater with a giant grinning snowman on the front. The snowman has bright red cheeks and black pom-poms for eyes. It's the kind of thing you'd expect to see on an old-school librarian, not a thirty-year-old man.

"Wow." I purse my lips, fighting back a smile. "That is quite a sweater."

"Don't mock me, Forrest." Jacob shakes his head, but there's a grin forming at the corners of his mouth. "You can't kick a guy down when he's wearing a light-up sweater. It goes against common decency."

"You're telling me this monstrosity lights up? You *have* to show me."

He looks like he'd rather eat a bowl of glass. "This may surprise you, but I have some self-respect."

"Self-respect is overrated, Jacob."

"I won't debase myself for your entertainment."

"What if I paid you?" I ask. It can't hurt to sweeten the offer, right? "Everyone has a price. Name yours."

"You're out of luck, I'm afraid. I left the remote at home."

"The *remote*?" Jacob is wearing a sweater that comes with a *remote*, and I can't see it in full effect. What did I do in a past life to deserve this kind of torture? "Oh, c'mon. Now you're just teasing me."

"That's what you get for finding amusement in other people's suffering," he says. "The sweater was an early Christmas present from my mom. She gets me one every year."

"Does she hate you?" I ask, dumbfounded.

"She thinks I love ugly Christmas sweaters. She bought me one a few years back, and I pretended to like it. It's sort of taken on a life of its own. I don't think I can stop it at this point without crushing her." Well, that clears things up a bit. It earns Jacob some respect in my eyes. It takes serious loyalty to commit such a heinous crime against fashion to avoid hurting someone's feelings.

"I'm obviously hiding in the kitchen to avoid being seen in this," he says, gesturing to his abomination of a sweater. "What are you doing in here?"

"Hoping to consume as much spiked eggnog as possible before my mom rakes me over the coals," I answer honestly. I'm already hiding the situation from Delia and Morgan. I don't have it in me to lie anymore. "She has strong opinions about my…everything."

Jacob gives me a sympathetic nod. "Then you should stick with me tonight," he says. "Your mom won't even notice you if you're standing next to me."

"*Izzy!*"

Morgan's voice rings through the house. I barely have a second to turn around before she comes barreling toward me, wrapping me in a hug that smells like her vanilla perfume.

"Hey, Morg," I say, returning the embrace.

She pulls back, excitement swirling in her eyes. My sister reminds me of a cartoon princess, all hopeful and starry-eyed. I only have two years on Morgan, but she has an exuberance that makes her seem much younger.

"When did you get back?" she asks. "Delia said you were out shopping."

"Only a few minutes ago."

Peeking over Morgan's shoulder, I see the attention of the party has shifted to me. My skin feels tight and itchy under the weight of everyone's eyes. Especially Mom's. I haven't looked directly at her, but her gaze feels like a sharpened blade.

It's at this moment, of course, that I say something ridiculous.

"Don't all rush to greet me at once," I tell the group. "Please form an orderly line."

No one laughs. Fantastic. I should just throw myself into moving traffic.

"It's good to see you, Izzy," Mom says. Finally, I force myself to look at her. She wears a strained smile as she assesses me carefully. With my mouth closed, I run my tongue along my teeth, checking them for food. I scarfed down a box of caramels on the drive home.

"You too, Mom," I say, matching her smile with one of my own. *Please don't let me have chocolate on my teeth.*

We stand several feet apart, staring at each other like strangers. I don't know what to do. Should I hug her? It's been a few months since I last saw Mom, and we aren't on the best of terms. Hugging her might be awkward. Plus, she hasn't come over to hug me.

The longer neither of us does anything, the more uncomfortable the situation becomes. I can't imagine how it must look to everyone else. We're acting like we've never been around each other before.

Luckily, Morgan is here to break the ice.

"Jacob, oh my god!" she exclaims. "I love your sweater!"

Her compliment diffuses the tension instantly. Brenda beams with pride when Jacob says his sweater was a gift from his mom. Everyone slips back into conversation, the light mood returning to the party. I pour myself a glass of eggnog and find a spot on the loveseat in the living room.

A few minutes later, Morgan plops down beside me. She asks me about work, and I tell her it's fine. I ask her about school, and she says she's relieved to be done with the semester. Morgan is a graduate student at Finlay University in Boston. She's getting her degree in data science. The past year has been stressful for her.

After I finish my drink, I take Morgan upstairs to my bedroom. I close the door behind us and tell her the box wrapped in shiny gold paper sitting on my bed is for her. She settles on the corner of the mattress, pulling the box into her lap and tearing away the thin paper.

She tugs the lid off the box. "Thank you, Izzy!" she cries out as she peers inside. I ended up getting her a few books from her reading wishlist. Morgan loves romance novels. She has stacks of them scattered all over her apartment.

"You're welcome," I reply. "I figured you'd rather open those in private to avoid having to give Mom a crash course in erotica."

Morgan's cheeks turn bright pink. "They're not all like that," she says. It's true, but it's still fun to tease her. Some of those romance books can be downright filthy.

By the time we return to the party, everyone's getting ready for dinner. We head to the kitchen, where a buffet of honey-glazed ham, buttered carrots, roasted potatoes, and green bean casserole awaits us. My mouth waters at the scents of butter and garlic.

I snag a glass plate off the counter and line up to serve myself.

"You've really outdone yourself, Delia," Tanner's mom, Ellen, says as she scoops carrots onto her plate.

Delia, hovering by the stove, looks pleased. "Thank you," she says, "but I can't take credit for the food. That was all Tanner."

He smiles at her. "Don't forget about the rolls, darling," he says.

"Oh, right. I popped a tray of frozen rolls in the oven."

"And what about you, Izzy?" Mom asks, coming up behind me to grab a plate. "Did you have any hand in this?"

"If having a hand in it means supplying the rum for the eggnog, then yes," I tell her. Mom doesn't seem to find it amusing. She lifts a brow, and the subtext is clear. *You're living rent-free in your sister's house, and you couldn't be bothered to make a fucking casserole?*

"Izzy offered to help, Mom," Delia insists. "Tanner and I had it covered."

Mom nods, though she doesn't appear convinced.

After I fill up my plate, I file into the dining room and slide into the empty chair between Jacob and Morgan. Immediately, I shove a forkful of green bean casserole into my mouth. I figure Mom is less likely to pick a fight with me if I'm chewing. She won't want me showering crumbs all over Delia's centerpieces, right?

The table fills up quickly, conversation humming in the air. Normally, I'm the type to pipe up at group dinners, but I think it's best if I take on the role of a listener tonight. Mom and Ellen spend most of the meal praising Delia for her decorations, a compliment I agree with wholeheartedly. She turned this place into a Christmas wonderland. I know how hard she worked on it, so I'm glad she's getting positive feedback.

As I'm finishing up what's left on my plate, Brenda turns her attention to me. She's sitting in the chair across from me, sipping a glass of red wine.

"Izzy, you work for Tanner, don't you?" she asks.

Nodding, I swallow a mouthful of potatoes. "I'm his office manager," I say. "The best in company history. Isn't that right, boss man?" I send a look to Tanner at the other end of the table. He rolls his eyes, though he's clearly unbothered.

"She's done a decent job," he admits.

It's not the most heartfelt of compliments, but I'll take it.

"What were you doing before you moved to Seaview?" Brenda asks.

"Working in graphic design. That's what my degree is in."

"How neat. I'm not very creative myself, but I admire those who are."

"I'll probably end up working in that space again eventually," I tell her. "My position at Ryan & Son is just temporary."

"Though I'm sure you'd make a terrific office manager in the long term," Mom chimes in. *Oh, great.* So we're doing this here.

Ignoring Mom's comment, I turn to Brenda and say, "I love art. I've always known I wanted to do something creative."

"What we love and how we make money aren't always the same thing," Mom says. "You think telemarketers are in it for the passion?" Annoyance rips through me. She's being demeaning. Making it seem like I'm a starry-eyed kid chasing an unrealistic dream. I have a *degree* in graphic design. I may have gotten fired from my last job, but that doesn't mean I'm completely talentless.

I don't want to make a big scene in front of everyone, but I need to get away for a second, or I might say something I'll come to regret.

I give Brenda a small smile. "Excuse me," I say, pushing out of my chair and exiting the dining room. I turn the corner, quickly locking myself in the half-bath on the first floor. I brace my palms on the edges of the laminate counter, forcing myself to take deep breaths.

I hate that I let Mom get to me like this. It happens every time. Whenever we interact, I revert back to the teenage version of myself, getting frustrated and storming out of family dinners. I haven't been that person in a long time, but being around Mom makes it feel as though nothing has changed.

It's only dinner, I remind myself. Mom may think I'm still in high school, but I'm a grown woman. I don't live under her roof anymore, and I don't cave to her demands. I can handle her criticism for one night. She's heading back to Boston tomorrow. I won't have to deal with her opinions for much longer.

Taking another deep breath, I decide it's time to rejoin the party. I unlock the bathroom door and step outside, surprised to find Mom waiting in the hallway. Her features are taut, and her arms are folded against her chest.

"Sorry," I tell her as I move out of the doorway. "I didn't know there was a line." I start to leave the hall, hoping she'll let me leave it at that, but it's *Mom*. It's never that easy.

"You're upset with me." She says it like it's an inconvenience. As tedious as cleaning the kitchen or getting groceries. It doesn't matter how she made me feel. My reaction is nothing but a pesky matter to be handled.

"We've been over this a million times, Mom," I say, trying to keep my frustration at bay. We might be in another room, but Delia's house isn't very big. "I wish you'd stop trying to make a thing out of it when you know I don't agree with you."

"I just don't understand why you won't at least consider it," Mom replies. "What's wrong with being at Ryan & Son for the long haul, Izzy?"

"It's not what I want."

"But it's a good job. You like it there, don't you?"

"Well, yeah. But that doesn't mean…" I trail off before I finish the sentence. What am I doing? What am I trying to prove? I've had this exact argument with Mom a dozen times before. It doesn't matter what I say—she's never going to change her mind.

Mom pinches the bridge of her nose. She shakes her head as though she's fully exasperated with me. "I wish you'd start taking your future seriously," she says. "Life isn't all fun and games, Izzy. You need stability. Ryan & Son is offering you that."

"I told Tanner this was only temporary."

"He's happy to let you stay on." *He's happy.* Not he *would* be happy. I don't miss the tense she uses or what it must mean.

"Hang on. You asked Tanner about this?"

"Well, not exactly," she says. "I was talking to him and Delia the other night, and he mentioned that you've been such a great fit at the company. All I said was that it would be nice if you stayed there permanently."

"Mom, please tell me you're not serious."

"I was only trying to get a sense of where his head was at," she argues. "For the record, he seemed very receptive to the idea." I hide my face in my hands. Tanner and I might not have the traditional boss-employee relationship, but he's still my *boss*. I don't need my mother pressuring him into making my temporary position permanent.

"Please don't be angry with me," Mom says. "I only did it because I care about you."

"Bullshit. The only thing you care about is trying to control me. I'm not fifteen anymore. You don't have a say over what I do with my life."

"I'm being realistic, Izzy. Someone has to be. You have a great opportunity in front of you, and you're throwing it away." I've had enough. We've done this same routine too many times now. I can't keep going in circles with her.

"I'm done having this argument with you," I tell her. "I'm an adult living *my* life. If you can't respect my decisions, then maybe you shouldn't be in it." Anger charts through my veins, hot and fluid like magma. It's a harsh thing to say, but

I don't know what else to do at this point. If Mom can't accept my decisions, why does she even want to be around me? I'm tired of the fighting and the tension. Of always saying the wrong thing.

Mom rears back as if I just slapped her. "If that's what you want, fine," she says coldly. "I wouldn't want to burden you with my concern." She turns and stalks back toward the dining room, leaving me to stew in my frustration.

Eight

Izzy

So, this is what dying feels like.

Knives slash in my temples when I wake up on Christmas morning. Cracking open my eyelids, I'm met by painfully bright light. I shut them immediately, burying my head under my pillow, where I remain for seconds or minutes or hours. I don't know how much time passes. It has no meaning at the moment. The only thing that matters is making the ache go away.

When my head finally stops feeling like it's being poked with a thousand tiny needles, I sit up. I'm not in my room. I wound up crashing in Tanner's guest room after the party last night. Delia thought it was for the best. I think she was afraid Mom and I might kill each other if we had to sleep under the same roof.

We haven't spoken since our argument outside the bathroom. Both of us went back to the dining room, acting as if nothing happened, but the friction between us was thicker than a cloud of smoke. The others had to notice. I may have had a glass or two of spiked eggnog to help wash down the awkwardness. It's a decision I've come to regret this morning, as my head feels like a marching band stomped all over it.

Fighting with Mom always leaves me feeling out of sorts. A mix of emotions has been stirring within me. Annoyance.

Sadness. Frustration. However, the feeling weighing heaviest on my mind is disappointment.

Mom and I have never had an easy relationship. We spent almost all of my teen years arguing, mostly over small things like my sneaking out or getting detention. Back then, I always knew on some subconscious level that she was right. I was reckless and selfish and irresponsible, and she was only trying to stop me from making mistakes.

But I've grown up a lot over the past eight years. I'm not a silly teenager determined to make the worst decision possible in every situation. I'm a grown woman, trying to figure out what to do with the rest of my life. While I may be uncertain right now, that doesn't mean I'm not taking my future seriously. Mom could at least try to be supportive. She doesn't have to agree with my choices, but she could say she loves me and that everything will be fine. Is that so much to ask? For a little reassurance?

I wish Mom and I hadn't gotten into that fight. But even more, I wish it hadn't happened at Delia's party. She wanted it to be perfect. Our bickering certainly wasn't part of her plan. Thankfully, Mom and I didn't seem to ruin the night. Everyone appeared to have a good time, praising the food and decor. Still, I hope I didn't cause Delia any stress. I know how much that party meant to her. I need to apologize and tell her that the night was amazing, even though Mom and I didn't make it easy.

Slowly, I push down the covers and roll out of bed. As I stand up, I glimpse at myself in the mirror on the dresser. My hair is a bird's nest, sticking wildly in every direction. My clothes are rumpled, and there are crease marks on my cheek from my pillow. I look like a woman who had one too many glasses of eggnog last night and woke up with endless regret. Maybe it's my comeuppance for being a bad sister.

I do what I can to fix my hair (which isn't much) before opening the bedroom door. Carpet squishes under my bare feet as I make my way down the hall. I'm halfway down the stairs when I hear Delia's and Tanner's voices coming from the kitchen.

"I hate your coffee maker," Delia says, followed by the sound of liquid being poured down the sink.

"You forgot to put on the strong setting again, didn't you?" Tanner asks, chuckling softly. "Darling, how many times are you gonna drink watery coffee before you remember?"

"Don't blame me. It's *your* coffee maker. That thing is a piece of junk."

"It works just fine if you use it correctly."

Delia harrumphs. "Don't start with me," she warns him. "I haven't had coffee yet. I may scratch your eyes out."

"But you think my eyes are so pretty."

"I'm gonna dump the rest of this on you. Better yet, I'm gonna exchange the sander I got you for Christmas for a new coffee maker."

Tanner laughs, footsteps echoing off the hard floor. "You know," he says, "there's an easy way to remedy this situation."

"Me smashing that machine with a sledgehammer?"

"If you lived here, your fancy coffee maker would be here, and you wouldn't have to rely on my crappy one." I freeze. Tanner is asking Delia to move in *right now*? No way I'm interrupting. I've been telling him to do it for weeks.

"It *would* be nice not to drink watered-down coffee every morning."

"We could turn the guest room into your home office," he says. "I could build you a big fancy desk."

Delia sighs. "It's tempting," she tells him, "but you know I can't right now. Izzy's in a bad place. She's dealing with some stuff, and she needs me. I can't leave her." *What?* No. Delia's words strike my ears like an out-of-tune piano. She is supposed to say yes, not turn Tanner down. Especially not because of me.

"It's okay if you're not ready," Tanner says. "I don't want to force you into anything."

"No, that's not it," she insists. "I want to. Really. It just wouldn't feel right abandoning Izzy right now. Not when she's going through something."

"Well, the offer still stands, whenever you decide. Though it may take a while for my ego to recover from your cold-hearted rejection."

Delia laughs. "Oh, please. You're gonna regret asking me when you hear what I have planned for the living room. I'm thinking lace curtains. Maybe new wall sconces."

"Darling, you can do whatever the hell you want with this place."

"Even wallpaper?"

"Okay, maybe not everything."

"But you just said!"

"Taking that stuff down is a nightmare. Your fingernails wouldn't last five minutes."

"Then it's a good thing I have a boyfriend to do my bidding for me."

Kissing noises echo through the kitchen, which I take as my cue to leave. I tiptoe back up to the guest room, quietly shutting the door behind me. With my back pressed against the door, I slide down to the carpet, dropping my face in my hands.

Delia rejected Tanner because of me. She won't take the next step in her relationship with a guy she loves so much because she is afraid of how it will make me feel. The knowledge hits me like a gut punch.

Being in Seaview has changed Delia a lot. She's happier, more relaxed. She found her place here, but instead of basking in her happiness, she's putting her future on hold. For my sake. I'm such a disaster that I'm actually holding my sister back.

It's shocking and embarrassing. I've never been as put together as Delia or Morgan, but I didn't think I was messy enough to raise this level of concern. Does Delia resent me for it? Is she secretly hoping I'll get it together so she can move on with her life?

I'm ruining her life, and I didn't even realize. How selfish am I? I've been so focused on my career that I didn't consider how my decisions affect the people around me.

I don't want to be a burden to my loved ones. Delia shouldn't sacrifice her happiness on my behalf. This *has* to be a wake-up call. I've been floating through life, aimless, like a piece of driftwood, for too long.

Something has to change. The question is, what am I going to do?

***

Getting your shit together isn't easy.

Most people spend the week between Christmas and New Year's lounging in sweatpants all day and eating sugar cookies for breakfast, but I've been devoting every minute to

76

figuring out how I can stop being such a nuisance in Delia's
life.

The day after Christmas, I dug an old self-help book out
of the back of my closet called "Reinventing Your Life:
Becoming the Best Version of You." Mom gave it to me a
couple years ago, a subtle middle finger. I never thought I'd
actually read it, but I needed to start somewhere, and a book
about self-improvement seemed like as good a place as any.

Unfortunately, I had a hard time getting through it. Jason
kept nibbling at my ankles, demanding my attention. It was
impossible to focus. I barely made it through two chapters
before I shoved the book back in my closet, never to be seen
again.

After I gave up on the self-help book, I spent some time
job hunting. I've glanced at a few openings for graphic
design positions since I started working at Ryan & Son, but I
haven't applied for anything. Getting fired from my last role
has made me hesitant to put myself out there. I don't want to
experience another work-related disaster. I have to be
particular in choosing my next job. It's the only way I can
ensure my success. I still haven't found anything I feel good
about.

Of course, there's an obvious solution here: leave town.
Delia only rejected Tanner's invitation to move in because
I'm living with her. If I weren't here, there'd be nothing
stopping her. I could always go back to New York. Cynthia
wouldn't mind me crashing with her.

Yet moving away would come with its own set of
complications. First, I don't have a job in New York.
Working at Ryan & Son might not be my idea of a long-term
career, but it's a steady paycheck. How would I afford an

apartment in the city without a consistent source of income? I'd be broke within weeks.

Second, it would feel wrong abandoning Tanner without any notice. He knows I'm not planning to stay at his company forever, but I want to be there until he finds someone to take over for me permanently. Tanner did me a huge solid by giving me this job. I don't want to return the favor by leaving him hanging.

Third, and probably most important, is that I *like* Seaview. I may have initially come here to escape my rapidly deteriorating life in New York, but I've developed an appreciation for this little town. I've gotten used to the quiet life, the mom-and-pop shops where the employees know you by name. Living here has been a nice change. I'm not ready to say goodbye.

There's also the fact that abruptly moving would seem impulsive and rash, validating Delia's concerns about me being a mess. I want to ease her worry, not add to it, which means I have no choice but to stay and prove to her I'm not a total disaster.

It won't be easy. My life is in shambles in every way imaginable. My floundering career. My strained relationships. Change is going to require something big.

I have to become the antithesis of myself. Someone organized and consistent and dependable. Luckily, I have the best example living under the same roof as me. Delia has a stable career and a loving boyfriend, so she must be doing something right. Maybe emulating some of her qualities will help me turn myself around.

A therapist would probably tell me not to change who I am. That I can find ways to improve my life without completely deconstructing my personality. But honestly?

Screw that love-who-you-are crap. I've been myself for twenty-five years. It's. Not. Working.

Several days after Christmas, I'm sitting at the kitchen table sipping a mug of coffee when Delia comes downstairs dressed in a black pullover and leggings. She quietly says "good morning" as she steps into the kitchen, carrying a pair of sneakers.

"Morning," I chirp back, anxiety twisting in my stomach. I haven't told her about what I overheard the other day. Admitting the truth would only make Delia feel guilty.

Delia pulls out a chair at the table and begins putting on her shoes. I watch her for a moment, an idea forming in my brain.

"Going for a run?" I ask.

She nods. "It's supposed to snow later," she says as she laces up her sneakers. "I want to get out there before the sidewalks get too slick."

"You doing that trail by the beach?"

"That's the plan."

I hesitate for a second, then say, "would you mind if I come?" Successful people like running, don't they?

Shock blankets Delia's face. "Seriously?" From the tone of her voice, you'd think I just asked her to commit arson with me.

I shoot her a pointed look. "I'll pretend not to take offense to that."

"I wasn't trying to offend you," she replies as she finishes lacing one shoe, then switches to the other. "The last time I invited you to come on a run with me, you told me you'd rather make snow angels naked." Okay, she may have a point there. I've never been shy about my hatred of running. I haven't gone on a run since last winter, when I stepped in someone's half-eaten burrito in Central Park. My sneakers stunk like onions for weeks, even after I washed them.

"Well, maybe I've had a change of heart," I say. "I can go by myself if you don't want me to come."

"No, I want you to," she insists. "We can hit the beach or do laps downtown."

"I thought you wanted to do the trail."

She pulls her dark hair into a tight ponytail. "It's pretty long. You haven't been running in a while, Iz. I don't want you to strain anything."

"What? No. I'll be fine." The whole point of me pulling myself together is so Delia stops inconveniencing herself for my sake. "Let's do the trail."

"Are you sure?" she asks, sounding uncertain. "I usually do three miles."

Fuck me. "Yeah. I'm positive."

Twenty minutes later, I'm clad in spandex, chasing Delia down the paved trail that runs along Beach Park. It's thirty-four degrees outside. Dark-blue waves ripple on the horizon, and a dusting of snow coats the beach like powdered sugar.

I thought the seaside views would make the run less terrible, but I was wrong. I'm too cold to appreciate the scenery. We've only been out here for a few minutes, but my fingers are already numb, and my lungs feel as if there's a boulder pressing down on them.

Truly, I don't understand what my sister finds enjoyable about this experience. The sore muscles? The sweat? Maybe Delia is a masochist. I can't think of a single reason anyone would like running unless they enjoy making themselves suffer.

As if she can sense me thinking about her, Delia glances at me over her shoulder. Her cheeks are flushed, but she doesn't appear to be out of breath at all. "You doing okay, Iz?" she asks, her ponytail swinging back and forth.

I'd laugh if I weren't gasping for oxygen. If "doing okay" means debating whether I should fake a hamstring injury, then I'm downright peachy.

"Yeah. I'm fine," I tell her, though I barely manage to get the words out.

"We can slow down if you need to."

"Delia, I'm *fine*." I know she's only trying to help, but I'm not in the mood for her patronizing. I'm going to finish this run, even if it kills me. Which it very well might. I'm already gassed, and we've only done a mile. At this rate, I don't know how I'm going to make it back to the car. Delia might have to drag me there.

"Izzy, watch out!" she exclaims.

I don't have a chance to react before I stumble over a crack in the pavement, instantly losing my footing. I throw up my arms, fighting to keep my balance, but it doesn't do me any good. I tumble forward, my palms and knees catching most of the impact as they scrape across the ground.

"Shit, Iz!" Delia shouts as she rushes to my side. Concern flashes across her features. "Are you hurt?" She offers a hand, but I don't take it, forcing myself to get up on my own. I wipe my stinging palms on the back of my leggings.

"Only my pride," I mutter.

I think I found a new level of rock bottom.

Nine

Izzy

Running, it turns out, is modern-day torture.

Despite my epic tumble, I've joined Delia on her morning run every day this week. I thought it would get easier with time, but it has only validated my hatred. If running on a daily basis is what it takes to fix my life, I may have to reconsider. I want to improve my life, not hate every second. And that's exactly what will happen if I keep this up.

Finding a way to change hasn't been easy. I've only been doing this for a few days, but nothing I've tried so far is going to cut it. I'd like to know I'm heading in the right direction. Right now, it feels like I'm running circles around a track, burning tons of energy but ultimately going nowhere.

I'm lying in bed on New Year's Eve, every muscle in my body screaming, when Delia knocks on my door. "Hey," she says as she lets herself inside. "Tanner and I decided we're gonna go out tonight. Seaview Tavern is having a New Year's Eve thing. Do you want to come with us? We're leaving in about an hour."

"No, that's okay." I'm already ruining Delia and Tanner's relationship by being in Seaview. The least I can do is let them enjoy a night out without me third wheeling. Besides, I already have my New Year's Eve plans figured out. I'm going to eat a frozen pizza by myself, then pass out on the couch. "Enjoy your date."

"Oh, we're not gonna be alone," she says. "Jacob's coming, too. It's his birthday tomorrow. I'm sure he'd appreciate the company."

Curiosity stirs in my brain. "What makes you think that?"

"I guess he had another bad date the other night. Tanner didn't give me all the details, but Jacob has been trying to meet someone for a while, and it hasn't been going well. I think he's bummed out." Jacob's been having dating problems? I had no idea. He always seems so put together when I'm around him. He has a house, a nice, stable job. From the outside, you'd have no clue that he's struggling with *anything.* It's almost hard to believe…

Oh my god.

I sit up straight, inspiration jolting through my veins. My sore muscles are going to have to toughen up because we are going out tonight.

"On second thought," I say, throwing the blankets off my body, "I'll come."

Delia's face brightens. "Awesome. Let me know when you're ready. I'm so excited."

I return her smile with my own. "Me, too."

***

Jacob

I'm almost thirty.

I could spend the first minutes of my thirtieth birthday ringing in the new year with a crowd of drunken strangers, but I step out of the bar instead. I'm not in the mood for celebration. I only came out tonight because Tanner insisted. If it were up to me, I'd be at home with Lulu, wallowing in my self-pity in peace.

It's quiet on the back patio of Seaview Tavern, the music and laughter muffled. A thin layer of snow coats the patio furniture, which has been covered for the winter, and a few empty beer cans and cigarette butts litter the icy pavement. It's freezing. I slip my hands into the pockets of my jeans to keep them warm. I wish I had the sense to bring my beer outside. Alcohol might've dulled the sting of the wind.

I breathe into the darkened sky, my breath unfurling like a cloud. When I was younger, I loved having a New Year's Day birthday. It was a guaranteed celebration. I always knew I would start the day surrounded by friends or family. But the older I've gotten, it feels more like a nuisance. Each birthday serves as a reminder of everything I failed to accomplish the previous year, and it's set against the backdrop of a party.

It was this time last year when I decided to fully commit to finding someone. I was tired of being alone, so I told myself I would do everything to meet the woman I want to spend the rest of my life with. I signed up for online dating. Asked friends to set me up. Went on countless unsuccessful dates. A year later, and nothing has changed. Despite my efforts, I'm no closer to getting married.

What if another year goes by, and I'm out here again? An entire year of active dating brought me nothing. What if my thirties look like this, too? Will I be by myself on the eve of my fortieth birthday, wondering what I did wrong?

What's the problem? Is it me? Maybe I've set my standards too high. I've been idolizing my parents' relationship for years. I've always thought I would find something similar for myself, but that could be that's the issue. Marriages like my parents' are rare. Most people don't meet the love of their life at fourteen. Hell, half of marriages end in divorce, don't they? And who's to say the ones that stay together are even happy?

Maybe I need to be more realistic. What I'm searching for is uncommon, like finding a sand dollar intact. People will spend years scouring the ocean floor and *still* never locate one. Is that what I'm doing? Holding out for the improbable? I'm a small-town actuary, for christ's sake. That's not exactly what great loves are made of.

Is it time to settle? I don't want to be alone forever. I'm sure I can still have a fulfilling relationship, even if it isn't grand and passionate. A good love may not be a great love, but it's better than no love, isn't it?

"Holy shit. It's *freezing*!"

A glance over my shoulder reveals Izzy stepping outside in nothing but high heels and a short sequined dress that fits her curves like a glove. The tops of her breasts spill over the neckline, which is something I *definitely* shouldn't be noticing about my best friend's girlfriend's little sister, so I quickly tear my eyes away.

She's carrying two shot glasses. She sticks one between her teeth, so she can use her free hand to shut the sliding door behind her, and then she heads toward me.

"I thought I'd come out and commiserate with you," she says, teetering across the icy pavement in her heels. "Of course, I didn't realize we were in the middle of another ice age. How have your nipples not frozen off by now?" I'm barely fazed by her outlandish words. I've spent enough time around Izzy to expect the unpredictable. Besides, I'm more concerned about her developing frostbite. Though hearing her talk about my nipples certainly doesn't help the whole don't-stare-at-Izzy's-rack thing.

"We should go inside," I say, pulling off my jacket to offer it to her.

Izzy dismisses my concern with a wave. "What's life without a little risk?" She hands me a shot glass, then clinks it against her own. "Cheers," she says before downing her shot. I do the same because it *is* freezing, and I *am* commiserating. The tequila burns its way down my throat.

We set our empty glasses on the railing. I offer her my jacket again, and she reluctantly accepts it, draping it over her shoulders. The yellow porch light shines over the top of her curly hair like a halo. She's exceptionally pretty, with wide blue eyes and full lips painted bright red. She has this knowing look about her, as if she's always in on a secret. She's the type of woman who demands your attention simply by being in your presence.

"Is there something specific we're miserable about tonight, or is this general misery?" she asks, giving me a sideways look. "Either is fine with me, but context would be nice."

"I think you might be projecting a little, Forrest," I tell her. Izzy might not be wrong about me being miserable, but I'm not about to share my deepest fears with a woman I hardly know.

"Are you gonna psychoanalyze me, Jacob?" She lifts a brow, intrigued. "I've heard I'm quite the case study."

"A woman who goes outside in freezing temperatures to take shots? I think that goes beyond my capacity."

"There's no harm in trying, right? What if I give you a dollar for each correct answer?"

"You *want* to be psychoanalyzed?"

Izzy shrugs. "We've got to pass the time somehow, don't we?"

I study her for a moment. Her tone is playful, but she seems serious.

"I don't know you that well," I remind her.

"Exactly. You can be objective."

Izzy stares at me expectantly. Is she really asking me to psychoanalyze her? I don't know enough about her to make an accurate assessment, but I doubt she's going to take that as an answer. I need to think of something to satisfy her.

"You've been living in New York for the past few years, right?" She nods. "That couldn't be more different from Seaview. I bet you're missing home. Wondering why you came to this small town in the first place."

Izzy makes an indignant sound. "Missing home? Seriously? *That's* your best guess? I asked you to speculate about the inner workings of my psyche, Jacob."

"Your psyche confounds me."

"Don't give me that. We have five minutes till midnight. How am I supposed to be a better person in the new year if you won't lay the truth on me?" I barely know Izzy, but what *do* I know? She's loud and impulsive. Deeply unserious. Prone to cracking jokes and toying with the people around her. Izzy likes to challenge others. Catch them off guard.

"I guess you seem a little indecisive," I tell her. "And that you make other people uncomfortable to avoid dealing with uncomfortable feelings yourself."

Shit. Did I say that aloud? It's been a while since I've done a tequila shot, but I didn't think the liquor would hit me that quickly.

I glance at Izzy, expecting her to appear (rightfully) offended, but she's looking at me with amused eyes, fighting back a smile.

"Now that, Freud, was some psychoanalysis," she says. "I owe you a dollar."

"I'm sorry. I wasn't trying to be so, uh—"

"Honest?" she supplies. "You shouldn't apologize. Honesty makes the world go round."

"I don't think that's how the saying goes."

"Well, it should. Because if you and I were honest and dealt with our shit, we'd probably be in there celebrating instead of freezing our asses off out here." She jerks a thumb back toward the bar, a contemplative expression on her face.

We're both quiet for a moment. Then curiosity gets ahold of me.

"What are you commiserating, Forrest?" I ask.

Izzy sighs. "Being the root of my sister's unhappiness."

"Some context would be nice."

"Tanner asked Delia to move in with him," she explains. "I overheard them talking the other day." This doesn't shock me. Tanner told me about his plan to ask Delia to move in a couple weeks ago. Honestly, I was surprised he hadn't done it sooner.

"It makes sense, right?" Izzy adds. "They're happy and in love. Of course they want to live together. Except Delia said no. Because of me."

I frown. "What? Why?"

"Apparently, she's worried about how it will affect me. She thinks I'm in a fragile state right now." Izzy shakes her head, appearing to be lost in thought. "The worst part is, I can't blame her. You saw what happened on Christmas Eve." I don't know anything about Izzy's relationship with her mom, but things were tense at that dinner party. I got the sense they've been having problems for a while.

"I was in a rough spot when Delia moved here," Izzy says. "I'd just gotten fired, and I had no idea what I was going to do. Delia offered to let me stay with her so I could figure things out. It seemed great, the idea of us living together. But I never would've done it if I'd known it was gonna ruin her happiness."

"I don't think you've ruined her happiness."

"It's my fault she's not living with him, Jacob."

"Can't you talk to her about this?" I ask. "Explain how you feel?"

"Delia's stubborn. When she makes a decision, she sees it through. She's not gonna move in with Tanner unless she thinks I can handle it. I need her to see me as solid, but it's hard to do that when every aspect of my life is a mess." I'm surprised Izzy is sharing so much with me. Our conversations are usually light and inconsequential. She must be feeling pretty defeated if she's willing to confide in a virtual stranger.

I give her an empathetic look. "I'm sorry. I wish there was something I could do."

At once, Izzy's spirits seem to brighten. Hopefulness shines in her light eyes. "Actually," she says, "I think we might be able to help each other."

"What do you mean?" I meant what I said, though I wasn't actually expecting Izzy to take me up on it. It's not like I can force her sister to move in with Tanner.

"I've heard about your women troubles."

My face gets hot. Izzy is the last person I want to talk to about my dating woes. Well, maybe second to my mother. She's constantly feeding me cheesy lines about how *there's always more fish in the sea* or *the right woman is just around the corner.*

"It sounds like it's pretty rough out there," Izzy says.

"No offense, Forrest, but I really don't want—"

"I bet I could help you."

I turn to her, perplexed. "How exactly?"

"I know women, Jacob. How we think. What we look for in a partner. With my help, I'm sure you'd find yourself having a lot more successful dates."

"You're offering to teach me how to pick up women?" I thought being out here alone on my thirtieth birthday was the ultimate low point, but no. It's this. Am I such a lost cause that someone wants to teach me how to date?

"All right, Forrest," I say. "I think I've had enough commiserating for tonight." I grab our empty shot glasses off the railing, then turn to head back into the bar.

"What? Where are you going?" she asks.

"To find out what a hangover in your thirties looks like."

"Jacob, wait!" Izzy grabs my forearm. When I look back, her features are rigid. "You didn't let me finish telling you about my proposal."

"Your proposal has already done enough damage to my ego."

"What's wrong with getting a little help with dating? It's just like anything else. If you want to improve, you have to figure out your weaknesses. Are you really gonna let *pride* stop you from finding someone?"

"Um, yeah, actually."

Izzy puts a hand on her hip like a teacher delivering a lecture. "You're self-sabotaging. I'm offering you a real solution here. You're a good-looking guy, Jacob. Nice. Funny. You should have a girlfriend if you want one. I can help make it happen." She sounds earnest. I don't think she's saying any of this to tease me, but it feels like a big joke.

"And what would you get out of this?"

"Your help in return."

"With what? *Men*?" I laugh and shake my head in disbelief. She's out of her mind. "Go look in a mirror, Forrest. You don't need my help."

"Not with *men*. You'd be helping me pull myself together."

"I'm not following."

"I need Delia to stop seeing me as a disaster," Izzy says. "It's the only way she's gonna move in with Tanner. You own a house. Have a stable job. You're, like, a testimonial in a brochure called 'How to Succeed at Life.' I want you to teach me your ways. It's a simple exchange of services. You help me. I help you."

It appears I'm not the only one who can't hold their liquor. Izzy's talking nonsense. "We should go back inside," I tell her. "I think that shot went to your head."

"Jacob, I could be plastered right now, and this idea would still make perfect sense. What do we have to lose? Neither of us is going to get what we want if we don't at least try to do something different. The worst that happens is nothing changes."

She's quiet for a moment, sawing her bottom lip between her teeth. I think she's waiting for a response, but I don't know what to say. I wasn't expecting *this* when she stepped onto the patio.

"You don't have to decide anything right now," she says. "Just think about it, okay? You know where to find me if you change your mind."

I nod because it's the only thing I find myself capable of doing. This night is weird.

"*Now* we should go inside," she says, tucking her arms against her sides. "I don't know about you, but my nipples are like ice picks." And it keeps getting weirder.

Izzy steps forward and opens the back door. Cheers erupt through the congested bar, followed by the screech of dozens of party horns.

It must be midnight.

Happy birthday to me, I guess.

Ten

Jacob
I'm thinking about it.

At work, when I should be analyzing spreadsheets. At home, when I'm scrolling through profiles on True Connections. Izzy Forrest planted a seed in my brain, and I can't dig it out for the life of me.

By all measures, her idea is terrible. Izzy and I barely know each other. How is she supposed to help me with dating? I value structure, stability. She stands outside without a coat in freezing cold weather, taking shots. Something tells me the two of us have very different thoughts on relationships. Izzy doesn't know me well enough to know what I want. Dating hasn't been going well for me, but she can't force something that isn't working.

And despite what she may think, I have no idea how to help someone get their act together. The things she pointed out as "evidence" of my successful life—my job, my house—mean nothing when I've failed miserably at achieving what I want most. I went on twenty-two first dates last year. Only a handful of them led to second dates, and none resulted in relationships. If Izzy knew the true extent of my dating failures, she wouldn't want any guidance from me.

Logic says Izzy's idea would be a complete waste of time, but that hasn't stopped me from considering it. Her proposal might be ridiculous, but it's something different, right? It can't be worse than what I've already been doing. My track record is abysmal. If my dating life were a problem I was analyzing at work, I'd be telling our company executives to cut our losses and get out while we still can.

Am I really in a position to turn anything down? Izzy's methods may be unconventional, but they'd probably give me a better chance at success than my current path. I haven't been on a date since *Marina*. I've tried talking to a few women on True Connections, but our conversations were drier than an instructional manual.

The thing is, I have to put myself out there again. It's the only way I'm ever going to meet someone. But I'm tired of the constant disappointment. It's not just about Marina—it's about all the bad dates that came before her. I feel like a boxer trapped in the ring with a vastly superior opponent. I keep taking punches, and each time it gets tougher to stand back up. It's getting old, opening myself up only to get clobbered.

Maybe I could use Izzy's help. She knows how women think, what they like. And she has no trouble speaking her mind. She might be able to figure out what's going wrong with my dates. A woman's perspective could be exactly what I need.

A heavy slap at the top of my cubicle jolts me from my depressing thoughts. "Jake, my man," Luke Daniels shouts as he hovers over the fabric wall that separates our desks. Our consulting firm moved into a bigger office space last fall, and I ended up next to him. I think HR wanted to avoid putting any women in his proximity. Luke has the greasy energy of a used car salesman. It's amazing he hasn't been fired yet.

"Hi, Luke," I reply, quickly closing the *Galactic Rush* tab in my browser. Normally, I don't play video games at work, but I've had a hard time focusing today. Still, I don't want

Luke to see my computer screen and get the impression I'm available to chat.

"How's the day treating you so far?" Luke asks. He takes a sip from a coffee mug that reads "Warning! My sense of humor might offend you." Christ, who did I piss off in HR to get stuck here?

"Fine," I tell him curtly. "How's yours going?"

Luke runs a hand through his overly gelled hair. You'd think the guy just climbed out of a pool. "Not too bad," he says. "But I might've overdone it last night at Seaview Tavern. Me and a few of the guys stopped by for happy hour. Someone suggested shots, and, well, you know how that goes." He grins, but I'm not sure what he's so proud of. Getting trashed on a random Wednesday night hardly seems like an accomplishment. "If you talk to Carmichael today, make sure you keep your voice down. He was in pretty rough shape."

"Thanks for the heads up," I say, letting my eyes trail back to my computer screen. Luke, naturally, does not take the hint.

"You should come with us for drinks sometime. We go a few times a month. It's a great way to blow off steam, especially with the way the bitch has been riding everyone lately." He gives me a conspiratorial wink, which might be the douchiest thing I've ever witnessed. Also, our office has an open floor plan, so I'm confident someone is already working on a complaint to HR about Luke loudly proclaiming that our CEO is a bitch.

"Maybe sometime." I'd rather spend every night alone for the rest of my life than subject myself to one of Luke's happy hours, but if making him think otherwise speeds up this conversation, then so be it.

Luke nods and promises to add me to a group chat with the other office assholes. "You and I have gotta look out for each other," he says. "We're a dying breed."

I frown, confused. "What?" Is this a setup for the offensive humor his mug brags about? Am *I* going to be the person complaining to HR?

"Single guys in this office," he explains, glancing around. "Derrick's engaged. Sam's getting married in the spring. You and I might be the only ones around here left with any brain cells." He offers a parting smile that makes my insides roll before ducking back into his cubicle. I stare at the space he occupied for several minutes after he's gone, unable to ignore the dread coursing through me.

I need to talk to Izzy.

***

It's a little after three when I step inside the lobby of Ryan & Son Construction. Izzy is sitting at the rectangular desk directly across from the entrance. Her curly brown hair peeks out from behind her large desktop monitor. She looks up from her computer when the bell above the door chimes, blue light washing over her pretty features.

"Jacob," she says, her tone a mix of surprise and confusion. As I start toward her desk, she clicks her mouse, presumably minimizing the tab she had open. "Well, this is unexpected. What happened? Did you get tired of crunching numbers and decide to play hooky? Seems a bit juvenile for you, but you know I approve." Her words are light, playful. My arrival might have caught Izzy off guard, but she doesn't miss a beat.

I stop in front of her desk, studying the candy dish on the edge. Uncertainty tugs at my mind. Maybe Izzy wasn't being serious when she suggested we help each other. I mean, she pitched the idea while taking shots on New Year's Eve. It's safe to assume she wasn't in her sharpest frame of mind. It could've been a drunken thought rather than a genuine idea. She might not even remember it.

Does coming to her about this plan almost two weeks later make me seem desperate? How awkward would it make things if she changed her mind? Izzy and I may not be friends, but we're not strangers either. She is Delia's sister. Plus, Seaview is a small town. I don't want to make things uncomfortable for either of us.

When I don't say anything, Izzy takes it upon herself to fill the silence.

"So, what do you want to do?" she asks, smirking like a deviant teenager. "Smoke a joint in the parking lot? Trash the principal's car? I don't have any eggs on me, but there's a tuna sandwich in the break room fridge that smells pretty ripe."

Izzy pauses, waiting for me to respond, but I'm trapped by indecision. Is it too late to leave? Maybe I can fake a work call and escape with a sliver of dignity intact. "Uh, Jacob," Izzy says, her brow furrowing slightly, "it's kind of hard to do the whole conversation thing when you're leaving me hanging."

Jesus, I need to get a grip. I made my decision already. I'm doing this. I shake my head, blinking several times to reorient myself. "Sorry," I say. "I'm trying to decide whether you actually egged your principal's car."

Izzy smiles. "I'm afraid I can't tell you that," she says. "Face it, Jacob. You have narc written all over you." Playfulness lights up her blue eyes.

I laugh, despite my nerves. "How so?"

She gives me a deliberate once-over. "For starters, you're wearing khakis."

"Wow, Forrest." I grab my chest, pretending to be wounded. "I didn't know you could be so judgemental."

Izzy shrugs, unapologetic. "I call it like I see it. And I definitely would've cheated off you in math class."

"You're doing unspeakable damage to my ego right now."

"Repress and compartmentalize." She pauses, giving the words a moment to linger before she changes the subject. "Well, if you're here for Tanner, I'm afraid you're out of luck. He's stuck in meetings the rest of the afternoon."

"Actually, I'm here to see you."

Izzy perks up. "Is that so? Tell me more, Jacob. I'm intrigued."

Instantly, my mouth feels dry. I'm overthinking this, aren't I? I just need to *talk to her*. If it doesn't go well, I might even be able to play it off as a joke. Izzy is always saying strange stuff. She'd probably find it funny.

"It's about New Year's," I say, "the, uh, idea you suggested."

Smugness settles over Izzy's face. "I knew you'd come around eventually," she says, leaning back in her chair. "It's been eating you alive, hasn't it? Turning me down? I've been known to have that effect on people."

She's ridiculous. It takes every ounce of my restraint to fight the smile forming at the corners of my mouth.

"You know what I admire about you, Forrest?" I ask. "The way you're always in a state of delusion."

Izzy clucks her tongue in disapproval. "This isn't the time to poke fun. This is the time where you tell me you were wrong and plead for my forgiveness."

"I haven't agreed to anything yet. I have questions."

She gives me a funny look. "What is there to question? Both of us are floundering, Jacob. We need to do something about it. It's quite simple."

"So you're serious about this?"

"I wouldn't have asked you about it if I wasn't," Izzy says. "Look, being with Tanner makes Delia really happy. I don't want to get in the way of that. If making myself seem more responsible is what it takes, then so be it." It's the most honest thing I've ever heard from Izzy, who never seems to take anything seriously, and it catches me by surprise. Obviously, she cares about her sister's happiness, but I didn't realize how much it meant to her. She must feel pretty guilty if she's willing to do all this just so Delia agrees to move in with Tanner.

"It's not like I'm against the idea," I admit. At this point, I'd try almost anything to improve my dating situation. "I'm just not sure what I could do for you, Izzy. I'm not a life coach."

"And I'm not a dating coach," Izzy points out, "but you think I might be able to help you. Otherwise you wouldn't have come here. We can figure out the details as we go, okay? The important part is that we'd actually be doing something about our situations. We'd be, like, each other's accountability partner."

Accountability partner? "This is getting weirdly cultish."

"Relax, Jacob. There will be no chastity belts in your future. Unless you're into that sort of thing. Because I'm not judging—"

"Please stop talking," I say, feeling my face heat up.

"I promise I won't say another word if you say yes."

"Somehow, I doubt that."

"*Please*, Jacob. Quit thinking so much. Just go with it."

"You're not making this any less cultish."

Sighing, Izzy grabs a yellow legal pad off her desk. She takes the cap off a thick black marker and writes *PLEASE!!!!* in giant block letters. She holds it up and turns it toward me, a pouty expression on her face. When I don't answer fast enough, she flips the paper back and adds, *I'm not in a colt.*

"Colt?" I ask, lips twitching in amusement.

Izzy frowns, then scribbles *CULT.*

"Your penmanship needs work," I tell her.

One of the many things you can teach me, she writes back.

Shaking my head, I finally relent. "All right. I'm in."

Her eyes sparkle. *Our alien overlords will be pleased.*

I chuckle slightly. This could be a disaster that blows up in our faces. Or it could be the solution to our problems. It's too soon to know anything…except for the fact that I just gave Izzy Forrest an open invitation to unleash chaos in my life.

What could go wrong?

Eleven

Izzy

Jacob caved.

It took longer than expected (men and their foolish, self-destructive pride), but he's going to help me become the New, Improved Izzy. I'm heading over to his place tonight so we can hammer out the details.

Although we haven't gotten started yet, I'm thrilled by this development. Jacob is a thirty-year-old homeowner with good friends and a stable job. Aside from Delia, he's the most self-actualized person I know. I bet he flosses regularly and has high-yield savings accounts. If anyone can help me figure my shit out, it's him.

I'm not sure what exactly I'm going to do for Jacob on the dating front, but I'm certain I'll be able to manage. Most single guys have at least one glaring red flag they're completely unaware of. Maybe Jacob talks about himself too much or spends his dates glued to his phone. Getting him a girlfriend should be easy once I weed out his flaw. Jacob is a total catch. Cute. Smart. Successful. Women will be jumping at the chance to be with him.

On my way to Jacob's house, I stop at the craft store to pick up a few art supplies. I like to sketch in my spare time. It gives me something to do with my hands when I'm watching TV or sitting in the waiting room at the dentist's office. My old sketchbook is almost filled up, so I figured I'd get a new one, along with some fresh pencils.

As a bonus, the craft store trip is getting me out of a FaceTime call with Cynthia. She's been pestering me about rescheduling since Dominic interrupted us, and I've been blowing her off. As much as I miss her, I don't want to risk seeing Dominic again. I need time before I can fake my way through another interaction with my insufferable ex.

I'm wandering through the aisle of drawing supplies when I pick up a pack of graphite pencils. I flip it over, checking for a price. Oh, wow. Cheaper than I thought. The place where I used to buy art supplies in New York was so expensive. Living here is going to save me a small fortune on craft supplies alone—

A loud crash echoes from the aisle over. It's followed by a series of gentle pattering noises that sound like raindrops hitting a rooftop. Listening closely, I hear someone muttering curse words under their breath. Curious, I set the pack of pencils back on the shelf and head toward the commotion.

When I enter the aisle, I see paint bottles everywhere. It looks like a bulldozer plowed through the aisle, knocking everything off the shelf. A dark-haired woman crouches on the floor at the other end, frantically picking up bottles and placing them back on the empty shelf. She looks like she's about to be sick.

"Need some help?" I ask.

The woman glances up, arms laden with paint. Relief floods her panic-stricken face. "Yes, please," she says, shoving an armful of bottles onto the shelf. "I don't know what happened. One second I was reaching for a bottle of paint, then the guardrail fell off, and bottles went flying everywhere." Luckily, none of the paint bottles appear to be open. And the woman seems to have managed to put the guardrail back in place on the shelf, so the only thing left to do is collect the bottles.

"It happens to the best of us," I tell her, bending down to pick up the teal bottle by the toe of my shoe. "You should've seen the fight I had with the face washes at Ulta one time." I bumped into a skincare display. Shoving bottles of face wash back onto the shelves while other shoppers gave me judgmental looks is a humiliation I wouldn't wish on anyone.

She smiles politely. "It's just my luck for something like this to happen. I haven't been to a craft store in years. Of course I accidentally destroyed the place."

"Take it as a sign from the universe. Maybe you were grabbing the wrong color."

"I didn't even have a specific color in mind," she admits. "I'm doing a painting project with my students tomorrow. My only goal was to find something light enough that it won't stain every square inch of my classroom."

I check the label on the bottle in my hand. "Well, these are acrylics," I say. "For kids, you probably want to go with tempera. It's easy to clean, and it dries quickly. Plus, most tempera paints are non-toxic."

The woman nods. "Good to know. The problem with first graders is that one of them is always gonna put something in their mouth or up their nose."

"Believe me, I know. I was one of those kids." When I was six, Mom bought stuff for me and my sisters to make macaroni necklaces, and I shoved an uncooked noodle so far up my nose she had to take me to the emergency room.

We make quick work of picking up the bottles. Within minutes, the paint aisle is back to normal, no sign of the recent disaster.

The woman stands up, wiping her palms on her long floral skirt. "Thanks for your help," she says. "I don't know if you could tell, but I was on the verge of a breakdown."

"Don't worry about it," I say. "And good luck with your students. Fingers crossed they don't totally wreck the place."

She laughs. "Fingers crossed."

Heading out of the aisle, I hold my chin high, a smile on my face.

Helping a stranger? I must be becoming a better person already.

***

"So, on a scale of one to ten, how much do you already regret this?" I ask as I wipe my snow-covered boots on the beige mat in Jacob's foyer.

He gives me a suspicious look as he closes the door behind me. "I don't know, Forrest," he says. "You tell me. Should I regret this?"

"Not at all," I assure him. "But you seem like an overthinker. I wasn't sure whether I'd have to do damage control when I got here." Jacob *just* agreed to my proposal, so I don't think he's ready to call it off, but I figure it's best to address any doubts he's having.

"My only concern is that you've been here for, like, thirty seconds, and you're already asking me if I want out," he says. "What exactly do you have planned for tonight? Don't tell me you're taking me to a tarot reading."

"Why would you need a tarot reading when you've got a psychic right in front of you?" I ask, gesturing to myself. I'm sure I look the part. Bundled up in my leopard-print coat with a hot pink scarf around my neck. Have I mentioned it's cold as shit in Massachusetts? "I've seen your future, Jacob. True love is headed your way."

"If your psychic abilities are anything like your acting skills, Forrest, then I think I'm doomed to a life alone."

"The universe is not kind to nonbelievers," I warn him. "I'd advise you to keep your skepticism to yourself."

"Noted." He folds his arms across his dark-blue T-shirt. "So, if it's not a tarot reading, then what is your plan?" My "plan" for tonight consists of skewering Jacob like a kebab about every aspect of his dating history. I need details if I'm going to help him get a girlfriend. However, I don't think he'd be thrilled to hear that tonight is going to be an interrogation, so I keep my plans to myself.

"I could ask you the same thing," I tell him. "This is a two-way arrangement, remember? I assume the reason you're hounding me about my plans is because you have something amazing planned."

Jacob winces. It seems I've got him there. "I don't really have anything."

"What?" I place my hands on my hips in mock outrage. "Jacob, if you're gonna Mr. Miyagi me, you need to have a plan."

"I told you, Forrest. I don't know what you want from me."

A faint bark echoes through the back of the house, capturing my attention.

"Is that Lulu?" I ask. Jacob mentioned having a dog at the Christmas Eve party. He nods. "Where is she?"

"I let her outside," he explains. "I didn't want her attacking you the second you came through the door."

"Well, let her back in."

"You sure? She's a little jumpy."

"I don't mind." Plus, I'm not going to be the reason she's kicked out of her own house.

"Don't say I didn't warn you," Jacob replies as he turns and heads to the kitchen. He unlocks the back door, and a tiny blur of light-brown fur bolts inside. Lulu finds me immediately, her collar jangling as she dashes across the room. She's an adorable boxer with a big pink tongue and sappy brown eyes.

I give Lulu a second to sniff my hand before I pet her. She tries to jump on me, but Jacob tells her to stay down. Then she flops onto her back, demanding a belly rub. "Oh my god. I love her," I say as I crouch down to scratch her exposed stomach.

"She's a little restless," Jacob says. "We haven't gone on a walk today."

A walk. Now there's an idea. "Why don't we take her?"

Surprise splashes over Jacob's features. "Really?"

"Yeah. Why not?" It might be easier to get information out of Jacob if we're doing something else. Though walking another person's dog does feel like the worst form of betrayal. Jason will sense my guilt the minute I get home. I'll give him plenty of bacon treats to make up for it. "But can I borrow a hat? And maybe some gloves? I'd like to keep my extremities for the foreseeable future."

Jacob grabs a knitted beanie and a pair of black gloves out of the coat closet, handing them to me. I slip them on while he puts on his own winter clothes. He calls Lulu over so he can hook her up to a leash. Then the three of us head out the front door.

It's dark and windy, and thick, wet snowflakes are falling from the sky. Jacob's neighborhood is lit up by street lamps. Lulu's tail swishes back and forth as she walks ahead of us, leaving tiny pawprints on the snow-dusted sidewalk.

"Well, I figured out the first thing you need to teach me," I declare. "How do you get Lulu to walk so well on a leash?"

Unlike Jason, Jacob's dog maintains a nice, slow pace. She isn't running or pulling or trying to sniff the bright red fire hydrant in the treelawn. "Jason tries to rip my arm off when I take him anywhere."

"I enrolled Lulu in obedience classes after I adopted her," Jacob says, holding the leash nonchalantly in his gloved hand. I wish I could be nonchalant with the leash when I walk Jason, but it's not impossible. Everything excites him. Squirrels. Cars. Bushes. I have to hold that thing in a death grip if I want to stay on my feet.

"Obedience classes. Now there's a thought."

"I assume Jason hasn't had any." Jacob tries to hide it, but I hear the amusement in his voice. See the slight uptick of the corners of his mouth.

"Spare me your judgment, Jacob," I say, hitting him with a glare. Well, the fiercest look you can give someone when you're arguing about animal names. "I'm aware Jason is a terrible dog name."

"I never said that."

"It's not what you said. It's how you said it." It's very clear how he feels about the name. Amusement is radiating off Jacob like a beacon right now.

"If you think the name is so terrible, then why did you pick it?"

"The volunteers at Seaview Animal Shelter did, not me." Why they couldn't go with fucking Fido is beyond me. "I tried changing Jason's name after I brought him home, but he wouldn't answer to anything else. It was either accept the terrible name or give my dog a complex."

"It's really not terrible."

"It is. It's like naming a baby Craig. It violates the laws of nature."

"I mean, there are babies named Craig."

Shuddering, I shake my head at him. "Don't say that. Babies are not named Craig. Craigs are forty-five-year-old men with office jobs and back problems."

He chuckles. "I didn't realize it would bother you." He switches Lulu's leash to his other hand. "I guess I shouldn't tell you about my ten-year-old cousin named Muriel then." Muriel? Do that child's parents hate her?

"I'm gonna pretend you didn't say that," I reply. "I don't want to offend you or your family." I pause for a moment, letting the silence hang between us before I move to another subject. "So, I'm curious. What made you change your mind about this? You seemed pretty unconvinced on New Year's Eve."

Jacob sighs. "Luke Daniels."

"I'm not sure I follow."

"He's this asshole who works in my office," Jacob explains. "He made a comment the other day about us being the only single guys left. I guess it hit me that if I don't do something different, I might end up just like him."

"I see. Luke made all your bad dates feel a little too real."

"I haven't been on *that* many bad dates."

"Oh, really?" I shoot him a doubtful look. "You know, the beautiful thing about this arrangement is we don't have to lie to each other. You can tell me you've been on hundreds of bad dates, and I won't judge you for it."

"There haven't been hundreds."

"Put a number on it for me." He looks like he wants to object, but I cut him off first. "How many dates have you been on in the past year? I can't help you if you aren't honest with me, Jacob."

He sighs as he does the mental math. "Around twenty."

It certainly isn't in the hundreds, but twenty is still a fairly big number. I try not to let my surprise show. Jacob doesn't come across like a serial dater. "Well, the problem isn't that you're not putting yourself out there, which is good." Too many people complain about being single when they haven't actually tried to find someone. They forget that dating requires dating. "Have you met all these women on dating apps?"

Jacob nods. "Mostly. I've gone on a few blind dates, but I try to steer clear of those."

"I get that." Blind dates are the worst. In college, a friend of mine set me up with her cousin, who spent the entire night talking to my rack. Telling her why it wasn't going to work out was incredibly awkward.

"So, what's the ultimate goal here? Marriage? Babies?"

He groans. "Do we really need to get into this?"

"Jacob, I need to know this stuff." How am I supposed to find someone for him if I don't know what he wants? "So, what are you looking for? A girlfriend? A wife? An emotionally manipulative situationship? If it's the last one, there might be some other issues we have to resolve before we get to dating."

He lets out a long breath that materializes in the cold air. Bits of snow cling to his forest green beanie. "I'm looking for something long-term," he says. "I'd like to be married with kids at some point."

I give him a light tap on the shoulder. "See? That wasn't so hard."

"Don't patronize me, Forrest."

"I'm not. It's good you know what you want. It puts you ahead of most guys." I pull my scarf over my nose, attempting to block the wind. "So, that's why you've been dating so much. You want to meet your wife and start making little Craigs and Muriels."

"I know that kind of thing isn't for everyone," Jacob says.

"And you assume I don't want a nuclear family?" A lot of people make the same assumption. My sisters joke that I was born to be a Cool Aunt. But I haven't ruled out marriage or kids. Helping someone learn and grow and become their own person actually sounds kind of nice. I just haven't met anyone I'd want to share that experience with. "What gives you that impression? Do I seem too dysfunctional to be someone's mother?"

Panic crosses Jacob's face. "What? No. I was only trying to say that I wouldn't judge someone if they didn't want kids. There's so much pressure on people to have kids, but no one should feel obligated to have a family. If that's not what they want, I mean. I wasn't implying that you would be a bad mom." I bite my bottom lip, holding back a smile. It's sweet, the way he's almost tripping over himself to make sure he didn't offend me.

"I think about half of that made sense."

"Seriously, Izzy, I don't want you to think—"

"Relax," I tell him. "I'm only messing with you. I'm sure it's hard to picture me telling a kid to eat their broccoli. Besides, it would probably be better for humanity if I didn't produce any offspring. I spent the first three years of my life biting anyone who came within a five-foot radius. My kids would probably be monsters."

"I actually think you'd be great with kids," he says. "You wouldn't tone yourself down for them. I bet they'd appreciate that."

"I mean, I'd probably try to avoid calling them monsters directly to their faces, but I see your point." Kids don't want to be babied. They want to be treated like people. They might be small, helpless, hopelessly confused people, but they're people, nonetheless.

What I don't tell Jacob is that this might be the first time someone has said they think I'm responsible enough to care for someone else. Most people see me as Fun Izzy. A woman who doesn't take anything too seriously. They don't imagine me carting kids to soccer games or packing school lunches. I get why. I probably don't exude the most parental energy when I'm making dirty jokes or complaining about what a mess my life is. But it's nice to hear someone talk about me like I'm more than just a good time.

"I'm so glad you deemed me capable of raising children," I say teasingly. "That's exactly what I needed. Validation from a Big, Strong Man."

Jacob groans. "I should shut up now, shouldn't I?"

"It might be for the best."

We finish a loop around the neighborhood, ending back in front of Jacob's place. My limbs feel like ice picks, and I think my toes might've succumbed to frostbite, but Lulu looks overjoyed, her pink tongue lolling out the side of her mouth.

"I'd say this has been a fairly productive evening," I announce.

"Productive?" Jacob repeats, looking confused. "How so?"

"Well, you helped me realize I need to enroll Jason in obedience classes." Getting my dog to stop tearing up Delia's things would certainly put me on her good side. "And I figured out what we need to do to solve your woman problem."

"Oh, yeah? And what's that?"

I grin. "You need to take me on a date."

Twelve

Jacob

Planning a date for Izzy Forrest isn't for the faint of heart.

She doesn't give any helpful advice. Over the last three days, I've sent her half a dozen potential date ideas, ranging from ice skating to wine tasting, but she hasn't told me whether she likes any of these options. She says it would be cheating. That the point of this outing is for her to evaluate my dating skills. Helping me plan the date would defeat the purpose.

Her logic is that off base, but it hasn't stopped me from trying. This afternoon, I spent my lunch break researching first date ideas. I stumbled upon a board game cafe located thirty minutes outside of Seaview and texted Izzy a link to the website. *Thoughts?* I asked. I know she likes board games. We played Jenga at a dinner party last summer.

When Izzy's reply bounces back ten minutes later, it's just as frustrating as I feared.

Izzy: You know I'm an admitted sore loser, right?

Jacob: Is that a no?

Izzy: It's a statement of fact. I WILL show up to the board game cafe prepared to crush you. It won't be pretty.

Jacob: Would crushing me be an enjoyable way to spend your evening?

Izzy: Nice try.

Jacob: Please, Forrest. Just tell me a few of your likes and dislikes.

Izzy: Likes include long walks on the beach and spending time with my loved ones. Dislikes include people who play games with my heart.

Jacob: I asked for your interests. Not the world's worst dating profile.

Izzy: I love strawberry-scented candles. I hate NASCAR.

Jacob: Those are extremely unhelpful responses.

Izzy: Don't take me to any auto racing events, and we should be fine.

Jacob: Give me something I can work with.

In response, Izzy shares a link to the registration page for a water aerobics class at the local rec center. *Maybe we'll find your future wife here.*

Shaking my head, I set my phone facedown on my desk. I can see why she's being coy, but would it hurt her to offer a few details? I don't want to subject us to a miserable night because I couldn't plan a decent date.

The easy solution is to play it safe. Dinner and a movie. A trip to the art museum. Something simple and inoffensive. Yet neither of those seems like a good option for a "date" with Izzy. She's loud and chaotic. She likes the unexpected. Something tells me she wouldn't enjoy a date that felt boring and overdone.

If I want to impress her, I have to plan a night that catches her by surprise. The only way to grab her attention is to do something she won't see coming. But how am I supposed to shock the unflappable Izzy Forrest?

It's the question on my mind several nights later when I'm sitting in my kitchen with Delia. Tanner came over tonight to finish the work on my back porch, so I invited the two of them for dinner. Tanner insisted he didn't have much left to do, but he's been outside for almost an hour, and the food arrived twenty minutes ago. Delia and I tried to be patient, but the combined scent of fresh garlic and tomato sauce got to be too much for us. We wound up opening the box of breadsticks.

"I want to feel guilty about this," Delia says between mouthfuls of garlic bread, "but it's so good that I can't." Stuffing our faces while Tanner works in the cold does feel wrong, but he said he didn't want help. Delia and I both offered, but he told us we'd slow him down, which is probably true. Before Ryan & Son became Tanner's company, it belonged to his father. He's been doing construction work since he was a teenager.

"We'll save plenty for him," I assure her.

Delia laughs. "You're better than me. I was gonna suggest we finish the box and hide the evidence." She reaches for another breadstick.

"You know, it used to be hard for me to believe you and Izzy are related, but I'm starting to see the resemblance," I say.

"That's right. I heard you've been hanging out with my sister."

I finish chewing before replying, "um, yeah. A bit." Izzy and I decided to tell Tanner and Delia we've been spending time together. There's no good reason to lie about it. Though we left out the part about me helping her pull her life together and her helping me figure out my dating troubles. As far as they know, we're simply friends.

Delia dabs the corners of her mouth with a napkin. "Well, you know I approve of this friendship," she says. "But I'm warning you in advance that Izzy is slightly unhinged."

"Oh, I've noticed," I say. "Izzy is making me plan something for us to do together, but she won't tell me what she likes to do. Every time I ask for suggestions, she sends me something unhelpful. Her latest idea was for us to take a water aerobics class."

"That's Izzy for you. Being unhelpful is her speciality."

"I don't suppose you have any ideas." Is asking Izzy's sister for suggestions cheating? Maybe. But Izzy has given me nothing. If this were a real date with a woman I met on True Connections, I'd have a profile to work off. Izzy has put me at a severe disadvantage here. I need to take any help I can get.

Delia taps her chin. "Have you considered taking her to water aerobics?"

"The classes at the rec are for seniors." I thought about making Izzy eat her words by signing us up for water aerobics, but the registration form mentioned the classes are geared toward older adults.

"That's too bad. I would've loved to see Izzy in a swim cap."

"You already started eating?" Tanner says as he steps through the back door, a blast of cold air rushing inside.

"Only the breadsticks," Delia replies. "And we saved you the best one."

"One? As in a singular breadstick?"

She winces. "Well, yes. But you weren't stuck here smelling them for the past half hour. You're lucky we had enough self-restraint to save you anything."

Tanner shakes his head as he heads to the sink to wash his hands. "A half hour with a box of breadsticks? That's all it takes to break your self-restraint?"

"I figured it was better to act now and beg for forgiveness later."

Tanner smirks. "I do like listening to you beg."

Jesus Christ. "I did *not* invite you over so you could terrorize me in my own home," I mutter, dropping a half-eaten breadstick back on my plate. Hanging out with Tanner and Delia is usually fun, but sometimes they say stuff that makes me want to scrub the inside of my brain with a cleaning brush.

"That's what you get for eating without me," Tanner says smugly as he strolls over to the kitchen table. He takes the seat next to Delia, draping an arm over the back of her chair as he grabs the last breadstick.

I know Izzy thinks Delia's decision not to move in with Tanner is hurting their relationship, but she has nothing to worry about. Tanner and Delia are fine. He told me about it the other night over beers. Understandably, Tanner was disappointed Delia said no, but he wasn't upset with her. Izzy is freaking out over nothing.

"You're just in time," Delia says, shifting her brown eyes toward Tanner. "Jacob was asking me for ideas of fun things he can do with Izzy."

"How am I supposed to help with that?" Tanner asks, looking perplexed.

"She works for you," Delia reminds him. "I thought you might have some insight."

"No offense, darling, but I don't think I'd be able to understand the way your sister's mind works, even if I had an instruction manual."

She smacks him playfully. "Not. Helpful."

"Forget it. We'll just go bowling or something," I say. Knowing Izzy, she'll probably spend the night making ball jokes.

Delia frowns. "Honestly, I wouldn't overthink it. The thing about Izzy is that she likes a good story. Just try to give her one."

A good story. I hadn't thought about it like that before. It's a great way to frame. Izzy won't care what we do on this date as long as it's memorable. She wants something to talk about later. Something that sparks her curiosity.

And suddenly, I think I know how to give that to her.

***

Izzy

On Thursday night, Jacob turns into the gravel parking lot of a small rustic building with wood shutters and a chimney. The place appears somewhat busy. Cars occupy most of the spaces in the lot, and groups of people file through the front door. A crooked sign that says "Off the Vine" in cursive script stands in the treelawn.

Jacob parks his sedan in an empty spot along the side of the building.

"What is this place?" I ask.

He kills the engine and unbuckles his seatbelt. "You'll see." His smile is faint, but the amusement in his voice is undeniable.

"Seriously? More secrecy?" Jacob texted me earlier to see if I was free tonight for our "date." When I responded yes, I expected him to follow up with more details, but he simply said he'd pick me up at a quarter to seven. I tried to press him for information, but he wouldn't budge, even when I tried to bribe him with candy. The man is a steel trap.

"Are we doing something illegal?" I ask. "I'm not necessarily opposed, but I'd prefer to know what I'm getting myself into."

"Is patience a foreign concept to you?"

I huff in mock offense. "I'm incredibly patient. I was so good at staring contests growing up that other kids called me the Death Stare." I usually won by making my opponent laugh and lose focus, but Jacob doesn't need to know that part.

Jacob's lips twitch with laughter. "Did you have a walkout song, too?"

"You laugh, but I was the stuff of second-grade legend."

"I would never disrespect the sanctity of second-grade legend, Forrest."

Shaking my head, I unclip my seatbelt and climb out of the car. Jacob gets out, pocketing his keys. He's wearing khakis and a navy blue crewneck. With him being so tight-lipped, I had no clue what to wear. I went the casual route, opting for a simple red turtleneck sweater tucked into a pair of jeans.

"You know, all this secrecy has really built up my expectations," I warn him as we walk toward the building's entrance. Salt crunches under the heels of my boots. "This date better dazzle me."

"I guarantee tonight will leave you speechless," he says.

"Please tell me it isn't the opera. I left my evening gloves at home."

"The opera seemed a little intense for a first date. Let's see how tonight goes, and then we'll talk. I can't let just anyone in my box."

"I'll be on my best behavior. Which means I'll refrain from making any unsavory jokes about you letting people into your box."

We follow the sidewalk up to the front door. Jacob gets there first and opens it, motioning for me to go ahead. I step into the lobby of what appears to be an art studio. It's a spacious room with tall windows and recessed lighting. Easels are scattered about the hardwood, and landscape paintings hang on the walls. A bar area takes up the far corner, surrounded by a cluster of people waiting for drinks.

It's a paint and sip. *Oh.*

"Class starts at seven," Jacob says as we shuffle out of the doorway to make room for the next group coming in. "You wanna find us an easel? I'll grab drinks."

"Sure," I reply. I shoot him a small smile, hoping it will mask my disappointment.

"What do you want?"

"An espresso martini, please."

With a nod, Jacob darts toward the bar, and I set out to find an empty easel. I snag an open spot in the back row by the window and take a seat on the small stool. I slip off my coat, setting it on the stool beside me to save a place for Jacob.

While I wait for him, I do a bit of people watching. A lot of couples seem to be in tonight's class. There's an older guy several rows ahead of me who keeps grabbing the butt of the woman next to him. I think he thinks he's being subtle. He looks around smugly every time he does it, as if he just got away with the filthiest act in public, even though I'm pretty sure people on the street can see it.

My eyes land on the back of Jacob's lanky frame at the bar. I hate that I'm feeling disappointed, but I expected more from tonight, especially with Jacob's secrecy. Bringing an artist to a paint and sip class isn't exactly groundbreaking. I've been on plenty of paint and sip dates, most of which were total duds. A guy once asked if he could give my painting to his mom as a birthday present since he forgot to buy her something.

I shouldn't be surprised that Jacob went a basic route for our date. I'm helping him improve his dating skills, after all. He wouldn't be looking for assistance if he didn't need it. Still, he seemed confident about tonight. I thought he had something up his sleeve. When he asks for feedback later, I'll have to let him down easy.

Jacob heads over with our drinks a few minutes later. He hands me my martini before taking a sip of his iced tea. Clutching the martini glass in one hand, I use the other to move my coat off Jacob's seat. To my confusion, he doesn't sit down.

"Don't let someone take your spot," I tell him. Other people are starting to look for their seats. "I got us great seats. Prime viewing for the ass grabbing in row three."

"Ass grabbing?" he repeats.

"The old guy in the baseball hat hasn't stopped grabbing the butt of the woman beside him," I explain. "He has the subtlety of a hand grenade."

Jacob looks forward, then frowns. "That's Mr. Erikson. He was my physics teacher in high school."

"Well, it looks like he's giving a lesson called 'How Horny Can You Act in Public Before You're Asked to Leave?' Take note, Jacob. There might be a quiz later."

Jacob tears his eyes away from Mr. Erikson, who goes for another squeeze. "I don't think you understand the damage this is inflicting on my teenage self."

"Then you'd better shield your eyes, prude. We've got front row seats."

"Now I wish I was gonna be blindfolded."

Wait. What? "Blindfolded? What are you talking about?" I ask, turning to face him. Jacob has a playful look in his eye, but he says nothing as he sips his iced tea.

The chime of a bell silences conversation.

An older woman with long gray hair stands at the front of the room. She can't be more than five feet tall, and she has on a flouncy cream dress that falls around her ankles. Several large pendant necklaces rest on her chest. And her fingers are decorated in so many rings it almost looks like she's wearing brass knuckles.

She shakes the silver bell in her hand again, demanding the attention of the room. "Good evening, everyone," she says in a low, calm voice. "Welcome to Off the Vine. For those who don't know me, my name is Aurora, and I will be your instructor tonight. Think of me as your artistic guide. Tonight's journey will be an exploration of intimacy and passion. I encourage you to be open and to embrace everything this experience has to offer."

My jaw drops like an anchor. What is happening right now?

"Jacob," I whisper, "what is this?" Did he bring me to an orgy?

He smirks. "You'll see." Son of a bitch.

"Our exercise tonight is designed for couples," Aurora says. "It's called Through Your Eyes. Each couple will be divided into two roles: the painter and the guide. Painters will be blindfolded throughout my demonstration. I won't be giving any verbal directions, so they will have to rely on their guides for instruction. This activity is all about trust and communication. Couples will need to work together to complete their painting."

Conversation resumes as Aurora slips her bell into the pocket of her dress and begins setting up her easel.

"You ready, Forrest?" Jacob asks, holding out a black blindfold.

"You want *me* to be the blindfolded one?"

"My date, remember?" I can't argue with him there. I reach out a palm, but instead of handing me the blindfold, Jacob puts it on for me. He drapes the dark fabric over my eyes and ties it at the back of my head. "Can you see anything?"

"Only the backs of my eyelids."

"Good. I'm gonna grab us a palette and brushes. Be right back."

He's gone in an instant, but he's back again before I even finish taking a sip of my martini. I listen as he arranges the supplies on the folding table beside the easel.

Aurora rings her bell, and the room falls quiet. "It looks like everyone is ready, so we'll get started," she says.

The first thing Jacob does is swap my martini glass out for a paintbrush. I twirl the wooden handle between my fingers as I wait for his instructions.

"Dazzled yet?" Jacob whispers in my ear. His breath smells like spearmint. I appreciate that he had the courtesy to pop a piece of gum before getting so close. Most guys wouldn't hesitate to give you a breathful of the tuna sandwich they ate for lunch.

"Let's not get ahead of ourselves," I tell him. "I need to see your guiding skills in action. I expect to leave here with a masterpiece."

"I'm right there with you. People will weep at the sight of our painting."

"Will these be tears of horror or jealousy?"

"That all depends on how well you listen. I'm your guide, Forrest. I encourage you to be open and to embrace everything this experience has to offer."

There's slight pressure on my wrist as Jacob wraps his long fingers around it, lifting my hand upward. "I'm dipping your brush in paint now," he says. I heard the quiet sound of bristles rubbing against the wooden palette.

"Oh, tell me more. I like it when you talk dirty, Jacob."

"I thought you were refraining from unsavory jokes tonight."

"That was before you got all freaky with the blindfold."

He chuckles softly. "So, the first thing you want to do is paint a thin line across the lower middle of the canvas." I raise the brush to the approximate height, which isn't easy with a blindfold on. Jacob guides me by the elbow to the correct spot. I press the brush to the canvas, sweeping across in a straight line.

"How are we looking so far?" I ask.

"Pretty good," he replies. "Next, you're gonna make two identical arches coming out from the sides of the line. The end result looks sort of bulbous."

"You can't use words like 'bulbous' if you expect me to take you seriously."

"Focus, Forrest. We're aiming for a masterpiece here." He dips my brush in more paint and then steers me to the ends of the line I just made so I can create a *bulbous* shape. I have no idea if it looks even, let alone like Aurora's example.

We continue at this pace for a while, Jacob feeding me directions and me cracking unhelpful jokes. Spa-like music plays on a loop throughout the room. When I ask Jacob how our canvas looks, he says it reminds him of a child's finger painting. Realizing we have no chance at making this painting look decent, I decide to have some fun instead. I start purposely messing up Jacob's directions, extending lines longer than necessary and putting pressure on my brush so that paint drips down the canvas.

"Make a very thin curve right here," he tells me, moving my elbow up so that the brush is aligned with the top left-hand corner of the canvas.

"Like this?" I ask innocently, painting a line I know is too thick. I end up turning that line into a circle and filling it in for good measure.

"I know what you're doing."

"I have no idea what you're talking about."

"Sabotage isn't cute."

"This isn't my medium, Jacob. I prefer drawing, not painting."

"That's good. Because I don't think either of us is gonna make it as a painter after this."

"I'm sure it looks amazing."

"Well, you'll find out in a second," he says. "We're almost done. You just have to sign the bottom."

I sign both of our names, because Jacob deserves just as much credit for the atrocity that is this painting.

"All right, everyone," Aurora announces. "Our session is complete. Painters, feel free to remove your blindfolds and view your work."

I yank my blindfold down instantly. What I find doesn't disappoint. Our painting is a mess of drip marks, lines, and scribbles. It looks like the painter sneezed and accidentally dragged their brush across the canvas.

I glance at Aurora's reference painting, which is sitting on an easel up front. We were supposed to paint a vase of flowers, but our canvas shows nothing of the sort. If anything, the tall vase combined with the bulbous flowers makes it look like a crudely drawn dick and balls.

Oh my god. I turn to Jacob. "Does that look like—"

"Something you'd find on a desk in a seventh-grade classroom? Yes."

Laughing, I let my eyes return to the painting. I can't believe I managed to do this unintentionally. It's incredible.

"And what do we have back here?" I look to my side to see Aurora coming toward us. She stops in front of our painting, resting her chin on the bridge of her knuckles as she studies it intently. I don't know how she manages to keep a straight face.

Her eyes widen. "Oh my," she says. "Well, there's no need to be embarrassed. This is a very sensual activity."

Aurora gives us a knowing smile before drifting off to look at another couple's painting. Jacob and I exchange looks of bewilderment before both of us burst out laughing. Crinkles form at the corners of his eyes as he shakes his head.

"You're unbelievable," he says.

Thirteen

Jacob
Both of us are starving by the time we duck out of Off the Vine, so we decide to stop at the taco place down the road for something to eat. It's a little after eight on a weeknight, so the restaurant is unsurprisingly quiet. The place has a simple but modern interior with brick walls and lights strung across the ceiling. The guy at the host stand tells us to sit anywhere we'd like.

We wind up grabbing a booth in the corner. A server appears almost instantly, handing us menus and dropping off a basket of chips and salsa. He takes our drink orders and then heads to the kitchen, leaving Izzy and me alone.

Wordlessly, Izzy reaches into the basket and plucks out a tortilla chip. She dunks the chip in salsa before shoving it into her mouth. Her blue eyes bounce around the empty tables that surround us, head bobbing softly to the pop music playing overhead. She looks pretty tonight in her dark-red sweater, her curly hair spilling over her shoulders.

Still, she's being weird.

"You're quiet," I tell her.

She crunches her chip. "And?"

"You're never quiet, Forrest." If there's one thing I've learned about Izzy, it's that she always has something to say. We've only just sat down, but the fact that she hasn't said a word strikes me as unusual. "What gives?"

"I'm still trying to process what I just experienced," she says. "I never thought tonight would involve a blindfold and a hippie. You're into some weird shit, Jacob." I can't help but grin at her words. I saw Izzy's face when we walked into Off the Vine. She thought I brought her to a normal paint and sip class, and she was underwhelmed. Keeping a straight face was hard, but it was worth the effort to see Izzy's baffled reaction to Aurora.

"As you can imagine," Izzy says as she goes for another chip, "I have a lot of questions."

"Lay them on me," I reply, leaning against the cushioned backrest.

"How long have you been into kinky paint and sip?"

"This was actually my first time. My mom is a physical therapist. Aurora is one of her longtime clients. She's been running Off the Vine forever, and she recently started these sessions for couples. I figured it would be interesting."

"And that it was," Izzy says. "I had no idea what was gonna happen, and I kind of loved it. Though it's good to know you haven't taken your previous dates there. I don't know if others would be so receptive to Aurora's style."

"That date was specifically tailored to you, Forrest."

"Well, I'm touched."

I grin. "You were disappointed at first, weren't you?" I grab a couple of chips as I wait for her response.

"Only because paint and sips are, like, the first thing every guy suggests after he finds out I'm a graphic designer," she admits. "I've been on a lot of paint and sip dates."

"And how does this one measure up?"

"It's in the top half, for sure. Might even crack the top five if you let me keep our painting. It would look nice in Delia's living room, don't you think?"

"I think Delia might kill you if you try to put that in her house." Delia is very particular. Her place is clean, minimal.

I can't imagine she'd take kindly to a painting that looks like a dick hanging on her wall.

"It could be the motivation she needs to accept Tanner's invitation," Izzy points out. "So, I'm curious. What made you think I would like something like tonight?"

I shrug, trying to figure out how to explain myself. "I don't know. It seemed fun and different. I guess I wanted to be the one to shock you for once."

"What's that supposed to mean?"

"C'mon, Forrest. You like shocking people." Spending time around Izzy makes that pretty obvious. Whether she's saying outlandish things or slinging back shots of tequila, she knows how to make people stop in their tracks.

"Do I?" she asks, blinking innocently.

I narrow my eyes, refusing to fall for her act. "The night we met, you asked me how much of a douchebag my best friend was on a scale of one to ten." We were at a cookout at Tanner's mom's place. Tanner and Delia hadn't gotten together yet, but it was clear they liked each other. Izzy and I were trying to give them time alone. She wasted no time before grilling me for information.

"All right. Fine." She raises her palms. "I'm a sucker for a little shock value."

Our server returns with a glass of water for me and lemonade for Izzy. He pulls a small notepad out of the pocket of his apron and asks if we've decided what we want to eat. I've barely glanced at the menu, but I've been here dozens of times, so I go with my usual order of steak tacos and rice. Izzy, meanwhile, asks for a chicken burrito with red chile sauce. After he scribbles down our orders, the server collects our menus and disappears again.

I look across the table at Izzy. Her eyes shimmer in the yellowish glow of the restaurant. "So, have you always been into art?" I ask.

She nods. "Pretty much. It's something I got from my dad. He used to draw funny little pictures and leave them in random spots around the house. A kitten in roller skates on the fridge. A flying robot on my bedside table. I started drawing my own and really fell in love with it. I double majored in graphic design and drawing in college." Tanner told me that Izzy and Delia's dad died of skin cancer years ago.

"I assume that's why you chose graphic design," I say.

"Yeah. My mom wasn't exactly thrilled."

"Why's that?" Izzy's career seemed to be the source of tension between the two of them on Christmas Eve, so I'm not surprised to learn it's been a longstanding conflict.

"It's a tough industry to break into. Mom wanted me to do something more practical."

"Like become an actuary?"

"Oh, she would've loved that." Izzy twirls her straw around her glass of lemonade. "Except I'm terrible at math, so I probably would've gotten fired and still ended up in this position."

"You want to go back to graphic design, right?" Izzy's position at Tanner's company isn't permanent. I know Tanner would let her stay if that's what she wanted, but Izzy has made it clear she doesn't see herself there for the rest of her life.

"Eventually, yeah," she says. "But getting fired doesn't exactly bode well for my future in the industry."

"People get fired, Forrest."

She raises a brow. "Have you ever been fired?"

I open my mouth, but no words come out. Truthfully, I haven't been fired or even reprimanded at any job I've had. That includes high school. I worked at a movie theater my junior and senior years. Most of my coworkers would sneak out back to smoke during slower times, but I was stressed out by the thought of leaving the cash register unattended.

Izzy smirks triumphantly. "That's what I thought. Model. Citizen."

"To be fair, I've never been passionate about any of the jobs I've had." Even my current one. My work is steady and predictable, but it's not like I wake up every morning eager to get to the office. "I go in, do my work, and go home." My focus is meeting expectations, not exceeding them. Work is nothing but a means to an end.

"It's a smart approach," she says. "Caring too much sucks. You internalize everything."

"Then why go back to graphic design?" I hope she's not offended by the question, but if she thinks she's better off not caring, then staying at a place like Ryan & Son makes the most sense, doesn't it?

Izzy traces a bright red fingernail around the rim of her drink. "Ryan & Son is great, but I get restless. I've always been that way. As much as it sucks, I need to care about what I'm doing, or I feel like I'm bouncing off the walls. Art is the one thing that's been consistent for me. I have to be doing it in some capacity."

I can't relate to the feeling she describes. I've always liked numbers and problem solving, but I've never needed fulfillment out of my career. Still, I sympathize with Izzy. We spend most of our time at work. Feeling miserable for forty hours a week would be exhausting.

"I wouldn't sweat it too much," I tell her. "You'll find what you're looking for. Isn't that why you took the job at Tanner's company? To figure things out?"

"That was six months ago. At what point does *figuring things out* just become an excuse for having no idea what to do with your life?"

"I don't think you can put a timetable on it."

"Don't get all inspirational on me, Jacob," Izzy says, folding her arms across her chest.

"I mean it. No one has everything figured out all the time."

"Easy for you to say."

"Is it though?" I ask. "Have you forgotten we're on a pretend date?"

She concedes that point. "Still, you're only looking to improve one aspect of your life," she says. "My entire life is a disaster."

I want to tell her that she's putting too much pressure on herself. Everyone feels directionless at times. She's no more lost than anyone in their mid-twenties. But I don't think it would be of any use. Izzy seems adamant about this. Nothing I say right now is going to change her attitude.

Our food arrives on piping hot plates, the scents of fresh herbs and sauteed peppers thick in the air. Izzy snatches a bottle of hot sauce from the edge of the table and starts drizzling it on her burrito.

"We've been talking about me too much," she says. "Let's talk about you. Why do you want to get married, Jacob?" She gives me a curious look from the other side of the table.

"I think we went over this already," I remind her. Izzy prodded me for details the other night when we were walking Lulu.

She shakes her head. "You told me you want marriage and children. You didn't say *why* you want those things."

"I've always wanted them." I can't remember a time in my life when that wasn't the objective. Even when I was a kid, I knew I wanted to have a family someday. "I like the idea of going through life with someone. Having that person you always know you can rely on." Izzy passes me the hot sauce, and I pour it on my tacos. "It could be the influence of my parents. They've been together since they were teenagers, and they're still happy."

"That's sweet," she says. "I've always been jealous of those couples. It must be nice to meet the right person when you're so young. They don't know how lucky they are. I'm convinced the older you get, the harder dating becomes."

"I tend to agree with that theory." Meeting someone only becomes more challenging as you enter new stages of life. I'm a prime example.

"I assume you've always wanted kids, too."

"Pretty much." I've always pictured myself with at least two kids. I don't have any siblings, so I like the idea of my kids having each other to depend on.

"You know, I could probably give you the same advice you gave me," Izzy says. "You shouldn't put so much pressure on yourself to meet the right person at a specific time. It's completely out of your control. Look at Tanner and Delia. Neither of them was interested in a relationship when they met, but they're perfect for each other."

"Are you saying I'm too desperate?"

"Not at all. I think you want it so much you think you can will it into existence. But that isn't how life works, is it? If it was, you wouldn't be on a fake date with a washed up graphic designer."

"I don't know. A lot of people get married." So many others manage to find relationships and make them work. Why can't I do the same?

"A lot of people get divorced, too," Izzy points out. "You shouldn't settle. Not if you want something special like your parents have. There's a woman out there who loves math and comic books and wants two point five kids. Your paths will cross. I'm sure of it."

My lips twitch slightly. "If you mention model trains right now, I'm leaving."

"Skipping out on *another* date? I think we might be getting to the root of your issues."

Forty minutes later, we've devoured a mountain of food—including a giant plate of churros that Izzy insisted on—and are ready to head out. We make the chilly trek back to the parking lot and then I drive Izzy to Delia's place. Within minutes, I'm pulling up the narrow driveway and putting my car in park.

I glance over at Izzy. "So, what's the consensus?" I ask. She hasn't given me much feedback so far. I wonder if she wanted to wait till the end of the night to lay everything on me. "If you think I'm a lost cause, all I ask is that you break the news gently."

Izzy taps her chin. "I honestly think you had the right idea for tonight. You should do more fun stuff like this with your dates."

"You mean bring them to Off the Vine?" My tone is skeptical. I know Izzy had a good time, but that's because we already know each other. Something tells me tonight would not have been a success if I had invited a woman I'd never met before.

"Aurora's style might not be for everyone," Izzy replies, "but I think it's a good idea to do something different. First dates are usually awkward. And they can feel formulaic if you've been on a bunch. This changes things up. Of course, it will inevitably crash and burn sometimes, but at least you'll make yourself memorable."

"That's actually not a bad idea." Normally, I opt for the traditional route on first dates. Before tonight, I never considered doing something other than the typical dinner or drinks. Maybe that's why nothing has worked out—I'm playing it too safe.

"I've been known to have those on occasion," she says as she unbuckles her seatbelt. "Don't worry, though. There's a flaw in you somewhere. We will find it." She promptly opens the passenger side door. Cold air whooshes inside. "This was fun, Jacob. I'll text you so we can figure out what to do next time."

"Sounds good," I reply as she hops out of the car. As Izzy goes to slam the door shut, realization dawns on me. "Wait. What should we do about the painting?" I gesture toward the backseat, where our heinous work of art (if you could call it that) sits in all its glory. "We never established who gets the misfortune of taking it home."

Izzy grins. "You keep it," she says. "And make sure you hang it somewhere nice. I'm looking for it next time I come over."

Fourteen

Jacob
Being friends with Izzy Forrest isn't good for my blood pressure.

"You're telling me you've never made a budget, *ever*?" I stare at her, horrified by the confession. "You are aware of the fact that you need money to survive, right?" By twenty-five, I had a favorite budgeting app. The thought that Izzy has never once created a budget for herself has my financially-oriented brain in a tailspin.

Izzy's bright red lips curve into a grin. "Not when you have charm and good looks," she says as she stretches like a cat on my couch. "The guy who ran my bodega in New York used to give me free Red Bull all the time. I think he wanted me to go out with his son. But he was, like, twenty, and I'm pretty sure he sold vapes to high schoolers."

"Saving three dollars on a can of Red Bull won't help you pay your bills, Forrest," I reply, handing her a glass of ice water before plopping on the couch beside her.

Izzy gives me a skeptical look over the rim of her glass. "You don't know what I'll do with the energy from that Red Bull. I could invent a new language or write the next great American novel." She crosses one fuzzy-sock-covered ankle over the other. "Actually, scratch the novel thing. I couldn't sit still for that long. But I bet my cool new language would catch on. It wouldn't have any of those asinine spelling-pronunciation discrepancies we have in English. Like read and read. Why did we do that to ourselves?"

I bite my tongue to avoid smiling, even if she *is* pretty and charming. After our pretend date last week, I figured it was time for me to hold up my end of our bargain, so I offered to give her some financial advice. I have no idea what Izzy's finances look like, but with my numbers background, I thought I could make a few suggestions.

I still don't know what Izzy actually wants out of this arrangement. Her request was for me to help her pull her life together, which is pretty vague. I'm not a counselor. I don't have the skills to fix her problems. What I can do, however, is provide solid financial guidance. Of course, I didn't expect Izzy to tell me that she's never budgeted in her life. The idea was to help her, not give myself heart palpitations.

"Do you know how much is in your bank accounts?" I ask.

She blinks. "Accounts, plural?"

Jesus Christ. "You might be the most terrifying creature I've ever encountered."

Izzy laughs, throwing her head back. "Oh my god. I'm kidding," she says. "You can relax, Jacob. I do, in fact, have a savings account."

"You can't joke about these things, Forrest. I'm in a fragile state right now."

"I promise I'm totally irresponsible," Izzy assures me. "I have a general idea of what's in my accounts. I just don't check them religiously." I can actually feel the hives forming beneath my skin. Izzy's nonchalant approach to her finances might be causing me to have an allergic reaction.

"With a basic spreadsheet, you'd know exactly what's coming and going from your accounts every month."

"My brain malfunctioned after you said spreadsheet."

I groan. She's not going to make this easy, is she? "You are a menace."

"I think the correct term is solid C student," she says. "The second you start talking about numbers, Jacob, my eyes are gonna glaze over. It's in my nature." She drums her shiny fingernails against the side of her water glass. "As much as I appreciate the budgeting advice, it's really not necessary. Delia's house is paid off. She insists on taking care of the utilities. Other than groceries, I don't have many expenses right now."

"It's still a good practice," I argue. "Unless you're planning to live at Delia's place forever, your expenses are gonna go up at some point. You might as well get in the habit of budgeting. Honestly, it's pretty straightforward. It'll only take me a few minutes to build you a simple budget."

Without further debate, I reach for my laptop on the coffee table. I need to make this budget, if not for Izzy, then for my own well-being. I cannot let her go home tonight without any sort of financial plan in place.

Izzy shrugs. "I guess that gives you something to do while I carry out phase two of Find Jacob's Future Wife."

"I'm almost afraid to ask," I mutter as I boot up my laptop.

"I'm scoping out your True Connections profile," she says. "I need to see how you're presenting yourself to the world so I understand the type of women you're attracting."

I shut her down immediately. "Absolutely not."

She looks shocked. "What? Why? It's a perfectly good idea." She's probably right, but the thought of Izzy looking at my True Connections profile seems about as desirable as a root canal. Online dating already makes me feel ridiculous. I don't need Izzy searching through my profile with a fine-tooth comb.

"Because, despite agreeing to this arrangement, I do have a modicum of self-respect," I tell her as the laptop screen glows to life.

She folds her arms over her chest, causing her breasts to press up along the neckline of her sweater. I try not to stare because *friends* and *respect,* but Izzy has a spectacular chest, so it's very hard not to.

"Spend enough time around me, Jacob, and I'll squeeze that self-respect right out of you," she says ominously.

I drop my gaze to the laptop screen as I open up a new spreadsheet tab.

Don't I know it.

***

Izzy

Tragically, I can't ignore the fight with Mom forever.

I want to. Believe me. I'm a big fan of avoidance. Why acknowledge something sticky and messy and uncomfortable when you can just…pretend it doesn't exist? Bury your problems deep, deep inside so they never return to the surface?

Unfortunately, my sisters don't subscribe to the same mindset. They're all about dealing with conflict, talking about what happened and how everyone feels about it. Morgan is the perfect mediator. Delia comes up with the best compromises. Me? I'm usually smack dab in the middle of the fight.

"She feels bad, Iz," Morgan insists one night on a FaceTime call. Delia and I try to chat with her once a week during dinner. We order takeout and catch up. Usually, I look forward to these calls. But I had a feeling something was up when I got home with the Chinese food and found Delia and Morgan already on the phone.

"I know the fight was bad," Morgan continues. She appears on Delia's laptop, which is positioned at the head of the table. "I'm not saying you have to talk to her or anything, but you should know she misses you. She asks about you constantly. She said she'd take everything back if she could."

"Even if you're not ready to forgive her, it might help to talk things over," Delia adds, giving me an encouraging nod from across the kitchen table. "Neither of you will be able to move past this if you don't communicate."

"Did you two rehearse this?" I ask, unimpressed. It sounds like an intervention on a crappy reality TV show.

Delia and Morgan exchange a quick look. "No," Delia says, "but we have talked about how weird things have been since Christmas. It's been over a month, and you haven't mentioned Mom once. What the hell, Iz? Are you just never gonna talk to her again?"

It sounds bad when she frames it like that, but it's sort of how we left things. I accused Mom of trying to change every aspect of my life, and she said she'd stop being part of it if I found her concern to be such a nuisance.

"I don't know," I mutter, prodding at my fried rice with my fork. Jason, a relentless beggar, is resting his slobbering jowls on the top of my thigh, watching my every move like a sophisticated predator. Begrudgingly, I grab a small piece of sesame chicken off my plate and toss it to him. He gobbles it up in half a second.

Delia scowls. "You shouldn't feed him at the table."

"Why not? It's not like it'll stop the begging." I haven't gotten him into obedience training yet. The place Jacob recommended doesn't have another session starting till spring, so we'll have to endure a couple more months of Jason's bad behavior.

"If you don't want to talk to Mom, will you at least talk to us?" Morgan asks, her voice laced with concern. "You haven't said a word about Christmas Eve."

Both my sisters fall silent, awaiting my response. It's hard for me to find the words for them. It's not as though I want a bad relationship with Mom. We don't have to agree on everything, but as long as she can respect my choices, I can deal with it. The problem is, she's incapable of doing that. No matter how many times we have this argument, she refuses to accept that I want something different from what she wants for me.

Morgan and Delia wouldn't understand, even if I tried to explain. Mom's scrutiny hasn't been shining down on them like a bright, hot spotlight their entire lives. They don't know what she can be like when she's disappointed, brutal and uncompromising.

"There's nothing to talk about," I say. "Besides, Mom hasn't apologized."

"She said you haven't been taking her calls." Okay, that part is true. I just don't see the point. We've been having the same disagreement for too long. Isn't it time we cut our losses and accept that we're never going to make our relationship work?

"Would talking to Mom be easier if Morg and I were there to mediate?" Delia asks. "We could call her right now if you wanted."

"I can't tonight," I say, rising up from the table to clear my plate. "I'm hanging out with Jacob." I dump the bits that remain of my dinner in the trash can, then set my empty plate in the kitchen sink.

Morgan frowns. "Jacob?" she repeats. "You mean Tanner's friend?"

"The very same." He hasn't budged on the True Connections profile yet, which makes zero sense to me. Online dating forces you to make snap judgments. If Jacob's profile has blurry photos or he lists his height followed by "because apparently that matters," then it doesn't matter what else he does. Women won't be interested.

"They're friends now," Delia explains. "But Izzy, please don't go if it's because of the Mom stuff. We can stop if it's bothering you." I'm actually not hanging out with Jacob tonight. He told me he has a work thing. But my good friend, avoidance, is telling me to get the hell out of here before this conversation goes any further.

"It's fine," I say. "But I can't stay."

Morgan frowns. "Are you mad at us?" I'm not. My sisters have good intentions—they just don't understand how deep my issues with Mom go. They wouldn't understand, but I know they genuinely want to help.

"Jacob and I made these plans a few days ago. I don't want to flake on him." I'm well aware that by not wanting to flake on Jacob, I'm flaking on my sisters, but I can't think of a better excuse, so I say my goodbyes and scurry out as quickly as I can.

Of course, leaving the house means I need to find something to do. And since Jacob, my only friend in Seaview, isn't free tonight, my options are limited. It's too cold to wander around the beach, and I don't feel like going to a bar alone.

After several minutes of internal debate, I realize my only solution is the craft store. I haven't drawn anything since the last time I went there, but it's close and warm and—most importantly—open.

Fifteen minutes later, I'm wandering through a long fluorescent-lit aisle of paintbrushes and canvases. I decided the best way to waste time was to scour every aisle. The store is the size of a warehouse, so it could take a while. So far, I've browsed the yarns and fabrics. And I found a keychain of a tiny silver steam train in the bargain bin. I'm thinking of getting it for Jacob. I'm sure it would annoy him.

Unable to resist, I pull out my phone and snap a picture of the keychain. I send it to Jacob, along with the words *belated birthday gift*?

His reply appears a moment later. *This is harassment.*

I laugh to myself. *Don't be so sensitive.*

I'm ending this friendship. I refuse to be a victim of your character assassination.

I type my next response without giving it much thought. *I used to have a thing for nerds.* Before I discovered douchebags in college, I dated guys who were a lot like Jacob. My first boyfriend, Carter, was quiet and bookish. He begged me to read *Lord of the Rings* for him, but I never got beyond the first few pages. Unlike Morgan, I'm not a big reader.

My thumb hesitates over the send button. Does this sound like flirting? I don't mean it that way. Jacob is funny and thoughtful, and he has a lanky sort of charm that some might find attractive, but I'm not interested in him like that.

Jacob is looking for someone to spend his life with. I'm trying to stop my life from combusting. We're in two different places. On two different planets. I don't want to give him the wrong impression.

"Oh my god. It's you."

Startled, I whip my head around. It's the woman I helped pick up paint bottles here the other night. She's standing at the other end of the aisle, dressed in a long navy skirt with pencils and apples printed all over it. She told me she was a teacher, right? That makes sense. Or else she has a very unique taste in fashion.

"I think you might be my craft store fairy godmother," she says, laughing to herself. "You always appear when I need help." I almost tell her that if I'm her fairy godmother, she's screwed in more ways than she could imagine, but that feels a little heavy to share with a stranger.

"What happened? Did you destroy another aisle?" I ask.

"Not tonight," she says, sounding relieved. "Your advice on the tempera paint was amazing, by the way. The kids got it everywhere, but it didn't leave a stain."

"I'm glad to hear it." A petty thought enters my mind. *See, Mom? My art degree isn't useless. I saved this stranger's classroom!* "Acrylic can be a nightmare to get out. I've ruined, like, a dozen sweaters with it."

"I think you saved me a lot of calls from angry parents."

"Happy to help. So, what's the issue tonight?"

The woman's dark eyes widen. "Oh, you don't have to do that," she says. "I'll manage on my own. My problems are not your problems."

"Are you sure? It's not a big deal. I'm here to kill time, anyway." I need to stay out of the house for at least a couple of hours to make Delia believe I'm hanging out with Jacob. Helping this woman might make the time go faster.

"If you *really* don't mind, I won't say no," she tells me. "I'm trying to come up with a new project for my students. We tried this craft I found on Pinterest today, and it did not go over well." She shakes her head as if revisiting a painful memory. "Let's just say six-year-olds do not respond well to complicated instructions. Anyway, I promised them we'd do another project tomorrow to make up for today's disaster, but I don't have an artistic bone in my body. And I'm afraid any ideas I see online might be too hard for them."

"So, you're looking for a project that doesn't require much artistic ability and won't cause a bunch of little kids to lose their minds," I summarize.

She bobs her head. "Exactly."

I tap my chin for a moment. This shouldn't be too hard. I used to do crafts all the time. We can just replicate something I did as a kid.

"How do your students feel about unicorns?" I ask.

"Unicorns are probably a no-go," the woman says. "I can already see one of the boys complaining about the project being for the girls."

"Well, that's ridiculous," I assert. "I mean, we're talking about a fucking flying horse."

"You're not wrong," she says, "except unicorns don't fly."

"They don't?"

"No, that's a pegasus. Unicorns just have the horn on their heads."

"So, what? They don't possess any magical qualities at all?" How have I gone my entire life without knowing this?

"I don't know. I'd have to read up on my mythical creature lore."

"I guess it's not important right now." Unicorns are out, which means we need to find other ideas. "What about puppies? Are they acceptable to everyone?"

The woman grimaces. "One of my students just mentioned their dog is sick. I don't want to upset them."

"Wow. Okay, this is harder than I thought."

"First grade politics are a minefield."

I rack my brain for a second. Think, Izzy. Put yourself in the mind of a first grader. "What about a moose?" I ask. "That can't offend anyone, can it?"

"I can't think of any reason it should."

"Great. Then follow me."

We zip through the craft store. The woman trails behind me carrying a plastic shopping basket, which I load up with brown construction paper, googly eyes, and paint. "I assume you have paper plates at home," I say. "Give each kid a plate and have them paint it brown. Once those dry, you can have them draw faces and glue on googly eyes. You should be able to find an outline online for antlers. Print that out, then trace it on the construction paper and cut it out. I wouldn't leave that part up to the kids." Something about tiny children with scissors unsettles me.

The woman looks at me like I just shared with her the secrets of the universe. "You have no idea how much you just saved my life," she says. "Seriously. Do you need a kidney or something? I feel like I owe you an organ."

"I'm not sure my idea was creative enough to deserve an organ," I tell her. Paper plate animals are hardly original, but they're simple enough for a bunch of six-year-olds to manage without sending their teacher over the edge.

"Then can I buy you a drink as a thank-you?" she asks.

"A drink sounds wonderful." And a lot better than loitering in this craft store for another hour.

"Perfect," she says. "Seaview Tavern is just across the street." She gives me a kind smile. "I'm Angie, by the way."

"I'm Izzy."

In a matter of minutes, Angie and I are sitting at a high-top table at Seaview Tavern, sipping espresso martinis. We spend a few minutes getting to know each other. Angie is a twenty-seven-year-old Seaview lifer. She's married to her high school sweetheart, Carly, and she's been teaching at Seaview Elementary for almost five years. I tell her that I'm relatively new to town and that I'm living at my sister's place until I figure things out career-wise.

"Delia Forrest. That sounds familiar," Angie says, her lips twisting in thought. "Is she dating Tanner Ryan?"

"That's her," I confirm over the rim of my martini.

"Tanner's a great guy. Carly and I hired him to redo our kitchen last fall. It looks phenomenal," she says. "I think I've seen your sister at Ralph's Diner a few times. She's a brunette who always dresses nice, right?"

"Ugh. Yes. And before you ask, yes, it was frustrating to grow up in her perfect shadow."

Angie laughs. "Sorry. I didn't mean to poke at old wounds."

I wave off her concern. "You're fine. I'm actually pretty close with Delia and our other sister, Morgan, who's just as perfect."

"Well, don't sell yourself short," she says. "You've been a huge help to me, and we barely know each other." She blows a strand of black hair out of her face. "Without you, I'd be having a breakdown at the craft store right now."

"Don't take this the wrong way, but if you're so terrible at art, why are you trying to do so many art projects with your students? Can't you leave that to the art teacher?" I hope I don't offend Angie, but I can't understand why she's putting herself through this if she knows nothing about art. It seems she's setting herself up for failure.

"Our art teacher moved to Florida at the end of December," Angie explains. "It happened suddenly. Her mom got sick, and she had to go take care of her. The district didn't have time to find a long-term sub before school started back up after winter break. With only half the year left, the board decided to hold off on hiring a replacement until next school year."

"So, the kids just don't have art class for the rest of the year?"

She nods grimly. "Me and a few other teachers have been trying to do projects with our classes," she says. "Obviously, it hasn't been working out so well. I feel awful. The kids deserve to have a creative outlet, but I can't give it to them." Sadness pulls at my chest. Losing art class would've devastated me as a kid. I was never good at math or science or language arts. The art room was the only place where I felt capable in school. I was about six or seven when I developed my love for drawing. I may be a mess, but I would've been a much bigger one if it weren't for art classes.

My mouth moves before my head has time to catch up. "I could do it."

Understandably, Angie looks confused. "What?"

"I could give your kids art lessons. I'm not a teacher, but I have degrees in drawing and graphic design." The elementary school is down the street from Ryan & Son. I doubt Tanner would mind if I stepped out during my lunch break. "I wouldn't mind coming in to do projects with them."

Shock blankets her features. "Seriously? You'd do that?"

It might seem a tad impulsive, but I can't stomach the thought of these kids not having art classes. Am I a competent substitute for a real art teacher? Not at all. But I should be able to handle myself better than Angie. Who knows? Maybe it could be fun. I like kids. They can be little shits, but they're also cute and excitable and imaginative.

"I appreciate the offer, Izzy," Angie continues, "but you know I can't pay you, right? This would have to be strictly volunteer."

I nod. I wasn't expecting any kind of payment. "Art class was really important to me as a kid," I explain. "I want to help your students. But if you're not into the idea, I totally get it. Like I said, I am not qualified."

She lets out a surprised laugh. "Are you joking? You have an art degree. That already makes you more competent than me." Excitement lights up her eyes. "You'll have to pass a background check, of course. I can't let just anyone walk into a building filled with children. But I would love to have you, and I'm sure the kids would, too."

Okay, well, it looks like I'm doing this. "You'll have to warn me if there are any biters," I say. "And I'm not cleaning up puke."

"Luckily, I don't have any biters this year, and I promise not to put you on puke duty," Angie replies. "This is amazing! Thank you so much, Izzy. I think I owe you another drink." She raises her hand to signal for the bartender while I try to ignore the nervousness suddenly climbing up my throat.

Teaching art. To kids.

I can do this, right?

Fifteen

Jacob

"Is something burning?"

Mom freezes in the middle of tug-of-war with Lulu. Realization flashes in her dark-brown eyes. "Shoot," she says. "I forgot about the pie." She drops her end of the frayed rope toy and scurries off to the kitchen, leaving behind a very confused Lulu. Climbing off the couch, I motion for Lulu to follow as I trail after Mom.

The kitchen is filled with smoke. As I walk further into the room, my eyes water. Mom stands in front of the open oven, frantically waving a dish towel. The burning smell is so strong I can taste it in the back of my throat.

Coughing, I rush to open the window above the sink, letting in a stream of cold, fresh air. Mom continues to swat away the smoke with her dish towel. After a few minutes, the room starts to clear. Mom slips her hands into a pair of oven mitts and pulls out a pie that looks like a giant hockey puck. She sets it on the stovetop.

"Unbelievable," she says, shaking her head in disappointment. "All that work for nothing. I went to the farmers market for those cherries."

"You could easily solve this problem if you used these things called timers," I tell her. Mom doesn't believe in timers. She claims her internal clock is sharp enough that she doesn't need them. I'll admit, her cooking is usually perfect. But now and then, her internal clock malfunctions, resulting in dishes that are undercooked or burnt to an absolute crisp.

Mom scoffs. "There's something wrong with this oven," she mutters as she picks up her ruined pie and carries it over to the trash. "I've been telling your dad that for ages."

"Well, now that pie is off the table, I guess me and Lulu should be heading out." Mom texted earlier when I was at work, asking if I wanted to stop over tonight for cherry pie. She emphasized that the invitation extended to Lulu as well. I'm completely aware of the fact that my mother bribes me for access to my dog, but she makes an incredible cherry pie, so I don't mind going along with it.

"Don't even think about running off," Mom warns me. "I haven't had a chance to see Lulu in the sweater I knitted for her. Besides, I want to hear how your day was."

"It's great to know I come after Lulu on your list of priorities."

Ignoring me, Mom gives Lulu a scratch on the head before settling at the kitchen table. She rests her chin on her palm, a contemplative expression on her face as she turns to look at me. "How are things, Jake?" she asks.

"Things are fine," I say. "Work is fine."

"Try not to use so many adjectives."

"I don't know what else to tell you, Mom," I say, slipping my hands into my back pockets. "I haven't gone through any dramatic life changes since we last saw each other." I'm not being curt on purpose. We had dinner just three days ago. Unless she wants to hear about the unsavory joke Luke Daniels told in the break room yesterday, I've got nothing new to report.

She arches a brow. "So, you're not seeing anyone?"

I groan, unable to help myself. Not the dating questions again. Didn't I endure enough after the whole Marina debacle? "Forget what I said," I tell her. "I'm perfectly content with second place on your list of priorities." I'd rather never talk about myself again than discuss my romantic failings with Mom.

"I'm not trying to pry," she insists, which I find hard to believe. What part of asking if I'm seeing anyone *isn't* prying? Unfortunately for her, there's nothing to share. I haven't been out with anyone since my fake date with Izzy.

"I think this is the very definition of prying, Mom."

She shakes her head adamantly. "I had to ask before I brought up what I really wanted to talk to you about."

I *really* don't like the direction this conversation is going. "Please tell me you aren't trying to set me up." My dating life might be bleak, but that doesn't mean I'm ready for Mom to play matchmaker.

"Sort of," she says. "You know my friend Eva? The one who works with me at the hospital? Her niece just moved to the area. Her name is Catherine. She's in her late twenties. Single. Eva mentioned that she doesn't know a lot of people around here. I wondered if you might be interested in showing her around. Maybe the two of you could hit it off."

I try the best I can to keep a neutral expression, even though that idea seems about as appealing as swallowing a handful of nails. I don't need Mom and her friends setting me up. Eva's niece might be a single woman around my age, but that doesn't mean we have anything in common. What if we went out, and it was stiff and awkward? Then I'd be forced to go back to Mom and share the gory details.

Still, I know she's only trying to help. I don't want to hurt Mom's feelings or make her think I don't trust her judgment. How can I let her down gently? I'm still trying to figure that out when my phone buzzes on the counter.

Picking it up, I see a text light up the screen.

Izzy: Do you think first graders would use these as projectiles?

A picture of plastic rainbow beads accompanies the message. I'm confused. Why is Izzy asking me about art supplies? Or whether children might use them as a weapon? She must've meant to send this to someone else. Three dots appear. She's typing. I wait for her follow-up message, expecting something along the lines of "sorry, wrong person." Her next words, however, leave me even more perplexed.

Izzy: If I need to ask that question, it's probably a yes, right?

Izzy: Beads are out. Too many unknowns.

Izzy: Better question. What would kids NOT use as projectiles?

The messages come in rapid succession. They're chaotic and unfiltered, like Izzy, but there's something about them that gives me pause. They seem frantic. As if Izzy is firing them off as soon as a new thought enters her brain. Is she…panicking? She sounds uncertain, which isn't like Izzy at all. She might not know what she wants to do with her life yet, but she never comes across as nervous. She's Izzy. Calm and witty.

My thumbs hover over the keyboard. I don't want to make Izzy uncomfortable, but I can't ignore the fact that she seems distressed.

Jacob: Are you all right?

Izzy: I'm fine! Sorry for all the texts. Just thinking out loud.

That response *should* settle my suspicions, but it only deepens them. Is she fine? It certainly doesn't feel like it.

Why else would she send a series of seemingly nonsensical texts?

Are you sure? I type. Something stops me before I hit send.

I'm not convinced Izzy is going to give me an honest answer. She knows how to charm people. Hell, she convinced me to go along with her crazy scheme. It wouldn't be hard for her to pretend she's fine when she's not.

Tightness spreads through my chest. I don't like the thought of Izzy keeping her feelings bottled up. We haven't been friends for very long, but we've spent a lot of time together these past few weeks. I care about her. I don't want her to feel like she has to put on a facade with me. While I can't force Izzy to open up, I can make sure she knows I'm here for her. And I have a feeling this conversation will be much easier in person. Without a phone for her to hide behind.

"What do you think?" Mom asks as I drag my eyes away from my phone screen. "I haven't mentioned it to Eva yet. I don't want you to feel pressured."

Honestly, I can't be bothered with Mom's setup right now. I'm too focused on Izzy. "I'm sorry, Mom," I say. "I've gotta go."

"What? Jake, please don't leave. I'm sorry I said anything."

"No, it's not because of that. I need to check on a friend."

She frowns. "Is everything all right?"

"That's what I'm going to find out," I answer truthfully. "You can tell Eva to give Catherine my number." I'm not interested in pursuing anything romantic with Mom's friend's niece, but being a new person in a small, tight-knit town must be tough. I wouldn't mind giving her an introduction to Seaview. Helping her learn the ropes of this place.

I call Lulu over so I can hook her up to her leash. Giving Mom a quick hug goodbye, I grab my coat and head out the door.

Five minutes later, I pull into Delia's driveway. I turn off the car and climb out. After I get Lulu out of the backseat, I start up the walkway that leads to the front porch. I press the doorbell before I can second-guess myself.

Izzy answers in a pair of baggy gray sweatpants and a long hoodie that almost touches her knees. Her hair is in a ponytail, but most of it appears to have fallen out, and her eyes are framed by dark circles. It's an odd look for Izzy, who's usually dressed in bright colors, dark hair spilling freely down her shoulders.

Nevertheless, she reacts to my unexpected arrival with her usual levity. "A gentleman caller," she says, smiling playfully as she meets my eyes. "I'm flattered."

I shake my head. "One of these days, you're gonna greet me like a normal person."

"This is how I greet all of my suitors, Jacob," she replies as she steps out of the doorway to let me inside. Her eyes widen when she notices the furry companion by my legs. "Oh my god. You brought Lulu."

Immediately, Izzy crouches down to pet her.

I scratch the back of my neck. I probably should've checked before I brought my dog over. "I hope that's okay," I say regrettably. "Sorry. I should've asked. We were at my parents' place. I didn't think about it."

Izzy laughs off my concern as Lulu gives her a slobbery kiss on the cheek. "It's fine," she says. "Jason doesn't spend much time around other dogs, but the people at the shelter told me he doesn't mind them. A little socializing would probably do him some good."

A wave of Izzy's floral perfume floods my senses as I enter the warm house. Jason appears immediately, bypassing me for Lulu. Izzy says it's fine to take Lulu off her leash, so I unclip the buckle to let her roam free. She and Jason sniff each other, tails wagging like propellers. It seems to be going well.

"You'll have to excuse my appearance," Izzy says, gesturing to herself. "My hair straightener and I got in a fight this morning." She shows me her index finger, which is sporting a small reddish burn. "I think we're breaking up."

"I never thought the two of you were right for each other." My tone is teasing, but I'm not totally lying. I like Izzy's curly hair. It suits her.

"Me neither," she admits. "So, if you're not here to call on me, then what brings you to my doorstep? Are you finally gonna let me see your True Connections profile?"

"Do the words 'never in a million years' mean nothing to you?" I ask.

"Sounds like a challenge to me." She glances around the house. "Delia is at Tanner's, by the way. I'm not, like, putting you on blast."

"I never thought you were." Izzy and I agreed to keep our arrangement a secret. I figured her sister wasn't home the second she brought up True Connections.

"Well, I'm running out of guesses. I suppose you'll have to just tell me." She gives me an expectant look. The problem is, I'm having a hard time finding the right words. Izzy is acting like everything's fine, but that wasn't how things felt over text. Maybe the best option is to just come right out and say it.

"I wanted to see if you were all right," I confess. "You seemed off."

Surprise flares in Izzy's blue eyes. She quickly drops her gaze to the floor. "That's why you shouldn't send someone a bunch of rambly texts," she says, forcing a laugh. "You probably thought I was here writing my manifesto. Rest assured, I'm fine."

Are you? The question sits on the edge of my tongue. Izzy may be talking like her normal self, but something is definitely wrong. It's like she's putting on a performance. Izzy can be theatrical, but that's who she is. Her jesting usually feels like a natural extension of her personality. This is different. Izzy's responses seem forced. Stiff.

She shifts her focus back to me, surprise replaced by calmness. "Do you want something to drink?" she asks. "I'm sure there's some of Tanner's beer in the fridge." She's en route to the kitchen before I can answer her, leaving me no choice but to follow.

Right away, I notice the mess on the table. It sticks out like a beacon in Delia's tidy kitchen. Paintbrushes, sketch pads, and colored pencils are scattered across the wooden surface. A massive tub of clay sits on one chair. And a faint trail of glitter appears to run from the table to the foyer. Did she...rob a craft store?

Izzy winces when she sees the direction my eyes have shifted. "Okay, this probably isn't helping me beat the manifesto allegations," she says. "I promise there's an explanation that proves I'm not a danger to society." Her joke lands with a whimper. I'm not buying it. Something is bothering her, and I'm not letting up until she admits it.

"Forrest, you know we're friends, right?" I ask, giving her a serious look. "That means you can tell me stuff, even if you are writing a manifesto."

She shakes her head. "I promised I wouldn't try to recruit you into a cult, Jacob. I think that includes any kind of indoctrination."

"Then this is me letting you out of that promise." She smiles, just barely, and it feels like a knife to the gut. I hate seeing her like this, all tense and strained. I want to help, but I can't do that if she won't let me. "Seriously, Izzy. It's obvious you're upset. Will you please tell me what's going on?"

Finally, mercifully, she drops the act. It's like watching a play from the side of the stage and seeing the moment the curtain falls, the way the actors suddenly stop pretending. Izzy's calmness vanishes instantly, a worry line appearing between her brows. Her shoulders slump, and the light in her eyes seems to dim.

"I made a spectacularly bad decision," she says in a voice fraught with panic. "And now I'm questioning all of my life choices." Without another word, she heads to the living room and drops onto the couch, letting out a heavy sigh.

I stare at her in a mixture of surprise and confusion. I've never seen her like this, and I think that's by design. Izzy doesn't seem like the type to let anyone see her unravel. I have to tread carefully here if I want her to talk to me. The best way to do that is to give her free rein of the conversation.

I quietly follow her to the living room, taking a seat on the opposite end of the couch as I wait for her to elaborate.

Izzy grabs the throw pillow beside her, resting it over her midsection. "I met this woman at the craft store the other night," she says. "She's a first-grade teacher at Seaview Elementary. She was there picking up supplies for an art project for her students. We got to talking, and she mentioned that their art teacher recently left the school, and the district isn't filling the position until next year. Which means those kids don't have art class.

"I felt terrible for them. I mean, this woman seemed lovely, but she knows next to nothing about art. One thing led to another, and I ended up volunteering to teach art to these kids." She pauses, twirling the tassels on the pillow. "Honestly, I don't know how it happened. I blame the martini."

I frown. "I don't understand. What's the problem?" It sounds to me like Izzy offered to do a nice thing for these students. Plus, she loves art. I don't see what part of this could be classified as a spectacularly bad decision.

"The problem," Izzy says, turning to face me head-on, "is that my first lesson is tomorrow, and I have no idea what I'm doing. Wanna know what my first project idea was? To have the kids make these cute little deer figurines out of wine corks. Wine corks. I was gonna waltz into a fucking elementary school with a bag of wine corks. Once I realized that was a no-go, I thought about having the kids make fairy houses out of construction paper. But they're first graders, so you know someone is gonna bring up the tooth fairy. And there's always that one little shit who knows the truth and wants to ruin it for everyone. So then I'll make a bunch of little kids cry."

She buries her face in the pillow, so her next words are muffled. "I don't know why I do this to myself," she says. "I make these impulsive decisions that end in disaster. You've seen me, Jake. I cannot be responsible for a group of children. Dominic wouldn't let me watch his baby nephew by myself for an hour. How am I supposed to keep track of twenty kids?"

"Who's Dominic?" I ask.

"My ex-boyfriend," she replies. "I broke up with him last spring. He never took me seriously. Dominic was a dick, but he was right about some things. I'm not made for the big stuff, you know? I'm Good-Time Izzy. I'm not the person you ask to lead a group of impressionable children."

Anger burns inside me. "The only thing you just said that's accurate is that your ex is a dick," I tell her. Who is this guy? I can't believe he made Izzy feel that way about herself. I've never actually hit someone, but I think I'd like to punch Izzy's ex in the face. "Forrest, you absolutely are made for the big stuff."

She lets out a watery laugh as she looks up from the pillow. "Did you not hear the part about the wine corks?"

"I heard everything, and I'm telling you none of it is true," I say. "You didn't bring wine corks into an elementary school because you realized it was a bad idea. People have bad ideas all the time. You can't beat yourself up over something you *didn't* do. And the tooth fairy thing? That's something I never would've thought of. The fact that you're worried about potentially upsetting the kids proves that you're taking this seriously."

She rubs her red-rimmed eyes. "I just…I know I'm gonna do something wrong," she confesses. "Screwing things up is kind of my speciality. My mom knows it. Delia knows it. I don't want to give them more evidence of how much of a mess I am."

I had no idea Izzy carried this much self-doubt. She constantly jokes about not knowing what she wants to do with her life, but I didn't realize those self-deprecating remarks were laced with such honesty.

Izzy really sees herself as a disaster. I need her to understand how untrue that is. She might not have her life sorted out, but most people don't. She isn't the first person to be unsure about her future. The pressure she's putting on herself is unreasonable. And she's much more capable than she gives herself credit for.

"You're not a mess, Forrest."

"Yes, I am. I'm messy and flighty."

"Being funny doesn't make you flighty."

Izzy's lips twitch ever so slightly. "You think I'm funny?" She's deflecting, but I'm still glad to get a smile out of her.

"You're letting your panic get in the way of logic," I say matter-of-factly. "You're dealing with kids. Of course something will go wrong. But that doesn't mean it'll wind up being a disaster. Besides, you said you're doing this as a volunteer. I'm assuming that means you won't be the only adult in the classroom."

Izzy nods. "Their teacher, Angie, will be there."

"Does she know it's your first time doing anything like this?"

"Oh, I made sure of that."

"Then she's probably expecting a few hiccups, anyway."

Izzy is quiet as she absorbs my rationale. "You're right," she says, hugging the pillow against her chest. "I know I'm working myself up for no reason. I just don't want to disappoint anyone."

"There's nothing wrong with being worried, Forrest, but you have to give yourself a little leeway," I reply. "Besides, they're first graders. If all else fails, bribe them with candy."

She laughs slightly. The sound makes the tight feeling in my chest finally loosen. "I'm sorry for spiraling," she says. "I'm sure you weren't looking to play therapist tonight."

"There's nothing to apologize for. You don't have to pretend with me, Izzy. If you're stressed, be stressed. Don't tell me you're fine if that's not how you feel." I'd rather talk Izzy through a thousand moments of panic than have her lie and say she's all right.

She clears her throat. "Well, I just realized we left the dogs alone," she says, "which means they've probably destroyed everything in Delia's house." *Oh, shit.* I was so focused on comforting Izzy I nearly forgot that I brought Lulu. She plays well with other dogs, but I have no clue how she's going to do with Jason, who Izzy claims is part demon. It's suspiciously quiet in the other room.

Izzy and I exchange concerned looks, then both of us scramble to the foyer. I round the corner, expecting to find broken vases and furniture. Instead, the dogs are playing harmlessly, Jason licking Lulu's ear affectionately.

Izzy smiles. "It looks like they're getting along pretty well," she observes.

She's right. They make an unlikely pair, but they seem to be doing just fine.

Sixteen

Izzy

Jacob might actually be a wizard.

Did his pep talk magically cure me of my self-doubt? No. But it calmed my nerves enough that I actually managed to fall asleep last night. Without him, I probably would've spent the evening pacing my bedroom, contemplating what sort of malady I could fake to get out of teaching Angie's class. Instead, I'm heading into my first art lesson with a full eight hours of shuteye. An unbelievable turn of events.

Truly, I don't know how he did it. I was a wreck when he showed up, panicked and incoherent. I'd started thinking about all the ways things could go wrong, and I completely fell apart. But Jacob seemed so certain about my ability to handle this.

Getting assurance from someone as competent as Jacob was exactly the boost I needed. He could've been placating me, but I think he was being sincere. After all, he's supposed to be helping me improve my life. I don't think he'd let me walk into a situation if he thought it would end in disaster.

And Jacob's confidence in me wasn't the only reason I left our conversation feeling better about myself. He also made me feel seen. He knew I was panicking without me even telling him. When I said it was nothing, he wasn't having it.

You don't have to pretend with me, Izzy.

Admitting my feelings has never been my strong suit. I prefer keeping the not-so-fun parts to myself, burying them beneath jokes and smiles. It's what everyone has come to expect from me. Dominic shut me down every time I tried to open up to him. Mom never takes my decisions seriously. Even Delia and Morgan don't know the true extent of my career struggles.

Talking to Jacob, however, was so easy. I feel better about the situation, having told someone my fears. It turns out being honest about your emotions has some benefits.

Who knew?

At a quarter past noon, I park in the visitors' lot at Seaview Elementary. I told Tanner I had an appointment during my lunch break and that it was probably going to become a regular occurrence. Jacob is the only one who knows about the art lessons. Telling anyone else felt like too much pressure. If I were awful, and word got back to Mom, I'd never hear the end of it.

The elementary school is a boxy brick building with long rectangular windows and a small playground off the parking lot. I stare up at the building, giving myself an abbreviated version of Jacob's pep talk. *Angie will be there. It's okay if things go wrong. If all else fails, give the kids candy.* I took the last piece of Jacob's advice very seriously. I raided my office candy stash, filling my purse with chocolate. At the first sign of trouble, I'm whipping out the good stuff.

When I grab my phone out of the cupholder in the center console, a message from Jacob appears on the screen. *Check your glove compartment.* How mysterious. What has Jacob gotten up to in the last fifteen hours?

Obeying his request, I pull open the glove compartment. Inside, I find a pink three-wick candle. I remove the lid to take a whiff of it. Strawberry. He remembered. On the bottom of the candle, there's a Post-It note.

Tickets to the Daytona 500 were too expensive.
P.S. You're going to kick ass.

Warmth spreads through my veins. I have no idea how Jacob managed to pull this off, but I'm touched, both by the gesture itself and the fact that he recalled things about me that I told him weeks ago.

I quickly text him back.

Izzy: How did you get in my car?

Jacob: I told Delia I left my jacket in the passenger seat.

Of course. Delia would think nothing of it. But that would mean he had to do it this morning before I left for work. Jacob left my place around nine-thirty last night. Did he seriously go to the store afterward to pick this up?

Izzy: Thank you.

My phone immediately starts ringing. Without bothering to look at the caller ID, I answer. "You had the opportunity to hot-wire my car, and you didn't take it," I say, grinning to myself as I trace a fingertip around the rim of the candle. "I don't know whether I should be flattered or offended."

"It's barely noon, Iz. How much have you smoked today?" replies a voice that most certainly doesn't belong to Jacob.

Shock waves ripple through me. "Cynthia. Oh, my god." I didn't think to check who was calling—I assumed it was Jacob. Now, I wish I'd taken half a second to look. I've been dodging Cynthia's calls for weeks. I imagine she's not thrilled with me.

"Were you expecting someone else?" she asks in a slightly confused tone.

"No, not at all," I say as I shift in the driver's seat. My jerky movement causes my elbow to bash against the car door. *Fuck.* Pain shoots through my elbow. I clutch the sore spot in my hand, the phone wedged between my shoulder and ear. "It's good to hear your voice. It feels like it's been forever since we last talked."

"It does. How long have you been ignoring my calls again? Five weeks? Six?"

Oh, she's pissed. To be fair, I didn't realize it had been that long. We haven't exchanged more than a few texts since our FaceTime got cut short by Dominic, and that was before Christmas. How did I let so much time slip away from me?

"Izzy, I've known you for seven years," Cynthia says flatly. "We've never not talked for this long. That includes the summer in undergrad when I went backpacking with my Swedish boyfriend."

"I forgot about Nils." He was a sweet guy. Definitely one of Cynthia's better boyfriends. Like me, she doesn't have the best track record with relationships. "I wonder what he's doing now. Do you think he started that meal delivery service company he always talked about?" Nils was a gym rat. He wanted to create a subscription service that specialized in protein-rich meals, which seemed like a very narrow market to me.

"Sadly, Meal Bros never quite took off," Cynthia replies, "but we're not talking about Nils' business failures right now. We're talking about why you suddenly decided to stop speaking to me. Are you gonna tell me what's going on, or do I need to guess?"

"I'm not blowing you off, Cynth." I cringe as the words leave my mouth. I hate lying to Cynthia, especially when I know she knows I'm bullshitting her. "All right, fine. Maybe I have been. But it's not because I don't want to speak to you. You're my best friend. That hasn't changed."

"So, why can't you be bothered to return a phone call?"

It's a fair question. I want to be honest with her. Hiding the truth about Dominic from Cynthia has put a huge strain on our relationship. I'm tired of giving my ex-boyfriend so much control over my life. I moved on a long time ago, but Dominic's presence looms behind me like a shadow. I want my friend back.

Still, it's impossible to sum everything up right now. I'm supposed to be teaching Angie's class in ten minutes. That doesn't give me enough time to justify why I've spent months deceiving my closest friend.

"It's a lot to explain, and I've gotta be somewhere in five minutes," I admit. "But I do want to talk to you about it."

Her response is surprising. "I want to come see you." Cynthia made a comment about making the trip to Seaview the last time we spoke, but I wasn't sure it would happen. "How does the first weekend in April work for you?"

"That's perfect." I don't have to bother checking my calendar. I'll make any weekend work.

This is exactly what I needed. A chance to be honest with her. Face to face.

I'm going to tell Cynthia everything.

***

"Let's all give a warm welcome to Ms. Forrest," Angie announces from the front of the classroom. She picks up a purple dry erase marker and scribbles my name on the massive whiteboard directly behind her.

Ms. Forrest. God, that makes me feel eight and eighty at the same time.

Rising from my wooden chair at the tiny circle table in the corner, I start toward the front of the room, twenty pairs of eyes watching me curiously. I stop beside Angie, who gives

167

me an encouraging smile before redirecting her focus to the students.

I stare into the sea of little faces. Kids are seated at tables of four scattered throughout the small classroom. Brightly colored bulletin boards line the walls, and an enormous polka dot area rug takes up a huge space in the back. The air smells like a mix of paper and cleaning products. These kids must be too young to have BO. I wonder if that's why Angie chose to teach first grade. It certainly would've been a factor in my decision. Who wants to be trapped all day in a room that reeks like armpit and Axe body spray?

"Ms. Forrest is going to lead today's art project," Angie says cheerfully. A little boy with sandy-blonde hair raises his hand. "Yes, Jace?"

"Is she our new art teacher?" he asks.

"No, Ms. Forrest is here as a volunteer," Angie replies.

"Then why is she teaching us?" another kid shouts.

"Ms. Forrest is an artist," Angie says. "I thought you would like to learn from someone who can draw more than stick figures. She's only here for forty minutes, though, so we need to let her get started. Please be respectful and use your listening ears. Ms. Forrest was kind enough to take time out of her day for us, so we want to show our appreciation."

With that, Angie promptly heads to her desk. My heart pounds like a hammer as I observe the students. I'm not shy. If this room were filled with adults, I'd have no trouble filling the silence, but these are young, susceptible children. I could scar them for life by saying the wrong thing, which means I have to be very careful.

"Hi, everyone," I say, slipping my hands inside my pockets so no one can see them shaking. I took a page out of Angie's book today, dressing in a long yellow skirt with a floral pattern and a light-wash jean jacket. That's teacher-y, right? "Like Mrs. Gomez said, my name is Ms. Forrest, and I'm excited to be here. Art was always my favorite subject in school. I hope we can have some fun and maybe learn a thing or two."

The same boy as before, Jace, raises his hand. "If you're not a teacher, then what do you do?" he asks.

"Well, I have degrees in drawing and graphic design," I reply, "but I'm currently working in the office at a construction company."

He frowns. "That doesn't sound like an artist."

Damn, Jace. Who would've thought a first grader could perfectly summarize my career crisis in a single statement? "Being an artist has nothing to do with your day job," I tell him. "Anyone can make art. Doctors. Plumbers. Nurses."

"My dad is a nurse. He can't draw."

"Being able to draw isn't what makes you an artist either. It's about having fun."

Jace doesn't look like he's buying what I'm selling, so I change the subject.

"Today, we're making robots." I open the giant cloth supply bag hanging over my shoulder and pull out my sample project: a purple robot made of construction paper with accordion arms and a pipe cleaner antenna.

The idea came to me shortly after Jacob left last night. I spent a couple of hours cutting arms, legs, heads, and torsos out of different colored construction paper, and I brought a bunch of markers, stickers, and googly eyes with me. I figured the kids would enjoy personalizing them.

"Does anyone want to help me pass out supplies?" I ask. A dozen tiny hands go flying. Thank god. Being rejected by a bunch of six-year-olds would've done serious damage to my ego.

After an adorable girl with curly pigtails helps me hand out the materials, I give the class a quick overview of how to put their robots together. I don't spend too much time giving instructions. The project is fairly simple, and there isn't a right or wrong way to do it. Besides, I want the kids to use this time to be creative, not listen to me drone on.

While the kids work, I float between tables, answering questions and offering guidance when needed. Most of them seem to be taking to the project. They ask me for suggestions and show off their progress proudly. When I get to Jace's table, however, he looks perplexed. He gives me a small frown.

"I don't know what to do," he says, nodding toward the assembled but undecorated blue robot sitting in front of him.

"You can do anything with it," I tell him. "It might help if you give your robot a backstory. Where does it live? Does it have friends? A family? What does it like to do for fun? What's its favorite food?"

"Robots don't eat food."

God, this kid is brutal. "Oh, really?" I say, raising a brow. "Because my robot loves chocolate chip pancakes." To no surprise, Jace looks like he wants to argue with me on that point, but he doesn't get a chance.

"Ms. Forrest!"

I turn my head to see a little girl with her hand raised. I quickly make my way over to her table. Her expression is distraught. "I made a mistake," she says, her voice thick and wobbly, as if she's about to cry. "I glued my robot's arm to his head."

Oh, crap. Not a crying child. That seems above my pay grade. I steal a glance at Angie's desk, but she's out of her seat, talking to a student on the other side of the room. It looks like I'm on my own with this one. Panic squeezes my throat. What do I do? I don't want to make the situation worse.

I give her robot a long, thoughtful look. "I don't know," I say, tapping my chin. "It seems pretty handy, doesn't it? Having an arm on your head would make headstands a lot easier." I have no idea if humor is the right approach, but it's the best I can do.

The girl, luckily, seems receptive to the idea. "I guess so," she says, letting out a small giggle. Relief pulses through me as her features brighten. Crisis averted.

Throughout the rest of the lesson, there's a feeling of lightness that carries over me, unraveling like a spool of ribbon.

This is kind of fun.

Seventeen

Izzy

"You gotta be kidding me, Forrest."

Jacob looks thoroughly unimpressed as he sets the bowl of popcorn on the coffee table. He crosses his arms over his chest, staring down at me through his wire-framed glasses at his ridiculously tall height. He might be in a sweatshirt and jeans, but he's channeling the energy of a disappointed professor with his haughty stare.

"What's the matter, Professor Howell?" I ask innocently. I'm sitting on the floor in Jacob's living room with my back pressed against the couch, alternating between petting Jason and Lulu. Jacob told me I could bring Jason over since he and Lulu got along so well the other night. At first, I was hesitant. Jason doesn't have the best track record with other people's belongings. But Jacob promised not to hold me liable for anything Jason damages. "Did I mess up the assignment?"

"Please don't call me that," Jacob says, shuddering. "Professor Howell is my father."

"Your dad's a professor?"

He nods. "He teaches English at Preston College." That explains so much. I've always thought Jacob had a hot academic vibe. Hold on—did I just call Jacob hot? I've acknowledged his attractiveness before, though I've never used the word "hot."

I take a moment to really examine him, like an artist taking in her subject. Jacob has warm brown eyes, strong brows, and a well-defined jaw. The tendons in his hands flex slightly as he gazes down at me. I've always appreciated a man's hands, and Jacob has great ones. Long, slender fingers with veins protruding beneath his skin.

Holy shit. He's a total smokeshow.

How am I only just discovering this? This must be how Isaac Newton felt when that apple clonked him in the head. One moment he's having a perfectly normal day, the next he's, like, duh. Gravity exists.

"It's never too late to follow in your father's footsteps," I tell him. "You could teach an introductory math class. I bet you'd set record attendance numbers."

"Why's that?" Jacob asks.

"Everyone wants a hot professor."

Surprise splashes over his face. "I-I..." He stammers, scratching the back of his neck in discomfort. "I'm, uh, not sure how to respond to that."

I grin like a kid on Christmas morning. "Oh my god. Did I embarrass you by calling you hot?" Oh, I'm loving this development. Jacob will never know peace again. "You're like a Regency-era debutante. Do you need a fainting couch?"

He shakes his head, eyes glued to the ceiling. "I hate you."

"There's no need to be so temperamental." I reach around him to snag the popcorn bowl, setting it on my lap. Jason and Lulu immediately get in my face, but I shoo them away. "Hot people and their egos."

"I know what you're doing."

"What's that?" I shovel a handful of popcorn into my mouth.

"Distracting me so I forget you took my phone."

I chew slowly. "I don't know what you're talking about."

"Forrest, there's a lump in your pocket."

"Maybe I'm just happy to see you."

Jacob looks even *more* unimpressed. I'll admit, it wasn't the most original joke, but he set me right up. "All right. Fine." Shoving a hand into the pocket of my hoodie, I pull out Jacob's phone and hand it over. "But I wouldn't have to resort to stealing if you weren't being so secretive about your dating profile."

He scoffs as he sets his phone on the couch's armrest. "This is about True Connections?" he says, surprised. "Are you ever gonna let that go?"

"Never. You're being stubborn for no good reason," I tell him. "Your profile is what women use to make their first impressions of you. There could be something that's throwing them off. What if the future Mrs. Howell swiped left because you used the wrong form of 'to' in one of your prompt responses?"

Jacob settles on the couch, giving Lulu and Jason each a quick pet. "If a misplaced modifier is what's keeping us apart, then it wasn't meant to be," he says dryly.

"We've talked about this, Jacob," I reply, giving voice to my growing frustration. "This arrangement isn't gonna work unless we're honest with each other."

He arches a brow. "I could say the same to you. You've been here for what…ten minutes? You haven't said a word about how the art class went yesterday." He snags the popcorn bowl off my lap, a triumphant gleam in his eye. I suppose he has a point. Despite my freakout the other night, I haven't exactly been forthcoming about the art lesson. I considered texting Jacob yesterday after I left the school, but I didn't want to be a nuisance.

"I've been waiting for an update, Forrest," he continues. "You've given me nothing."

"I didn't wanna annoy you," I tell him truthfully. "I thought you earned some well-deserved silence after I dumped my problems on you."

"I wouldn't ask if I didn't wanna know." The look he gives me is a mix of curiosity and sincerity. Aside from Jacob, I haven't told anyone about my volunteering. Not even Delia. I didn't want the pressure of having to explain myself if things ended badly. But I have been itching to tell someone about it, and if Jacob insists…

"The lesson went really well, actually," I admit. "The kids were sweet. None of them stuck candy in my hair, and only one made an unintentionally disparaging remark about my career. They seemed to like me. Angie said they've already been asking when I'm coming back. I think we're gonna make it a weekly thing."

Jacob beams. "Forrest, that's amazing." I try not to let those words go to my head. He's just being polite. I helped a bunch of six-year-olds make robots out of construction paper. It's not like I solved a world crisis.

"It's not hard to impress first graders. I'm sure they were just happy they got out of reading time," I say as I extend a hand toward the popcorn on Jacob's lap. I can't quite get there, so I slap lazily at the side of the bowl until he begrudgingly tips it my way.

"You do that a lot, you know," he says.

"Why move when I know you'll eventually give in?" I ask, scooping up a fistful of popcorn, then dumping it in my mouth.

Jacob frowns. "No, you like to downplay things. You did it the other night when you pretended you were fine. And you're doing it now by acting like this great thing you did for those kids isn't a big deal."

"We're back to psychoanalyzing each other, I see. We should trade places. I'll lie on the couch while you take notes."

He gives me a cut-the-bullshit look. "Forrest."

"Ugh. Fine." I guess fixing my life entails getting to the root of my problems. Boring. "I've never liked making a big deal out of stuff, but it's not what people expect from me, anyway. I'm Fun Izzy, remember?" I'm the person you look to for a smile or an ill-timed joke, not an emotional heart-to-heart.

"Is this about Dominic?" Jacob asks. Oh, yay. Talking about my ex-boyfriend. That's certainly going to make this psychological assessment more fun.

"No, this stuff predates Dom," I tell him. "Though I'm sure he'd love to think he had that much influence on my life. At this point, he's just a rash I can't quite get to go away."

"You still talk to him?" Jacob's tone rings with shock. The not-so-friendly way I talk about Dominic probably makes it hard to believe we're on speaking terms.

"Not by choice. He's part of my friend group back in New York, which means I have to endure his presence on FaceTime now and then."

"Your friends still hang out with him?"

"He's my best friend's cousin. Plus, he was their friend before we started dating. And they don't know what went down in our relationship. When I dumped Dominic, we agreed to tell our friends it was a mutual decision. We didn't want the breakup to make things uncomfortable for them. At least I didn't. Looking back, I think Dominic was mostly concerned with preserving his reputation. He wasn't exactly the most supportive boyfriend."

Jacob doesn't say anything. Only watches me with thoughtful eyes. His unspoken reply hangs in the space between us. *You can keep going.*

Hesitant, I bite the tip of my thumbnail. Admitting these things feels gross but oddly freeing. Like plucking a stray eyebrow hair or popping a pimple. Or tossing the stuff that's been bothering me out into the world like, "here you go, universe. It's all yours. Now please leave me alone."

"I don't think I ever loved him," I finally confess. "That sounds bad when I say it aloud, but it's the truth. I was in a weird place when Dominic told me how he felt. It was around that time when things at work started to feel off. I didn't like my job anymore. It was as if all the passion had been drained from me. And then Dominic said he loved me. It was…something different. Something new. And I needed something to feel good about.

"I thought if Dominic loved me, that meant he had to understand me. I expected our relationship to magically fix my problems, which is a red flag itself. A photographer from Brooklyn has never fixed anyone's life. But the real problem was that Dominic never saw me as a person. I was a party trick to him. Something fun and interesting. When I tried to open up to him about work or anything remotely serious, he acted like he didn't know me anymore.

"We agreed to stay friends after the breakup, and I didn't think much of it. We were friends for a long time before we dated. I figured things would just go back to the way they once were. But being around him was painful. I may not have loved Dominic, but I cared about him. The fact that he invalidated everything I was feeling at such a difficult time in my life…it stung. I didn't want to be friends with someone like that. It was eating me alive, but I couldn't say anything to Cynthia. It's one of the reasons I left New York."

When I finish speaking, I can barely bring myself to look at Jacob. I feel itchy, vulnerable. Saying those words may have felt liberating for a moment, but it's a level of exposure that I'm not used to. Like I'm standing in front of Jacob with a layer of skin removed. My insides feel raw. I'd very much like to pretend it never happened.

"That's a lot of Feelings Talk for one evening," I say, sighing. "We should talk about something else. Literally anything else. Automation. True crime documentaries. Remember that time when everyone was obsessed with mustaches? What *was* that?" Oh my god. I need to stop talking. This is the consequence of me being unable to keep my mouth shut.

"I concede," Jacob says.

I stare at him, confused. "What?"

"I'll let you see my True Connections profile."

***

Jacob

I didn't invite Izzy over for the sake of humiliating myself, but that's where this night seems to be headed. She pulls herself off the floor, then drops beside me on the couch, mischief dancing in her pale blue eyes.

"Hand it over," she says, making a *gimme* gesture with her left hand. "I promise I'll be gentle, Jacob. I know it's your first time."

Rolling my eyes, I grab my phone off the armrest and cue up my True Connections profile. Until two minutes ago, I had no intention of ever showing it to her. It felt too personal.

178

Profiles on dating apps are meant for strangers' eyes only. Letting Izzy see how I present myself online seemed like giving ammunition to a much stronger opponent. I could hear the jokes writing themselves already.

But then, she told me about Dominic. Her words confirmed a lot of the suspicions I already had based on our conversation the other night. Dominic made Izzy feel like shit simply for existing. It surprised me to learn that Izzy has stayed in contact with him. Then again, her dismissing her real feelings to maintain a sense of normalcy with her other friends makes complete sense. One thing I've quickly discovered about Izzy is that she'd rather suffer in silence than cause the people she cares about the slightest inconvenience.

Izzy doesn't like to divulge anything intimate. I could tell how difficult it was for her to open up about her ex-boyfriend. It only seemed fair that I give her something in return. If giving her control over my dating app profile makes her feel better about her decision to confide in me, then I'll gladly take the humiliation. I don't want Izzy to regret putting her trust in me. Especially when I know how hard it is to earn that trust.

Wordlessly, I pass her my phone. Izzy's face lights up. If there's one consolation for embarrassing myself for her entertainment, it's that she looks beautiful when she's happy. Her cheeks turn soft pink, and her features are unguarded, as if she has laid down her armor and surrendered to her feelings. It's how I was able to confirm she was upset when I showed up at Delia's place a couple nights ago. When Izzy is really, truly happy, she is joy in its purest form. A firecracker exploding across a pitch-black sky. Absolutely captivating.

I pet Lulu and Jason as I wait for her to finish scoping out my profile. Though I haven't had much success on the dating front, I'd like to think I put a decent profile together. It includes several photos of me with friends and Lulu, and my responses to the prompts show off my hobbies (reading, watching baseball, hanging out with friends) and make clear that I'm looking for a long-term relationship.

Yet I have no idea what Izzy is going to think of it. She's probably going to accuse me of playing it safe and say I need something that helps me stand out from the thousands of other profiles just like it. While there's surely some merit to that argument, I don't see myself making any drastic changes. My profile may be simple, but that's who I am. I'm not going to pretend to be someone else to get a woman's attention. It wouldn't bode well for our future together if she only liked me because she thought I was someone different.

"Well, I'm not seeing any photos of you posing with a fish so far," Izzy says, her red-painted fingernail continuing to swipe. "That's always a good sign." Her eyes connect with mine for a moment. "But Jacob, there are other people in all of these photos. Why aren't there any of just you?"

"I was under the impression that that's how you prove you aren't some creep living in their mom's basement," I tell her. Isn't that standard dating profile protocol? No friends or family sends the message *I might keep your used napkin so I can use your DNA to clone you.*

"Well, it isn't *Where's Waldo,*" Izzy argues. "You're not supposed to make women hunt for you. How is anyone gonna know which person here is you?"

"These were the best photos I had of myself."

"And not a single one was a selfie?" Izzy's expression is clouded in doubt. "You're telling me if I scroll through your camera roll right now, I won't find any pictures of you posing with model trains?" Without warning, I swipe my phone out of her hand. She gasps and tries to snatch it back, but my arms are much longer, so I hold it up and out of her reach.

"I wasn't finished!" she objects.

"Too bad. I've taken enough of your abuse."

Izzy sighs. "You're right," she says. "I'll admit, the train thing was uncalled for, but my point remains. We need new source material, Jacob. You're a catch. But how are women supposed to know that if your profile doesn't show them?" There's some logic to her argument. Any woman who studied my profile for long enough would eventually be able to tell who it belongs to, but why would they bother taking the time to do that?

Online dating is about making quick decisions. There's no reason for anyone to spend time sorting through my profile when they can easily find another.

"The only pictures I have of myself are from my college graduation," I say. "Won't those just make me look like a guy who can't let go of his glory days?" It's been eight years since I graduated from college. I think it's time to let that chapter of my life go.

Izzy is undeterred. "I can take a new one for you," she says. "I don't mean to brag, but I'm very good at staging a candid."

"Do you not hear how nonsensical that sounds?"

"Hush, old man. Everyone does it."

"A famously good reason to do anything."

Izzy grabs the throw pillow from behind her back and tosses it at me, hitting me square in the shoulder. "Keep this up, and you're gonna wind up alone forever," she says tauntingly.

"I think I'd rather die alone." I was wrong before. Letting Izzy go through my dating profile isn't the lowest it can get…letting her stage a candid for me is. "At least I have The Lieutenant to keep me company."

"The Lieutenant?" she repeats.

Oh, right. Izzy doesn't know the origins of my dog's name. "That's what Lulu is short for. She's named after a character in—"

"*Galactic Rush*," she says. "I know."

"You're a fan of *Galactic Rush*?" I try not to sound too surprised, but it's hard to contain my shock. Izzy doesn't seem like the typical sci-fi fan, and *Galactic Rush* has a notoriously dorky fan base. A group of fans created an unofficial language guide to Plesch, the native language of the desert planet Plesco. Every year, they host a fan convention over the same weekend as the official *Galactic Rush* fan convention, except theirs is spoken entirely in Plesch. I think it's supposed to be some sort of protest.

Izzy bobs her head. "I've never seen the movies, but I'm slightly obsessed with the video game. And by slightly obsessed, I mean I spent fifty dollars of actual U.S. currency on coins so I could buy a pet dog with laser eyes. It was worth it, though. Her name is Nebula, and she incinerates her enemies with the blink of an eye."

"It happens to the best of us," I say with a chuckle. "The first *Galactic Rush* game came out during finals week of my last semester of college. I became so obsessed that I played through the final exam for my poly sci class. My professor let me do a makeup test, but I also had to write a three-page paper on the negative effects of video games."

"Oh, sweet Jacob. That is why you should never be honest with your professors. Do you know how many sick relatives I had my freshman year? I used to change the time zone on my email so professors would think I was on the other side of the country instead of nursing a killer hangover in my dorm room."

"Forrest, that is a supervillain level of commitment."

"It's called dedication," she argues. "A couple professors were suspicious of my frequent absences, so I had to really sell it. And I can promise you, I never had to write a paper about the negative effects of doing too many tequila shots in a frat house living room."

"If only I had been around to corrupt you," Izzy says, brows raised suggestively.

"If only." Though I honestly doubt Izzy and I would've become friends had we met when we were younger. I only went out a handful of times in college. Drunken nights surrounded by obnoxious strangers in hot, sweaty places weren't my thing.

"I can't believe I've been tormenting you about model trains all this time," she says, shaking her head as if disappointed in herself. "You're so clearly a sci-fi nerd." Immediately, I throw the pillow back at her. She lets out a giggle as it smacks her in the shoulder.

"So, what level are you on?" she asks.

"Forty-seven. I've been stuck in a sandpit on Lovia for days. What about you?"

"Oh, I don't do quests."

"Isn't that how you play the game?"

"Not if your objective is to collect coins and steal cool stuff from other players."

"Please tell me you aren't one of those hellions who terrorizes people in the live chat." I assumed those players were twelve-year-old boys, but I wouldn't put it past Izzy to be complicit in a little virtual name-calling.

"Only if the other person deserves it," she tells me. "Like, the other day, I was scoping out the wreckage of a ship crash when some dick tried to take my spoils. That is an act of war, Jacob. Of course I had to call him out on it."

"I cannot believe this," I say, giving her a reprimanding look. "What you're saying right now goes against everything I believe in as a player and a person."

She returns my reproachful expression with her own. "You may not approve, but it is an effective strategy," she says, holding her chin high. "You're looking at the proud owner of a rocket launcher." I don't want to let my excitement show, but owning a rocket launcher is a big deal in the context of *Galactic Rush*. They cost tens of thousands of coins. I don't have one, and I've almost certainly been playing this game longer than Izzy.

Naturally, she sees right through my attempt to seem unaffected. "You want to see it, don't you?" she asks, a slow smile spreading across her face.

I absolutely do. But I can't just admit it. "Not really."

"God, you are such a bad liar, Jacob," she says. She lunges for my laptop, which is lying on the coffee table. Resting it on the tops of her thighs, she flips open the screen, light splashing across her face.

"What are you doing?" I ask, leaning over so I can see the screen. Izzy has opened the *Galactic Rush* app and is entering a username and password on the login page.

"What does it look like I'm doing?" she asks. "I'm giving your nerdy heart a chance to run wild." She finishes logging in to her account, then picks up the laptop and drops it on my lap. "Go ahead. But do *not* piss off Nebula. She needs to eat every couple of hours, or else she'll get cranky and start biting people."

There's no reason to say no. Besides, I'm probably never going to have another opportunity to try out a rocket launcher, so I might as well take advantage. Izzy wasn't kidding about not completing any quests. Her avatar, Hela, an alien the color of a grape, is listed as a level one player, despite possessing more coins than anyone I've ever seen.

Izzy begrudgingly gives me permission to complete the first quest so I can see the rocket launcher in full effect. It's a fairly simple quest, taking out a small group of enemy combatants. With the rocket launcher, it's easier than slicing through hot butter.

"Unbelievable," I say, my eyes fixed on the screen. "You have no idea the things you could do with this, Forrest. Especially on the more difficult levels." It probably isn't the smartest move to criticize the playing style of the woman who's letting me borrow her rocket launcher, but I can't help myself.

Izzy's arm brushes against mine. "It's turning you on, isn't it?"

I laugh, turning to steal a glance at her. Izzy has her phone ready, taking a picture before I even have a chance to react. She grins smugly as she studies her handiwork. "See," she says, passing the phone to show me. I have to hand it to her—it's far better than any of the pictures on my True Connections profile. I'm wearing an easy smile, eyes crinkled with laughter. "This is a good one."

We play for a while, Izzy and I making mindless conversation about the characters we love and the planets we've yet to explore. After I clear a few levels, Izzy convinces me to try things her way. We switch to live mode and begin searching for shipwrecks to ransack. At one point, Izzy engages in mild trash talk with another player after they try to take Nebula, but we come across a deserted fueling station flush with coins that makes up for it. Izzy's method of play may not be conventional, but I have to admit it's pretty fun.

"I may have been a little harsh in my judgment earlier," I say after a stretch of long but comfortable silence. I'm expecting a self-satisfied response from Izzy, so when I get nothing, I turn to look at her, curious.

She's asleep. Her cheek rests on the couch cushion, just a few centimeters from my shoulder. Her proximity makes me very aware of her…everything. Her full lips, parted gently, stained by her faded red lipstick. Her sloping nose, and the long, dark eyelashes lying against her cheek. The tiny brown freckle just below the corner of her left eye. And her floral perfume, fresh and light, is suddenly everywhere.

Izzy always smells good. I wonder how she manages it. Where does she apply her perfume? Her wrists? Her neck? I imagine tracing my nose along her soft skin, feeling her pulse pound as I breathe her in. Heat stirs in my veins at the thought of my face pressed to her neck, Izzy's heartbeat loud and fast, her fingers curled into my shoulders, and her voice a soft and pleading whisper. *Jake.*

Still asleep, Izzy makes a soft humming noise. The slight disruption is enough to shatter the illusion in my mind, which breaks like a chandelier on a concrete sidewalk. Realization swirls in the pit of my stomach.

I like Izzy.

Eighteen

Jacob

In retrospect, I don't know how I managed to go this long without realizing I was into Izzy.

Hindsight has a rather annoying way of connecting clues you never picked up on, almost like a roadmap, and shoving them in your face. *Wanna know how you landed here, jackass? it asks. Take a look.*

The evidence, unfortunately, is pretty damning. I spent hours panicking over where to take Izzy on a *pretend* date, which turned out to be the best one I've had in a long time. I invited her bulldozer of a dog into my house, despite his history of wrecking furniture. I hung a somewhat obscene floral painting in my living room, which will no doubt earn the ire of my mother, because I knew it would make Izzy smile.

Oh, and I can't stop thinking about kissing her red lipstick off.

My feelings for Izzy have certainly intensified since we started hanging out, but I think I've liked her for a while now. I always said yes to dinner or drinks with Delia and Tanner if I knew Izzy would be there. At the Christmas Eve party, I kept looking at the door, waiting for her to show up. Our conversations, though brief, never failed to be the highlight of my night.

Izzy is funny and beautiful, and she smells like a meadow. She has this innate way of making everyone around her feel comfortable, like you should tell her your deepest secrets or say something outrageous because you want to be interesting enough to hold her attention. She is warm and captivating, and she is the worst person for me to have feelings for.

First, Izzy is a self-proclaimed disaster. She's not nearly as messy as she believes, but still. Someone who feels as uncertain as Izzy does about the general direction of her life won't want to be with someone who's ready to settle down. And given how things ended with her ex, I doubt she's planning to rush into another relationship any time soon.

Second, and most important, is that these feelings are definitely not mutual. Izzy is helping me meet someone. I may not have the best track record in terms of romantic relationships, but I don't think she'd be actively trying to find the future Mrs. Howell if she was interested in me herself.

Based on everything Izzy has told me, I couldn't be further from her type. She says she likes raging douchebags. So unless I really lack self-awareness, or I've already started morphing into Luke Daniels, I'm not her idea of a romantic interest. I don't think Izzy, who admitted she once jumped into a pool from a second-story balcony on a dare, pictures herself with a guy who likes crossword puzzles and reads Reader's Digest (some of the home improvement tips are actually pretty good).

Unless I want to cut Izzy out of my life, I have no choice but to ignore my feelings and hope they go away. I care about her too much to lose her friendship. And I promised her I would help her figure out her life. Ditching her immediately after she started opening up to me would just reinforce her fear that she's too much for people. I don't want to make Izzy doubt herself more because I can't control my emotions.

"What are we here for exactly?" I ask as I follow her down an aisle of the craft store one night. The place smells like the potpourri my grandma used to make, and dated pop music plays over the loudspeakers. I try not to stare at Izzy's ass as she strides ahead in her flamingo pink leggings because friends do *not* do that.

"Clothespins," Izzy replies, giving me a quick look over her shoulder. She asked me to come with her to pick up supplies for her next art lesson, claiming she needed her tallest friend to help her reach the highest shelves.

I was more than happy to tag along. Izzy seems to love teaching art class. Last night, she texted me a picture of a pile of drawings that the kids made for her. And she looked so giddy on the drive here when she told me about how one of the quieter students gave her a hug at the end of yesterday's lesson. It's good to see her this excited. Izzy is incredible, and she deserves something to feel passionate about.

"I'm making clothespin dragonflies with the kids next week, but I need to test them out first," she says. "I can't have a bunch of first graders getting splinters on my watch. Your freakishly long arms should be able to reach them."

"If you want to use my arms, don't you think you should refrain from calling them freakish?" I ask in an amused tone.

"Jacob, you're, like, six hundred feet tall. Your arms are like hoses."

"That's height discrimination, Forrest."

She makes a dismissive sound. "Oh, please. I haven't once asked you how the weather is up there or what it's like to see the tops of people's heads."

"Balmy and you can really tell when someone has dandruff."

Izzy laughs. "You know, I made the mistake of telling one of my ex-boyfriends he had dandruff. I tried to be sensitive about it. I even bought him a nice dandruff shampoo. But he was so mad that he didn't talk to me for a week. I really wasn't trying to hurt his feelings. But Wyatt was the type of guy who smashed things after his team lost in fantasy football, so maybe I should've known."

I raise a brow. "The fantasy football thing wasn't your first red flag?"

"I was nineteen," she says in defense. "I ran on energy drinks and gas station pizza. My brain wasn't functioning properly. I'm sure you missed some major red flags with your exes, too." She stops all of a sudden in the middle of the aisle. "Oh my god. I just realized we've never talked about any of your exes."

Discomfort prickles along the back of my neck. "I think you've subjected me to enough emotional torture, Forrest," I quip back, hoping she doesn't press me any further. I don't feel like delving into my romantic history with Izzy, but she has a talent for recognizing when I'm being secretive and forcing the truth out of me.

Arms folded, she scrutinizes me. "How is that fair? You know all about Wyatt's dandruff and Dominic's emotional manipulation. I deserve a few details." Knowing Izzy, she isn't going to let this go until I give her something.

I decide the best course is to be honest…and vague.

"There's not much to say," I tell her. "I dated a woman named Hailey a couple years ago. She was a nurse from Pembroke, but we weren't together for long. Before that, I was with an accountant. Danielle. We dated for almost a year."

Izzy bobs her head, processing the information. "So, why did you break up?"

"Both relationships sort of fizzled out." Hailey and I didn't have enough in common to build anything lasting, and Danielle wanted to focus on her career. The breakups were mutual and uncomplicated. No screaming matches or hurt feelings. One day, we just stopped talking to each other, and that was that.

"And before that?" Izzy asks. "Was there anyone before Danielle?"

"Just Maggie." She stares at me, waiting for more, so I reluctantly share the rest. "She was a childhood friend. We dated in high school and most of college."

"Wow. So you were childhood sweethearts."

"I guess so."

"What was that like? I didn't have a long-term boyfriend in high school. It must've been nice to grow up with someone."

"It was good. Maggie and I had known each other for most of our lives, so we were comfortable together."

"So, why did it end?"

Tension coils in my stomach. "She went to school out of state and, uh, met someone else. A guy in her major. She broke up with me a few weeks before graduation." My tone is flat, emotionless. The last thing I want is Izzy's pity.

The color drains from Izzy's face. "Maggie cheated on you?"

I nod quickly. "She married the guy, so I guess it worked out for the best." I googled Maggie a few years back out of morbid curiosity. She and John were living somewhere in Connecticut with an ugly chihuahua.

Izzy twists her lips. "Shit, Jake. I'm sorry."

"It was a long time ago." I spent more than enough time moping over Maggie, wondering what I could've done differently. Was I too attentive? Not attentive enough? Did I miss any warning signs? The questions piled up in my head. But eventually, I came to terms with the truth. Maggie didn't want to be with me anymore. Nothing would've changed that.

"Still, Maggie sucks," Izzy says. "I will hire a witch on Etsy to put a hex on her if you want me to."

"I'm all right, Forrest." The Maggie stuff is ancient history for me. Talking about her is awkward, but I don't care enough for it to hurt anymore.

"If you ask me," Izzy continues, "you dodged a massive bullet. You shouldn't be with someone who doesn't appreciate you, Jacob. You're a good guy. You don't use empty liquor bottles as decorations, and you've never tried to lecture me about my taste in music. Those qualities are hard to find. Anyone who doesn't realize that doesn't deserve you."

She gives me a genuine smile, and she's just so pretty that it knocks the wind out of my lungs. I stare, speechless. My brain feels like it's short circuiting. Then Izzy clears her throat and glances down the aisle.

"You know what?" she says. "I bet the clothespins are over by the buttons. Follow me."

She's dashing out of the aisle a second later, leaving a wave of her perfume behind.

Being friends with Izzy might just kill me.

***

Izzy

If there's one thing I've learned about first graders, it's that they hate being told no. A few kids wanted to use glitter for our dragonfly craft yesterday. They saw a bottle of chunky blue sequins poking out of my craft supply bag and asked if they could give their dragonflies a little sparkle.

Initially, I tried to stop it, but the kids became really animated. They started telling me stories about their dragonflies coming from magic fairy lands where sparkles give them the power to fly. They were being creative and imaginative because of something *I* taught them. Denying them glitter would've been like stomping on their artistry. I

192

couldn't do it. Not when I'm constantly encouraging them to use their imaginations.

Of course, their imaginations led to an absolute mess. The kids got glitter all over Angie's classroom. Luckily, she had a vacuum in the closet, and we were able to clean most of it up. But I'm still finding sequins everywhere. My purse. My car. One day and two showers later, I'm still plucking glitter out of my hair. I wonder if this decision is going to haunt me for the rest of my existence. At my funeral, there will probably be tiny flecks of teal sparkles peeking out of the casket.

When I finish towel-drying my hair Wednesday night, I step out of the steamy bathroom and scurry down the chilly hall to my bedroom.

Closing the door behind me, I reach for my phone on the nightstand. I fire a quick text to Angie. *I'd like to apologize again for glitter bombing your classroom. If it's any consolation, I still haven't managed to get it all out of my hair.*

Angie responds with a string of crying emojis. *My thoughts and prayers are with your hair. No worries about the classroom. It's first grade. Things get messy. You should've seen the place after we made applesauce last fall. I never thought we were going to get the smell of cinnamon out of the carpet.*

I smile slightly. *You made APPLESAUCE with those children???* I know just how many of those kids pick their noses. Trusting them to prepare food is certainly a choice.

Is that judgment from the woman with glitter in her hair? Angie writes back.

Okay, she may have me beat there.

I toss my phone on my bed and slip into pajamas. Relief flows freely through my veins. I was a little worried about how Angie would react to the glitter incident. None of my other projects resulted in such a mess. At school, she told me it wasn't a big deal, but I thought it might cause her to second-guess this whole arrangement. Her easygoing responses put my mind at ease.

Things get messy. The words remind me of something Jacob told me when I was panicking about my first art lesson. Things can't go right all the time, especially when you're dealing with tiny children who cry when they don't get the color paintbrush they wanted. I can't slip into panic mode every time something goes slightly wrong. Mistakes will happen, and I need to embrace that if I want to make this work. And I really do.

Teaching these kids is the most fun I've had with anything art-related since I started my first graphic design job. I don't want anything to get in the way of it.

After I finish getting dressed, I flop into my bed. I expect Jason to join me right away—he's usually eager to get to bed. However, he stays in his curled up position on the floor, his back facing me. Is that a nibbling sound I hear? I scramble off the bed immediately, suspicious of the slurpy noises coming from Jason's side of the room. He definitely has something he shouldn't. I just hope it doesn't belong to Delia.

When I get to Jason's side, he abruptly sits up, guilt swimming in those big eyes of his. Something dark and circular sits in the space between his front paws. Oh my god. It's a potato. How in the hell did he get that?

Jason seems to recognize the moment he gets busted. He gobbles up what's left of the potato before I can snatch it from him. Licking his lips, he stares up at me with a triumphant gleam in his eyes. *Take that, bitch.*

I'll give him credit. This dog never fails to surprise me. Accepting defeat, I head back to my bed. I have to tell someone about this, don't I? Without thinking, I grab my phone and call Jacob. He answers on the second ring.

"You'll never guess what Jason did."

I hear him smile through the speaker. "I can't even imagine."

"He ate a giant raw potato. I just watched him polish off the rest of the skin. Jacob, I don't know how he got it. I put the potatoes in the fridge as soon as I got back from the grocery store. The little shit either snuck into my bags when I was bringing them inside, or he's a lot smarter than he's letting on."

"I watched Jason run into a glass door the last time I was at your place, Forrest. I don't think he has any intelligence to hide."

"Or maybe that's just what he wants us to think," I reply as I fall back on my pillow. Jason quickly jumps on the bed, taking his usual spot by my feet. I let him up, despite his transgression. He nuzzles against my ankles. "So, how was your day? I assume Lulu didn't get into any raw vegetables."

"She was with my mom most of the day, so I can't say what she got up to," he says. "But my day was all right. Though Luke Daniels kept forcing me to watch unfunny clips of athletes falling on their faces edited to trap music."

"Making someone watch a video should be outlawed." I had a coworker at my graphic design job who was obsessed with showing me videos of her cat. Maintaining an awkward smile for those two minutes was easily the most painful experience of my life.

"He played them at full volume in the middle of the office."

"That should carry jail time."

We share a laugh as I pull the comforter over my legs. Jason has already fallen asleep, his soft snores filling the room. He rarely crashes that quickly, so he must be tired. I wonder what time it is. My eyes widen when I check the clock on my phone.

"Oh my god. It's eleven."

"So?" Jacob says.

"So I just called you at eleven o'clock on a weeknight." I run a hand over my face, suddenly embarrassed. I didn't even think about the time when I hit the call button. "Respectable people do not call people after eleven."

"Since when were you a respectable person, Forrest?"

"Since never, apparently." I'm the kind of animal that calls people at inappropriate hours. What is wrong with me? "Were you asleep?"

It's quiet on the other end. "No."

"Jacob, you're *such* a bad liar."

"I really wasn't," he insists. "I just got in bed. I was watching a documentary about marine life. Did you know the blue whale is the largest known animal to ever live?"

"Admitting you stay up to watch nature documentaries doesn't help your nerd status."

"Your abuse doesn't faze me anymore."

I smile, picturing Jacob in a pair of plaid pajama bottoms, the TV light reflecting off his glasses. For a second, I imagine myself there with him, Jacob twirling a strand of my hair around his long finger while we watch a documentary, but the image dissolves faster than a snowflake melting on the sidewalk.

What the fuck was that?

It's weird that we're on the phone in bed, isn't it? Maybe it's messing with my brain. Jacob doesn't know I'm under the covers, but he probably suspects as much, given the time. If he's imagining me right now, I hope the mental picture is more flattering than reality. I'm dressed in an old T-shirt and a ratty pair of underwear that I usually save for the heaviest day of my period.

"I'm still sorry about calling so late," I say earnestly. "I didn't even think about it. We hadn't talked all day. It felt wrong, you know?" I've gotten used to talking to Jacob on a daily basis, even if it's only a few texts. Not having any sort of communication with him all day struck me as an error that needed to be corrected.

"Izzy, I wouldn't have answered if I didn't want to talk," he says in an earnest tone. I know he means it when he calls me Izzy, not Forrest.

"Well, you know the rules of late-night phone calls, don't you?" I ask. "Nothing you say tonight can be held against you. So if you have any murders or other nerdy hobbies you'd like to confess to, I suggest you get them out now."

Jacob chuckles. "I know you too well to trust that you'll keep your word." That's probably fair. I have been known to break the rules, so I can't blame him for expecting me to do the same thing now.

"I guess I'll go first then." I pause for a moment as I collect my thoughts. "You might already know this, but you're the only person I've told about the art classes. I want to tell Delia and Morgan, but I'm having such a hard time actually doing it. With you, it was a lot easier. Sometimes, it feels like you're the only person I can talk to."

My heart hammers in my chest. Oh, god. Was that too much? The problem with always saying the first thing on your mind is that you put your foot in your mouth. A lot. I hope my confession didn't make Jacob uncomfortable. It might've been too heavy for eleven-fifteen on a random Wednesday night. And the longer he doesn't say anything, the more it seems to confirm my suspicions.

"Please don't respond to that," I quickly add. "Like I said, late-night calls come with immunity. I can't be held accountable for any of it."

Jacob's reply lands like a bomb. "I was going to propose to Maggie."

My stomach drops. *Maggie.* As in Jacob's ex-girlfriend/childhood sweetheart, who cheated on him after she left for college. At the craft store, Jacob had been vague about their relationship. I suspected there was something more, but I didn't think it was that he had been planning to ask her to marry him.

"We always talked about getting married after college," he continues. "Like my parents, Maggie's folks were from Seaview, and they'd gotten married when they were young. Maggie and I both wanted something similar. I bought a ring a couple months before graduation. I was planning to ask her the night after the ceremony. I had no idea her feelings had changed. The breakup came as a total shock."

I'm speechless. The fact that *Jacob* was cheated on is awful enough. Learning that he was going to propose to this woman? It almost decimates me. Jacob is thoughtful and funny and supportive. A five out of five-star human. He deserves the very best. And that certainly isn't someone who could so easily discard him.

I'm almost afraid to ask my next question, but it rolls off my tongue before I can think better of it. "Do you still have feelings for her?" He said before that he was over it, but he also made it seem like their relationship was nothing but a blip in the past. Maybe the reason he's been unable to settle down is because he hasn't gotten over Maggie.

"No," he says. "Izzy, you're the last person I want to think that. I haven't felt anything for Maggie in years. When you asked about my previous relationships, I was caught off guard. I don't talk about Maggie often, so I didn't say much, but afterward I felt weird about it. I wanted you to know all of the truth, not just part of it."

Relief sweeps over me instantly. I wish I could see him. I can't imagine saying any of that was easy, and I want Jacob to understand how much it means to me. That he would trust me with such a vulnerable piece of himself. I have the urge to wrap myself around him like a koala.

"Thank you for telling me," I say in a hushed voice. I don't know why I'm whispering. Delia is sleeping at Tanner's, so I'm the only one home, but it feels like a secret that needs to be closely guarded, even in an empty house.

"I mean, how could I pass up immunity?"

We're silent for a while. At some point, my breathing deepens, as if I'm drifting to sleep, but I'm still wide awake. I didn't know it was possible to feel this wired and this relaxed at the same time.

"Forrest," Jacob says.

"Uh-huh?"

"You know I think you're really great, right?"

Something kicks in my chest. "I think you're really great, too."

Nineteen

Izzy

"How's it look, Iz?" Delia asks, her expression uncertain as she glances down from the top rung of the step ladder. She's holding a massive happy birthday banner with a confetti border against the back wall of the kitchen. "Be honest. I'm gonna spend the whole night fixating on it if it doesn't look right."

She means it. On Delia's twenty-first birthday, Morgan and I rented the party room at her favorite restaurant, where we hung a giant balloon banner. Halfway through appetizers, Delia's eye started twitching. When I asked her what the problem was, she said she couldn't stop focusing on the crooked "y" in birthday. She ended up pulling up a chair and fixing the banner herself.

I eye the perfectly straight banner from the other side of the kitchen. "It looks good from here," I tell her. "Do you need me to get a ruler?" I hope not. Delia's need for perfection doesn't normally bother me, but she's been trying to hang this banner for ten minutes. I'm ready to be done with it.

"No, no. I trust you." Finally, she climbs down from the ladder to give her own assessment. Satisfied, she dusts her palms on the backs of her black jeans. "You're right—it looks great. Now, do you wanna help me set up appetizers?"

"As long as you don't make me wait till everyone gets here to eat." The charcuterie board she picked up has been taunting me from the back of the fridge all afternoon. I skipped lunch today since I left work early to help Delia get ready for Tanner's birthday party, which she insists is not a party. Tanner didn't want her to do anything big, so it's only going to be the three of us and Jacob, but there are decorations and appetizers and a giant fudge cake. I'm pretty sure that qualifies as a party.

"You can have a few cashews," Delia says.

I wrinkle my nose. "Cashews? Seriously? Shouldn't helping you set up at least get me a cracker?" Everyone knows that nuts are the worst part of a charcuterie board, unless it's one of those boring healthy boards filled with sprouts or turnips.

My sister relents. "Fine. You can have a piece of cheddar or a slice of salami. But watch where you take it from." She points a finger at me, a warning gesture. "That board was expensive. It needs to look nice when Tanner gets here." She's entirely serious, despite Tanner being the last person who would care about the appearance of a charcuterie board. This is just Delia, wanting to make things perfect for the people she loves. It's an endearing, and sometimes frustrating, aspect of her personality.

"You know, you didn't have to go through all this hassle," I say. "I think Tanner would've been happy if your birthday plans consisted of a push-up bra and a bottle of wine."

She rolls her eyes. "He can have that next year if that's what he wants. This is our first time celebrating it together. I don't want it to suck."

You could always move in with him. The words threaten to leap off my tongue, but I keep my mouth shut. Delia still has no idea I overheard her conversation with Tanner after Christmas, which was almost three months ago.

As far as I'm aware, she's not any closer to moving in with him. I don't know if my spending time with Jacob has affected her perception of me, but she did say the other day that she was happy I made a friend in Seaview. Hopefully, she's starting to realize I don't need a babysitter.

For a moment, I consider telling Delia about the art classes. She'd probably worry less if she knew I found something I really care about. But something else is keeping me from opening up to her. Uncertainty, I think.

While I'd like to believe Delia would be supportive, I don't know how she would react. What if she had doubts? Or laughed at the idea? I'm just getting comfortable teaching the kids. Seeing myself as competent. A negative response from Delia would deflate my progress faster than a hole in a balloon. Maybe it's for the best if I hold off until things feel more certain.

The doorbell chimes, causing Delia's shoulders to perk up. "That must be Jacob," she says. "Mind letting him in? I'll take care of the food."

Nodding, I turn on my heels and head to the front door, where Jacob is waiting on the other side of the frosted glass. I open it to find him dressed in blue jeans and a gray sweater, clutching a bottle of red wine.

"I'm sorry, honey," I say. "We're not interested in buying any popcorn today."

"Are you kidding me, Forrest? I didn't wear khakis today specifically to prevent you from making a Boy Scout joke," he replies, shaking his head in disapproval.

I move out of the doorway so Jacob can come inside. Immediately, Jason comes rushing to the foyer, rubbing up against Jacob's leg as if he's never known human contact. "If it makes you feel any better, I'm absolutely seething over the fact that my dog likes you better than me," I tell him.

Jacob chuckles softly, clutching the neck of the wine bottle in one hand so he can scratch Jason's head with the other. Our eyes meet, and a warm feeling spreads through my body.

We haven't seen each other since our phone call a couple of nights ago. Confiding in him felt strange, in the sense that I don't open myself up to people. But in another sense, it felt very natural, the way talking to him always does. The more I've gotten to know Jacob, the more I've come to appreciate his friendship. Honestly, it's getting harder for me to understand how he's single. Jacob is head and shoulders above other guys on the dating market.

"I take it the party hasn't started yet," he says.

"Don't say that word in front of Delia," I warn him. "It's a gathering, not a party. She's told me that at least a hundred times today."

He quirks a brow. "Is there a difference?"

"Delusion, maybe? She wasn't clear on the specifics."

I walk Jacob to the kitchen, which looks incredibly festive for not a party. There's a tablecloth laden with balloon-shaped confetti and a vase of fresh violets. Delia is at the counter, adding a sleeve of crackers to her charcuterie tray. I swipe a bit of salami from the glass serving dish, along with a piece of cheddar. Company has arrived, so I shouldn't be in violation of any hostess protocol.

Delia's attention whirls to our guest. "Hey, Jacob. Thanks for coming."

"Of course," he replies. "Tanner hasn't done anything for his birthday in years. I wouldn't miss a chance to make him uncomfortable."

"This isn't supposed to make him uncomfortable," Delia objects.

"What is a birthday party if not a ritual in public humiliation?" I ponder.

As if on cue, Tanner suddenly knocks on the sliding glass door in the back of the kitchen. He steps inside, brushing snowflakes out of his brown hair. His eyes roam the decorated room before landing on Delia. "Hey, darling," he says, "what have you gotten—"

The push pin holding up the right side of the birthday banner pops out of the wall, and the banner drops, hitting Tanner in the side of the head.

"What the hell?" he says as he shoves the dangling cardboard away.

"Dammit," Delia whispers, scurrying over to grab the banner. "Go back outside." She pushes Tanner toward the door. "You need to get the full effect."

The party (or gathering, depending on your perspective) goes off without a hitch. After charcuterie and drinks, Delia pulls out the lobster rolls she picked up from Tanner's favorite restaurant, and we gather around the kitchen table for dinner. I have a shellfish allergy, so Delia got me a fettuccine alfredo entrée instead. It probably would've put a damper on things if I started choking and breaking out in hives mid-meal.

After we eat, we move to the living room for presents. Delia bought Tanner a woodworking toolkit, which she's been itching to give him for weeks. He thanks her for the gift and pulls her into his lap. They do that annoying thing couples do where they kiss and whisper to each other as if nobody else is in the room. Jacob and I exchange eye rolls. Delia and Tanner aren't too bad compared to other couples I know, but they have their moments.

While Delia and Tanner are still loved up, Delia asks if I can warm up the hot fudge for the ice cream sundaes. I jump at the chance to escape their coupley bliss, dragging Jacob with me. In the kitchen, I snatch the jar of fudge from the pantry, pop the lid, and stick it in the microwave.

"Doing okay, Forrest?" Jacob asks, a slight dip between his brows. He stands beside me against the side of the counter.

"Yeah. I'm fine. Why?"

He shrugs. "You haven't said much the past hour."

"Is that how you judge the way I'm feeling?" I ask, giving him a playful smile. "By whether I can keep my mouth shut?"

"I mean, you once told me that you always have something to say, even if it's nothing good." Okay, so Past Izzy might've been telling the truth there.

"It's nothing, really," I reply. "It's just hard not to think about how you're ruining someone's happiness when it's right in your face." Seeing Delia and Tanner all over each other serves as a bitter reminder that I'm the only reason they're not living together.

Jacob shakes his head. "I've gotta say, Forrest, I've always known you had a bit of an ego, but you're giving yourself way too much credit for this one."

"How so?" I have a tendency to be dramatic, sure, but I don't think it gets any clearer than Delia outright saying she won't move in with Tanner because of me.

"First of all, Delia is her own person, and she makes her own decisions," Jacob says. "Even if she said no because of you, that was her choice. It's completely out of your control. Second, she said she couldn't move in with Tanner right now, not that she never wants to. I've known Tanner since we were kids. He's never felt this way about anyone. He'll wait as long as Delia needs him to, so you don't have to worry about this affecting their relationship. Given the fact that they're mauling each other over on the couch right now, I'd say they're doing fine.

"And the third thing," he adds, "is that you're underestimating how much you matter to people. Necessary or not, Delia said no to Tanner because she wants to be there for you. She wouldn't have done that unless she really cared about you. I know you think you're ruining her happiness, Forrest, but part of what makes her happy is you."

Emotion clogs my throat. That might be the nicest thing anyone has ever said to me. So why do I feel like crying? I'm not a crier. I haven't shed a tear in front of another person since I sprained my wrist falling off a kids' jungle gym in college (don't ask). I refuse to bawl like a baby because someone told me I'm not ruining my sister's life.

The microwave dings, saving me from myself. Dismissing the weird mixture of emotions churning within me, I snag a set of potholders off the counter, then open the microwave door to pull out the steaming jar of fudge. The rich scent of melted chocolate floods my nose as I carefully place it on the stovetop. As soon as I drop the potholders, I reach for the utensil drawer and grab a big spoon.

"Forrest, what are you doing?" Jacob asks as I dunk the spoon in the hot fudge jar, swirling it around.

"What does it look like?" I say, lifting my fudge-coated spoon. "I'm having a little taste test." I'm a sucker for sweets, especially chocolate. Delia had Mom mail fudge from our favorite ice cream shop in Boston. It's quality shit.

I bring the spoon toward my mouth, but Jacob grabs my wrist, stopping the utensil before it reaches its destination. "Are you trying to give yourself a third-degree burn?" His expression is chastising. He's standing over me at his ridiculous height. "That stuff is still bubbling. You won't have any taste buds left."

I mimic his judgemental look. I don't think I'm doing a very good job because he seems to be fighting off a smile. "They're *my* taste buds, Jacob. I can burn them off if I want to."

"Isn't stopping you from making bad decisions the basis of this arrangement?" He leans his hip against the counter. He's still clutching my wrist, but his grip isn't strong. I could easily break free and shove the spoon in my mouth if I wanted to. "C'mon, Forrest. Save both of us a trip to the ER. Blow on it."

"You'll have to be more specific. What exactly do you want me to blow on?"

Jacob shakes his head as if he can't quite believe this is what he's dealing with. "You are so—" Before he can finish maligning my character, I turn the spoon and push it past his lips, forcing him to have a taste.

His eyes widen in surprise. The fudge is warm, but contrary to Jacob's dramatics, it isn't magma. He seems to enjoy it.

"Good, isn't it?" I say teasingly. I yank the spoon out of his mouth, then set it on the counter. Afterward, I notice a small blob of chocolate on the outside of my thumb and shamelessly lick it off. Jacob watches my movement with the same astonished look, his Adam's apple bobbing slightly.

"Hey, is the fudge ready?" Both of us turn at the same time. Delia is standing in the kitchen doorway, her eyes darting suspiciously between me and Jacob. Nodding, I step away from the stovetop to reveal the jar of fudge.

"Yeah, it's all good," I tell her.

"Great. Thanks." Delia walks around the counter, joining us on the other side. Her expression is unchanged. "Jacob, would you mind grabbing the candles?" she asks. "They should be in the hall closet."

"Sure thing," he says, heading out of the room. As soon as he disappears, Delia grabs me by the arm and tugs me close, her body language urgent. "What the hell was that?" she whispers.

I stare at her puzzled face. "What do you mean?" I ask, feeling lost myself.

"You and Jacob. I don't know what I just walked in on, but it looked flirty."

"You're kidding, right?" Delia cannot seriously believe Jacob and I were *flirting*. "That was nothing. We were messing around."

Delia folds her arms against her chest. "Izzy, how many times have you spoon-fed chocolate to a friend?" Okay, when she puts it like that, it seems suggestive. But that wasn't what was happening with Jacob just now. We're friends, and we like to joke around. It's not like I was feeding him chocolate-covered strawberries on a fuzzy rug by the fireplace.

"Drop it, Delia. You're making this into something that it isn't."

She frowns. "Does Jacob know that?"

Twenty

Izzy

When Jacob Howell invites you to accompany him to a random dive bar on Thursday night, you don't ask questions.

You say yes. Obviously.

I have no idea what Jacob has planned tonight. He claims it's related to my quest for self-improvement, but I did a quick Google search on this place, the Golden Pub, after he sent me the name. The food is cold, the music selection sucks, and the drink menu is limited, according to several uninspiring Yelp reviews. How it's going to help me remains a mystery, but I've trusted Jacob's judgment so far, and he's yet to steer me wrong.

That doesn't stop me from asking questions, though. On the Uber ride to the bar, I admit to my internet sleuthing. "Don't take this the wrong way," I tell Jacob, "but this place kind of seems like a trashy bar." It's possible I'm missing the bigger story. Maybe the Golden Pub is a Seaview landmark. Or the rather unimpressive space houses a cool speakeasy in the basement. Hopefully, Jacob will clue me in.

He chuckles in the back of the darkened car. "It *is* a trashy bar."

"So, why are we going there?" Make no mistake—I love a good dive bar. I practically lived at the spot around the corner from my apartment in New York. Cynthia and I used to dominate on trivia nights. Well, Cynthia used to dominate. She's a human encyclopedia. I would sit there with my cocktail, cheering her on like the good supportive friend I am. Or was.

Still, a place like the Golden Pub doesn't seem like Jacob's scene. One Yelp reviewer described it as the sort of spot people stumble into rather than seek out. I'd hardly call that a ringing endorsement. "I hope it isn't for eight-dollar prime rib night," I add. "Some deals are too good for a reason."

"Patience, Forrest," is all he replies. It looks like we're in for a repeat of the night at Off the Vine. I can only imagine what's going to happen tonight.

The Golden Pub turns out to be exactly what I expected. A small, crowded bar with poor lighting, dated furniture, and the stench of stale beer. After we enter, we find seats at the sticky wooden counter and order drinks from a surly-looking bartender. I ask for a cosmopolitan instead of my usual espresso martini. Something tells me this guy doesn't do complicated drinks.

"Okay, I have my first theory," I announce a few minutes later as I take the first sip of my cosmo, which burns on the way down my throat. I've got to hand it to Angry Bartender—he didn't hold back on the liquor.

Jacob grabs his beer off the bar top, wrapping his long fingers around the bottle. "You're not gonna guess this one, Forrest. You might as well give up now," he says.

His dismissiveness only fortifies my resolve. "I underestimated you before with the paint and sip," I tell him, "but that was a long time ago. I know you now, Jacob. It won't be so easy for you to surprise me this time."

"Let's hear your theory then." He raises the bottle to his lips.

Oh, he's being smug right now. I've never seen him this cocky before. He's that confident I won't be able to figure it out? I hope he's playing it up, or else I might be in trouble. "I think you bought this place to launch your new career as a restaurateur, and you want me to run it with you," I say.

"I think *restaurateur* is a generous word to describe the owner of this place," he replies, which is probably true. Half the items on the drink menu are listed as unavailable, and based on the smell, someone is definitely vaping in here.

"We could have a good partnership, you and me," I say. "You'd take care of the books. I'd make the ambiance a little less…dumpstery."

"I'm glad we've reached the stage in our relationship where we're talking about what it'd be like to own a bar together."

"The true testament of friendship." I clink my glass against his bottle.

Jacob smirks. "Got any other ideas?"

"My other thought is that you're secretly a health inspector, and we've come here to shut this place down."

"You think I'd subject you to drinking somewhere I know is in violation of health codes?"

"You know I like to live dangerously."

"Rest assured, I'm not a health inspector. And I'm not looking to make a career change."

That brings me back to square one. Despite my bravado moments ago, I'm not really confident I'm going to get this right, so I decide to say something that I know will get a strong reaction from Jacob. "You said this was about me, but maybe that was a lie to throw me off your scent," I speculate. "Maybe the real reason you brought me here is so I can observe your flirting technique in the wild."

To no surprise, Jacob doesn't seem to like the idea. "It's amazing how your guesses continue to get worse," he says.

"It's not a bad idea, actually." Though I suggested it in jest, it could have some real benefit. I've seen what Jacob is like on a pretend date and glanced over his online dating profile, but it doesn't get more authentic than watching him flirt with a woman he has genuine interest in. How have I never thought of this before? "What better way to put your skills to the test?"

"You weren't kidding about squeezing all the self-respect out of me, were you?"

"Oh, c'mon." I give him a playful nudge with my elbow. "We're here. We might as well give it a try. There's gotta be someone here you find attractive."

"I'm not doing this, Forrest."

"You're right. I should pick someone for you. It's more fun that way." I scan the bar for potential candidates, though most of the people here seem to be couples or middle-aged guys. The only suitable option is the woman beside me at the bar. She's in conversation with someone, but she looks to be in her early thirties. Perfect.

"Excuse me," I say, turning to face her before Jacob can stop me. "I'm sorry to interrupt, but I wanted to compliment your necklace." I nod at the shimmery pendant dangling at the base of her throat. "A beautiful necklace on a beautiful woman. Those were my friend's exact words." I jerk a thumb in Jacob's general direction. He looks absolutely mortified. He kicks my shin under the bar, and I return the move with equal gusto.

The woman grins. She's very pretty, which I didn't notice at first. "A man with good taste," she says, eying Jacob like he's been served to her on a silver platter. "That's something

I can get behind. I'm Sarah." She does that thing where you sip your drink without breaking eye contact. Bar flirting 101.

Jacob smiles politely. "It's nice to meet you. I'm Jacob."

Something bristles in my chest. Suddenly, I'm getting bad vibes from this woman. It's like there's a speaker in my head shouting "abort mission!" I struggle to figure out what's wrong until my eyes lock on the navy blue wristlet with a Yankees logo sitting in front of her on the bar. Oh, no. I just set Jacob up with a devil worshipper. I need to put a stop to it right away.

Impulsively, I push out of my stool, capturing both of their attention. "Well, Jacob, we've been here long enough," I declare as I swipe my drink off the bar top. "I think it's time for a game of darts." I grab his wrist, tugging him out of his seat. He barely has time to pick up his beer before I'm dragging him to the other side of the bar.

"She had a Yankees wallet," I explain. "Obviously, I had to intervene."

Jacob shudders. "Nice catch, Forrest."

The darts suggestion was merely a ruse, but we end up playing a game, anyway. Unfortunately, Jacob is a lot better than me. He consistently hits the high-scoring spots while my darts end up all over the board. I won't accept defeat, though. And I'm not above resorting to childish tactics to improve my chances. When Jacob goes up for a turn, I whisper things in his ear to throw him off his game. The results are mixed, but he does miss the board completely when I say "nipples," which I consider a success.

While we're playing darts, we order a second round of drinks, along with a basket of fries to share (neither of us trusts meat from this place). I'm gearing up for a throw that is destined to earn me a pathetic number of points when a deep voice booms across the bar.

"Jacob *fucking* Howell."

A man with enough product in his hair to ignite a small forest stalks toward us, beer in hand and a massive grin on his face. He reaches Jacob, clapping him on the shoulder. "It's about time you showed up for happy hour!" the man exclaims, much louder than necessary. We might be in a crowded bar, but he's standing right beside us.

Jacob gives him an uneasy smile. "It's good to see you, Luke." My eyes widen in surprise. As far as I'm aware, Jacob only knows one Luke, and it's the asshole coworker who convinced him to take me up on my deal in the first place. I've only seen him for thirty seconds, but this guy certainly fits the bill. The way he strode over here and interrupted us screams grade A douchebag.

"Why didn't you say anything in the group chat?" Luke asks. "Me and the guys are at a table over there." He nods toward a high-top in the back occupied by three guys wearing button-downs. "We're about to order a round of shots. That bartender chick with the nose ring is super into Carmichael, I'm telling you. We're trying to get him to make a move."

"I'm here with someone, actually. This is my friend, Izzy," Jacob says by way of introduction. Luke not-so-subtly checks out my boobs before he meets my gaze. I think it's safe to say this is definitely Jacob's dick of a coworker.

"He means girlfriend," I clarify, sidling up to Jacob. I lay a hand on his chest and wrap my other arm around his waist. Amusement dances in his eyes when I turn to look at him. *What are you playing at, Forrest?* All I do is smile.

"Girlfriend?" Luke repeats, sounding confused. He levels Jacob with a frown. "I didn't know you were seeing anyone."

"It's new," I interject. If this man is going to openly stare at my tits, then I see no problem with interrupting. "We've only been seeing each other for a few weeks, but when you know, you know. Isn't that right, honey?"

Jacob sets his chin on the crown of my head. "That's right. I've known since the day I met Izzy that she was the one for me," he says dryly. Jacob is a terrible liar, so it seems like it's up to me to really sell it. I rest my head in the crook of his neck.

"It's hard for me to wrap my head around it sometimes," I say in a gushing tone. "I thought I was going to be alone forever, then here waltzes this perfect man into my life. We just get each other, you know? Somewhere deep in my heart, I know he's my person."

From the look Luke gives me, you'd think I just confessed to having a contagious disease. "Yeah. Okay," he says, taking a small step backward. "Well, congrats on that." His eyes clearly say "dude, dump her." I cling to Jacob even tighter. "We're over there if you decide you wanna do something else, Jacob."

As Luke walks away, the two of us erupt in laughter. Tears form in the corners of my eyes. I have to cling to Jacob's arm for support because I'm laughing so hard. Without it, I'd be nothing but a pile of limbs on the Golden Pub's beer-soaked floor.

"You know he's over there formulating a plan to rescue me, right?" Jacob says, his cheeks flushed, eyes bright.

"Maybe he'll set you up with the cool bartender chick with the nose ring," I reply, my sides aching from laughter. We crack up for another minute before we finally pull ourselves together. I release Jacob from the clutches of his clingy new girlfriend.

"So *that* is the infamous Luke Daniels," I say. It feels like I met a supervillain. Well, an incompetent supervillain whose biggest crime is using too much hair gel.

Jacob nods. "In the flesh."

"Did you know he was gonna be here, or was this a happy coincidence?"

"Some of the guys in my office do happy hour. Luke has been bugging me to come to one for ages," he says.

"And you couldn't face them without me here for moral support?"

"Not exactly." Jacob directs my attention toward the group of his coworkers. "The guy on the end in the blue shirt? That's Steven. He's a consulting manager at my firm. Last year, he accidentally CC'd an employee he was going to fire on an email chain with HR about severance pay. It was a huge mess. The guy in the white, Carmichael, got drunk at the holiday party and told everyone that his wife was leaving him. Evan, the one in the black tie, caught the microwave in the breakroom on fire once after he tried heating up tinfoil. And Luke? Well, I don't think he requires an explanation."

"Okay, so you work with a lot of incompetent people," I say. The anecdotes are amusing, but I don't see what they have to do with anything. Maybe Jacob wanted to make me laugh. Help me take my mind off things.

"Those guys are in charge of important shit, despite being certified disasters."

"Douchebags failing upward. That's always lovely to see."

"Those guys have the things you think make someone put together," Jacob says, "and they're the furthest thing from that. This idea you have that you need to achieve certain things to be a successful person is nonsense. No one has everything figured out. If anything, the people who act like they do are usually the biggest messes. I know you think you're not as together as everyone else, Forrest, but most people feel lost all the time. That's just living."

I let his words sink in. I've built up this idea in my head that I'm not good enough. That I'm failing this imaginary test that everyone around me seems to be acing. My career is a giant question mark. Most of my relationships are strained. And I don't know what life holds for me in the long run. Solving these problems, I assumed, would make me feel better about myself. But what exactly would it change? I've felt this way since I was a flaky high schooler. My circumstances have changed over the years, but my perception hasn't.

Who's to say anything would be different if I got a new job or mended my fractured relationships? I'd probably find new things to pick apart about myself. Other reasons to deem myself not enough.

I might not be perfect, but I still get up every morning. Feed my dog. Go to work. Try not to be an asshole to the people I encounter. The rest of my life might not be sorted out yet, but I'm doing the best I can. Shouldn't that count for something? I'm not the first person not to have their shit together. But at least I'm trying to minimize the harm it's having on other people. The same can't be said for everyone.

"You wanna get out of here?" Jacob asks. "I only wanted you to see the guys. I'm not forcing you to spend an entire evening in this place."

If he'd asked me the same question thirty minutes ago, I probably would've said yes and made a beeline for the exit.

But I'm having a good time. The drinks are flowing, and though I'm not getting any better at darts, I'm enjoying the company.

"Actually, I think we should stay for a while."

***

Jacob
Izzy insists on dancing.

Around nine, a band called Total Dynamite hits the rickety wooden stage in the back of the bar. The group consists of three guys who appear to be in their mid-forties. Their set is *not* total dynamite. They play a bunch of Bruce Springsteen covers, the occasional modern hit thrown in, but their playing skills are slightly below mediocre, and the lead singer is stretching his voice beyond its capabilities.

Still, the guys seem to be having a good time. They've made several pleas to the crowd for requests, but no one in the packed bar wants to give them any time of day, and Izzy feels bad.

After Total Dynamite finishes another cover with a lackluster crowd response, Izzy drags me over to the open space in front of the stage. She tells the lead singer to play anything Springsteen, and as the music starts, she forces me to dance with her. By dance with her, I mean we sway in a very pathetic slow dance that doesn't match the tempo of the song. I step on Izzy's toes at least three times. I feel like a baby calf learning to walk.

"You're gonna leave scuff marks on my shoes," she says teasingly.

"You picked a bad partner, Forrest," I mutter.

She smacks me on the shoulder. "I picked a great one." Our unimpressive dancing brings attention to the band.

Within a few minutes, several couples have joined us, and the tables surrounding the stage appear more engaged in the music. It's a perfect example of how Izzy's enthusiasm, her infectiousness for life, makes everything better. Instead of a crappy set, this band is going to walk away from a fully engaged crowd, and it's all because of her.

Shortly after eleven, Izzy complains about her feet being sore. We've been at the bar for nearly four hours, and it's a work night, so it feels like a good time to call it quits. The crowd has started getting rowdier, people drunkenly singing and shouting requests at the band. Neither Izzy nor I have had that much to drink, and we've had enough of the commotion.

I order an Uber for us. We decide to wait outside, free from the hot, noisy bar. We stand under the overhang on the empty front porch. Cold air wraps around my body like a glove. I shift from one foot to the other, trying to keep my blood flowing. Beside me, Izzy wraps her leopard-print scarf around her neck, her teeth chattering.

"How cold are you right now?" she asks.

"I'm rapidly losing the feeling in my toes."

"I'm beginning to wonder if all our problems might be self-inflicted," she says, a smile lifting her pink-stained cheeks. "We spend too much time on porches in the dead of winter."

"Do you want to go back inside?"

Izzy quickly dismisses the idea. "I don't think my ears could handle another minute of the terrible singing. The guys at the bar were asking Total Dynamite to play *Piano Man*, Jacob. You know how that would've gone."

"What is it with drunk people and piano ballads?" I ask. Play a sad song on a piano for a crowd of drunk strangers, and they'll sing together like a group of old friends.

"The power of Billy Joel is bigger than all of us," she says.

We share a laugh as I study the sky. It's pitch black tonight. If it weren't for the light coming from inside the bar, we'd be surrounded by total darkness, aside from the occasional passing headlight.

"So, I have a question," Izzy says, turning to face me head-on.

I groan. "I beg you to reconsider it."

"But I haven't asked you anything yet."

"You only warn me when you're about to ask something you know I won't want to answer." Izzy's previous questions have been about my dating history and my True Connections profile. Whatever she wants to ask now must be equally embarrassing.

In true Izzy form, she proceeds with her question, anyway.

"Are you a bad kisser?"

Izzy blinks up at me, and I can't stop the indignant noise that comes up my throat. I should be used to it by now—her being so direct and outrageous—but she continues to mystify me. How does she always manage to say something completely unexpected? Izzy Forrest is a puzzle that constantly changes and evolves.

"I'm having a hard time understanding why you're single, Jacob," she continues. "Everything has checked out so far. You're a good conversationalist. You don't have a podcast. And you know exactly what you want. Those aren't qualities you find in single guys."

"Which leads you to believe I'm a bad kisser?" I don't know whether I should be offended by Izzy's assessment. It doesn't seem as though she's trying to be cruel, but the implication doesn't sit well with my pride. I don't want *her* of all people thinking it.

Izzy shrugs. "It's a safe assumption, right? You don't have any obvious red flags. There has to be a problem somewhere. Maybe it's your kissing. What would you rate yourself on a scale from one to ten?" Her eyes are light and playful. She's pleased with herself. Izzy likes challenging people. Making them uncomfortable. Conversation is a game to her, but it only works if she has another player.

"What are we talking here?" I ask. "Tongue? Groping? I need you to be more specific."

"I'm looking for a composite score," she says. "You like numbers. You should know what that is. Or else you might not be very good at your job."

"Don't pretend you know anything about my spreadsheets, Forrest," I tell her, tugging on a strand of her curly hair. She swats my hand away, nudging me in the ribs with her elbow.

"I'll ignore the obvious double entendre if you answer me honestly. This is a judgment-free zone, Jacob. I encourage you to be open and to embrace everything this experience has to offer."

I raise a brow. "You're quoting Aurora now?"

"What can I say? She's a wise woman."

A wise woman? "I'm pretty sure she makes her own toothpaste."

Izzy clicks her tongue. "Deflect all you want, but you aren't getting out of this question. I can be very single-minded. I will annoy you until you answer me."

We stare at each other for a moment, neither of us budging. Izzy might be insistent, but I don't know how much I want to divulge here. Despite going on dozens of dates this past year, I don't have a ton of experience with women. Maggie was my first everything. And I've never been a hookup person, so my experience is limited to relationships. I'm not sure I want to make Izzy privy to all the details.

"I don't need your help in that department," I tell her.

"Oh, really?" She cocks her head to the side. "You're *that* confident?"

"I've never had any complaints."

She laughs. "Just because you've had no complaints doesn't mean they aren't complaining," she argues. "Women talk, Jacob. Your bedroom skills could be the subject of a very lively girls' night right now."

"I suppose I'll just have to live with that risk."

Izzy gives me a sly grin. "Or you could kiss me."

My pulse stops, then starts again. "What?" I say, letting out an uncertain laugh. I know she must be joking, but this feels bold, even for Izzy.

"I'm serious," she says, taking a step closer. "Go ahead. Plant one on me." She closes her eyes and puckers her lips, looking almost cartoonish.

I shake my head, turning away. "You're ridiculous."

"How so?" she asks. "You say you're not a bad kisser. I don't believe you. There's a very easy way to figure out who's right." It's an awful idea, but Izzy seems determined. She puts her hands on her hips, staring up at me in challenge.

"I'm not gonna kiss you just to prove a point," I say.

Her smile turns devious. "You don't need to be scared, Jacob," she says tauntingly. "I'm an excellent kisser, but I won't judge you too harshly."

Heat bubbles under my skin. "You need your head examined."

"I could probably teach you a thing or two," she says. "I bet with some direction you could become a great—"

Before I can second guess myself, I grab her chin, tilt her face toward mine, and press my lips to hers. Her mouth is soft and warm, and her floral scent fills my lungs. I pull back after only a few seconds, finding myself face-to-face with Izzy's stunned expression.

I expect her to respond with her usual sense of humor, but she says nothing, lips parted, eyes wide in disbelief. Worry infiltrates my thoughts instantly. Did I completely misread the situation? The way she was egging me on made me think she wanted me to kiss her. Was she only joking? Did I make things uncomfortable?

Panicked, I begin to apologize. "Izzy, I didn't—"

This time, she is the one to cut me off. Izzy wraps her hands around the back of my neck and crashes her lips against mine. Our first kiss was hardly anything, a feather of a kiss, but this is an avalanche, a thousand tons of bricks hitting me at once.

Our mouths collide hungrily. It feels like we're trying to inhale each other, lips moving, hands roaming. Somewhere in the back of my mind, I'm aware of the fact that we're making out in front of a busy bar, but I don't care. We could be standing in the middle of a funeral procession, and it wouldn't make me peel away from her.

Izzy tastes like cranberries. Her lips mold against mine, and I wrap my arm around her waist, pulling her closer. My other hand dives into her soft, thick hair, the way I've been dying to for ages. I nip her bottom lip slightly, and she opens her mouth, allowing me to slip my tongue inside. She lets out a small noise that sends all my blood rushing south. Fuckfuckfuckfuck. I need to hear that again.

There's a sense of desperation in this kiss. As if a set of floodgates has been opened, and we're finally acting on something we've both spent hours imagining, trying to consume as much of each other as we can at once. Kissing Izzy is all I've been thinking about lately, so I'm not surprised by my own eagerness, but *hers* catches me off guard.

Has she been thinking about this, too? The possibility makes my head spin. I need to be careful, or I'm going to start spouting a bunch of stuff you definitely shouldn't say to someone the first time you kiss them. *You're perfect.* Kiss. *You smell like fresh flowers.* Kiss. *I want you more than I've ever wanted someone.*

A car horn blares through the parking lot, loud enough to startle us. I pull back from Izzy to see a black car idling along the sidewalk, presumably our Uber. The timing couldn't be worse. I wouldn't mind strangling the driver with my bare hands, even though it's my own fault for ordering the damn car. But it is freezing, and getting hypothermia would probably ruin the mood.

Izzy and I lock eyes for a moment, both of us breathing heavily. My pulse hammers in my ears. My hand is still resting on her lower back, fingertips pressing against the warm strip of skin above the waistband of her jeans.

There's an unguardedness in Izzy's eyes. It's there for a second, like a firefly or a flash of lightning, but she conceals it quickly.

Her expression becomes amused.

"Well, you were right," she says, letting out an unsteady laugh as she steps back from me. Her lipstick is smudged, and I'm sure there's a bunch of it all over my mouth, but I couldn't give less of a shit. My head is on another planet right now. "Your kissing skills are up to snuff. You don't need any help from me in that department."

I stare at her, speechless. Is that really what she's going to do? Pretend as if *that* was nothing? The Uber driver honks a second time, and Izzy turns on her heels, heading toward the car. I watch her go until my feet finally catch up. My legs feel wooden as I trail after her.

Thirty seconds ago, this seemed like the best moment of my life.

Now, I've never felt worse.

Twenty-One

Jacob's palm skates up my rib cage. "God, you're beautiful, Forrest," he whispers before his lips meet mine in a blistering kiss. I loop my arms around the back of his neck and pull him closer, wanting to feel him everywhere. Stars explode behind my eyelids when his warm mouth drops to my neck, heat building low in my stomach. Jacob's long fingers curl around my back, reaching for the clasp of my bra…

I shoot up in bed, sheets tangled, pulse pounding like a freight train. Jason's soft snores fill my dark bedroom as I take deep breaths, waiting for my heart rate to return to normal. My skin is hot and sweaty, the desire coursing through me impossible to deny. Groaning, I slip the pillow out from beneath my head and smack myself in the face with it.

"Fuck me," I mutter. This is the third horny dream I've had about Jacob in the past week. You'd think my brain would've gotten the memo by now. *Not gonna happen.* Instead, my mind seems determined to torture me with dirty scenarios.

It's bad enough that our *real* kiss is permanently burned in my memory. I don't need fake ones fueling this ill-conceived attraction.

It's been twelve days since I kissed Jacob. If you really want to get technical about it, *he* kissed *me*. But it was my idea, and I initiated the second kiss, the one with the tongue and the roaming hands. Both of us are at fault here, but I'd say I'm sixty-five percent responsible. There wouldn't have been any kisses without my badgering.

I still don't know why I asked him to kiss me. I've thought about it before in passing. For a good-looking guy, he's had unusually bad luck in the dating department. I wondered if it had anything to do with his kissing skills. Plus, Jacob had such a strong reaction to the idea of kissing me. I couldn't help but tease him. I didn't expect him to actually do it. Or maybe I did. Because my brain hasn't stopped feeding me filthy fantasies of the two of us since.

I remember everything. The way Jacob tugged my bottom lip between his teeth. The sweep of his long fingers over my skin. It's been almost two weeks, but the sensations are still fresh in my mind. And it's a terrible, terrible thing.

Because no matter how incredible our physical chemistry is, I can't do anything about it. Jacob is my friend, and I'm supposed to be helping him meet the love of his life. Sleeping with him wouldn't accomplish anything, even though I know it would be good. And it's been a long time since I've had good sex.

With Dominic, things were awkward. I never felt an intense attraction toward him, which made sex feel like a chore. I thought our lack of physical compatibility had to do with us being friends first. That I knew Dominic too well to experience that burning desire you feel when you start dating someone new.

Of course, Jacob proved that theory wrong. Friendship does not negate sexual chemistry. I mean, he and I barely did anything, but the memory alone makes my blood heat. Imagine what might have happened if our car arrived just a few minutes later…

Nope. No. No. No. I have to stop this. I care about Jacob. He's a great guy, and he clearly knows what to do with his hands, but starting something with him would be a disaster.

Jacob is searching for a stable, long-term relationship. I have no idea where I'm going or what I'm going to do with the rest of my life. I need to deal with my own shit before I can be in another relationship. It wouldn't be right to pursue this attraction when I know I can't give Jacob the consistency he wants.

For both our sakes, we have to put the kiss behind us. I hope Jacob understands. I've been keeping my distance since that night. I know it's childish, but I'm afraid of what might happen when we see each other again.

I don't want to hurt him or make him think I'm toying with his feelings, but we can't dwell on it. That kiss has to be nothing but a mistake, an impulsive moment between friends caught up in the drinks and dancing. That's all.

If only my imagination would catch up.

I lay awake for the rest of the night, scared of what I'll see if I close my eyes.

***

"You're sure you don't want another?" Angie says, gesturing toward my empty martini glass. "It's my treat tonight, remember?"

I bob my head. "I'm positive." I've only had two espresso martinis, but I'm already thinking about things that I shouldn't. Like the way Jacob's hands felt in my hair. Another drink would take away what little remains of my mental filter.

Jacob. God, I need to quit thinking about Jacob. But it's hard to do that when there's a text from him waiting on my phone. *Seaside Cinema is showing the first Galactic Rush movie tomorrow night. You in?*

It's been two hours since he sent the message, and I still haven't responded. I feel horrible for ignoring him. We've barely spoken for two weeks. Jacob obviously extended this invitation in an attempt to patch things up. I wish I were mature enough to take him up on it.

I miss him so much. We spent almost every day together. On those rare days when we didn't see each other in person, we texted constantly. It's weird not asking him how his day was or telling him about how Jason nearly broke the back door trying to go after a squirrel in the yard this morning.

Over the last couple months, Jacob has become the person I go to for everything. I hate us being out of sync. But we need this time apart. After that kiss, we need to reestablish boundaries. At least I do. My brain still hasn't accepted that Jacob shouldn't be starring in any sexy thoughts. Steering clear of him is the only way I force myself to let this go.

Opening Jacob's message, I quickly write back. *Sorry. I can't.* After I hit send, I drop my phone in my purse, where it should stay the rest of the night. I'm not here to lament Jacob—I'm celebrating with Angie. She offered to take me out for drinks to thank me for one full month of volunteering in her classroom.

One month. I can't believe it. In some ways, it feels like I just started giving art lessons. In other ways, it feels like I've been doing it for ages. I'm proud of myself for sticking with it this long. Frankly, I expected the kids to run me out of the building on my first day. But I'm holding my own there, and I'm having a lot of fun while doing it. The kids are sweet, and I love coming up with projects for them every week.

Smiling, Angie twirls the stir stick around her martini. "Jace tried to pull a fast one on you today, didn't he?"

"No kidding." My lesson got off to a rough start this afternoon when Jace raised his hand to let me know he wouldn't be painting a seascape with the rest of the class. Apparently, he hates the beach. It's too hot. Too sandy. And his mom never packs enough snacks. He was ready to stage a protest when I announced the project.

"There's always one kid who wants to fight everything," Angie says. "This is my sixth year teaching, and I've had a Jace in every class. You handled him pretty well, though." Instead of making Jace participate, I gave him paper and a pencil and told him he could draw anything he wanted. At first, he was thrilled. But his smile gradually faded when I started passing out paint supplies to the rest of the class. It wasn't long before he said he was willing to give the beach another chance.

"I pulled stunts like that all the time at his age," I say. Unfortunately for Jace, I'm very familiar with acting out for attention. He thinks he's being clever by being difficult. The easiest way to make him realize he's wrong is to give him what he wants.

"Well, I can't thank you enough for everything you've done," Angie says. "The kids adore you. A few of them have asked me if we could have art class every day."

Warmth stirs in my chest. It's nice to know I'm having an impact. Though I'm quite certain it's the subject matter more than it is me. "That's because they'd rather play with paint than do subtraction," I say dryly.

She shakes her head. "I don't think so. My students liked their old art teacher, but they weren't begging for more art classes. You have a real knack for this. Did you ever think about becoming an art teacher?"

A surprised laugh slips out of my mouth. I'm not trying to be rude, but seriously? Me? A career in education? My former teachers would be in hysterics.

"Never. I was a terrible student. In high school, I spent so much time in the principal's office that he called the chair in the corner Izzy's spot."

Angie shrugs. "Well, I wasn't an angel in school, either. Carly and I used to sneak out of study hall to make out in the closet in the band room. Our band teacher, Mrs. Wilson, caught us one time after we knocked over a box of sheet music. She never looked me in the eye during ensemble rehearsal again."

"The band room closet. How scandalous."

"Everyone used to make out in there," Angie replies with a wistful look in her eye. "That closet was a breeding ground for infectious diseases. But anyway, I think you'd make a great art teacher. I don't know if that's something you'd ever consider, but I'd be happy to put you in touch with the district if you ever wanted to shadow someone."

Oh, wow. She really means it. I thought she was just talking. Sort of like when you bump into an old friend and tell her you should catch up sometime, even though you're still pissed at her for abandoning you at a party for a guy who vaguely resembled the Brawny Man.

"That's sweet of you, but I'm not looking to go back to school anytime soon." Working with Angie's kids has been a blast, but getting a master's degree sounds stressful and expensive. Morgan has been busting her ass in grad school for the past two years. She's much more driven than me, and she still gets overwhelmed. I'd shrivel up faster than a T-shirt that's been left in the dryer for too long.

"You don't necessarily have to go back to school," Angie says. "There are teaching certification programs you could look into. I know some people who did them while working full time. Most finished their programs in a little over a year."

That's interesting. Still, do I really want to make a drastic career change? Graphic design may not be perfect, but I know it. Teaching would be something entirely new.

The plan has been for me to move back to a designer role. It seems like a natural move. Then again, I've been saying that for months, and I've barely applied for any jobs. I told myself I needed to be patient, waiting for the right opportunity to come along. But maybe I've been hesitant because I don't want another graphic design job.

Should I be looking at alternate career paths? "Oh, I don't know." I slump back in my chair. I'll admit, the idea is intriguing, but I don't know how realistic it is. "I'm twenty-five. Do I really want to start my career all over?" I know I need to get back to something art-related, but getting a teaching license would be a serious commitment. I'm not sure it would be worth the inevitable hassle.

"Exactly, Izzy," Angie says, nodding encouragingly. "You're twenty-five. You're gonna be working for the next forty years. You've got to think about what will make you happy in the long run."

I sit with her words for a minute. Maybe she's right. The prospect of starting over is terrifying, but would I rather be stuck doing something that makes me miserable for the next four decades? Feeling like I'm in a rut for the rest of my career?

I'm not making any life-altering decisions tonight. Certainly not when I'm tipsy. So I tuck the idea in the back of my mind.

There's a lot to consider. But for the first time in as long as I can remember, thinking about my future fills me with curiosity instead of dread.

Twenty-Two

Jacob

"We're out of popcorn. Sorry."

The wiry teenager behind the register at the concession stand delivers the news with a mildly apologetic look. A movie theater without popcorn. It seems unnatural. Like salt without pepper or peanut butter without jelly. For a second, I wonder if this kid is messing with me, but the apathetic glaze over his eyes tells me he doesn't care enough for that.

Seaside Cinema is bustling tonight. People scutter about the small rectangular lobby with neon lighting and a patterned carpet that hasn't been updated since the early 90s. Some are dressed in metallic bodysuits and antennas, their faces painted to resemble characters from *Galactic Rush*. Others opted for more subtle regalia, wearing hoodies and backpacks with the franchise's blocky logo.

I had no idea *Galactic Rush* had such a committed following in Seaview. Based on the lack of available concession items, the theater owners didn't either.

"That's fine," I reply, despite my disappointment. Watching a movie in a theater without popcorn feels almost sacrilegious, but there's a long line behind me, so I'm trying to be sympathetic. Plus, I worked at this place in high school. I know how difficult customers can be when they can't get what they want. "I'll take Twizzlers instead."

The employee winces. "We're out of those, too."

No Twizzlers either? What happened? Did someone rob a supply truck on its way in? "What *do* you have?" I ask. It's probably easier to get to the point than to continue playing this guessing game.

"We have Raisinets. Or I can get you a fountain drink."

I laugh slightly, unable to help myself. "I'll have a Coke and Raisinets then." Those lackluster options are fitting for the miserable night I'm having.

Tonight, I had two choices: sit at home and think about Izzy or sit in a dark theater and think about Izzy. *At least the latter has popcorn,* I thought as I booked my ticket. I've become so unlucky that even something as reliable as a movie theater with popcorn has failed me.

Nothing has gone right since Izzy stopped talking to me. Yesterday, I noticed Lulu pawing at her ear, so I brought her to the vet. Turns out she has an ear infection. The vet prescribed her an antibiotic, but she said it could be a week or two before Lulu is back to normal. And then this morning, Luke Daniels trapped me in the break room for twenty minutes to talk about the clingy chick I was with the other night at the bar. He thinks I should dump her immediately. *She's hot, man, but the way she was grabbing onto you? Run.*

All I wanted to do when I escaped that conversation was text Izzy. She'd find the whole thing hysterical. But I knew there was no point in trying to communicate with her since she decided to cut me off.

She's been blowing me off for two weeks. Every text I've sent to her has gotten a curt response…if it's gotten one at all.

Normally, Izzy is the kind of texter who writes in paragraphs. She sent me five consecutive messages when I asked her what toppings she likes on her pizza. *That's a loaded question, Jacob. Is it a sweet sauce? How heavy is the cheese? Are we getting sides? Is it from a local place or a chain?*

I wasn't surprised when she turned me down on the movie. I sent her a follow up, asking when she's free to hang out, but that text has gone unanswered.

What she's doing is obvious. Izzy could barely look at me after we kissed. When the Uber pulled up Delia's driveway that night, she jumped out before the driver even put it in park, offering me a dismissive goodbye before scurrying inside.

I knew the kiss would change things, but I wasn't expecting Izzy to ice me out. I figured we'd be back to talking after a few days. Once she had a moment to process. Now, I'm beginning to fear the distance she has put between us is meant to be permanent.

The worst part is that kissing her only solidified what I already knew. I like Izzy. More than I've liked any woman I've ever been with. Certainly more than anyone I've gone on a date with over the past year. Initially, the way she responded to the kiss made me think she feels it, too. This connection. But the lingering silence suggests otherwise.

Maybe she's not interested in a relationship right now. Given what she's told me about her ex, it makes sense that she would be hesitant about dating. Then again, Izzy knows I'm nothing like that guy. *Sometimes, it feels like you're the only person I can talk to.* That's not the sort of thing you admit to someone if you have conflicting feelings about them.

The only reason that makes sense is that Izzy doesn't feel the same. The kiss was an earth-shattering moment for me, but I've been fantasizing about getting Izzy's lips on mine for weeks. *Of course* it was going to be like that. Maybe she sensed the intensity of my feelings, and they spooked her. She could be sitting somewhere right now, panicking about how she's going to let me down without hurting me.

If only she'd talked to me. Izzy has become one of my closest friends. Talking to her is a daily ritual, akin to brushing my teeth or making coffee. I don't want to lose our friendship, even if she isn't interested in me. I've kept my feelings to myself for this long. So what if I have to keep doing it? I'd take any Izzy in my life as opposed to none.

Maybe I should text her again. Put it all out in the open. She's already ignoring me. What's the worst that could happen?

Impulsively, I pull my phone out of my pocket and type the first words that come to mind. *Are we good? Things have been weird since the night at the bar. I miss you.* I reread the message, then delete it right away.

What am I thinking? I can't tell Izzy I miss her. That would only make me seem more desperate. I'm acting like a lovesick puppy. It's the exact kind of behavior I'm trying to avoid.

I need to get a grip. Izzy is my *friend*. That's all. I can't keep getting tangled up in thoughts of her hair or her eyes or the way her entire face lights up when she's laughing—

"Do you want to share mine?" asks the woman beside me.

I don't respond, assuming the question is meant for someone else. But when I glance her way again, she's blinking at me with a curious expression.

She lifts the massive tub of popcorn cradled in her arms. "I ordered a large, but I'm here by myself," she explains. "I don't mind." She's pretty, with light-brown hair and green eyes, dressed in a black *Galactic Rush* T-shirt and sneakers.

My head feels dazed. I shake the thoughts of Izzy from my brain like cobwebs. "That's okay. I ordered something else, but thanks, anyway."

The woman tilts her head skeptically. "Are you saying no because you really don't want to share with me, or are you doing it to be polite?" she asks. "Because I'm not gonna finish this by myself. I'd hate to waste perfectly good popcorn."

"I—" I start to make up an excuse, then freeze. She's right. I only rejected her offer because it seemed like the polite thing to do. But my dog is sick, the woman I'm obsessed with won't text me back, and the smell of movie theater butter is taunting me. What's the point?

"You know what? That actually sounds great."

Her face brightens. When the kid at the counter hands me my Coke and Raisinets, I ask for an empty popcorn bucket. Together, the woman and I head over to the condiment counter on the opposite side of the lobby. She dumps half her bucket into mine.

"I feel much better now," she says. "Something about watching a two-hour allegory of power and greed with a giant bucket of popcorn while everyone else had none didn't sit right with me."

I chuckle softly. "Who would've thought there'd be such a big turnout?" Honestly, I expected the audience to consist of me and four other guys dressed as aliens.

"Never underestimate the dedication of *Galactic Rush* fans, right?" She gives me a small smile. "Well, anyway, thanks for helping me clear my conscience. Enjoy the movie." She turns on her heels and starts toward the screening rooms.

I'd hoped the movie would help take my mind off things, but I'm barely able to focus. Even something as loud and bright as *Galactic Rush* isn't distracting enough to get Izzy out of my head. She's still there, tormenting me.

I hate that she won't just have a conversation with me. Does our friendship mean that little to her? It has to if she's able to kick me out of her life so easily.

My misery gives way to frustration. I've gotten so worked up over Izzy that I nearly forgot what brought us together in the first place. She's helping me meet someone, and I'm helping her with her goal of self-improvement. I'd like to believe our relationship has evolved since we made our initial agreement, but the basis is still transactional. We only became friends because both of us wanted something from each other.

I claim I want love and commitment, but what have I done to show that since Izzy and I started hanging out? The only time I've been on True Connections was when she insisted on seeing my profile. I haven't been making dating a priority. I've gone stagnant. It's not getting me any closer to a relationship.

When the credits roll, I gather my trash and join the line of moviegoers shuffling toward the exit. I toss my empty popcorn bucket in the garbage, then step into the crowded lobby. Conversation buzzes as I make my way to the doors. I get there at the same time as the woman who shared her popcorn with me earlier. The two of us exchange smiles, then I open the door, motioning for her to go ahead.

"Thanks," she says as she heads outside.

"It's the least I can do," I say as I follow her out the door. We're standing on the sidewalk outside the theater. It's a cool, dark evening, and the marquee glows like a spotlight above us. "You saved me from a depressing, popcornless night."

She lets out a quiet laugh. "I couldn't let you sit through *Galactic Rush* with just Raisinets. That would've been cruel."

"Well, I owe you one. When *Galactic Rush 2* plays, popcorn is on me."

"Does this theater do a lot of re-releases?"

I nod. "The place is owned by an older couple. They've been running it for decades. Both of them are huge cinephiles, so they show a ton of classics."

"I love that." She zips her sweatshirt as a gentle breeze passes over us. "I'm new to the area, so I'm still learning my way around."

"Oh, yeah? How long have you lived in Seaview?"

"About two months."

"Well, I've lived here my whole life." I ball my hands in my jacket pockets. It is chilly. "It's a small community, but I couldn't imagine living anywhere else."

"You sound just like my aunt," she tells me. "She's lived here for fifteen years and swears I'm gonna fall in love with this place." Something occurs to me as I process her words. This woman looks like she's in her late twenties, she's new to Seaview, and she has an aunt who lives here. She sounds a lot like the woman my mom tried to set me up with. Could this be her friend Eva's single niece?

"By any chance, is your name Catherine?" I ask. It can't be her, can it? Seaview is a small town, but the odds of me unknowingly crossing paths with the woman my mom told me about weeks ago seem slim.

Surprise splashes over her features. "Um, yeah. How do you know that?" Her expression is one of concern. I should probably clarify that I'm not a stalker.

"I'm Jacob. I think your aunt is friends with my mom." I leave out the fact that our relatives have been scheming to get us together.

Catherine's eyes widen. "Oh my god. You're the nice Seaview guy Aunt Eva won't stop talking about." I guess I didn't have to leave out anything. It sounds like Catherine got the same spiel about me from her aunt. "This is so funny. Your mom gave my aunt your number. She's been begging me to text you for weeks. I haven't done it because…well, my aunt doesn't always have the best judgment. She once tried to set me up with her dentist's son, and he kept his taxidermied dog in his living room."

"Well, I can promise you I don't have any pets on display in my house."

She laughs. "That's a relief. I'll have to give Aunt Eva credit on this one. She should've led with the fact that you like *Galactic Rush*."

"I don't know. Giving credit to our scheming families is a dangerous game."

Something curious twinkles in her eyes. "But it might be worth it. Don't you think?"

She catches me off guard. I haven't thought about dating since I realized I liked Izzy. Probably longer, if I'm being honest. While I've only recently become aware of how desperate I am for her, I think I've had these feelings for a while. They're probably the reason I've had such a hard time meeting someone. I thought I was putting myself out there, but my mind has been wrapped up in one woman this entire time.

Izzy, who lights up any room she enters. Izzy, who could talk for hours and never be boring. Being around her feels like coasting down an empty road on a quiet summer evening. It's warm and open and comfortable. You can't help but want to stay in the moment. Commit every detail to memory so you can replay it later.

Izzy is the kind of person who makes the crappy commute after a tedious day of work seem worth it. She's the sunshine that turns the bad days into bearable ones and gets you through the slog of daily life.

Except Izzy doesn't feel that way about me. I can't ignore the signs when they're as large as billboards. She isn't interested. I need to let it go. I'm supposed to be looking for someone I can picture spending the rest of my life with, but it's been months since my last date. I've let my feelings for Izzy blur my focus.

I want marriage. Family. I can't spend the rest of my life pining after someone who doesn't want those things with me.

Catherine may not be my forever, but going out with her would be good for me, wouldn't it? It would force me to get back out there *and* show Izzy that I haven't let our kiss derail my plans. Maybe she'll finally talk to me once she hears I'm dating again.

It's for the last reason that I tell Catherine she should use my number.

Twenty-Three

Izzy

Preston College is *really* pretty.

Photos from the college's website show a picturesque campus with plenty of green space and collegiate gothic architecture. It has plenty of coffee shops, and it's only a twenty-minute drive from Delia's place.

But most importantly, Preston College offers a master of the arts in teaching. It's a two-to-three-year program that starts in the fall and can be completed through a mix of online and in-person courses. And it's geared toward part-time students, which means I'd have no issue taking classes while working full time.

But Angie was right—getting a master's degree isn't my only option for becoming an art teacher. I've been looking at alternative accreditation programs like she suggested.

The state education department has dozens of programs on its website. Angie told me that a lot of districts provide tuition reimbursement. Theoretically, I could obtain my initial license through a certification program and then go back to get my master's after I get a job in a school.

I've been doing a borderline obsessive amount of research on education programs since Angie threw out the idea. At first, it seemed impractical. But the more I read, the harder it is to convince myself why I shouldn't do it.

Living with Delia these past few months has allowed me to build up my savings account. And I'd only be in school part time, which means I'd still be able to work for Tanner.

I'm not trying to downplay the amount of work it will entail. I know it will be overwhelming for a while. But I'm thinking about the end goal here.

What will my life look like years from now? Will I be happy with it?

It's hard for me to imagine sitting in a cubicle for the next forty years. When I think back to my old graphic design job, the thing that sticks out is how miserable I was being in front of a computer all day. I hated the quiet. The stillness. Working in that environment sucked up my creativity faster than a drop of water in the desert.

A school would be a total change of pace. It certainly wouldn't be quiet or still. And if I like teaching half as much as I like working with Angie's class every week, then I know it would be a good fit. Isn't that what matters? Long-term satisfaction? I don't want to spend the rest of my career feeling restless, wishing I was doing something else instead.

These last few months have been about improving my life. Originally, I thought that meant making general changes, like working out more or spending less time playing video games, but I'm beginning to think that real growth is much more than that. It's about doing the hard work, digging deep into your problems and asking yourself what isn't right.

A self-help book isn't going to make my life better. The only way to do that is through big changes. They might be difficult and messy, but isn't that the point?

I've been browsing accreditation programs for almost an hour when my phone buzzes. I glance at the glowing screen to see a text from Delia. *Have you eaten already? Tanner is making homemade pizzas. Come over if you're hungry!*

My stomach growls. It's almost seven, and I haven't eaten since noon. I'm starving. Normally, I'd make dinner for myself, but Delia's offer is too tempting. Tanner is an excellent cook. Besides, I haven't been grocery shopping in almost a week. The cabinets look like the shelves at the grocery store the night before Thanksgiving. Unless I want canned corn with a side of stale pretzels for dinner, heading to Tanner's place is my only option.

I text Delia back, letting her know I'll be there soon. Closing my laptop, I throw my hair in a ponytail and slip on a pair of sneakers. I pour Jason a bowl of kibble and then make the short trek over to Tanner's house. Light swims in the windows as I head up the back porch. I knock once before entering—Delia said it was open, but she and Tanner are touchy-feely, so I'd rather not catch them mid-makeout.

The heavenly aroma of roasted garlic and tomato sauce greets me as I step inside. In the kitchen, Tanner is pulling a bubbling margherita pizza out of the oven. Delia is perched at the island, a glass of white wine in hand. Her brown eyes land on me, and she smiles warmly, lifting her glass in greeting.

"Hey, Iz. Have a seat." She pats the cushioned bar stool beside her. "Jacob just went to grab another bottle from the garage. I'll get you a glass." She hops down from her stool, padding barefoot across the tile. She skirts past Tanner and opens a tall cabinet, plucking a stemless wine glass off the shelf.

My stomach takes a nosedive. "Jacob's here?" That's the problem with entering through the back door—you don't see whose car is in the driveway.

Delia nods as she shuts the cabinet. "I'm surprised you didn't know that already. I was just telling Tanner that I think you've taken his spot as Jacob's best friend. He's feeling a little sensitive about it."

Tanner raises a brow as he sets the steaming pizza on the stovetop. "A little sensitive?" he repeats, looking down at her.

"Oh, c'mon," she says playfully. "Don't tell me you aren't at least a little worried about Jacob replacing you with Izzy."

"When was the last time you saw a doctor?" Tanner asks, lifting Delia's chin with his thumb. He tilts her head from side to side as if he's conducting a medical exam. "You might wanna get your head checked."

"There's nothing to be embarrassed about," she says in a patronizing tone. She climbs up on her tiptoes so that her face aligns with his. "Just because Jacob has other friends doesn't mean he cares about you any less."

Tanner smirks. "It's a good thing you're pretty, darling," he says, "or else it would be hard to overlook this level of delusion."

He kisses her. I can't even bring myself to be annoyed by their public display. I'm too busy spiraling over the fact that Jacob is here. Why didn't Delia say anything? *Probably because she doesn't know you made out with him, genius.*

Telling Delia would've made it an ordeal, which is the last thing I wanted, especially after the comment she made about us being flirty on Tanner's birthday. But she can't help me avoid Jacob when she doesn't know I'm avoiding him to begin with.

This situation is yet another reason I can't pursue things with Jacob. Our lives are connected through Delia and Tanner. I'm probably going to see him at parties for the rest of my life. Imagine how awkward it would be if we tried to be together, and it didn't work out. It's simply not worth the risk. I moved to another state to avoid interacting with one of my ex-boyfriends. I don't want a repeat of New York.

Still, I do miss Jacob. Cutting him off hasn't been easy. I've lost count of the number of times I've had to fight the urge to text him. The other day, I saw Aurora at the grocery store. It took every ounce of my self-control not to call Jacob when I got to the parking lot.

The door to the garage rattles, then swings open as Jacob walks inside clutching a bottle of white wine. "You're out of chardonnay, Tanner." He hasn't noticed me yet. His eyes are fixed on the bottle. "But I found a bottle of riesling in the back."

Jacob hands the bottle to Delia, then, finally, his gaze lands on me. His lips part in surprise. My heart feels like it's in my throat as his eyes trail over me.

Anxious energy courses through me. I wish I could hear what's running through his head. Is he angry? Hurt? Happy to see me? I'm usually good at breaking the silence in these types of situations, killing the tension with a funny comment. Right now, however, it feels like my mouth has been sewn shut. Are Delia and Tanner picking up on the weirdness? Is it obvious something happened between us?

Jacob's shocked expression fades suddenly. He hits me with a friendly smile. "Hey, Forrest," he says casually before taking a seat at the island. His attention switches to Delia. "Mind pouring me a glass, too?"

"Sure." She already has the cork out of the bottle and is filling a glass for me.

All right. So Jacob and I are keeping things amicable. That's good. Great, even. It would've been hard to get through the night with him flat-out ignoring me. Though there was some distance in his tone. Polite but aloof. Hearing Jacob talk to me like an acquaintance felt weird, but I'm responsible for our fractured relationship.

Delia passes me a wine glass before moving on to fill Jacob's. "I'll have to pick more chardonnay before Morgan gets here," she says. "We have to have a wine night."

Our younger sister is staying with us next week while she's on spring break. It's her last spring break of college—she's graduating in the spring. The three of us have been texting nonstop about what we're going to do while she's here.

"All three Forrest sisters in Seaview seems dangerous," Tanner says.

Delia laughs. "Maybe you can hire her, and we can make it permanent."

We end up eating outside on the porch. It's an unusually nice night for March, warm and light, and Delia says she doesn't want it to go to waste.

We sit around the glass table, trading stories and nibbling on pizza crust. Fairy lights twinkle along the porch railing, a Delia signature. The night is unexpectedly pleasant. With Delia and Tanner present, it's easy to pretend my problems with Jacob don't exist. It's as if we've entered a bubble, an escape from reality.

But eventually, that bubble has to pop. After we finish eating, Delia and Tanner gather our plates to bring them back inside. Jacob and I offer to help clean up, but they tell us they've got it handled. The two of them head inside, leaving us alone for the first time.

For a moment, we sit in silence. I try to remain calm, despite the fact that my skin feels like it's being prodded by tiny needles.

"So, how'd it go today?" Jacob asks.

I stare at him, confused. "Huh?"

"Your art class," he explains. "It's Tuesday, isn't it?"

"Oh, right." *Jesus, Izzy. You make out with a guy one time, and suddenly you forget how to act like a normal person in front of him.* "It was a good one."

Today, we did our first group project. Each of the kids designed their own lily pad, then we glued them onto a giant piece of shiny blue construction paper that resembled a pond. "Only three kids glued their fingers together, which I see as a success." The first time we used glue was a nightmare. Half the class glued their fingers together. Angie and I had to take turns helping kids wash their hands in the sink in the back of the classroom.

"I glued my fingers together working on a science project in second grade," Jacob says. "The other kids called me Elmer for the rest of the year." Smiling, I picture a tiny Jacob with glasses too big for his face, sitting at a desk with glued fingers.

"I bet that was traumatizing for you."

"I turned out fine. Mostly."

My lips twitch. "Mostly?"

"There are the invisible scars, Forrest," he says, clutching his chest in mock agony. "I still carry those with me." Both of us laugh, and the feeling is as light and natural as ever. God, what was I so worried about? Jacob and I never had trouble talking. I thought the kiss might ruin our dynamic, but it seems as if nothing has changed.

His casualness makes me question everything. Was I too hasty in cutting him off? I assumed Jacob would interpret the kiss as the start of something romantic. Ignoring him seemed like the only way to kill that idea. Then again, he's sensible. Logical. Jacob has a specific idea in his head of what he wants from a relationship. He has to know that I don't fit it.

Right now, it feels as though our impulsive makeout didn't happen.

A seed of hope sprouts in my chest. Does this mean Jacob wants to put the kiss behind us? If he can recognize it for what it was—a hasty moment between friends—then nothing has to change. We can resume our friendship. Go back to normal.

I'm thrilled about the possibility of getting Jacob back, but there's also a sense of guilt stirring in me. I kicked him out of my life based on an assumption. I acted like an asshole toward the one person who has been there for me over the many ups and downs of the past few months.

Jacob's reassurance has helped me so much. Without him, I never would've had the nerve to step foot in Angie's classroom. And I certainly wouldn't be considering a career change. He deserved better from me.

The best way to make it up to him, I quickly decide, is with honesty. Jacob has told me on numerous occasions that he doesn't want me to lie to him. The least I can do is let him know how much his friendship means to me.

"Angie says I'm a natural teacher." My throat suddenly feels tight. My palms are slick enough that I have to wipe them on my legs. I'm nervous. It's a rare emotion for me. Probably because I avoid talking about things that make me uncomfortable. I feel hot and gross, like I'm sitting in biology class after fourth-period gym, trying not to think about the way my sweat sticks to my clothes. I hate it. So I tell myself to quit being weird and spit the rest of the words out already.

"She thinks I should get my teaching license," I say. "Isn't that wild? My tenth-grade homeroom teacher would have a heart attack if he heard that." Mr. Simmons used to tell me I was the cause of his premature worry lines.

Jacob doesn't let me hide behind humor. He studies me with a thoughtful expression that makes my pulse speed up. "Are you thinking about it?" he asks. There's nothing funny or dismissive in his tone. Just genuine curiosity. I knew he'd take me seriously. But that doesn't stop my insecurities from rearing their ugly head.

Am I competent enough to be a teacher? Things with Angie's class might be going smoothly, but it could be that specific group of students. Would it be a different story in another classroom? What if I got my teaching license and completely bombed? All that work, all that money would be for nothing.

I kick those worrisome thoughts to the back of my head. I'm not making a decision right now. All I need to do is answer the question. Besides, if I can't admit the truth to Jacob, then how do I expect anyone else to believe in me? "Sort of," I admit. "I want a career that fulfills me, but I don't know. It's a lot of work."

"But if it's what you want to do, then you should do it." Sincerity shines in Jacob's eyes. "There are always going to be challenges, Forrest, but if you think this could make you happy, then you shouldn't hesitate. That's what really matters." He folds his lips, pausing for a beat before adding: "You'd be an amazing teacher."

Warmth floods my body. I knew Jacob would be encouraging—he always is. His belief in me means everything. It calms something within me. "Thanks for always being so supportive," I say, hoping he can hear just how much I appreciate it. "I wouldn't have gone through with the first lesson if it weren't for you."

He smiles. "Yes, you would've, Forrest. You don't need me to do anything."

But I do. You make everything easier.

Our eyes lock for the briefest moment before Jacob shifts his gaze to the yard. "I should probably be thanking you, too."

I shoot him a surprised look. "Don't tell me you've decided to give up your precious numbers for a career in teaching." Though he would easily fit in in an academic setting, Jacob seems settled in his career.

"No, but I met someone," he says. "Her name's Catherine. We started talking the other night at the *Galactic Rush* showing at Seaside Cinema."

I frown. "You started talking? At the movies?" Have neither of them heard of a concept called theater etiquette?

Jacob laughs. "It was before the movie. The place was so busy that the theater ran out of popcorn. Catherine was there by herself, so she offered me some of hers. Coincidentally, she's the niece of my mom's friend. They've been trying to set us up for a while, but neither of us was interested. Until now. We've been texting for a few days. We're grabbing drinks next week."

My stomach feels like a ball of lead. "Well, that's…awesome." Awesome. It sounds wrong, even in my head.

So Jacob found someone. Isn't that great? All this time, I've been worrying that he built the kiss up into something that it wasn't, and he's been getting to know another woman. Safe to say there was no issue there.

I laugh, feeling uneasy. "I bet you're glad I couldn't make it to that showing, huh?" It's a good thing I turned him down, isn't it? If I hadn't been so determined to push him away, then he would've been there with me. He wouldn't have had the chance to chat up some woman.

"I wouldn't have gone alone if it weren't for you," Jacob says. "You helped me realize that I need to push myself out of my comfort zone more often."

Oh, yay. You could almost say this happened because of me. How terrific.

A mix of emotions rolls through me. Surprise. Confusion. Embarrassment. Why did I assume Jacob wanted to be with me? He's looking for his wife. A woman to build his future with. Of course he doesn't see that future with me. I can't believe I was so presumptuous. That I nearly destroyed our friendship for no reason.

But it's okay. My sabotage paid off. Jacob met someone. He's probably been so busy thinking about her that he hasn't given a second thought to the way he gripped my waist, the way it felt when our mouths collided, the pure want and desperation.

None of that matters. It's all in the past. Gone and practically forgotten. And I'm *so* happy for Jacob. Because I know how much he wants this. How many bad dates he's suffered through. He wouldn't be telling me about Catherine unless he thought there was a chance with her. He deserves it. Someone who makes him happy. I'm ecstatic.

So ecstatic I'll probably cry myself to sleep tonight.

Twenty-Four

Really, I'm *fine*.

Finding out the friend you've been having not-so-friendly dreams about is going on a date with someone else would send most people plunging into a deep, dark abyss. Me, on the other hand? I'm taking it like a champ. A gold fucking medalist. I'm demonstrating record-breaking levels of self-restraint, and no one even knows it.

It's been a few days since Jacob dropped the Catherine bombshell on me, and I'm slowly—*very* slowly—coming to terms with it. For the most part, things have gone back to the way they were before we kissed.

We've been hanging out and texting like normal. Yesterday, Jacob mentioned that he and Catherine were having their first date tonight. Like any good friend, I offered to help him pick something to wear. Jacob tried telling me it wasn't necessary, but I insisted on stopping by his place after work.

Am I happy to be dressing him to go out with another woman? Of course not. It took me five whole minutes to work up the nerve to get out of the car. An impulsive part of me wanted to drive as far away as possible and never come back. *Nice knowing you, Seaview. It's been real.*

But as much as it pains me, I need to be realistic. Jacob is dating. It's happening, and I have to be okay with it, even if my feelings haven't caught up yet. I promised I would help him with his dating life, and that's exactly what I'm going to do. Which is why I've been digging through his closet, a surprisingly spacious walk-in with mahogany built-ins and recessed lighting, for the past half hour.

"All right, Forrest. What do you think of this one?" I stop flipping through hangers as Jacob steps through the doorway, dressed in a simple collared shirt and dark jeans.

"It's perfect," I tell him. Just as I suspected, the cool gray tone of the shirt brings out the warmth in his brown eyes. The jeans make him look casual yet put together, the perfect balance between caring and not trying too hard.

"You sure?" Jacob asks as he adjusts the buttons on his sleeve. He's probably expecting me to change my mind, since I've done that with at least six outfits already.

"Absolutely. Catherine is going to love it." The words taste like ash in my mouth, but my chipper tone gives away nothing. "I'd say my work here is…oh, wait. Hang on." Hurrying over to him, I grab a fistful of his shirt and sniff. I breathe in Jacob's fresh laundry scent.

Releasing his shirt, I pat him squarely on the chest. "Okay. Now you're good."

"Did you just sniff me?" he asks.

"Smell is everything, Jacob. You wouldn't believe how many guys show up to first dates stinking like sweaty gym socks."

His lips twitch in amusement. "So, did I pass the smell test?"

"With flying colors." With my palm still resting on his chest, I steal a glimpse of us in the full-length mirror. Our eyes lock, and my heart thumps furiously. That is, until I notice something that has me jumping back in surprise. "Oh my god. Your face." Jacob's glasses are nowhere to be found. He must've put in contacts when he was in the bathroom.

He gives me a strange look. "Are you talking about the contacts?"

"You don't wear contacts." I've known Jacob for almost a year, and I've never seen him without his wire-framed glasses. The sight is shocking. It's like being a kid and seeing Mall Santa light up a Marlboro outside behind Sears. I can't believe I didn't notice it right away. I must've been so focused on the clothes that it slipped by me.

Somehow, Jacob doesn't see the big deal. "I do sometimes," he says. "For dates and other stuff." Important stuff, he means. I've never met Glassesless Jacob because he doesn't feel the need to dress up for me. Unlike Catherine. He put in those contacts because he wants to make a good impression on her. On their date.

Which I'm totally cool with, by the way.

"I like your glasses," I blurt before I can think better of it. Shit, that sounded weird. Quickly, I try to recover. "I mean, you were wearing them when you met Catherine, weren't you? She's probably expecting you to have them on. What if she doesn't recognize you?" My sisters barely recognized me when I cut my bangs last summer.

Jacob chuckles. "I think you might be overthinking it. It's just contacts."

But it's not just contacts! I nearly scream. *You're going on a date! After we kissed! And I know it's my fault, but I still hate it!*

Except I can't say any of those things. If I want Jacob in my life, I have to get used to him dating other people.

My feelings are temporary. They're going to fade over time. Someday, I might even help Jacob choose an outfit for a date without feeling like I'm being run over by a semi-truck.

In the meantime, I'll be a good friend. A great one.

I'm fine, really.

***

Morgan won't stop blubbering. Tucked beneath a throw blanket on the other end of the couch, she cries silently at the TV. She thinks she's being sneaky, dabbing her wet eyes with a tissue every now and then, but I've been watching her, and it's been a steady stream of waterworks for the past fifteen minutes.

Annoyed, I snag the remote off the couch arm and press pause, leaving Claire Danes' distraught face on the screen. "Seriously, Morgan?" I level a glare at my younger sister. "You swore you wouldn't cry if we put this on."

"I'm not!" she objects, which is frankly ridiculous. Morgan's face is flushed, and her eyes are glassy. She looks like she just left back-to-back screenings of *Marley & Me* and *Old Yeller*.

"There are tear stains on your cheeks, Morg." Delia chimes in from her spot in the oversized armchair. I'm glad she's not letting Morgan get away with this nonsense.

Morgan arrived in town yesterday. She was wiped after the two-hour drive from Boston, so she crashed shortly after she got here, but she was up and ready to go this morning. It's her first time in Seaview for something other than a holiday or special occasion, and she says she wants the full tourist experience.

We spent the day exploring shops around town. Naturally, Morgan fell in love with the beach-themed bookstore, decorated with surfboards and chaise lounges for customers

257

to sit and read in. We ate lunch at Ralph's Diner and even signed up for a candle-making class at Wax & Shells tomorrow night. It was interesting experiencing Seaview through the eyes of a visitor. I haven't lived here for long, but it feels like home.

My days of playing tourist won't be ending anytime soon. Cynthia is supposed to arrive Friday night. She already sent me a mile-long list of things she wants to do. A lot of it overlaps with things on Morgan's itinerary, but it doesn't bother me. I'd happily do the same things over again if it means spending time with my favorite people.

After a long day of shopping, my sisters and I decided to unwind with pizza and a movie. Delia and I agreed to let Morgan choose what we watch. It's her spring break, after all.

I figured she'd put on something light and easy, not *Romeo + Juliet*. Blood feuds and teen suicide don't exactly scream "spring break fun." Delia and I tried talking Morgan out of it, but she was insistent. She swore she wouldn't cry, even though she's the type to tear up at commercials with puppies in them.

"Okay, fine," Morgan admits, holding up her balled-up tissue. "So I cried a little. But Delia was wiping her eyes, too."

I turn to my older sister, who shrugs. "It's a sad movie," she says, unabashed.

"Traitor," I mutter before turning off the TV.

"It's not over yet!" Morgan protests.

"You've seen it enough times. Use your memory to fill in the blanks." Morgan is only in Seaview for a week. We should be having fun, not sobbing uncontrollably. Besides, if

I wanted something to cry about, all I'd have to do is picture Jacob and Catherine.

"What do you suggest we do then?" Morgan asks.

"Jason could show you some of his new tricks." The dog's ears twitch at the sound of his name. Jason finally started obedience classes last week. He's only had two sessions, but I've been practicing with him at home.

Delia laughs. "Jason barked at his own reflection the other day. He's not going to learn anything." I'll admit, Jason hasn't shown much sign of progress yet. He sort of knows "stay" and "sit," but sort of knowing something isn't that helpful. I wouldn't want a surgeon who *sort of* knows how to perform open-heart surgery.

Still, I have faith in him. Jason's instructor, Louise, said training takes time. And it's a lot harder for dogs like Jason, who are older and already settled into a routine. It's going to be a while before we see any results.

"Don't underestimate him," I say. "He might surprise you."

"I'll believe it when I stop finding his teeth marks in my shoes," Delia grumbles. But when Jason approaches her, she runs a hand through his dark fur, petting him gently. Delia can deny it all she wants, but she loves him.

Morgan's phone buzzes on the coffee table. She picks it up and frowns. "It's Mom," she says, sounding oddly guilty. "I told her I'd call tonight. I completely forgot." Looking at me, she appears apologetic. "Sorry."

"Why?" I ask. I haven't spoken to Mom in months, but it's no secret that my sisters still talk to her.

Morgan fiddles with the phone in her lap. "I don't want to make things uncomfortable."

"Saying her name won't send me into a fit of rage, Morg." Honestly, I'm offended she'd even think that. I haven't asked either of my sisters to stop mentioning Mom around me. She's our *mother*. It's not like we can pretend she doesn't exist.

"I know," Morgan says. "That's not what I meant. I just don't want to hurt your feelings." She winces, and I feel like an asshole. Of course she's thinking about me.

"You won't," I assure her. This thing with Mom isn't going to affect my relationships with Morgan and Delia. I won't let it. "You should answer the phone."

Morgan's eyes round in surprise. "Really?"

"Yeah. You said you'd call her, right? We both know she isn't gonna stop blowing up your phone till she gets a hold of you."

"You're sure about this, Izzy?" Delia asks, caution in her voice. I get why she's worried—my conversations with our mother usually end in shouting—but Mom's shadow can't loom over me forever. The two of us will have to interact again at some point. Morgan's graduation is only a few months away. I highly doubt she wants her family sitting on opposite sides of the stadium. I might as well practice being civil with Mom.

"I'm positive," I say.

Biting her bottom lip, Morgan slides her thumb to accept the call. "Hi, Mom," she says, putting the phone on speaker mode.

"Hi, honey!" Mom says. "How's it going? I assume you made it to Seaview all right."

"Everything's great," Morgan replies. "We went shopping today and saw the cutest bookstore! I spent way too much money, but it was amazing. Anyway, we got back to the house a while ago and decided to watch *Romeo + Juliet.* But Izzy turned it off because my crying annoyed her."

"Why would you watch *Romeo + Juliet* on vacation?" Mom asks. Unfortunately, I don't get a chance to tell Morgan I told her so. "Are your sisters there? Can I say hi?"

"They're here. You're already on speaker."

"Great. Well, hi, Delia. Hi, Izzy."

Delia responds first. When it's my turn, my throat suddenly feels tight. "Hi, Mom."

Silence follows. It's months of tension unfolding at once, the kind of awkward that makes you want to bury your head under your pillow. I feel my sisters' eyes on me, but I don't look at them. I don't have to see their faces to know they're filled with worry.

After a moment, Mom ends the standstill.

"Izzy, do you think we could talk privately for a second?"

Her request catches me by surprise. What is there for us to say to each other? The last time Mom and I spoke, I told her she shouldn't be in my life anymore if she can't respect the way I choose to live it. Unless she's had a change of heart, there's nothing to talk about.

I almost say no. Chatting with Mom is at the very bottom of my list of desires at the moment. But do I *really* want to pick a fight with her in front of Morgan and Delia? After I just told them this phone call wouldn't be a big deal?

"That's fine," I reply reluctantly. Delia and Morgan wait for me to give them the go-ahead before getting up to leave. Once I make it clear that I'm okay, Morgan passes me her phone, which feels like a ticking time bomb, and then she and Delia walk out the door.

It's silent again. I decide to let it linger. Mom was the one who asked for this, so it only seems fair that she be the one to carry the conversation.

"So, how have you been? Are things still going well at Ryan & Son?"

Translation: have you gotten fired from another job?

"Things are fine," I say. With Mom, less is always better. "How are you?"

"Good," she says. "I've mostly been taking care of things around the house. I deep cleaned the basement for the first time in ages. You wouldn't believe how many candy wrappers I found buried beneath the couch cushions."

Actually, I would. Teenage Izzy liked to hide in the basement whenever she got the munchies, so those wrappers are probably mine. But bringing up my troublesome past when Mom and I are already struggling to make conversation feels like a terrible plan.

Mom lets out a shaky breath. "Listen, Izzy," she says, "I wanted to talk to you so I could apologize for what happened at the Christmas party. I never meant to upset you. I only wanted to express my concerns. Still, Delia's party wasn't the appropriate setting. I never should've put you in that position, and I'm sorry."

It's not often that Mom apologizes, so I know that she really means it. While it's great to hear her taking accountability for her actions, it doesn't sound like she understands the real problem here. I'm not mad that she brought up the work stuff at Delia's party. I'm mad that she brought it up, period. I've asked her not to.

Her comments did so much more than upset me. It feels like she's constantly trying to undermine me, treating me like a child in need of a lecture instead of a grown woman with the right to make her own decisions.

Mom is entitled to her opinion, and I can respect that. But I can't have her questioning everything I do. If she wants a relationship with me, she has to respect me enough to let me make my own decisions. I don't know if she's capable of that. My mom has always loved being in control. Is she able to let it go for me?

"Thanks, Mom," I say, somewhat guarded. I want to believe this is genuine, but I just don't know with her.

"You're welcome," she replies. "I've missed you, Izzy. I hate fighting. You have to catch me up on everything. How has the year been going?" Her question presents me with an opening. I could use it to test her. Give her a chance to show me that she really is sorry and wants to do things differently from now on.

"I've been busy. I actually made friends with a teacher at Seaview Elementary. The school's art teacher quit unexpectedly in December, and the district hasn't replaced her, so her students have been without art classes. I started coming in as a volunteer once a week to do projects with her first graders."

"Izzy, that's wonderful!"

"I know. It's been going on for a while now, and I love it. Angie thinks I'd make a good teacher. She asked me if I ever considered going into education. At first, I wasn't sure. But I've been thinking about it lately."

"About what? Getting a teaching license?"

"Yeah. I've been looking into some alternative programs. There are ways to get my license without going back for my master's. Most programs only take a year or two."

"Well, that's not what I expected to hear."

"I have a good feeling about this, Mom." *Trust in me. Believe in me. That's all I want from you.* "I've been hesitant about applying for new graphic design jobs. I thought I was nervous, but I think it's because I need to do something different."

She says nothing. I'm silently begging her to hear the meaning between my words. This is the olive branch. Mom can take it and prove to me that she actually intends to be supportive, or she can shove it back in my face, the way she has many times before.

"You know I'm all for trying something different," Mom says. "But, honey, are you sure becoming an art teacher is what you want? Getting a teaching license is expensive. You'll have course and exam fees. And you may enjoy working with those students now, but who knows how you'll feel ten years from now? You used to love graphic design, remember?"

I close my eyes. "So, you think it's a bad idea."

"No," she insists, "not necessarily. I like the idea of you exploring different career options. But why don't we focus on ones that don't require a bunch of classes and a license? You never liked school, anyway."

Disappointment rains down on me. She just can't help herself. The minute I open up to her, she pokes holes in me. "I wasn't asking for your opinion, Mom. You wanted to know what I've been up to, so I told you."

"Izzy, I—"

"This isn't going to work." I'm sick of arguing with her. Sick of her not trying to understand. Mom claims she wants to fix things, but she isn't going to change. She simply expects me to become more receptive to her ideas.

She's saying something now, probably trying to convince me of her perspective, but I'm blocking her out. At this point, I'm not even angry. I'm just done. So done.

So even though she's still rambling, I hang up the phone.

Twenty-Five

Izzy

Morgan is wine drunk.

She hardly ever drinks, so when Delia cracked open a fancy bottle of wine to celebrate Morgan's last night in town, I knew it wouldn't be long before Morgan started slurring her words and moving with all the gracefulness of a baby deer. While Delia and I polish off the last few drops of our second glasses with ease, Morgan is flushed and rambling about how pretty the stars are in Seaview.

"It's so clear and open here," she gushes, sandwiched between Delia and me under a blanket on the bench on the back porch. She tilts her head back to marvel at the sky once more. "It's like we're camping or something."

Delia and I exchange smiles. "We've never been camping, Morg," she says.

"Well, maybe we should try it." Morgan blinks a few times, as if she's ruminating on the idea. "Yeah. We should. Wouldn't that be fun?" Her eyes brighten with enthusiasm. She glances at Delia and me to gauge our reactions.

"Oh, yeah. That'd be a real blast," I mutter. Camping with my sisters would be a veritable nightmare. The three of us are city girls at heart, and we aren't too proud to admit it. Morgan would be terrified of the bears and bugs, and Delia would be annoyed about getting dirt on her nice hiking boots, and I would be bored out of my mind.

Morgan, in her inebriated state, doesn't pick up on my sarcasm. "Let's do it then," she says. "This summer. The

Forrest sisters go camping. Ha. Forrest. Forest. It's like it's meant to be." She grins, obviously proud of her word play.

Neither Delia nor I feel like crushing Drunk Morgan's dreams, so we tell her it's a plan.

We sit in silence for a few minutes. I take the time to appreciate the niceness of the evening, the full feeling in my stomach and the fresh air in my lungs. My life has felt like a roller coaster lately, but I know I have a lot to be grateful for. It's nights like these, taking in the salty breeze, talking nonsense with my sisters, that I remember how lucky I am.

Wow. Maybe I'm drunker than I thought.

Morgan clears her throat, her expression suddenly serious. "Thank you both for making this week so fun," she says. "I would've spent it holed up in my apartment if the two of you hadn't invited me here."

I wrap an arm around her shoulders, squeezing her. "It's been great having you here."

It's been an amazing week. We had a blast at our candle-making class. We got to select our own scents. Originally, I wanted to go with a fresh linen scent, but when I realized I was inadvertently recreating Jacob's smell, I scrapped that idea. My strawberry cupcake candle was the best of the three, hands down. Morgan mixed too many scents together, and Delia didn't put any fragrance in hers. She hates scented candles.

We did plenty of other touristy things during the week: touring local lighthouses, taking nature walks, and grabbing seafood at Saunders' restaurant. On Wednesday, it was even warm enough for us to have a picnic on the beach. We tried to do the same thing last summer, but our sandwiches got sandy. Delia thought we'd have better results if we brought pre-packaged snacks instead. Unfortunately, we still ended up with mouthfuls of sand. It turns out, the concept is much better in theory than in practice.

I've loved having Morgan around. The three of us don't get to spend that much time together, so I've been soaking up every minute.

"You're welcome here anytime, Morgan," Delia says, taking the words from my mind.

Morgan smiles. "I might just take you up on that. By the time I get through finals, I think I'll be ready for another vacation."

"Have you thought about living here after you graduate?" Delia asks. "Your lease expires in June, doesn't it? And you don't have a job lined up yet. You could stay here for a while if you wanted, you know."

Surprise sweeps over Morgan's features. "Seriously? But this place is a two-bedroom."

"You can take my room," Delia says. "I stay at Tanner's place most nights, anyway. You might have to share with me if I get mad at him, but other than that, it's all yours."

Morgan rolls her lips. She looks excited but also uncertain. My younger sister isn't a big risk taker. She probably has a million questions racing through her head, so I do what I can to reassure her.

"It'd be awesome if you stayed for a while," I say honestly.

She smiles slightly, as if toying with the idea. "I'll think about it."

***

Finding a hole in my sweatpants five minutes before Cynthia is supposed to arrive is less than ideal, especially when I'm still rushing to get things ready.

268

As I bend to grab a pile of blankets from the bottom shelf of the closet, I notice a hole in the middle of my thigh. It's nothing too egregious—a penny-sized rip revealing a slice of skin—but it's visible when I'm crouching. I used to wear these sweats during movie marathons with Cynthia back in our Kells College days. After seven years, I shouldn't be surprised they've started to deteriorate.

Unfortunately, I don't have time to change clothes. Cynthia has been sending me status updates since she left New York this afternoon. Her last update said she'd reached Seaview, which means she'll be here any minute.

It looks like Cynthia will be seeing my hole-ridden sweatpants in all their glory. It's far from the worst state she's ever seen me in. She once held my hair back while I threw up on the sidewalk after taking one too many shots at a frat party.

A tiny hole in my pant leg? That's nothing.

We're having a casual night, anyway. It's a long drive from New York, so I figure Cynthia will be exhausted. I gathered everything we need for a cozy night at home. Snacks. Booze. Blankets to wrap ourselves in while we watch crappy movies in the living room. Neither of us will be thinking about what I'm wearing when we're stuffing our faces with candy.

My heart drums as I carry the blankets to the living room. Tonight is the night I'm finally going to tell Cynthia about Dominic. She's here for the entire weekend, but I figure it's best to get the uncomfortable stuff out of the way first.

I know she's eager for answers. I wonder how she will react when she finally learns the truth. Will she be upset with me for lying? Hurt? Hopefully, she'll understand why I did it. I honestly believed concealing the details of the breakup was best for everyone.

The uncertainty of it all has my stomach doing backflips. Still, I'm ready for it, and I'll weather whatever reaction she has. I've let this lie carry on for too long. I owe Cynthia the truth. Maybe then we'll get back to being us again.

A car door slams. Jason jumps up from the kitchen floor like a shot, running toward the door. Scurrying to the living room, I peek out the front window. A black hatchback idles in the driveway. Cynthia stands beside it, stretching her back. She's wearing an old Kells College sweatshirt and her hair is in a frizzy bun. She looks so…Cynthia.

Seeing my best friend for the first time in ages puts a lump in my throat. I can't wait any longer. Rushing to the foyer, I shove my feet into the first pair of shoes I find and bolt out the door. My footsteps get Cynthia's attention immediately.

A smile stretches across her face. "Izzy!"

We run toward each other, meeting in an embrace. It's warm and comforting and—oh my god—I can't believe it's been almost a year since I last hugged Cynthia.

We break apart seconds later. Cynthia glances at the Kells College emblem on my sweatpants. "I guess we were both feeling nostalgic," she says, grinning.

My insides feel soft and mushy. "You have no idea how happy I am to see you." The last few months I spent living in New York were awful. I felt so disconnected from Cynthia. I hated lying to her. Standing in front of her now, I can't remember why I kept the truth from her at all. She always has my back. Always.

"I'm starting to see why you ditched New York," she says, eying the quaint neighborhood around us. "This place is adorable. We have to get up early tomorrow, so we can start crossing off items on my itinerary."

"The beach picnic is a bad idea," I tell her. "I'll do it because I love you. But Delia, Morgan and I tried to do the same thing earlier this week, and you wouldn't believe—"

The passenger door abruptly opens, and Dominic emerges in a pair of cargo shorts and flip-flops. "Shit, I thought it'd be warmer," he says, shivering in the mid-forties air. He breaks into a wide smile when his eyes land on me. "Izzy, hey."

Everything inside me freezes. Dominic. In Seaview. I almost don't believe it. It seems like a fever dream. A horrible nightmare that jolts you awake in the middle of the night, shaking and covered in sweat.

When I don't say anything, Dominic takes my silence as an invitation. He steps toward me and pulls me against him. I feel like a ragdoll as he wraps his arms around my back, overwhelming me with the scent of his cologne.

Revulsion rolls in my stomach. Has his cologne always been so potent? Dominic smells like he bathed in it. God, how did I sleep in the same bed as him for months?

Dominic lets go, and I take a step back. I'm stiffer than a board, my muscles tight and tense. "What are you doing here?" I ask when I find my voice again.

He looks at me like I'm making a joke he doesn't understand. "What do you mean? You think I'd pass up a chance at a free vacation? I thought you knew me better than that." Chuckling to himself, he gives me a playful punch on the shoulder, which adds to my annoyance. Was the step back not clear enough? I don't want him touching me.

I fold my arms against my chest. "I didn't know you were coming."

"You invited us." Is he being serious? I figured he'd hear about the trip from Cynthia, but I never invited him. And I certainly didn't expect him to have the nerve to show up here. It should go without saying that my *ex-boyfriend* isn't welcome to spend the weekend at my sister's place. I can't decide if he's being deliberately obtuse or if he's really this naïve.

Cynthia glances between us, perplexed. "You said you talked to Izzy about this," she says, turning a critical eye toward Dominic. Satisfaction blooms in my chest as he shifts on his feet, visibly uncomfortable. *Yeah, asshole. Explain yourself.*

"I swear I mentioned it the last time we texted," he says. "Didn't I?" Bullshit. The last time I heard from him was over a month ago. He sent me a message on a random Tuesday night saying he missed me and hoped I was doing well. Given that I *don't* miss him and *don't* wish him well, I chose not to respond. No reasonable person would take that text to mean that he was planning to crash Cynthia's trip.

I grit my teeth. "No, you didn't." There's a definite edge to my voice. It's been a while since I've had to pretend to be Dominic's friend, so I'm out of practice. Cynthia appears to pick up on the tension.

Dominic runs a hand through the back of his hair. "Can we talk for a sec?" he asks, nodding toward the porch.

I'd really like to yell at him, so I say yes. Once we're far enough that Cynthia won't be able to hear us, I let my anger fly. "What the hell, Dominic? You know I didn't invite you." I'm still processing it. My ex-boyfriend is in town, and he's planning to spend the weekend at my house. What did I do to deserve this?

"I didn't think it was a big deal," he insists.

"Oh, really? Is that why you kept it a secret?"

"C'mon, Izzy." He says my name like I'm being unreasonable. It's bold of him to try to control my reaction when he's the one who ambushed me. All this could've been avoided had he stayed in New York. "I didn't come all this way to fight with you."

"You shouldn't have come at all."

Dominic sighs in frustration. "Can we please just have a good time tonight? Cynthia has been talking about this trip for weeks. I don't want to ruin it for her." The audacity of this man is something. He wants to blame *me* for ruining the weekend?

"I—" I steal a glance at Cynthia, who's watching the exchange with a deep line between her brows. For a second, I imagine things from her perspective. She just drove four hours to see me, and now I'm arguing with our friend. Our friend who I had a totally amicable breakup with. She must be so confused.

Irritated, I turn back to Dominic. "Why did you come here? Really?"

He shrugs. "We're all friends. Why shouldn't I be here?"

He's acting like it's no big deal, but I think I know what this is about. Dominic probably got spooked when he found out Cynthia was coming here. With us together, and him hours away, it would've been so easy for me to tell her everything. Dominic knew what might happen, and he tagged along to stop it.

The way I see it, I have two choices: blow everything up right now or pretend I'm fine. Getting the truth off my chest would be so satisfying, watching Dominic's face turning red as I skewer him for being a horrible boyfriend. But where would it leave me?

Cynthia knows nothing. If I go off on Dominic, then she'll realize I've been hiding the truth from her. There's a reason I wanted to talk to her about this in person. She's going to be upset. She might even feel betrayed. Acting rashly could cost me our friendship. Do I really want to take that risk?

After a moment of hesitation, I decide Dominic isn't worth it. Swiveling away from him, I follow the porch steps back to Cynthia.

"We should go out tonight," I say.

She frowns. "Really? I thought you wanted to stay in."

A few minutes ago, nothing sounded more appealing than a quiet night at home, but that isn't a viable option with Dominic here. It creates too many opportunities for us to interact one on one. And if I'm going to survive this weekend, then I need to keep my direct contact with him to a minimum. Which should be easier to do in a busy bar.

"Yeah. There's a great bar in town. I'd love to take you there."

"That's good with me," Cynthia says. "But I'll need some time to get ready. I did spend the last four hours in the car."

"Why don't we plan for seven, then?"

"Sounds perfect."

As Cynthia goes to collect her bags from the trunk, Dominic brushes past me.

"Thank you," he whispers.

I don't acknowledge him. I didn't do this for him. I don't want him to be under the false impression that we're on the same side. I might not be interested in causing trouble tonight, but that doesn't mean I'm ready to let our past go.

I'm burying it. For now.

Twenty-Six

Izzy

"They've been hooking up since at least Christmas," Cynthia tells me as she swirls her cocktail straw around her gin and tonic. "I saw Ron coming out of her apartment one morning in a pair of candy cane pajamas. I don't think he was there to fix her garbage disposal."

I shake my head in disbelief. "My brain can't process this." How can Ms. Torres, the sweet woman who lived across the hall from me for years, be dating Ron, the building's crotchety manager? Ms. Torres used to bake us bread and let me and Cynthia play with her French bulldog. Ron, on the other hand, tried blaming us when a pipe burst in our apartment, ruining everything in our pantry. "I don't know what's more horrifying: the thought of them as a couple or Ron in candy cane pajamas."

Cynthia laughs. "He hasn't made direct eye contact with me since. I guess he was embarrassed to be caught doing the walk of shame."

"Well, this explains why Ms. Torres never got in trouble for Sadie." My old apartment building has a strict no-pets policy, and Ms. Torres' dog has a loud bark. I never understood how she got away with having her there. "Ron must've been playing the long game."

"You'd think he'd be less cranky now that he's getting some," Cynthia says, "but he still leaves passive aggressive notes in the lobby whenever someone tries to put a welcome mat outside their door, claiming it's a fire hazard." She makes a pouty face as she drops her straw in her near-empty drink. "I thought love was supposed to bring out the best in people."

I shrug my shoulders. "It turns some people into assholes, I guess."

Dominic materializes at the side of the table, sporting an easy grin. "Reinforcements have arrived, ladies," he says smugly, handing me an espresso martini and Cynthia a fresh gin and tonic. He plops onto the chair beside me, swallowing half his beer in one gulp.

His elbow bumps my arm when he wipes his mouth with the back of his hand. I scoot my chair toward the edge of the table. I hate that we ended up next to each other. I purposefully stayed away from him when we were walking into the bar, but he got to the table first and pulled out the seat beside his and offered it to me. I've been inching away from him all night, wanting every inch of distance possible.

Frankly, I'm amazed we even got a table—Seaview Tavern is jammed. Clusters of people mill around the bar area, searching for an open seat. Some have taken to the small stage normally used for live music, sitting cross-legged between pieces of band equipment. Chatter buzzes in the air, though it's overwhelmed by the music blasting over the loudspeakers. Cynthia and I have had to repeat ourselves on more than one occasion.

We've been here for about an hour, and it's only gotten busier. That should excite me. The bar is noisy and chaotic and distracting, which is exactly what I wanted. Except the commotion isn't helping the way I thought it would. I'm trying not to focus on Dominic, but it's hard when I can smell the beer on his breath and feel the heat radiating off his body.

I haven't said a single word to him, but he has still wormed his way into every conversation. He even took a sip of my last espresso martini. Just picked up the glass and put his mouth on it as if it was no big deal. I think he's trying to overcompensate for my obvious discomfort by being overly friendly, and it's getting on my nerves.

Dominic's presence, combined with the bar's frantic energy, has me feeling edgy. Instead of taking my mind off things, the crowd is overwhelming me. I haven't stopped sweating since we got here, and my stomach is in knots. The alcohol isn't doing me any favors.

"All right, Izzy," Cynthia says, tipping her glass toward me. "Let's hear about you."

I drink my martini. "You'll have to be more specific."

"I just told you all about my drama. Now, I wanna hear yours."

"I don't think Ron and Ms. Torres' relationship qualifies as your drama."

Cynthia rolls her eyes. "You know what I mean. You moved to a new town in a different state. Got a new job. Yet you've barely told us anything. I want details."

I drop my gaze to the rim of my glass. How much do I tell her with Dominic sitting here? Obviously, I can't talk about what's really on my mind. But I don't feel like giving him any other insight into my life either.

I could share something simple, like how strange it feels living in a small town after years in a massive city, or what it's like being a first-time dog owner, but those topics feel too generic. Cynthia wants something honest and real. She isn't going to let up till she gets it.

"Well, my focus lately has been on keeping a bunch of kids from eating paint," I say, garnering baffled looks from the table. "I'm friends with a teacher at the local elementary school. I volunteer doing art projects with her students."

Cynthia smiles. "That's great, Iz."

"I know. The kids are awesome, though there's this one who likes to give me trouble. Still, I love being in the classroom."

"You're volunteering in a *school*?" Dominic says, his eyes going as wide as dinner plates. "Christ, what planet is this?" Irritation bristles in the back of my mind.

You can't kill him, Izzy. Murder equals bad.

Ignoring Dominic's slight, I redirect my attention to Cynthia. "I've been doing it once a week for a couple months."

"I bet those kids love you," she says as she goes for a sip of her gin and tonic. "So, what else has been going on? Any other exciting news?" She rests her chin on the bridge of her knuckles, her expression thoughtful and open.

I know what she's waiting for. When she told me she was coming to visit, I promised I would finally come clean. My new hobby as a part-time volunteer art teacher doesn't explain why I've been distancing myself from my best friend.

Unfortunately, the reason for our fractured relationship is sitting right beside me. I can't admit the truth with Dominic breathing down my neck.

"Not really," I reply, fiddling with the stem of my glass. "I'm still working for Delia's boyfriend, so it's been a lot of the same old." Cynthia's face falls, and it crushes me. I hate Dominic for this. For making me lie again. This was supposed to be the weekend I got my friend back, freed myself from the heavy weight of this secret. Dominic swept in like the Grim Reaper and destroyed my chances at repairing this relationship.

"I had the craziest experience on a shoot the other day," Dominic says suddenly. Of course he would change the subject from my career to his own. "These parents hired me to shoot their kids fishing in Central Park. And let's just say you do *not* want to know where this kid put his fishing hook…"

My attention fades as Dominic rambles, and my eyes wander. A group of middle-aged guys chat around the pool table. A cluster of kids celebrating someone's twenty-first birthday takes up the corner booth. My brain skitters to a halt when I reach the back of the bar, catching sight of a familiar face.

Jacob's here. He's sitting across from a dark-haired woman at a table along the wall. Nodding at something she says, he wraps his long fingers around the tall glass in front of him, picks it up, and takes a drink. He looks casual, comfortable. Happy.

Seeing Jacob at Seaview Tavern shouldn't surprise me—this is, after all, the best bar in town. But I didn't know he had plans tonight. He didn't say anything when we were texting this afternoon. I wonder why.

Slowly, I begin to connect the dots. Jacob isn't wearing his glasses. And I don't recognize the woman he's with, but she's pretty in that fresh-faced I-rolled-out-of-bed-like-this way. It has to be Catherine. She looks like the kind of woman who would want a simple yet elegant wedding, two kids, and a dog. And she's staring at Jacob with a hopeful gleam in her eye, like maybe he's the one who will give those things to her.

Emotion tears through my organs like a hot knife. Knowing Jacob was dating someone stung, but seeing it with my own eyes is a different form of pain. He didn't say much about his first date with Catherine the other night, so I assumed it didn't go well. Clearly, that wasn't the case. Not if Jacob brought Catherine to his favorite bar. You wouldn't introduce someone to a place you love unless you planned on seeing them again.

My stomach rolls. What's going on in his head right now? Is he thinking about having sex with her? Picturing their future together? And why didn't he tell me he was going on another date with her? I'm supposed to be his dating advisor. Shouldn't I be in the loop on these sorts of things? Why would he hide this from me?

Maybe their first date went so well that Jacob doesn't think he needs me anymore. Maybe he had an instant connection with Catherine, and he knows deep in his bones that this is the woman he wants to marry.

My vision goes blurry as Catherine slides her hand across the table, placing it over Jacob's. Something hot and sharp pops in my chest. I can't watch any more of this, so I tear my gaze away from them.

I'm lightheaded. My skin feels tingly and feverish. There's a funny ringing sound in my ears, like I knocked my head against something hard, and I'm struggling to reorient myself. It's so hot in here. The lights are too bright, the noises too loud.

Everything is too much.

"Izzy, are you all right?" Cynthia asks, her voice fraught with concern. It feels like I'm seeing her from underwater, her features warped and blurry.

"I'm fine," I insist as I stumble out of my chair. I catch the side of the table before I fall and manage to stay on my feet. "I just need a minute."

Before she can respond, I'm heading out the back door, tears building in my eyes.

***

Jacob
I'm not staring at Izzy.

Okay, maybe I am. But it's hard not to when she's visibly uncomfortable. Her friend keeps angling his chair in her direction, seemingly oblivious to the fact that she's been acting like he has something contagious for the past hour. He took a sip from her drink earlier, and she looked like she wanted to be sick.

Who is he? Izzy told me her friend Cynthia was visiting for the weekend, but she didn't mention anyone else. The guy beside her has blonde hair and is wearing cargo shorts. Does this douchebag not realize it's March?

The guy says something to Izzy, and heat flares in her eyes. She's livid. I don't think I've ever seen her this angry. I wonder if that guy is Dominic. Izzy's ex is part of her old friend group, but there's no way she invited him here. She left New York to get away from him. He wouldn't show up unannounced, would he?

Then again, this is the guy who made Izzy feel like shit for talking to him about her feelings. His judgment is garbage.

The more I watch Izzy, the more concerned I become. She was excited about Cynthia's visit. So, why does she look so dejected? Izzy's emotions aren't usually this transparent.

Every impulse in me is firing. *Go over there. Find out what's going on.* I tap my foot, my body whizzing with adrenaline.

"So, is she friendly?" Catherine asks. "I've wanted a dog forever." Her expression is open and curious as she waits for my response. I've been so focused on Izzy that it takes a few seconds for me to recall what we were talking about. Oh, right. Lulu.

"Very friendly," I reply. "The kids in my neighborhood always want to pet her when I take her on walks. She loves the attention." Lulu will happily lie down on the cold sidewalk if it means getting a few belly scratches.

Catherine's smile lights up her entire face. "My neighbor had a boxer when I was growing up. She was the sweetest."

"I can connect you with the shelter where I got Lulu. They're really helpful to first-time pet owners."

"That would be amazing. Maybe Lulu and my future dog can be walking buddies." Smiling, she reaches for a chip in the little plastic basket sitting between us. Tossing it in her mouth, she crunches softly.

I know I should be the one to fill the silence, but I've had a hard time making conversation since I realized Izzy was here.

Catherine is great. Kind and pretty and smart. We have a lot in common. A love for dogs and *Galactic Rush.* A desire for a quiet, simple life with the right person. Going on a second date was a no-brainer. With the awkwardness of the first date behind us, I figured we'd have a nice time getting to know each other.

Then I saw Izzy, and everything went to hell.

I'm trying to get over her. I'm on a date with a wonderful woman, one who's actually interested in me, but instead of asking her questions, I'm obsessively checking a table twenty feet away. Going out with Catherine seemed like the easiest way to move on, but it isn't working. That's because moving on requires you to want to move on. And I'm holding onto my feelings for Izzy like they're something precious.

I've never had feelings like this. So strong and certain. When I look at Izzy, there's a sense of rightness, of belonging. *That's it*, my brain says. *That's her.*

My dad once told me that he realized he loved my mom when she was mad at him. He got the time of a date wrong and accidentally stood her up. *I'd rather fight with her than have a good time with someone else*, he said.

That's how I feel about Izzy. I want to be with her, even if it involves something as awkward as having drinks with her asshole ex-boyfriend.

The fact is, I'm in love with her. Perfection with someone else is nothing compared to complicated with Izzy. A pleasant date with a nice woman isn't going to make feelings like these go away. Not when I'm gripping the edge of the table to stop myself from running over there to ask Izzy what's wrong and what I can do to fix it.

It's bad. So bad. Izzy has made it clear she isn't interested, and we just got our friendship back on track. I don't want to ruin things, but I can't keep pretending my feelings don't exist. How can you expect to get over someone if you don't accept that you want them first?

I'm going to need time—and lots of it—to deal with all this. I'm nowhere near ready to be in a relationship with someone else. Catherine is nice, but she isn't Izzy. She deserves better than my pathetic attempt at getting over Izzy.

As if she can sense me thinking about her, Catherine stretches her hand across the table, placing it over mine.

"Should we order another appetizer?" she asks, nodding toward the near empty chip basket.

Guilt lodges in my throat. I didn't mean to lead her on. I wish I would've had this epiphany before I agreed to a second date. "Catherine," I say, "you seem like an amazing person, and I've really enjoyed getting to know you, but I—"

She groans. "Those words are never good."

"I don't think this is gonna work out. I'm sorry."

Nodding, Catherine pulls her hand back to her side of the table. "Was it the dog thing?" she asks. "Because that wasn't me implying that we should, you know, adopt one together."

I shake my head firmly. "Not at all. This is on me. I thought I was ready to date, but I'm not. I'm sorry for wasting your time."

Catherine looks disappointed, but she tells me she understands. Within two minutes, she gathers her purse and coat and heads out the door. Once she's gone, my focus returns to Izzy. When I glance back at her table, however, she's not there.

I take a quick scan of the bar, but I don't see her anywhere. Her friends are still at their table, which means they haven't left yet. So, where is she? I spend a few minutes searching, but she's nowhere to be found.

When the server comes back to my table, I quickly pay my bill. Izzy still hasn't gotten back to her friends. I wonder if she's outside. That's where she was on New Year's, after all. I can't leave until I talk to her, so I decide to check.

Setting my sights on the door, I make my way through the crowded bar. I push open the sliding glass, and then I step into the night.

Twenty-Seven

Jacob

Izzy's here, and she's crying.

She hunches in a metal patio chair facing away from the bar. Her shoulders shake as her muffled cries drift into the quiet night. There's only one light source, a small bulb glowing by the back door, so it feels dark and secluded.

At the slide of the door, Izzy glances over her shoulder. Her face is mostly concealed by shadows, but I catch a glimpse of her red-rimmed eyes and the makeup smudged around them like war paint.

I observe her for a minute, frozen. Seeing her like this hurts something fierce. My heart pounds furiously, my brain pleading with me to do something. It feels like I'm trapped in a room rapidly filling with water. I have to act now.

At first, Izzy seems embarrassed to be caught in a vulnerable moment, but her reaction changes when she registers it's me standing behind her. She lets out a deep, unsteady breath. "Jake." There's relief in her voice, unadulterated and raw. She isn't hiding anything. I've never seen her this unguarded before. I don't know if she's doing it intentionally, letting me see her this way, but it knocks the air out of my lungs.

Instinct takes over. Without thinking, I rush toward Izzy, kneel in front of her, and cradle her face between my palms. "Hey. Hey. What's going on?" My voice is calm but urgent. I want to help, but I don't want to overwhelm her. So I let Izzy take her time, trailing my thumb along her wet cheek as I wait for a reply.

I want to be this person for her. The one she turns to at her lowest. The one she feels comfortable being open with. I've never wanted anything more. The need is so strong it feels as though it's clawing out of my chest.

Her chin wobbles. "Dominic's here."

The words land like a missile. So my suspicion was right. "I'm guessing he's the guy who was sitting next to you."

Izzy nods. "He came with Cynthia. She didn't bother to warn me. Cynthia thinks we're cool, but Dominic is still my ex-boyfriend. I didn't think I needed to clarify that he wasn't invited to stay at my house. He's acting like everything's fine, and I just have to sit there and deal with it."

Anger twists in my gut. "You shouldn't have to deal with it."

"I know. But Cynthia drove all this way, and she's only here for a couple days. I don't want us to be fighting the entire time. Wanna know the worst part? I was going to talk to her. Be honest about Dominic. It seemed like the perfect opportunity for us to reconnect. But now, he's here, and everything is ruined again."

I hate this so much. I'd gladly tell that guy to get the hell out of town, but I think it would only make Izzy more upset. "Why don't I take you home?"

She clutches my forearm as if she's holding me in place. She doesn't have to worry—I'm not going anywhere. But I like the way her hand feels on my skin, the light press of her fingernails.

She lowers her head against my shoulder. "I can't leave Cynthia," she mutters. "Besides, I've already pulled you away from your date for long enough. Catherine is probably wondering what happened to you."

"She left, actually. It's not going to work out with her."

Izzy pulls back to look me in the eye. "What? Why?"

Because she's not you. "It's just not a good fit."

Something snaps in Izzy's eyes. The vulnerability evaporates, replaced by worry. She untangles herself from me immediately, pushing out of her chair to step away. "She left because you came out here to talk to me, didn't she? God, I'm *such* an asshole."

At once, I'm on my feet. "She left because I told her it wasn't going to work. And you didn't make me come out here, Forrest."

Izzy shakes her head. "No, you came out here because you're a good guy," she says, sighing. "You mean well, Jacob, but I can't keep letting you take responsibility for my problems. I'm officially ending our deal, okay? I'm actually sabotaging your chances of finding someone." She paces the length of the patio.

"I'm not out here because of the agreement we made. I care about you. I had to make sure you were okay." I'm irritated by her trying to dismiss my concern using the deal we agreed to. I haven't thought about it in months. This—*us,* we're so much more than that.

"That's the problem," Izzy insists, her pacing growing more frantic. "This is not a healthy friendship. You're not on a date right now because of me. And that woman was into you. She touched your hand, and she was trying to play footsie with you under the table. You don't do those things unless you think it's gonna work out."

"Exactly how much of my date were you watching?" The question tumbles out of me instantly. While I spent most of my night sneaking glances at Izzy's table, I didn't realize she was doing the same.

She scoffs. "It was obvious. Anyone in the bar could see it." Her tone is sharp and defensive, and she isn't meeting my eye. Clearly, she wants to drop the subject, and under normal circumstances, I would let it go. But something's telling me to press her.

Why was Izzy paying attention to my date? Shouldn't she have been focused on her friend, the one she hasn't seen in almost a year?

"I know why I've been looking at your table all night, Forrest. Why were you looking at mine?" I'm tired of dancing around the truth with her. Being direct is the only way I'm ever going to get answers.

She crosses her arms. "Jacob, please don't make this a thing."

"It already is a thing," I tell her. "I'm sick of pretending that it's not. You didn't talk to me for two weeks after we kissed, Izzy. What was up with that?"

"I was afraid it was going to ruin our friendship! We needed time apart for the awkwardness to subside," she argues, determination set in her brow.

I press harder. "No, that isn't how you work."

"What is that supposed to mean?"

"You thrive in awkward situations. Half the time, you purposefully create them." Izzy loves pushing people's buttons. Seeing how they'll respond to it. "If this was about you feeling awkward, you would've had no problem addressing it. You only deflect when you feel vulnerable." I know Izzy. She runs when she feels like she's headed into deeper emotional territory than she's comfortable with.

"I don't know what you're trying to get at here," she snaps, "but you went on a date with someone weeks after we kissed. If it was that big of a deal, then why did you go out with Catherine?" My irritation deepens. I won't let her make me the one who has been in denial. Not when I've been losing my mind trying to figure out what's going on with her.

"Because I thought it was what you wanted! You wouldn't talk to me. Do you know how miserable I was? I needed to do *something* to get you to stop shutting me out. It was the only thing I could do to make you stop avoiding me."

She parts her lips, but nothing comes out. For the first time, I've rendered Izzy Forrest speechless, and I have to use it to my advantage.

"But I get it now," I say. "I get why you were ignoring me. It's because you knew what I was going to say, isn't it? And you didn't want to hear how long I'd been thinking about kissing you. How I haven't stopped thinking about it since. You didn't want to hear about the way you've completely changed how I experience happiness."

"Jacob, please. Don't." Her bottom lip trembles, but her eyes remain fiery, an icy-blue heat that scalds my veins. I take a step closer to her, refusing to let up. I've held these words in for too long already. There's no way I'm stopping now.

"Everything revolves around you, Izzy," I tell her. "Whether you're happy. Whether we've talked during the day. I'm always trying to get your attention." How can you not see how utterly obsessed with you I've become?

She looks both furious and frightened, like she wants to lob my head off, and at the same time, lock herself inside a closet to avoid me. Pissing her off may seem like an odd way to confess my feelings, but if I drop this now, we'll never do it again.

"Did seeing me with someone else bother you?" I ask bluntly.

Izzy explodes. "Of course it did! Is that what you wanted to hear so badly? Christ, Jacob, I don't get what you're trying to accomplish. You know none of this changes anything."

"What are you talking about? It changes *everything*." I run a hand through my hair, my own frustration rising. If Izzy feels the same way, then we should be together. What reservations could she possibly have? Is she worried her feelings are temporary? That they'll fade, and she'll get bored of me?

"No, it doesn't." She shakes her head adamantly. "You know what you want, Jacob. You need someone who can meet you on that level. I'm the furthest thing from ready for marriage. How could I be with you when it means keeping you from that?" Her eyes fill with tears again. She wraps her arms around herself. "I'm not what you want."

"You don't get to decide what I want," I say, hands flexing at my sides. "Did you not hear me before? Everything is different because of you. If the only thing that mattered to me was getting married, then I'd be with Catherine right now. But I was miserable tonight, because she's not you. You're what I want, Izzy. All the time. You're the only thing I think about. The only person I want to be with." We could make this work. I know it. But she needs to let go of her fears and trust me, which is not an easy feat for Izzy.

"But I'm a mess," she says, seemingly a last-ditch effort to drive me away. Instead, I move closer, leaving us separated by inches. She's beautiful, even with tear stains running down her cheeks. Full, bright red lips. Curly hair.

The delicate slope of her shoulders. Her chest rises and falls unsteadily as I brush the side of her jaw with my thumb. The muted thumps coming from inside the bar seem to disappear. There's no one but us for miles.

"Izzy, I see all of you," I say in a low voice. My pulse is so fast it feels like my heart might explode. "I like all of you. Especially the messy parts."

There's nothing left to say. So I stop using words. Angling her face toward mine, I lean down and press my mouth to hers.

***

Izzy

Jacob's kiss is like gasoline. It instantly sets my body ablaze. There's no way to stop myself from getting wrapped up in it. It overrides any logic I possess.

Kissing him back, I thread my fingers through his hair. It's just as soft as I remember. I love the way it feels between my fingers. Jacob seems to like it, too. He makes a low sound in the back of his throat and wraps an arm around my waist, hauling my body against his.

We spend a few minutes like that. Devouring each other. I can't recall the last time I took a breath, but I don't think I need oxygen anymore. Just Jacob's mouth. And hands.

When we break apart, my head is spinning. Then the warm press of Jacob's mouth descends to my jaw, my throat. He's moving urgently, as if he's up against the clock. His hands roam with a similar franticness, touching the bare skin where the back of my shirt has ridden up.

He's everywhere. Invading my senses with his clean laundry scent and his explosive touch. All I can do is wrap my hand around the back of his neck and lose myself in sensation.

"Jake, you feel so good," I whisper as his wet mouth covers the side of my neck.

He pulls back for a second, breathing ragged. "I love it when you call me that."

"Jake?"

"Mhmm." He's kissing my neck again. "It makes me think you're out of control, too. If you feel even a fraction of this, Izzy…that's all I need." A fraction. I feel so much more than a fraction. Everything and then some. A whole fucking pile of numbers.

I'm about to correct him on this, but then Jacob's mouth finds mine again, and I lose the thought entirely.

"You have no idea how much time I've spent thinking about this," he says against my lips. "The things I'd do if I got my hands on you again. It's been killing me not to touch you. I've been waiting for you to notice."

"I noticed." The truth comes out without me even thinking about it. Apparently, Jacob has scrambled my brain. "I didn't want to admit it, not even to myself, but I've always seen the way you look at me. And I've always liked it."

He grins. He has such a nice smile. So warm and open and Jacob. My pulse quickens. I never want him to stop smiling at me. Ever.

Jacob's mouth travels to my ear. "Then let me show you what I've been thinking about." I suddenly become aware of his hardness between us.

Okay, maybe he can stop smiling to do *that*.

I kiss him fiercely on the mouth. "We have to get out of here," I say. Or else I'm going to have sex with him on this porch. And I don't want us to spend our first night together in a jail cell. "Let's go to your place."

Jacob reacts right away. Grabbing my hand, he leads me down the porch steps and around the side of the building to the parking lot. He already has his keys out of his pocket, the lights on his sedan flashing briefly as he unlocks it. He doesn't let go of my hand until we get to the car. Even then, he follows me to the passenger side, planting a firm kiss on my lips before scrambling over to the driver's side.

Jacob flings open the door and climbs inside, quickly starting up the car. I'm inside a second later, pulling my seatbelt on.

We're out of the parking lot in less than a minute. The drive to Jacob's place isn't long, but every second we're not touching makes my skin itchy. How did I go so long without kissing him? It's only been a few minutes, and I'm already desperate to touch him again.

Unable to help myself, I reach across the center console, placing a hand on his thigh. I circle my thumb against the hard muscle.

Jacob glances at me briefly. His grip on the steering wheel is stark white. "Forrest, I'm going to crash the fucking car if you don't stop," he says through gritted teeth. He sounds like he's in pain, and I love that he's this keyed up because of me, that I affect him so much.

When we get to the house, we make it to the porch slowly and clumsily, pausing to kiss every few feet. I'm pressed against Jacob's side as he tries to unlock the front door, and my wandering hands seem to make it hard for him to slide the key in. He groans in frustration, and I laugh, and he pinches my side.

Once the door is open, we stumble inside and take the stairs up to Jacob's bedroom. His mouth and hands are all over me as he walks me toward the bed. The backs of my legs hit the mattress, and I fall back onto a plush comforter, dragging Jacob with me. He props himself up on his elbows, caging me in as his lips feather along my jaw. I can feel him smiling against my skin, so I grab the sides of his face and force him to look me square in the eye.

"What?" I ask.

He shakes his head, still smiling to himself. "I convinced myself you didn't feel this." Those words send a wave of emotion barreling through me. I don't want to think about it, the way he must've felt when I was avoiding him, so I kiss him instead.

Jacob's hands glide up my sides, drawing out goosebumps. He gives me a look. *Is this okay?* And I nod wordlessly, lifting the upper half of my body so he's able to pull the sweater over my head. His eyes darken when he realizes I'm not wearing a bra. He spends a moment drinking in my bare skin, the heat in his gaze scalding me alive.

Seeing the raw desire on Jacob's face does something to me. My limbs feel like they're charged with electricity. Has anyone ever looked at me like this before? I've never felt so desired, so seen. For some reason, it makes me want to cry.

And because I'm incapable of handling a serious moment like a normal person, I say something crass. "I have a nice rack, don't I?"

Laughing, he says, "shut up, Forrest." Then his mouth lands on mine again. He slips his tongue inside as his warm palms move to my chest. He cups my breasts in his hands, and it feels so good.

"You're so beautiful," he whispers before his lips descend to my neck.

A soft gasp leaves my throat when Jacob's open-mouthed kisses reach my breasts. He pulls one nipple between his teeth while palming my other breast. His ministrations make my head go fuzzy. I tangle my hands in his hair and hold him close.

When he's finished lavishing my chest with attention, he kisses a line down the center of my stomach. He pops the button on my jeans and tugs them down my legs. Blood roars in my ears as he kisses around the edges of my panties. I'm practically panting by the time he pushes my underwear aside and finally puts his mouth on me.

Jacob plays my body like an accordion, his mouth and fingers working in perfect tandem.

I thrash in the bed sheets as the heat in my core grows hotter, threatening to burn me from the inside. Jacob pins my thighs to the bed as he works me over. I moan his name as the pressure builds. More. More. More.

"Jake. Oh my god." Stars swirl behind my eyes as I completely fall apart. I drop back on the pillows, a sweaty, breathless mess. My bones feel like they're made of jelly.

Jacob crawls up the bed and stretches out beside me, propping his head up with his elbow so he can watch me come down from my high. "That was perfect," he says, brushing a sweaty lock of hair behind my ear. "You're perfect." His tone is pure adoration. And even though I feel boneless and satiated, it's still not enough. I need more of him.

Pressing my lips to his, I climb into his lap. Jacob sits up, resting his back against the headboard. "My turn," I tell him as I pepper kisses along the underside of his jaw.

My hands slip under his shirt, feeling the planes of his stomach. He's still wearing clothes, which is ridiculous. I quickly remedy the situation, tugging his shirt over his head and tossing it on the floor. Seconds later, Jacob shucks off his jeans. He's all long limbs and warm skin, and he feels like mine.

Jacob grabs my wrist when my hand dips beneath the waistband of his boxers. "I can't handle that right now, Forrest," he says. "I think it would actually kill me."

I can't help but tease him. "Quick to the trigger, are we?"

He kisses the corner of my mouth. "I'd tell you to shut up again, but I liked hearing you." Tension once again builds in my center.

Instead of responding, I shove down Jacob's boxers. Letting my thighs fall on either side of his waist, I kiss him urgently. "Condom," I say breathlessly against his bottom lip.

"In the drawer on the nightstand."

I quickly retrieve a square packet from the drawer. Jacob's gaze feels like a pile of bricks as I tear it open and slip it on him. His eyes are wide, and his breathing is shallow.

This is new territory for us, thrilling and nerve-wracking, but it also feels comfortable and natural. Because it's us. And everything with Jacob feels right.

Heart hammering, I slowly lower myself onto him. Both of us groan as he fills me, pressure coiling like a spring. Bracing my palms on his shoulders, I begin to move my hips. Holy shit. Pleasure scatters through me as I work faster, eventually finding a rhythm that has black spots flooding my vision. Jacob closes his mouth over my nipple. The wet heat of his mouth, combined with the intense fullness, has every cell in my body on fire.

"*Fuck*, Izzy." Gripping my waist, Jacob suddenly flips our positions, caging me to the bed as he thrusts into me. I dig my nails into his shoulders, losing myself to the feeling of Jacob's skin on mine and his scent surrounding me.

With every move, the pressure inside me grows tighter, a string being pulled from either end, and then it snaps. Waves of euphoria wash over me as I break apart. Jacob is right there with me, burying his face in my neck and telling me how good I feel as he finds his own release.

In the aftermath, we stare at each other, both of us struggling to regain our breath. The room is dark, hiding parts of Jacob's face, but the intensity of his gaze is impossible to conceal. I see everything. The emotion. The sincerity. There's no going back from this. Things for us will never be the same.

And as good as it feels to have given into my feelings for him, I can't ignore the pinch of fear spreading through my chest. *There's no going back from this. Things for us will never be the same.*

Twenty-Eight

Jacob

Holy shit. *Holy. Shit.*

Izzy's head rests on my shoulder, her body pressed against my side and her soft breaths brushing over my skin. One of her hands is locked in mine, lying in the center of my chest. Izzy lifts our joint fingers, relinquishing her grip so she can press our palms flat together, before intertwining our fingers again.

"You have nice hands," she says, sweeping her fingertips over my knuckles. She pulls my hand toward her face as if she wants to inspect it more closely, and I let her. Izzy Forrest can do whatever she wants with me. I'll gladly be her rag doll.

Turning my head, I press a kiss to the outside of her palm. "Thanks."

"You're also good at sex," she says. "Very good. Even better than in my dreams."

Heat stirs in my veins, disrupting the lazy mood. "You've dreamt about me?" I'm not playing it cool at all, but I don't care. The thought of Izzy dreaming about me feels like a drug entering my bloodstream.

Hearing the eagerness in my voice seems to unlock her playful side. She grins mischievously as she presses her cheek to my pillow. "Oh, yeah," she confirms. "They were some dirty dreams, too. There was this one where we were back at the bar playing darts, and you tried to distract me by getting on your knees and—"

I cut her off with a kiss. I want to go again, but I won't last long if she keeps talking like that. Her lips vibrate against mine with laughter. I bet she knows exactly what I'm thinking.

Izzy pulls back after a second, a sleepy smile on her face. She curls her fingers around the back of my neck. "I'm a little offended you haven't been dreaming about me," she says, pursing her lips as if annoyed.

Propping myself up on my elbows, I hover directly over her. Her floral perfume washes over me, sweet and all-consuming. "I don't need to dream about you," I tell her, tucking a strand of hair behind her ear. "You're every waking thought."

Lowering my face to her neck, I let my lips explore her skin. "Your laughter keeps me up at night." Her breathing hitches as my mouth reaches her pulse point. "At work, all I'm thinking about is when you're going to text me. And seeing you upset at the bar tonight destroyed me. Honestly, I don't know how we got home. I think I might've run a red light or two."

Izzy laughs quietly. "I'm glad we made it back to the house. I didn't want to be the second girl you've hooked up with at that bar." I give her a teasing pinch on the side when she references our first meeting.

"I've liked you since then, you know."

Her eyes widen. "Really?"

"I didn't realize it at the time, but yeah."

Looking back, it's obvious I've been obsessed with her since we met.

***

Eleven months ago

I forgot the damn shrimp.

I slam the door to my sedan as I step out at the end of Ellen's driveway, cursing myself for leaving it behind. Tanner's mom told me not to worry about bringing anything, but I didn't want to show up empty-handed, so I picked up a shrimp cocktail platter…then immediately forgot it on top of the fridge in my garage.

Should I run home and grab it? I'm already late to Ellen's cookout, but I don't want my garage to stink like rotten seafood. It's eighty-five degrees outside. That shrimp is basically in a pressure cooker. Who knows how long that smell will linger?

Besides, I'm not in a party mood. Work has been a nightmare this week. I found out my annoying coworker, Luke Daniels, is going to be put next to me when our company moves into a new office space in the fall. Luke reheats seafood in the office microwave and has no sense of personal boundaries. Being in his proximity is going to make it impossible to get anything done.

I'd much rather spend tonight commiserating at home with a beer. But I promised Tanner I'd be here, and Ellen is like a second mother to me, so blowing off her cookout isn't an option.

I'm still standing there when I hear footsteps on the pavement. I turn to see Delia Forrest coming up the sidewalk with a bottle of wine. At least she had enough sense to remember her contribution to the party.

I cast aside my frustration, giving her a polite smile. "Hey, Delia. Tanner said you were coming tonight. I wasn't sure whether to believe him." My friend won't admit it, but he likes this woman a lot. I wonder how much convincing it took to get her to come tonight.

"I was kind of strong-armed into it," Delia admits as she stops by my car. I chuckle at her response, not surprised in the slightest.

"He can be pushy."

"Actually, it wasn't by Tanner."

Delia shoots a sharp look at the short, curly-haired woman beside her. The other woman seems annoyed by Delia's anger. "Don't listen to her, Jacob," she says, rolling her eyes. "I'm paying for this tremendously."

I study her for a moment, puzzled. I've never seen this woman before. I'd know it if I had. She has a smattering of freckles across her nose and the brightest blue eyes I've ever seen. Her bow-shaped lips are redder than cherries. Everything about her says "notice me." There's no way I wouldn't remember her. So how does she know my name? And why is she talking to me like we're old friends?

"I'm sorry. Have we met before?" I ask.

The woman grins. "I'm afraid you haven't had the pleasure. I'm assuming you're Tanner's friend, Jacob. Unless there's another guy Delia failed to mention."

I glance between the two women, noticing their dark hair and similar noses. The resemblance suddenly becomes obvious. "You're Delia's sister."

The woman pats me on the shoulder like I'm a child who just figured out how to spell their own name. "They raise them sharp in Seaview, don't they?"

"Ignore her, Jacob," Delia says. "She was dropped on her head as a baby."

Their dynamic is amusing. I'm guessing they bicker a lot. Something tells me Delia is the older sibling. "The two of you are certainly...different."

Delia's sister laughs. "You can admit you like me better than Delia. You wouldn't be the first." She puts her hands on her hips, making me notice the way her dress hugs her waist like a second skin. She has round hips and the tops of her breasts peek out from her neckline. I tear my eyes away from her as soon as I realize what I'm doing. I can't check out Delia's sister. Tanner will kill me if Delia bails because I weirded out her sister.

I shift on the balls of my feet and then head up the driveway. Delia and her sister follow me to the front door, and I let us inside. I've been coming to the Ryan household since before I could talk. I've never once used the doorbell.

The party is well underway when we step inside. Clusters of people are gathered in the kitchen and living room, conversation pulsing in the air. A group of kids crowded around the TV lets out a collective cheer as they play Mario Kart. I don't see Tanner right away, but Ellen is standing by the island, talking to a woman with red hair. She catches my eye from across the room and gives me a quick wave.

Behind me, Delia and her sister are having a hushed exchange. I can't make out anything they're saying until Delia's sister suddenly proclaims, "my new friend Jacob is gonna keep me company," and shoots me a warm smile.

Confusion settles over me. "Uh, what?" Maybe Delia wasn't kidding about her sister hitting her head as a baby. Figuring she isn't going to bother with an explanation, I study Delia's tense body language. Her gaze darts to the bay window for the briefest second. That's when I see Tanner out by the grill on the back porch.

The situation immediately becomes clear. Izzy is trying to convince Delia to go talk to him. I don't mind her using me as part of her strategy. I'm in support of Tanner and Delia.

I've never seen him care so much about a woman the way he does with her. So I wait there silently while Delia's sister whispers in her ear.

Eventually, Delia straightens her shoulders. Raising her chin, she starts toward the back door. Delia's sister wastes no time before sidling up to me.

"I need you to be honest," she says, blinking up at me with wide eyes. "On a scale of one to ten, how much of a douchebag is your friend? Because if I told Delia to go out there, and he's more than a seven, then my head is on a spike."

Her bluntness catches me off guard. It's probably why my response comes out a jumbled mess. "He's not…Tanner isn't a douchebag. He can be a dick sometimes, sure. But he's definitely not a douchebag." Jesus. That was a terrible answer. I hope this conversation never gets back to Tanner. I might have to let him knee me in the balls.

"Really, he's a good guy," I add, hoping I can somehow salvage this.

Delia's sister nods slowly. "A dick, but not a douchebag. Delia can work with that." Her eyes sweep around the busy kitchen, landing on the island covered in appetizer trays. "I don't know about you, but I'm starving."

Immediately, she makes a beeline for the island. Grabbing a plate off the counter, she begins filling it with appetizers. It doesn't seem she needs me to keep her company, but I follow her over, anyway.

"So," she says as she adds a stuffed mushroom to her plate, "has this thing been going on since Delia got here? She claims she told me everything, but, knowing her, I'm guessing she left out a few details."

Heat creeps up the back of my neck. I'm not sure how much to tell her. Tanner has hardly talked to me about Delia. I don't think he'd be thrilled to hear me gossiping about their relationship with Delia's sister. "I really don't know much."

She rolls her eyes. "C'mon, Jacob. You've gotta give me something. I found them in a very interesting position this afternoon, but I'm not telling you anything unless you return the favor." Interesting position? Did Tanner hook up with Delia? He didn't say a word to me, but that might explain why he invited her to his mom's cookout.

"You probably know more than I do. Tanner's not saying much."

She frowns. "That's a shame. I guess I'll have to keep my observations to myself then." She holds her full plate out to me in offering. I shake my head, politely declining. Shrugging, she pops a sliced bell pepper into her mouth and crunches loudly.

"So, is it just me you're not interested in talking to, or do you not want to be here?" she asks between bites. "Because if it's the first thing, I can find another way to entertain myself. I'm sure those women would let me sit in for a round." She motions toward the kitchen table, where Gloria Thompson and her knitting club are playing poker.

"I doubt it," I tell her. Despite her sweet, grandmotherly appearance, Gloria is fearsome with a deck of cards. Her poker prowess is something of Seaview legend. Rumor has it Gloria hasn't paid for a drink in town in twenty years. She always runs into someone who owes her money. "Gloria likes to keep her poker games small."

"I bet she'd take mercy on me if she knew how much you wanted me to go away," she argues. "Seriously, you won't hurt my feelings if you tell me to leave you alone." Once again, I find myself stunned by this woman's directness. Does she always say the first thing that crosses her mind?

"It's not you."

"What is it, then? Do you prefer awkward silence over conversation?"

"I had a long day. And there's a mountain of shrimp rotting in my garage."

She arches a dark eyebrow. "Is that some sort of idiom?"

If only. "I didn't realize till after I got here that I left the shrimp platter I meant to bring in my garage." My stomach rolls at the thought of going home to that smell.

Delia's sister wrinkles her nose. "No wonder you're not interested in conversation," she says, looking disgusted. "How attached are you to this house?"

"I bought it six months ago. I'd say pretty attached."

She sets her half-empty appetizer plate on the nearest counter. "C'mon," she says, motioning for me to follow her.

"Where are we going?"

The look on her face makes me feel ridiculous, despite it being a perfectly reasonable question. "We're saving your garage from certified disaster. I can't in good conscience let you leave shrimp in there. How would I sleep at night?"

"You want to come to my house?" It seems a little rash. We've known each other for all of ten minutes.

"I'm not coming inside," she says, as if taken aback by the suggestion. "I don't even know you. We're just going to dispose of the shrimp. Well, you're going to dispose of the shrimp. I have a shellfish allergy, so I'll be staying in the car. I assume you don't live far from here."

I bob my head. "I'm only a few blocks away."

"Good. We'll have to take my car, since I'm not getting into yours. Stranger danger and all that." She reaches into her purse and pulls out a bright red keychain. "Let's get out of here. You've got stuff to deal with, and I want to get in on the next poker game. Oh, and I'm Izzy, by the way. Not that you bothered to ask."

She turns toward the front door, giving me a look over her shoulder. *What are you waiting for?* her eyes seem to ask.

Honestly, I don't know. But somehow, I find myself following a virtual stranger out of the party, feeling confused and intrigued.

Two minutes later, I slide into the passenger seat of a pale blue beetle. The interior smells like flowers, and the floor is covered in sketch pads and empty coffee cups. "Ignore the mess," Izzy says as she sticks her key in the ignition. The car rumbles to life. "I live in New York. I haven't driven this thing in ages."

"It's no big deal," I tell her. "I don't think you could've anticipated driving someone to deal with a shrimp-related emergency."

As she pulls off the curb, I give Izzy directions to my place. We ride in silence for a few minutes, a pop song playing through the speakers of the car. We blur past the tree lawns of the quiet development before Izzy turns onto a main road.

"So, are you a local?" Izzy asks. Her eyes flicker to me briefly.

"Yeah. I've lived here my whole life."

"That seems to be the story with everyone," she says. "Are Delia and I the only outsiders to visit Seaview *ever*?"

"We don't see a lot of new faces outside of tourist season," I reply. "Wait till next month. This place will be crawling with new people."

The start of summer isn't so bad, but it gets old, waiting in line at places where you usually walk right in. By September, I'm ready for the tourists to clear out.

"Growing up in a resort town must be wild," Izzy remarks. "I can't even imagine the trouble I would've gotten into as a teenager if new kids were coming to my hometown every week looking for a good time. I bet you have some crazy stories."

"That wasn't really my thing." I'm honestly surprised she assumed otherwise. Between the glasses and the khakis, I don't exactly give off the impression of a partier.

"You're telling me you've never taken your top off dancing on a table? Drunkenly sung karaoke until your friends started ordering earplugs online?" At the stoplight, I instruct her to take a left turn.

Chuckling softly, I shake my head. "Tourists leave. The regrettable choices they made on vacation stay behind. If you live in Seaview, anything you've done can and will be held against you. People in small towns are nosey, and they don't forget anything."

"So, what? You've lived a squeaky clean life?"

"I didn't say that. I've just learned from my mistakes."

"I want at least one story out of you, Jacob. That's my price for the ride."

My first thought is to keep it vague. Feed her a basic story about getting drunk on a boat or going to a party at a massive beach house. But neither of those options seems good enough. For some reason, I want to impress Izzy. Tell her something that will actually grab her attention. So I find myself sharing the most interesting story from my youth.

"There's this bar in town. Seaview Tavern. It used to be owned by a middle-aged guy named David. He had one of those terrible landing strip goatees and drove around with a bumper sticker that said brakes for MILFS."

"Sounds like a real class act," Izzy observes.

"You have no idea. That bumper sticker was a source of controversy for years. The PTA tried to organize a boycott of Seaview Tavern to get David to remove it. But the tavern is the only decent bar in town, so they couldn't get anyone to commit to it. Though David eventually ended up selling the place and moving to Ohio.

"Anyway, Seaview Tavern is a popular spot. During spring break, it's packed with college kids. When I was a senior in high school, my girlfriend really wanted to go, so she got her older cousin to hook us up with fake IDs. We were wandering around when we stumbled across David's office. The door was unlocked, so we went inside. A few seconds later, we heard someone at the door. We hid in the closet right before David came in. He was on the phone, telling someone he wanted to take their clothes off."

"You heard goatee man having phone sex?" Izzy lets out a surprised laugh.

"Luckily, it didn't get that far. An employee knocked on the door needing David's help at the bar." Unfortunately, I did hear some of the worst dirty talk I've ever heard. "I used to see David at the gas station all the time. I never looked at him the same."

"Of course not. You heard how he talked to his MILFS. That would scar anyone." She gives me a playful look across the center console. "So, what did you and your girlfriend do? Were you bold enough to stick around or did you hightail out of there?"

Heat rushes to my face. I didn't expect her to ask that question. Before I even tell her, I'm trying to justify my behavior. "We were teenagers," I explain. "The place was jammed, so we knew it would be a while before David made it back to the office, and both of our parents were home."

"Oh my god." Izzy looks like she's about to lose it. Her eyes sparkle with amusement. "Please tell me you didn't lose your virginity in David's office."

"God, no. This was strictly over-the-clothes action."

"That's a relief. I don't know if I could've looked at you the same," Izzy says, pretending to shudder. "Though that is a great story. I guess you weren't so squeaky clean."

"It's my only story," I tell her honestly. The only other person I've shared it with is Tanner, and he's been my friend for ages.

"It's not half as bad as the stuff I did as a teenager," Izzy replies matter-of-factly. "I was a menace. A demon sent to torment my mother. There was this neighbor boy I was friends with. Bobby. My mom saw him vaping at the park one time and banned me from seeing him. Which, of course, made me like him more. His parents were gone one night, so he invited me to hang out in his hot tub. Except Bobby's parents unexpectedly came home. I couldn't get caught at his place—my mom would've killed me. So I ran all the way home in my soaking wet two-piece bathing suit."

I chuckle at the mental image. I haven't known Izzy for even half an hour, but that story seems to suit her.

"I think swapping secrets means we're friends now," Izzy says. "Which is good. I don't know how long I'm gonna be in town, but I could use a friend." She pulls into my development, driving slowly until I finally tell her to stop at my place. Putting the car in park, she turns to me with a smile.

"Now hurry up and deal with your shrimp," she says.
"I've got a poker game to get to."

Twenty-Nine

Jacob

I kiss her when she tries to leave the car.

"Jake," Izzy says. Despite her exasperated tone, her lips curve against mine in a smile. "I have to go." Pressing her palms to my chest, she gently shoves me away. She looks beautiful in the hazy glow of the streetlight. It makes me want to kiss her again.

Instead, I slide a hand through Izzy's hair, letting my thumb brush along the edge of her jaw. "It's late," I remind her. "Your friend is probably exhausted after that drive. You should stay at my place. I can bring you back in the morning."

I tried making this argument before we got in the car, but I figure it's worth another attempt. I like the idea of waking up with Izzy. Smelling her perfume on my sheets. Seeing her messy hair sprawled across my pillow case. I picture her in nothing but one of my T-shirts, perched on the kitchen counter while I make us breakfast in the morning, and my blood sizzles.

Sighing, she falls back in her seat. "Cynthia has texted me, like, a million times. I feel bad about ditching her at the bar. She drove all this way to see me." Izzy has a point, but that doesn't mean I like it. If it were up to me, we'd still be at my place, and we'd be wearing a lot less clothing, but Izzy insisted on me bringing her home. Her phone wouldn't stop pinging while we were lying in bed. Apparently, Cynthia and Dominic had left the bar, and they wanted to know Izzy's whereabouts.

We've been sitting in Izzy's driveway for ten minutes. Every time she tries to open the door, I kiss her. I don't want her to go yet. It's only been a couple of hours since we slept together. I want to savor it a little longer.

Plus, I'd be lying if I said I wasn't scared of what might happen after Izzy heads inside. She seems relaxed now, but what if that changes? What if she second-guesses everything?

Izzy admitted she had doubts about us. I don't think those went away just because we had sex. Maybe she's hiding her uncertainty from me. Waiting till she can get away to let herself panic about what all this means.

I want to believe Izzy won't shut me out again, but she hates dealing with big emotions. She might decide it's easier to cut me off, a possibility that terrifies me. I can work with Izzy's indecision. Talk through her worries and assure her we make sense together. But I can't do that if she ignores me.

For all we confessed tonight, we didn't make any promises to each other. I need to make sure Izzy knows what I want and where I stand. "Can I see you tomorrow?" I ask, not caring if it makes me sound desperate. I *am* desperate. I don't want her to doubt my feelings for a second.

Izzy saws her bottom lip between her teeth. "I should probably spend the weekend with Cynthia," she says. "She's only here till Monday."

Disappointment pulls at my chest like a rip current. I get why she wants to spend the limited time she has with her friend, but I hate the thought of not seeing her for the next two days. Tonight was a major development in our relationship. We didn't just have sex—Izzy told me she has feelings for me. That's a big deal for her. Izzy isn't the type who lets herself be vulnerable. Being apart could easily stir up doubts in her head.

"This weekend is going to be the longest of my life," I mutter.

Izzy grins, amused by my agony. "Men have been known to lose their grip on reality after sleeping with me. Consult your doctor if you start to feel disoriented or have difficulty concentrating."

I kiss her because she's ridiculous but also completely right. I don't know how I'm supposed to go back to a normal life after hearing Izzy orgasm. I'm pretty sure the noises she made will echo in my brain for the rest of eternity.

Worry trickles through my thoughts as her lips mold against mine. Everything seems good now, but Izzy could change her mind. Her ex-boyfriend is in town. Seeing him might remind her of all the reasons she wasn't interested in another relationship. What if she decides it's too complicated, or that she doesn't want to make any commitments?

She doesn't even know the extent of my feelings. At the bar, I almost told her I'm in love with her, but I was afraid that confession might overwhelm her. Izzy dodged me for *weeks* because she didn't want to hear that I liked her. How will she react when I tell her I love her? That when I envision my future, she's at the very center of it?

It's too soon for such bold declarations, even if they're true. With Izzy, I need to take baby steps. She's only starting to let me in, giving me a small crack in the doorway to slip through. I don't want to push too hard and risk her slamming the door again. Which means I need to play it cool. Give her the reassurance she needs without overloading her.

When the kiss ends, Izzy looks at me sternly. "Seriously, I have to go."

Begrudgingly, I untangle myself from her. The two of us get out of the car, and I walk her to the front door. She kisses me one last time, then says she'll see me later. Grabbing her keys out of her purse, she unlocks the door.

Before she walks inside, I impulsively call out to her. "Izzy?"

She glances over her shoulder. "Yeah?"

Please be in this with me. Please don't shut me out again. I love you. I need this to work. I've never felt like this before, and I'm never going to again.

"Call me if you need anything, okay?"

She nods. "Of course."

As she closes the door behind her, I wish I could say I believed her.

***

Izzy

Cynthia pounces the minute I get inside.

She strides into the foyer with her arms folded over her chest. Her features are stony, and she's wearing a thick pink bathrobe and slippers. She looks like a disgruntled mother catching her daughter sneaking in during the early hours of the morning, which would be funny if she wasn't totally pissed.

"Hey," I say enthusiastically, hoping to ease the tension. Though it will probably take a lot more than a friendly greeting to get back in Cynthia's good graces. She drove four hours to see me, and I returned the favor by ditching her at a bar.

"Hey," Cynthia says, her tone much colder than mine. "I thought you would've been back already." I texted her when Jacob and I left Seaview Tavern. I told her I wasn't feeling well, and that I ran into a friend who was going to drive me home. She gave the message a thumbs up, but she didn't say anything.

"Sorry," I say as I shrug out of my jacket. "My friend wanted to stop for food. He thought it would help me feel better." I slip off my sneakers on the mat by the door.

"And do you feel better?"

"Much better. Though I really am sorry about tonight. I thought the bar would be fun, but when I started feeling sick, I knew I had to get out of there."

Cynthia nods stiffly. "It's fine." Nothing about her body language feels fine. She's all pursed lips and rigid shoulders. But I act as though everything is normal.

"So, how was the rest of your night?" I ask. "Did you stay at the bar for a while?"

"We ordered an Uber right after you texted," she says. That means she's been sitting at the house, waiting for me, for at least a couple of hours.

I whip my phone out of my purse. "How much was it?" I'm responsible for Cynthia's bitter mood. It seems reasonable that I pay for her ride home.

She waves me off. "Don't worry about it."

"No, you're my guest. That ride is on me."

"It doesn't matter."

She's being stubborn, but I'm not going to let this go. "Well, I'm sending you twenty bucks." That should be enough to cover the short ride from Seaview Tavern back to the house. "Feel free to steal from my purse if it was more."

"Drop it, Izzy," Cynthia snaps. "I don't want your damn money." Her nostrils flare, and she pulls her folded arms tighter against her body.

It looks like we're doing this tonight. I really hoped she'd let it go till morning. After everything that's happened over the last few hours, I don't think I have the mental bandwidth to fight with her. And truthfully, I'm getting annoyed.

I haven't said anything about her bringing Dominic here without telling me. Both of us messed up, but forcing someone to spend the weekend with their ex is much worse than leaving them for a few hours. Can't Cynthia give me a break?

"I said I was sorry, Cynthia," I reply. "What else do you want from me?"

She laughs humorlessly. "Some honesty, for once, would be nice. Who's the guy?"

"What?"

"Who's. The. Guy. I saw you making out with him outside the bar. You didn't look sick to me." She saw me and Jacob? Shit, I had no idea. But her accusatory words only add to my irritation.

She thinks I ditched her for a guy, but we were only at the bar tonight because *she* brought my ex-boyfriend here. Does Cynthia not realize how inconsiderate that was? Did my feelings cross her mind for even a second? I'm hurt, too. But she only seems to care about her own anger. Both of us have made mistakes, yet I'm the only one apologizing. It's hard to keep my cool when I'm being met with open hostility.

Naturally, Dominic chooses this moment to make his presence known. Sauntering through the doorway, he enters the foyer, waving a bottle of tequila. It looks like he raided the liquor cabinet while I was gone.

"Izzy's back," he says excitedly. Clearly, he's not reading the room. "Excellent. I need someone to do a shot with me."

I wrinkle my nose. Getting drunk with my ex seems like the worst way to cope with fighting with my best friend. "No, thanks," I say. "I'm actually kind of drained. I think I'm gonna go to bed." It's late, and a heavy ball of emotion is sloshing around my stomach. I need to be alone for a while, or else I might say something I'll later regret.

Dominic whines. "Oh, c'mon. Just one shot." He shakes the glass bottle as though it will entice me. "I'm on vacation, Iz. I can't drink by myself."

"I said no," I reply sternly. Dominic can be persistent, and I don't have the patience for him right now.

His expression turns sour. "All right. Whatever." Letting the bottle fall to his side, he releases a long sigh. "I thought we were finally getting the old Izzy back, but I guess not."

"The *what*?"

He shrugs. "You know, the old Izzy. The one who used to have fun."

My ears are ringing. With those words, Dominic takes me back to another lifetime. Living in New York. Feeling lost and unhappy. Trying to talk to my boyfriend about it only for him to get annoyed with me. *Lighten up, Izzy. Since when did you become so serious? Can't we just have a good time without you bringing down the mood?*

Dominic acted like my feelings were a burden. If I wasn't cracking jokes or having fun, I was killing the mood. His flippant attitude made me not want to share things with anyone. I built a perimeter around my emotions, and I've stayed there ever since. Lying about the way I feel. Trying not to cause trouble for anyone.

And all it's done is make me feel worse. I'm tired of pretending all the time. Of tying myself in knots so everyone around me feels more comfortable. Cynthia has been my best friend for years. I love her, but I can't keep making myself miserable for her. Our relationship can't come at the expense of my happiness.

"I'm just teasing you, Izzy," Dominic says, giving me a carefree smile. He's expecting me to perk up instantly. To let his dig roll off my back, the way I always do. But I've had enough of his bullshit already.

"Get out of my house."

Dominic's jaw drops. "Izzy, what—"

"You can't stay here," I say firmly. "I don't want you here."

He raises his palms in surrender. "Hey, I'm sorry if I upset you with the shot thing," he says, injecting his tone with humor. He still thinks he can fix things. That if he uses his charm and his smile, I'll stop being difficult. He has no idea how finished I am. "I was only kidding. Can we talk about this before you throw me on the street?"

"There's nothing to talk about. You're not welcome here."

"I can't tell if you're being serious or not."

"I'm dead serious. Do I need to order you a car, or can you handle that yourself?"

His eyes turn stormy. I'm not playing by Dominic's rules anymore, and he doesn't like it. So he looks over at Cynthia. "Can you please reason with her?" he asks.

She touches my arm gently. "Izzy, I don't think he meant to upset you." Her tone is calm and rational, none of her anger to be found.

Ignoring her, I direct my next words at Dominic. "You need to leave."

"Where do you expect me to go?"

"There are plenty of hotels around here. I'm sure you'll find something." As long as he's not in my house, I don't care where he sleeps tonight.

Dominic throws his arms up, frustrated. "You've gotta be fucking kidding me."

"C'mon, Izzy," Cynthia says. "You're being unreasonable."

The rage simmering in me suddenly comes to a boil. "No, what's unreasonable is you inviting my ex-boyfriend to spend the weekend here. What were you thinking?"

Cynthia's face drains of color. "He told me he talked to you about it."

"And you didn't think it was worth mentioning to me even once? We've been texting about this trip for weeks, Cynthia. Didn't you find it weird that I never mentioned Dominic? You should've talked to me."

"That's all I've been trying to do for months!" she exclaims. Her anger is back and in full force. "But you ignore my calls and barely respond to my texts. I drove all this way to see you, and you still found a way to ditch me. So don't you dare accuse me of not communicating with you. I'm the only one putting any effort into this friendship."

"That's what this weekend was supposed to be about! So why did you bring Dominic?"

"Why do you keep talking about him like he's a random ex-boyfriend? You're friends, Izzy. The three of us hung out almost every day *after* you broke up. Did something happen when you left New York?" She glances between us frantically, as if she hopes to find the answer in our facial expressions.

"The issue," I say, "is that he and I aren't good, and we never will be."

Dominic shakes his head. "We said we wouldn't do this."

"I only agreed to that because I thought it was the right thing." I was afraid that telling the truth would cost me my relationship with Cynthia. The thing is, I'm losing my relationship with her, anyway. Lying has made everything worse. "You can stay tonight, but you have to be gone by morning." Even though I want to kick him out tonight, Dominic has been drinking for hours. I can't in good conscience throw him out.

As I head up the stairs, Cynthia asks me to wait. "Where are you going?"

"To pack a bag. I'm staying in Tanner's guest room." I can't kick Dominic out, but I'm not sleeping under the same roof as him either.

"Izzy, please don't leave," she says. "We should talk about this."

"Not tonight." My brain has reached its breaking point. I've had enough emotional upheaval for one night. I'm not subjecting myself to any more.

So I head upstairs, toss a few things in a duffel bag, and walk out the door.

Thirty

Izzy

"I'm gonna kill her."

At one in the morning, Delia paces the length of Tanner's dimly-lit guest room, the black lace sleeves of her robe swishing against her sides. Her nostrils flare, but even in her enraged state, she looks elegant. Her dark hair sits in a low bun, and her velvet slippers make a soft scraping sound as she walks across the wooden floor.

"Who invites their best friend's ex-boyfriend for a visit?" she asks, digging her manicured fingernails into the flesh of her palms. "I don't care if Dominic is Cynthia's cousin—there was *zero* reason for her to bring him here."

Saying nothing, I run a hand through Jason's fur. He's sleeping with his head on my thigh, his quiet snores filling the room. Delia hasn't even commented on the fact that he's sprawled across the bed, which lets me know just how angry she is.

"Can I kick Dominic out?" she asks. "I bet I could scare the shit out of him using Tanner's power tools." The mental image of Delia terrorizing Dominic with an electric drill brings a faint smile to my lips. But I don't see how it will help me.

"Maybe we should try coming up with some less violent solutions." Morgan's suggestion rings through the speakerphone. She drove back to Boston this afternoon, but Delia insisted on calling her when I got to Tanner's place. Even though it was after midnight, Morgan picked up. I told her and Delia everything that happened tonight with Cynthia and Dominic. Morgan seems just as upset as Delia, but she's less likely to turn that rage into violence.

It feels good talking to my sisters. Cathartic, even. Jacob is the only other person I've told about the Dominic situation. Hearing Delia and Morgan say that they've always disliked Dominic and never understood why I was with him is exactly what I need.

Their support means everything. And it makes me feel ridiculous for keeping so much from them for so long. Both of them are awake in the middle of the night because they want to hear about my problems. Why have I been shutting them out?

"I hate the thought of Dominic sleeping in our house," Delia says with a disgusted look on her face. "You shouldn't have let him in, Izzy. I would've locked the doors and drawn the blinds until he went away."

I shake my head. "I couldn't do that to Cynthia. Not after she drove all this way."

"Why not? Cynthia obviously wasn't thinking about you when she invited Dominic. You would've been well within reason to slam the door in both of their faces."

Even though I'm mad at Cynthia, I still feel an urge to defend her. "She didn't do it to hurt me." I've known Cynthia since we were eighteen. She isn't vindictive. Bringing Dominic to Seaview was a careless move, yes, but she wouldn't have done it to hurt me intentionally.

"He's your ex, Iz. It's weird."

"I know. But Cynthia doesn't know everything."

Delia frowns. "What do you mean?"

"Well, she thinks the breakup was mutual," I say as I continue to pet a sleeping Jason. "Dominic and I told her we were better off as friends."

"But why?" Morgan asks.

The answer is obvious, isn't it? "Dominic's her cousin. He's part of our circle of friends in New York. I didn't want to make things awkward for everyone. But I know I should've been honest with her. That's what I was planning to do this weekend. But then Dominic showed up, and everything went to hell." I recall the sinking feeling I had when Dominic stepped out of that car. I didn't know it was possible to shift from excitement to misery so quickly.

"Cynthia has no idea how hard it was for me to see him every day and pretend everything was fine," I add.

"Wait. You saw Dominic *every day* after you broke up?"

"Pretty much. Like I said, he's part of our friend group. Everyone thought we were cool, so they invited us to the same stuff. He had dinner at my place all the time."

"Oh my god, Izzy. What were you thinking?" Delia asks, sounding horrified. "Spending that much time with an ex, especially a recent one, would make anyone want to gouge out their own eyeballs."

"Seriously?" I figured she would give me some credit for trying to get along with Dominic. Sure, it was a spectacularly bad idea, but I still had good intentions. "I thought I was being mature."

Delia arches a brow. "By lying?" She places her hands on her hips, visibly unimpressed. "You have to be honest with people, Iz. That's what makes relationships function."

"Do you think that's why Cynthia brought him here?" Morgan asks. "I mean, if you were hanging out with Dominic all the time in New York, then I can see why she might've gotten the impression that you wouldn't care." That theory sounds a lot like what Cynthia said last night. It's not a totally unreasonable assumption. After all, I did spend the past year trying to make Cynthia believe Dominic and I were solid.

Delia turns to me. "Why would you keep this stuff from your friends? Didn't it just make you miserable?" She delivers the question in a way that feels curious and thoughtful. She isn't judging me—she just wants to understand.

I take a second to compose my thoughts. I could reiterate everything I've already said. *I didn't want to make things awkward. It was the only way to keep my friend group together.* Those responses, while true, feel like excuses. They're surface-level answers. They gloss over the basis for my decisions without getting to the root of the issue.

And I don't want to keep lying. I'm sick of putting on a front all the time. Which means I need to be honest. No more deflecting from the truth.

With a deep breath, I let it all out. "I know I can be a lot," I say. "I'm loud and stubborn, and I make terrible decisions all the time. That's what people expect from me. I'm Fun Izzy. Interesting and unfiltered but not someone you'd ever take seriously. And I'm usually okay with that. I like having a good time. Making people laugh. It's who I am. But sometimes, it feels like a performance.

"Last year was really hard for me. Work was making me miserable, and I didn't know what I wanted to do with the rest of my life. I felt directionless. And I didn't think I could talk to anyone about it because that's not what people want from me. I'm fun and flighty, not the kind of person who needs emotional support. I didn't want to make myself a burden."

"Why would you think that?" Delia asks.

"Well, Dominic shut down every time I tried to talk to him about anything serious. But honestly, I've felt this way for ages. Mom acts like I'm a complete disaster. I guess I'm scared of proving her right."

Sadness clouds Delia's eyes. "Shit, Izzy. I had no idea you felt that way."

"I'm sorry we didn't see it," Morgan says.

I shake my head. "It's neither of your faults." My sisters aren't mind readers. They couldn't know about any of this without me talking to them.

"No, but we could do more," Delia says. "Especially with Mom. I know she's hard on you, but I thought it was just the kind of relationship you had. I didn't realize how much it actually affected you."

"How could you? Your relationship with her is so different from mine. So is Morgan's. Growing up, you were her perfect straight-A students, and I was getting sent to the principal's office every day. Mom still sees me as the kid who won't listen to her."

"Would it help if we talked to her?" Morgan asks.

"I don't think so." The problem is, Mom doesn't treat me like an adult. I don't want her to only start taking me seriously because Morgan and Delia told her to. She needs to listen to me. Hear me. "This is between me and Mom."

"I'm sorry if we ever made you feel like you couldn't talk to us," Delia says. "Morgan and I don't see you as a burden, Izzy. We want to be there for you, no matter what you're feeling. Being a fun person doesn't mean you have to be fun all the time. You're allowed to feel heavy shit." Hearing those words is like being wrapped in a warm blanket. Why didn't I do this sooner? I should've known my sisters would be supportive.

"No, it's nothing you did," I reply. "This is on me. I can't expect you to know how I'm feeling if I don't communicate it. I'm sorry for keeping so much from you."

Delia tilts her head. "Have you been keeping other secrets?"

Well, shit. I just decided that I need to be more open with them, but I didn't think about everything else that would entail. If I'm going to try this honesty thing, I have to commit to it, don't I? I can't start off with another lie.

So I bite the bullet. "I slept with Jacob."

"*What*?" Morgan screeches.

Delia pounces on the bed, waking up Jason. "I knew it!" She wags a finger at me like a smug teacher who caught a student cheating on a test. "What did I tell you, Morg? She was spoon-feeding Jacob hot fudge like a sweet, doting girlfriend."

I roll my eyes. I knew she would bring that up. "I'm not his girlfriend. We're not—" God, I don't even know what the fuck we are at this point. *Friends* feels too small, but it's not like we're together. Then again, Jacob kissed me when he dropped me off. And he asked when he could see me again. Does *he* think we're together? "It only happened a few hours ago. I haven't had time to process it, so I would appreciate it if both of you could be normal about this."

Delia laughs. "Oh, because you were so normal when I started seeing Tanner."

"That was different." It's really not, but now I'm the one under the microscope, and I'm feeling the heat. "And I don't know how much I can tell you if you're going to squeal like middle schoolers at a slumber party."

"Oh, you're telling us everything," Delia insists. "How did this happen?"

"Honestly, I have no idea." One moment, I was outside crying. The next, Jacob's tongue was in my mouth. It all happened so fast. "It was an accident."

"Izzy, you can't accidentally sleep with someone."

"I don't know how else to describe it."

"Is this the first time anything has happened with Jacob?" Morgan asks.

"No, we made out one time. But that was also an accident."

"Oh my god, Izzy. How long have you been hiding this?"

Exasperated, I drop back on the pillows. "We've had this thing for a while, I guess." I told myself it was platonic, but upon further reflection, I don't know how I convinced myself of that. "I'm pretty sure we've been flirting for, like, a year."

I start from the beginning. The little conversations we had at parties. How we just seemed to connect right away. Then I tell them about the deal we made. I leave out the part about overhearing Delia turn down Tanner's invitation to move in with him. That feels like something I should address with her privately. So I keep it simple. I wanted to become more responsible, and Jacob needed help in his dating life. It seemed like the perfect setup.

"When I saw Jacob on a date, I just freaked out," I say. There's no other way to put it. I hated seeing another woman put her hands on him. It was pure jealousy. "I went outside, and he followed me. We started arguing and then we admitted we both had feelings for each other and, well, you know the rest."

"I don't understand," Morgan says. "If you both like each other, why aren't you together?"

"Our feelings aren't the problem, Morg." I've always felt drawn to Jacob. And that connection has only deepened the more time we've spent together. Jacob knows me better than anyone, and I know him the same way. Which is why we can't be together. "Jacob wants marriage and family more than anything. I'm still figuring my life out. We're in completely different places. It would never work."

"But don't you owe it to yourselves to at least try?" It's a tempting thought. Letting go of my concerns and exploring things with Jacob. I've never felt so seen, so comfortable and loved. And he insisted that his feelings for me were more important than anything else.

You've completely changed how I experience happiness. It would be so easy to put my trust in those words, to give this a real shot. But the feelings Jacob has for me, no matter how intense, can't possibly compare to a lifetime of wanting a family.

I want one, too. At some point. But I don't know when that will be. Jacob is ready for his future now. I can't be the reason he delays his happiness.

"It would only hurt us more in the long run," I say, pulling a pillow to my chest.

"Are you sure?" Delia asks cautiously. "If you don't pursue this, Izzy, then he's going to move on. Do you really want to watch Jacob fall in love with someone else? Get married? Have kids?" It's a horrible thought. Jacob, married to someone else. Picturing him with a wife and a baby makes me want to throw up. But there's one scenario that seems worse. Jacob coming to resent me. Seeing me as the reason he doesn't have what he really wants. I don't want to be a regret to him. A mistake he wishes he could take back.

He's the only person who understands me. All of me. My quirks and flaws. The insecurities I keep tucked away from the rest of the world. How could I recover if I lost him? If the person who means the most to me suddenly stopped caring? I'd rather have part of him always than all of him for a limited amount of time.

"I'll just have to deal with it." Simple as that. But I don't feel like talking about Jacob anymore. Not when everything hurts, and my brain feels like it's been wrung out like a dishtowel.

I'm a word away from sobbing uncontrollably.

Luckily, Delia senses this. "You should get some sleep," she says, climbing off the bed. "Unless, you know, there are other secrets you need to confess." She's joking, but there is, in fact, one more thing I haven't told them about. The art classes. And given everything else I've admitted tonight, it feels like they deserve to know.

"Well, there is one thing."

Delia smacks my arm. "Are you *kidding* me?"

***

Jacob

My phone lights up on my nightstand, and I flip to my side to grab it. It's almost two in the morning, and I haven't gotten a minute of sleep. Nor do I expect to. Not when my sheets smell like Izzy's perfume, and my brain is playing the tiny noise she made when I kissed her neck on a loop.

There's enough energy coursing through my veins right now to power a small city. I'd take a walk to burn some of it off if Lulu weren't sleeping soundly at the foot of my bed.

Waking her would throw off her routine. So, if I'm stuck with all this adrenaline, I might as well find something to keep my mind occupied.

It's probably a text from Izzy. I don't know who else would be messaging me at this time of night. I wonder if she's having trouble sleeping, too. Maybe she changed her mind about spending the night with Cynthia and wants me to come get her. I could be at her place in ten minutes…less than ten if I forgo shoes and a shirt and don't lock my door.

When I check my notifications, however, there are no new messages from Izzy. Instead, I have a text from Tanner. *Did something happen with you and Izzy?*

My stomach sinks. Why is he asking that? Tanner knows I like Izzy, but I haven't told him about tonight. As far as he knows, I went out with Catherine. Anything he heard about Izzy and me he got from someone else.

The thing is, Tanner isn't a gossip. He wouldn't text me at this hour just to find out if I slept with Izzy. Something must've happened to make him think he needed to reach out. I have a feeling it isn't good.

What's going on? I write back.

Izzy's here, he replies. *I think she's staying the night. She and Delia have been talking for a while. She seemed upset.*

Immediately, my concern turns into dread. Izzy's upset. Why? Is it because we slept together? She seemed fine when I dropped her off, and it's only been a few hours. How much could've changed since then?

Is she already having regrets about us? I thought we'd make it through at least a night before she started to second-guess everything.

Stop it, I tell myself. *It could have nothing to do with you.* Izzy's ex-boyfriend is staying with her. Maybe he's the reason she's upset. Or maybe she confronted Cynthia about her bringing him to town. Izzy's distress might have nothing to do with me.

But if that were the case, then why wouldn't she come to me about it? I told her to call if she needed anything. I would've been there. She knows that. So why am I hearing about this from Tanner instead of Izzy directly?

All I've done is try to make her comfortable. I held back when I thought she wasn't interested, then opened up when I realized she felt something for me. I've let her set the pace, and I've had no problem with it. Izzy's uncertainty has never intimidated me. I want to know about her doubts. How else can we work through them? But I can't meet Izzy where she's at when she keeps running from me.

After tonight, I thought we were finally getting somewhere, but maybe I was wrong. We might be even further off course than before.

Thirty-One

Jacob

Lulu's tail thumps against the carpet as Mom pets her stomach, adoration shining in the dog's eyes. I don't know when Mom replaced me as Lulu's favorite person, but I'm guessing it has to do with the bag of peanut butter treats sitting on the end table.

"We need to set a limit on how many treats you give her," I say. Lulu doesn't have this much of a reaction to anyone, not even Izzy. Lulu loves her, but she isn't stuck to her side like plastic wrap every time she comes over. "This behavior has to be the result of you feeding her excessively."

Mom casts me off with a wave. "There's nothing wrong with a little spoiling." She scratches the underside of Lulu's chin. Lulu sits up so she can rub her face against Mom's shin. It's absolutely pathetic.

"Does that mean you'll clean my car if she gets sick on the ride home?"

Mom narrows her eyes. "You should be nicer to your mother." With a quick pat on Lulu's head, she walks back over to her chair. Sitting down, she picks up her needle and embroidery hoop and begins working on her floral cross stitch. Mom recently moved on from knitting to embroidery, but I don't think this hobby is going to stick. Mom claims it's too tough on her eyes, even though she wears glasses.

"Thanks for watching her for me," I say. When I texted Mom this morning to see if she was up for a Lulu visit, she told me I could bring her over any time. At nine-thirty, I got Lulu leashed up and drove to my parents' place. It's early for Saturday activity, but it wasn't like I was getting any sleep. I was up agonizing over Izzy all night.

"Of course," Mom replies happily. "What big plans do you have today?"

Truthfully, none. But I thought it was a good idea to get out of the house today. Drive around. Maybe run a few errands. Sitting around would only amplify the dread lingering in my stomach. Besides, I need to talk to Mom about Catherine.

Last night, Mom sent me a text wishing me luck on my date. I didn't tell her anything about Catherine, which means she must've heard something from her friend, Eva. I should give her a heads up that things with Catherine aren't going to work out. Better she get the news from me than someone else.

When I don't respond right away, Mom takes it upon herself to fill in the blanks. "Are you going on another date with Catherine?" she asks, looking up to gauge my reaction.

"Uh, no," I reply, scratching the back of my neck. *This* is why I was against going out with her friend's niece. Who wants to explain to their mom why their date didn't go well? At least Catherine was cool about everything. I can't imagine how much more awkward this would be if she'd gotten upset.

Mom looks surprised. "Really? I thought you two had a lot in common."

"We do. But, you know, not everything is about that." The fact that I was sitting across the table from Catherine but thinking about another woman should've been the first clue that it wasn't going to work. "We got along just fine, but there wasn't really a connection."

"That's too bad," Mom says, making a disappointed face. "The way Eva talked about Catherine made her sound like the perfect woman for you."

"Catherine's great," I assure her. "It's nothing personal. But I wasn't going to lead her on when I didn't see a future there."

Mom nods slowly. "Is this about Izzy Forrest?"

My pulse spikes. "What?" I try not to let my shock show, but I'm sure I look like a gutted fish. How would Mom even guess that? I haven't told her anything about Izzy.

"You spend a lot of time with her," she says, by way of explanation. "I wondered if something was going on. Your reaction tells me everything I need to know." Satisfaction gleams in her eyes. Did my own mother just play me? "Does Izzy know how you feel?"

I run a hand over my face. "I really don't want to talk about this, Mom." My situation with Izzy is too fragile. Too fresh. I have no idea where we stand. Talking about it will only give voice to the doubts circling my head. "It's complicated with Izzy. She's hesitant about relationships because of how a previous one ended."

Mom shrugs. "Well, so are you."

"Is that a joke?" First, Mom plays me for information. Second, she teases me about my dating failures. Is this some kind of retribution? Maybe she really was offended when I accused her of buying Lulu's love with treats. "You know I went on more than twenty first dates last year, right? I'm not hesitant about anything."

I've always known what I wanted. Why else would I be crushed about being single?

"Don't take this the wrong way, Jacob," she says, "but do you honestly put yourself out there? Twenty dates is a lot, sure. But none of them led to relationships. Don't you think you would've dated at least one of those women if you were serious about marriage?"

"They weren't good dates, Mom. I would've tried if I thought there was even a slight chance of one of them leading somewhere. I wanted them to work out more than anything."

"Do you truly believe that, or are you telling yourself that?"

"Are you trying to make a point, or are you just asking leading questions?"

Mom sighs. "I know you want to find someone," she says. "But I think you're afraid to let anyone in. You're using these bad dates as excuses. Face it, Jacob. If your only goal was to get married, you would've found a way to make it work with at least one of these women, even if it wasn't perfect. Instead, you've latched on to any reason you can to explain why the two of you wouldn't be a good fit."

Mom is usually pretty intuitive, so I'm surprised to hear her say something so off base. What is she talking about? "Why would I do that?" Of course I'm not sabotaging myself. No reasonable person would put themselves through dozens of True Connections dates if they weren't serious about meeting someone.

"So you can convince yourself you're making an effort without actually opening up to anyone," she replies matter-of-factly. "You've been hurt in the past. I think it has affected you more than you want to admit."

"You think this is about Maggie?" I stare at her, baffled. "I haven't thought about her in ages, Mom." My relationship with Maggie seems like it was from another lifetime. I'm not hung up on the woman who cheated on me when I was twenty-one. I don't even feel angry about it anymore. I don't feel anything.

"You were serious about her, and she walked away," Mom says. "You don't think that changed the way you approach relationships?"

I shake my head. "This is different." I thought I loved Maggie, but that was before I knew what it meant to love Izzy. What I felt then was only a fraction of what I feel now. I'd give her everything if she'd let me.

Mom blinks. "So Izzy knows how you feel?"

"Yeah. She—" Well, she knows I want her. That I see her as so much more than a friend. That I don't want to be with anyone else. But I haven't told her the most important thing. That I'm in love with her and can't imagine a future without her in it.

I told myself it was too soon to drop the love bomb. Izzy already has doubts about us, and finding out I love her might overwhelm her. What if it drives her even further away? Everything with us is so fragile. Saying "I love you" would be like hitting a glass vase with a hammer and then acting surprised when it shatters. I don't want to destroy what we have.

That said, is it really fair to say that Izzy knows how I feel? She has a general sense of my feelings, but she doesn't know the true extent of them. I gave her part of myself, not all of me. Yet I'm standing here, frustrated that she hasn't given me everything.

How can I expect that when I haven't done the same?

Maybe Mom has a point. I convinced myself that Izzy wasn't ready to hear that I love her, but maybe I'm the one who wasn't ready. I'm terrified of her rejecting me. Of flaying myself open to her, and it still not being enough.

Sometimes, it feels like Izzy is a firefly moving through the night, and I'm a desperate kid with a jar trying to catch her. Does she even want my love? Is it enough for her? She's pure magic. I work a boring job and live a simple life. Maybe Izzy, fierce and wild and bold, is searching for more than what I can offer her.

Losing Izzy before I've ever really had her…I don't know if I could recover from that. She consumes me in a way that no one has before. She's completely rearranged my molecules. And if I'm all in on her, on us, then I need to be honest with her. I can't ask her to put her trust in me when I'm holding myself back.

She needs to know everything. Even if it destroys me in the process.

***

Izzy

Cynthia: We'll be gone by eleven.

Cynthia: I really am sorry. For everything.

Uncertainty sloshes around my body as I stare at Cynthia's messages. I woke up to her texts this morning, and though I've reread them a hundred times, I still haven't decided whether I should respond.

I've been restless all morning. When I got out of bed, Delia offered to pick up breakfast, but I wasn't in the mood for conversation. I needed to be alone, so I took Jason to the beach. It's a chilly morning, but the fresh air feels good on my skin, and the sound of waves lapping against the shore is peaceful and soothing.

We walked around for a while, then I laid out a towel and sat down. The occasional runner passes by, but other than that, there's no one here but me and Jason. I study the expanse of dark-blue water in front of me as my mind repeats the same question.

What do I do about Cynthia?

I'm still furious about last night. Cynthia crossed a line by bringing Dominic here without talking to me first. She had no right to blindside me like that. But after my conversation with Delia and Morgan, I'm seeing things more clearly from Cynthia's perspective.

I haven't given her any reason to suspect I have problems with Dominic. In fact, I've done the opposite. Hanging out with him. Texting in our group chat. Cynthia had no way of knowing that things weren't right with us.

Plus, she's been trying to maintain our friendship since I left New York, even though I haven't made it easy on her. If I'm honest with myself, I haven't been a very good friend to Cynthia recently. I've hidden things from her. Blown off her calls and texts. *I'm the only one putting any effort into this friendship,* she said last night. With the way I've been acting, I can't blame her for thinking that.

I read her texts again. They feel so cold and final. Could this be it? The end of seven years of friendship? Cynthia and I have had plenty of fights before, but this one is different. We're not roommates anymore. We don't have proximity holding us together. What happens if she goes home today, and we don't talk? Something tells me I might never see her again. That isn't what I want. But where do we go from here?

Dominic is Cynthia's cousin. She's connected to him in a way that I'm not. What if she decides it's easier to take his side and let go of our friendship? She already thinks I don't care about our relationship. She's probably tired of putting in all this effort and getting nothing in return.

It all comes back to me, doesn't it? I've been lying to the people who matter most, pushing them away to avoid being seen as messy or complicated. I thought it made me a better friend, but it's actually tearing my relationships apart. I put up roadblocks where I meant to add bridges. The distance is all my fault.

Footsteps swish across sand. Glancing over my shoulder, I see Jacob coming toward me. Wind sweeps through his dark hair as he closes the gap between us. He looks focused. His eyes are locked on me, steady and determined.

My heart pounds. What is Jacob doing here? It can't be a coincidence that both of us ended up at the beach this morning. Seaview is small, but it isn't that small. Besides, most people have enough sense to avoid the ocean when it's thirty-seven degrees—hence why there's no one else in sight. Delia must've given Jacob my whereabouts. Which means he went to see me.

Panic grips my throat. This isn't supposed to happen. Jacob thinks I'm spending the rest of the weekend with Cynthia. I'm supposed to have two days to figure out what I'm going to say to him before we see each other again.

I needed that time. Last night still feels so fresh. I haven't had a chance to process what it means for us or how we're going to move forward. Being away from him was supposed to help me sort my shit out. What am I going to do now?

When Jacob reaches me, I say nothing. It's better to let him talk first. Maybe it'll give me a sense of where his head is at.

"Hey," he says, giving me absolutely nothing. Fuck.

"Hi." My voice sounds wobbly. "How did you…?"

"Delia told me you were here. Mind if I sit?"

Shaking my head, I pat the empty space beside me on the towel. He settles next to me, and there's barely an inch of space between us. I feel the heat radiating off his body.

After a few seconds, Jacob turns to me and frowns. "Why do you have so much sand in your hair?" he asks, dragging a finger through a grainy piece of hair near my face. His fingertip grazes my cheek, and my skin feels like it's on fire.

I drop my eyes, not wanting him to see how much a small touch affected me.

"Jason wanted to dig when we got here," I tell him. "It wasn't pretty." It took about fifteen minutes of coaxing Jason with treats to get him to stop. But first, he showered me in enough sand to fill a child's sandbox.

Jacob stares at me, his jaw flexing. I try smiling at him, but he isn't buying it. "Are you all right?" he asks. How did I forget about his built-in Izzy Bullshit Meter?

There's no point in lying, so my response is as honest as it can be. "I didn't get much sleep last night." *Mostly because I was thinking about you.* I tried to banish Jacob from my mind, but being alone in a dark bedroom made that impossible. I kept remembering how good it felt having his hands on me.

Jacob and I have this raw intimacy. An invisible force that seems to connect us. It's been here this entire time, long before I even realized how much he meant to me.

I always thought I went to him for conversation during parties or nights at the bar because I was bored and needed someone to talk to. But it wasn't someone I needed—it was him. And that need has only gotten stronger the more I've gotten to know him.

Still, we can't be together. Not with so much working against us. Jacob wants a woman with a clear vision of her future. I'm not that woman. I won't be the reason he doesn't get everything he deserves.

"Last night is what I want to talk to you about," Jacob says. The intensity in his eyes is too much, so I look at the horizon instead.

And Jacob knows, without me uttering a word, exactly what's happening.

"You're already doing it," he says. "It hasn't even been twelve hours, and you're already shutting me out."

Feeling exposed, I tuck my hands against my sides. He's right, and I feel terrible, but that doesn't change anything. "Jacob."

"Tanner told me you were at his place last night," he says. "He said you were upset." There's pain in his voice. He thinks I was worked up about us, doesn't he? "Things seemed good when I dropped you off. Were you…do you regret what happened?"

"No." My answer is immediate. I can't let Jacob believe I spent the night devastated over us sleeping together. It wouldn't be fair to him. "It wasn't about us. After you left, I got into a fight with Cynthia and Dominic."

"Oh," he says, and I sneak a peek at him. At first, he looks relieved. But within seconds, that look is replaced by disappointment. "You could've called me."

I wanted to. When I walked out of the house last night, Jacob was the first person I wanted to call, but I couldn't go to him for comfort when I knew this was coming next. It wouldn't have been fair. "I know."

He's expecting more. An explanation. Some assurance. "Please talk to me, Forrest," he says. He'd take anything. I'm sure of it. All Jacob wants is for me to show any sign that I'm still with him. To make it clear we're on the same page. But I can't do that.

"I don't know what you want me to say," I tell him.

Jacob closes his eyes. "I don't know why you keep doing this. You give me an inch and then take away a mile. I'm not asking you to have all the answers here, Forrest. I just need you to stop pushing me away every time you feel uncomfortable."

Emotion is a knife plunging into my abdomen. I hate hurting him. "Jake—" He shakes his head, and I immediately stop talking.

He pulls my hands into his. His touch is warm and right, and it makes me want to climb into his lap and press my face against the side of his neck. Instead, I sit there, motionless, while he draws circles on the back of my hand with his thumb.

"Last night, I wasn't completely honest with you," Jacob says. "I told myself it would scare you, but the truth is, I was scared. I talk about wanting to be in a relationship, but I haven't given myself to anyone since Maggie. I was afraid of putting myself in a position to get hurt again. But I can't expect you to open up for me if I won't do the same. You deserve to know exactly what you're getting, Izzy.

"I love you. It took me a while to realize it, but ever since we met, I've been desperate for you. Your attention. Your laughter. The things you don't share with anyone else. Everything you give me is a privilege. Sometimes I think I'd be happy just existing for you. It's hard for me to fathom how you doubt yourself. The world is different with you around. It's brighter. More fun. You're magnetic, and I don't know how I functioned before you were in my life. I don't want to know what it's like to function without you again. I want you. All of you. Or whatever pieces you're willing to give me."

When he finishes, Jacob's chest is heaving, and I'm dead. Gone. If he weren't gripping my hands, I'd think I had melted. That I was nothing more than a puddle on this beach.

"I know that's a lot," he says, running his thumb over my hand reassuringly. "I don't expect you to say it back, Iz. I know you're figuring things out. I'm sure this isn't what you imagined for yourself. My life is simple, I know. So if you have doubts, I get it. But all I want is to make you happy. Let me do that for you. Please."

Leaning forward, Jacob rests his forehead against mine. Our noses brush, his familiar scent flooding my senses, and I want to kiss him. To tell him that no one has ever touched me this deeply and that nothing about us is simple. But there's still that reservation in the back of my mind. As good as this all sounds, it doesn't change things, does it? We're still haunted by the same problem.

"You have direction, Jacob," I remind him. "You know what you want." I can't ask him to wait for me while I piece my life together.

He shakes his head. "I don't have everything figured out, remember? I thought I knew what I wanted, but that was before you completely upended things. Neither of us is ever going to have everything figured out. But we can work on it together. I just need you to let me in." He cradles my face as his pleading words wash over me. My heart feels like it's fracturing into a million pieces.

Tears burn in my eyes. "Jake, I—" The rest of my response gets stuck in my throat, but Jacob seems to understand where it was headed. Closing his eyes again, he breathes in deeply. As he breathes out, he opens them. Then he lets go of my jaw.

He stands. He's barely a foot away, but it feels like a mile. When he meets my eyes again, the intensity is gone, replaced by emptiness. My jaw begins to shake, so I clench my teeth. I can't lose it in front of him. Not after I just wrecked us. He offered me everything, and I crushed him. There's no going back from that.

"I love you," he says, except it's colder this time. Sadder. Resigned. "That isn't going to change. So if three days or six weeks or ten months from now you figure that out, you come find me."

He walks away. And I watch him go, feet firmly rooted to the sand, even as everything in me screams that I just made a terrible mistake.

Thirty-Two

Izzy

I'm a blubbering mess.

The walk back to the house is brutal. Sobs racket through my body as I lead Jason down the sidewalk. I'm making a spectacle of myself in public, but I don't care. Not when I just lost the most important person in my life.

Jacob is gone. I have no one but myself to blame. I pushed him away again. And though I had my reasons, the only thing I can think about is the look on his face when I shot him down. He seemed disappointed, but not surprised. Like he was expecting this type of reaction from me, and yet he still put himself out there.

I just need you to stop pushing me away every time you feel uncomfortable. His words flash across my mind. That's what our dynamic has been, isn't it? We get close, then I shove him away. Hurting Jacob has never been my intention, but everything I do seems to cause him pain. He's a victim of my self-destructiveness, bearing the brunt of every bad decision I've made in our relationship.

When I get back to the neighborhood, it feels like I'm under a fog. I walk toward Delia's house, but then I see the black car in the driveway and remember Cynthia and Dominic are still there. I can't go inside with a puffy face and red eyes. But it's not like I want to go back to Tanner's place looking like this.

I'm frozen at the bottom of the driveway. I don't know how long I stand there before the front door opens, and

Cynthia steps out wheeling a pink suitcase. She looks tired. Her hair is in a messy ponytail, and she's wearing the same Kells College sweater she had on yesterday.

Initially, she doesn't see me. But as she drags her suitcase down the porch steps, she looks up, and her eyes meet mine. Frowning, she takes me in. Her expression goes from guarded to concerned.

"Izzy?" she says, worry swirling in her voice. Releasing the handle of her suitcase, she starts toward me. When she's just a few feet away, the pain in my gut deepens. Tightness spreads through my chest, making it hard to breathe. I'm losing her, too. My best friend. Everyone in my life is going to be gone because I can't figure my shit out.

Panic overwhelms me, the weight of my choices crashing down on me at once. I can't let Cynthia leave here, thinking our friendship doesn't matter to me. I won't.

"I'm so sorry, Cynthia," I say, the truth bubbling out of me. "I shouldn't have lied to you about the breakup. Not being honest with you has been killing me. It's no excuse for the horrible way I've treated you, but I only did it because I was afraid of screwing up our friendship."

Nodding, Cynthia wraps me in a hug. Relief courses through me. I hug her back like she's a lifeline. "I'm sorry, too," she says over my shoulder. "Bringing Dominic here was a mistake. Given how weird things have been with us lately, I thought he could be a buffer. I had no idea the two of you weren't on good terms, Izzy. I never would've invited him if I'd known that. Please don't think I did it intentionally to hurt you."

"I don't think that." Even if she had suspected something wrong between me and Dominic, Cynthia wouldn't have asked him here as some sort of cruel test. She isn't like that.

"My plan this weekend was to come clean to you about Dominic. That's why I was so upset last night. Him being here made it impossible to talk to you."

"When you're ready, I want to hear everything," Cynthia says. "I grilled Dominic last night. He admitted that he never asked you for permission to stay here. I might not know what happened between you two, but I promise it won't change our friendship. I made that very clear to Dominic. You're a permanent part of my life, Izzy. I don't want this to come between us."

Sometimes, it's hard to know how much you need to hear something until you actually hear it. "You're a permanent part of my life, too."

Cynthia pulls back to look me in the eye. "Let's go inside," she says. "I'll tell Dominic to get lost for a while, and we can really talk."

So that's what we do. For hours, we sit on the couch, swapping stories from the past year. I tell Cynthia about my work problems and how Dominic never listened. She tells me how nervous she was when we first got together because she's known Dominic her entire life and wasn't sure he'd be a good boyfriend. She wanted to be supportive, so she didn't say anything to me. She would've said something after we split, but Dominic and I seemed fine, and she didn't want to cause unnecessary conflict.

Once we get through the Dominic stuff, Cynthia wants to know about Jacob. I explain he isn't a random guy I met at the bar and that we've had this push and pull going on for a while. She's stunned when I fill her in on what happened at the beach this morning. And while she doesn't seem to understand why I turned Jacob away, she says she's here for me whenever I want to talk.

By the end of the conversation, I feel a lot better about me and Cynthia. It's going to take some time for us to get over a year's worth of secrets and lies, but at least we know where we stand with each other. I wish she could stay for the rest of the weekend, but she has to start driving back to the city. Dominic can't spend the weekend here, and they drove together. But we make a plan for Cynthia to come back over the summer by herself. And I promise to visit her in New York, which I should've been doing all along.

When Cynthia finishes packing her bags, we hug one last time in the driveway. "Call me as soon as you get back," I tell her.

"I will," she assures me. "It was so good to see you, Iz."

"You, too." She lets go and climbs into the driver's seat. Dominic is already in the car, but I haven't made eye contact with him once.

With a wave, Cynthia backs out of the driveway. I watch her car disappear, feeling good for a moment. But then I'm alone, and there's nothing to distract me from the grief of losing Jacob.

I cry all weekend. The sobbing starts again as soon as Cynthia leaves, and it doesn't stop. I make it back to the couch before I collapse, but it feels like my body is shutting down. My limbs are heavy and lifeless, and there's a deep ache in my chest that refuses to go away. Is this what dying feels like? It hurts so much that I honestly wonder.

My sisters text me, wanting to know how I'm doing. Delia offers to come over, and Morgan volunteers to drive to Seaview, but I'm not in the mood for company. I let them know Cynthia is gone, but that we made up and that I need to be by myself for a while. I can't rehash this morning with Jacob again, but I'll tell them everything later.

I fall asleep on the couch, and when I wake up the next day, I barely leave it. I only get up to eat or let Jason outside. By Sunday night, my back is stiff from so much lying down, and I haven't changed clothes in twenty-four hours.

On Monday morning, I cry in the shower. I nearly call off work, but I know that won't help things, so I force myself to get dressed and make coffee. I head to the office with puffy eyes and suds in my hair. I look like the disaster that I feel like, but I can't be bothered to put on a smile and pretend.

I'm usually good at hiding things. But nothing feels right. And I have a feeling it's going to be like this for a while.

I have to keep going until I feel okay again.

***

"Do we have eggs?" Delia asks as she throws open the refrigerator doors.

"I think so," I reply. "Why?"

"I'm in the mood for French toast." After a minute of shuffling through the fridge, Delia pulls out a long cardboard container. She sets it on the counter, then goes to grab a loaf of bread from the pantry. "Do you want some?"

My eyes flicker up from my laptop screen. "No, thanks."

"Are you sure?" she asks as she opens the tall cabinet where we store the mixing bowls. "We have berries and whipped cream." She snatches the strawberry container out of the fridge, holding it out to show me.

I give her a small smile. Delia knows I'm in a funk, and she's been trying to cheer me up all week. Last night, she invited me to eat pizza and watch reruns of her favorite drama series, *Twisted Hearts*. And the night before, she dragged me with her to the nail salon. French toast is just her latest attempt to make me feel better.

Despite her support, I still feel like a sack of garbage. I cried in the shower again this morning. It's starting to feel like part of my morning routine. Face wash. Cry till I feel like puking. Get dressed.

I got myself into a presentable shape for work, but I don't remember most of the day—it's like I was on autopilot. I answered calls, chatted with clients, but I was a shell of myself, empty and hollow.

All I wanted to do when I got home was crawl back into bed. But getting in bed would've meant spending the rest of the night sobbing into my pillow, and I've already shed enough tears to raise the sea level. I need to try to be a functioning human being again.

So instead of going upstairs after work, I took a seat at the kitchen table. I've been on my laptop for a couple of hours, putting together a list of education programs in Massachusetts. I want to compare everything. Enrollment timelines. Pricing. Length of programs. It's a time-consuming task, but it's what I need to take my mind off things.

"You know, I'm gonna burn the shit out of this if you don't help me, right?" Delia says as she sets a frying pan on the stovetop. She isn't exaggerating. Delia's cooking skills leave plenty to be desired. She tried making chicken a few weeks ago, and she set off the fire alarm. It took forever to get the burnt smell out of the house.

Delia is really trying to help me here, and I don't want to leave her hanging, so I push out of my chair. "I guess I'll save the fire department the hassle," I tell her as I head to the sink to wash my hands. Admittedly, French toast sounds good right now.

Delia doesn't even pretend to be offended. She steps away from the stovetop so I can take over, and I quickly get to work. Grabbing a couple of eggs, I crack them in the mixing bowl. Then I added a splash of vanilla and whisk everything together.

Once the egg wash is ready, I turn on the stovetop. I cut a hunk of butter and drop it in the pan to sizzle as I coat slices of bread in the egg wash. When the rich, creamy smell of melted butter fills the kitchen, I drop my first two pieces of French toast in the pan.

Delia, meanwhile, is over at the sink, washing the strawberries in a plastic strainer. "So," she says over the sound of running water. "How's the research going?"

I pause, spatula in hand. "Huh?"

"I saw your screen earlier," she admits. "You were looking at education programs. Have you found one you like yet?" The question takes me by surprise. We haven't talked about my career since the night I crashed in Tanner's guest room.

"I haven't settled on one yet," I say. "But basically, I have two options: get an alternative license or get my master's degree. Right now, I'm leaning toward the first one." Getting an alternative license takes less time than the traditional master's degree. Plus, most of the programs are structured for people who work full time.

"How long does that usually take?"

"A year or two. The programs are flexible, so I could keep working at Ryan & Son while I'm getting my license."

Delia nods. "Well, I think it's a great idea. You've always been good with kids. I'm sure you'll make an amazing teacher." The smile she shoots my way is warm and earnest, and it hits me hard. Delia's opinion means a lot. Switching careers is a big move. As much as I want it, I'm a little intimidated by the idea. Having Delia, the most organized person I know, say she believes in me is just what I needed to hear.

"I'm sorry if you felt like you couldn't talk to me about this," she adds, frowning slightly. "I know how hard it can be, making decisions about your career. I was up for a promotion last year, remember? Turning it down felt strange, but I knew it was the right decision for me. That's what matters most, Iz. Making the choice that's best for you."

God, why did I keep the truth from her for so long? Delia went through a career crisis last spring. She knows what it's like to doubt yourself and the direction you're headed.

"Thank you," I say. "That means a lot." She's making me realize just how much I hurt myself by lying. Delia would've been there for me when I was struggling at the design firm. If I'd opened up to her, then maybe I would've realized sooner that I needed to make a change.

Isolating myself from the people I love has made me feel so alone. I don't want to keep secrets anymore. Which reminds me that there's one thing I didn't bring up the other night that I've been meaning to talk to Delia about.

"Del," I say calmly, "there's something I need to tell you."

She gives me a wary look. "Okay. I'm listening." I can't blame her for her suspicion. With all the bombshells I've dropped lately, she probably has no idea what to expect.

"Do you remember how I stayed at Tanner's house on Christmas Eve after that fight with Mom?" She bobs her head, so I continue. "Well, when I woke up, I overheard you and Tanner in the kitchen. He asked you to move in with him, and you said you couldn't because you were worried about me."

Instantly, Delia's face falls. "You heard that? Oh my god. Izzy, I'm so sorry."

I shake my head. "You don't have anything to apologize for." Delia was talking to her boyfriend in his house. It's not her fault I was eavesdropping. "I should've told you this sooner, Delia, but I don't want you to hold yourself back because of me. Your life is your life, and you should live it. Move in with Tanner if it'll make you happy."

"Well, I *am* sorry, even if you don't want me to say it. But I'm not holding myself back because of you, Izzy. I love you, and I care about what's going on with you."

"I know. But I don't want my problems getting in the way of your happiness."

"They're not," she insists. "*I* said no to Tanner, not you. Looking back, was it unnecessary? Of course. I don't need to live with you to be there for you. Still, that was my decision. You can't hold yourself responsible for it."

"I don't want to cause any problems between you and Tanner." I know how happy he makes her. I'd hate to play a part in any conflict between them.

Delia dismisses my concern. "You haven't. Things are good with us. Really good, actually." Smiling to herself, she lifts her left hand, which has a *ring* on it. "Tanner asked me to marry him."

"What?" Grabbing her hand, I gape at the marquise diamond on her finger. It's beautiful and elegant, which is so Delia. "Holy shit. Tanner picked that out himself?"

Delia laughs. "I know. I couldn't believe it either."

"Did you know this was happening?"

"We've talked about getting engaged, but I had no idea when he was going to propose. You should've seen it, Iz. He texted me asking if I could bring him something while he was working in his woodshop. When I got there, it was all decorated with flowers and candles. It was so romantic."

I'm stunned, but also elated for her. "When did this happen?"

Delia bites her bottom lip. "Sunday night."

"You've been engaged for *five days*, and you didn't tell me?"

"I know. But you've been down lately, and I didn't want to make things worse—"

"Delia, you getting engaged is not going to make me sad." If anything, this engagement is a bright spot. It means I haven't screwed things up for Delia and Tanner. "This is amazing. Congratulations."

Her cheeks turn slightly pink. "Thank you."

"So, are you moving in with Tanner, then?"

She nods. "That's the plan."

"Well, let me know what your timeline looks like," I tell her. "It should only take me a few weeks to find a place." I'll have to start apartment hunting tonight. Hopefully, I'll be able to find something in Seaview that's dog friendly and fits within my price range.

Delia laughs. "What do you mean?" she asks. "You don't have to go anywhere. You're keeping the house, Izzy."

"Seriously?" Our grandma left the place to all three of us when she died, but Morgan and I agreed to let Delia keep it since she did most of the work to fix it up.

"Of course. It's *our* house, remember? Besides, I'm hoping Morgan decides to stay here this summer. It'd be fun having her around, don't you think?"

"Oh my god, Delia. Thank you." I don't know what else to say, so I hug her. Everything feels good for a second, and then the burning smell hits me.

In all the excitement, I forgot about the French toast.

Delia grins. "It looks like I'm not the only one who burns things."

Thirty-Three

Izzy

Offering to plan an engagement party for my Type A sister might be the most impulsive thing I've ever done. And that's coming from a girl who tried piercing her own cartilage when she was seventeen (I actually passed out because of all the blood. Morgan found me on the bathroom floor. Later, Mom made me scrub the tile as punishment).

But I wanted to show Delia just how excited I am for her. She's engaged to the man of her dreams. That deserves to be celebrated. Delia never skimps out on the people in her life— it's time for someone to return the favor. Which is why I found myself volunteering to organize her and Tanner's engagement party. Delia should be wrapped up in engagement bliss, not stressed with party planning.

Of course, I underestimated the amount of work that goes into putting on a party like this.

When I hosted friends back in New York, all I did was buy a few bottles of wine and order pizza. An engagement party? Not so simple. There are guest lists and decorations and catering options, and every decision needs to be run past Delia. She says she trusts me, and that I don't need her permission on every detail, but I'm not leaving anything up to chance.

My sister is going to love this party, dammit.

And Tanner will hopefully have a good time, too.

So far, Delia has been surprisingly laid back about everything. She wants something small and intimate, so we decided on an outdoor brunch in the backyard. Tanner redid the porch last year, and it's gorgeous. With a few tables and floral arrangements, I'm confident I can transform the backyard into a beautiful party venue.

I've tried getting Delia's input on the flowers and color scheme, but she keeps telling me that whatever I pick will be fine. Those are strange words to hear from Delia. My sister color codes her grocery lists. She isn't the type to have no opinion about her engagement party. When Delia told me last night that she didn't care what appetizers we serve, I had to text Tanner to ask if she hit her head recently. If she weren't so obviously happy, I'd be concerned.

One nice thing about planning the party is that it's keeping me busy. I don't have much time to think about Jacob. Or how dull my life feels without him. It's been two weeks since he said "I love you," and we haven't talked since.

While Jacob and I never dated, this feels a lot like a breakup. I keep waiting for that moment when things start to get easier. The morning you wake up and realize you're going to be okay. But it hasn't happened yet.

I'm doing a better job of pulling myself together for work, but I still cry in the shower. My days are slow and lifeless, and it takes everything in me just to get up in the morning. I'm a shell of myself, cold and hollow. And it's worse than I ever could've imagined. I knew losing Jacob would crush me and that it would be a while before I felt good again. But I thought, eventually, I would start to feel less shitty.

I wonder if this is who I am now. Did Jacob alter me as a person? Because it doesn't feel like I can go back to the Old Izzy, the one who stuffed her feelings in boxes and laughed when she felt like sobbing. I'm still figuring out this new version of myself. Trying to understand what my life looks like now that Jacob isn't in it.

With so much change happening at once, it's hard to find consistency. But there's one constant I can always count on.

Mom's doubt.

She called me as soon as she found out that Delia let me take over the engagement party. We hadn't talked since that phone call over Morgan's spring break, but Mom glossed over the weeks of silence like they were nothing.

What's the venue? Have you settled on a caterer yet? When are you sending out invitations? Her questions never stop coming. All day, every day. Mom always has details to hammer out, which means we're in constant communication.

I'll admit, Mom's help isn't all bad. She knows Delia's tastes, so some of her ideas have been useful. But I can't help but think Mom only got involved because she was afraid of me messing things up for Delia. At times, her questioning can feel like an inquisition. It seems like she's waiting for me to screw up so she can swoop in and take over.

"Is Tanner's sister bringing her kids?" she asks during one of our *many* party planning calls. "We should make sure we have something for them to eat."

I try to suppress my sigh as I drop back on the couch. "Mom, it's brunch," I remind her. "The kids will be fine with donuts and waffles."

Mom sucks in through her teeth. "I don't know. Shouldn't we have something substantial for them? We don't want to give them a sugar high. You should get Tanner's sister's number from Delia so you can find out what they like."

"We're gonna have plenty of food." Given Delia's lack of direction, I thought it would be best to serve a little of everything. I'm planning for a full breakfast buffet. "If we get desperate, we can just order a pizza."

"Kids are picky, Izzy. You don't want to leave anything to chance."

My grip on the phone tightens. It's one thing for Mom to voice her opinion, but it's another thing for her to continue arguing with me after I've made a decision. We've been playing the same game since I began working on this party, and it's grating on my nerves.

"Would you be questioning every decision if Morgan was the one planning this?" I ask. I've kept things civil with Mom until now. My sole focus has been making this party amazing for Delia. But everyone has their limits.

She huffs. "It was just a suggestion."

"Really? Because it feels like you're trying to take over. Delia trusts me, Mom. Why can't you?" Why do you think I'm incapable of making a good decision? "I know I was a hot mess as a teenager, but I'm twenty-five. I know how important this is for Delia. I won't screw it up."

"I never said you would," she replies defensively. "I was giving you my opinion."

Mom doesn't realize this is about more than the engagement party—it's about her inability to give me the benefit of the doubt. Ever. How am I supposed to succeed at anything if she always has something negative to say? Everything with us is so tense because I'm constantly waiting for her to cast judgement.

I've tried to raise this issue before, but it's always come from a place of anger. I've accused Mom of being unfair and threatened to cut her off, but I've never said how much it hurts, knowing she doesn't trust me. I don't let her see the way I've internalized her doubt.

I'm trying to be more honest with the people in my life. Shouldn't that include Mom? Our relationship is fractured, and I don't know if the truth will be enough to repair it, but at least I'll be able to say I laid it all out there.

"It hurts, you know," I say, emotion stirring in my chest, "being a disappointment to you. Knowing that every time I tell you something, you're going to find a way to make me doubt myself. Sometimes it's hard to tell if you even like me as a person."

I don't wait for her response. I hang up the phone, feeling like a raw nerve. I've never been that vulnerable with Mom before. Will she be angry or defensive? Saddened or frustrated? I want to give her some time to sit with those words before we talk again. I don't know if what I said is going to make a difference, but at least I can walk away knowing I did everything I could to make our relationship work.

I stay on the couch for a while, staring at the ceiling. At some point, my mind drifts to Jacob. I want to call him. Tell him what happened with Mom. But I can't do that, so instead, I grab my phone and open my camera roll.

I scroll back to the picture I took of him the night I let him play on my *Galactic Rush* profile. I caught him at the perfect moment. He's grinning at me, eyes crinkled behind his glasses. His smile is so warm and open. You can't help but want to keep looking at him.

I meant to send him this photo to use for his dating profile, but every time I went to do it, something held me back. Jacob gave me that smile. It wasn't meant for someone else. Certainly not some woman mindlessly scrolling on a dating app.

My stomach flips. Jacob loves me. And he's going to be at this engagement party. And I have to pretend that every part of me doesn't fiercely love him back.

***

Jacob

Luke peers over the wall separating our cubicles. My fingertips fly across my keyboard as I attempt to ignore him, but he doesn't take the hint. "Hey, man," he says. "We're doing happy hour tonight. You in?"

I glance his way for half a second before my focus goes back to my desktop monitor. "Not tonight. Sorry." I'm being shorter with him than usual, but I don't have the patience for Luke's bullshit right now.

I've had a terrible day. This morning, I woke up to find the contents of my garbage can scattered across the kitchen. Lulu must've gotten into it overnight, a rare act of disobedience for her. After I finished sweeping the floor, I realized I forgot to pick up coffee beans on my way home yesterday, which meant I had nothing to brew. And my drive to work took an extra twenty minutes, thanks to a water main break on Main Street.

I can't decide if a wave of bad luck is hitting me at once or if I'm only noticing these inconveniences because I'm already miserable. A minor thing like a crappy commute wouldn't have fazed me three weeks ago. Now, it has the power to sour my mood. I guess that's what happens when the love of your life stops talking to you. The small stuff feels a lot less tolerable.

The past couple weeks have been hell. I've tried my best to keep up a routine—walking Lulu, visiting my parents, grabbing beers with Tanner—but it hasn't helped. Life seems

361

so small and dull without Izzy. It's like the sun suddenly disappeared, leaving me in darkness. How am I supposed to go on as if that light never existed?

Luke frowns. "You haven't come out with us in forever."

"Been busy, I guess."

"What's the deal? Are you still seeing that girl from the bar?" My mind instantly flashes back to the night, the first time Izzy and I kissed. How good it felt to have her body pressed up against mine. I was so confident in that moment we were finally going in the right direction. I had no idea how much disappointment lay ahead.

Still, I can't say I regret telling Izzy the truth. She needed to hear that stuff, and I needed to say it. I didn't realize how much of myself I had been holding back. Izzy deserved to know everything. If she was going to have doubts about us, it wasn't going to be because she wasn't sure where my feelings were.

I don't want to talk about Izzy with Luke. And I certainly don't want to do it in the middle of the office. So I keep my reply cold and vague. "It's complicated."

Luke gives me a knowing smile. "No doubt. She seemed sort of…" He circles his pointer finger around the side of his head. A pang of sadness echoes through my chest. Izzy would lose her mind if she knew Luke was saying this. She put on quite a performance that night. Too bad I won't be able to tell her.

"If you ask me," Luke says, dropping his voice to a whisper, "you might wanna cut the cord on that one. Get out while you still can."

I might laugh if I weren't so deeply unhappy. Cut the cord? Is he joking?

With Izzy Forrest, that cord is as deep as it can get. And I
don't think it's coming out.

Thirty-Four

"They're so perfect it's actually disgusting," Morgan says, gazing despondently at Delia and Tanner. They stand several yards away from the rest of the party, looking like a couple in a bridal magazine. Tanner whispers something in Delia's ear. She rolls her eyes and shoves him playfully as her cheeks turn bright pink.

We're sitting at a circle table in the backyard. Around us, partygoers mingle, sipping mimosas and checking out the photos of Tanner and Delia that I hung with fairy lights around the porch. I was a little nervous when I decided to have the party outside, but thankfully, the weather has cooperated. It's a warm, sunny day, perfect for an afternoon of celebration. And it better stay that way. I refuse to give Delia anything less than a flawless engagement party. The universe does not want to fuck with me on this.

Morgan takes an aggressive bite out of her French toast. "Bitterness looks weird on you, Morg," I tell her. Unnatural, even. The girl is made of sunshine. When I broke my toe in middle school, the first thing she said to me was at least I wouldn't have to participate in gym class. Morgan always looks on the bright side. Which is why it's so bizarre to see her cynical at our sister's engagement party.

Morgan winces. "I'm sorry," she says, setting down her fork. Sighing, she slumps back in her chair. "You know I'm happy for her. It's just…every time I see couples all perfect and in love, I can't help but think about the fact that I'm not, you know?"

"You'll find that someday," I assure her. Morgan is thoughtful and kind, and she loves romance. There's no one more deserving of a happy ending.

She gives me a weak smile. "What about you?"

"Me?"

"You think you'll find that someday, too?" Curiosity shimmers in her dark brown eyes. I know what she's thinking. I had that. With Jacob. And I totally screwed things up. But I've avoided him so far at this party. There's no way I'm going to tempt the universe by bringing him up.

Across the yard, I spot Mom. She's talking to one of Delia's friends, champagne glass clutched in her hand. Her eyes lock with mine for a moment, and she smiles. *Everything is beautiful,* she mouths, raising her glass as if to salute me for a job well done.

A shot of warmth rushes through my veins. It's been a few weeks since the phone call, and things between us feel a lot more…settled. We had a real, honest talk about our relationship. Mom apologized for the way she had been treating me and promised she would do anything she could to make it right.

So far, she has lived up to that promise. Mom still helped me with the party planning, but she took a backseat, deferring to me instead of trying to override me. She even complimented the pink chrysanthemum bouquets I picked out for the tables.

Our relationship didn't magically change overnight, but Mom is trying. *Really* trying.

That's all I ever wanted. For her to actually listen.

"Everything is amazing, Izzy," Delia gushes as she and Tanner approach our table. She looks beautiful in her white lace dress with spaghetti straps and a long, flowy skirt. She comes up to my chair and pulls me into a hug. "Seriously. I can't thank you enough."

"I'm glad you're having a good time," I say over her shoulder, giving Tanner the death stare.

He shakes his head. "You're still on this?"

"I'm never not going to be on this." Tanner and I ride to work together every morning, and he never mentioned that he was shopping for rings. As he and Delia's biggest supporter, I feel deeply betrayed. "You've made an enemy for life, boss man. I hope you enjoy getting fruitcake for Christmas for the rest of your life."

"Worth it," he says, "since it kept you out of my business for once." I bite my tongue before something snarky can come out of my mouth. It's wrong to fight him at his own engagement party, isn't it?

I turn to Delia. "I'm going to get the dessert before I do something rash like murder your fiancé," I say, rising out of my seat.

She laughs. "Do you need any help?"

"No. You relax. Have fun. I'll be back in just a second." Grabbing my champagne flute off the table, I make my way through the party. I climb the porch steps and enter the house through the back door. Jason runs up to me as soon as I step inside, desperate for attention. He's never been around so many people before. He's wild and energetic, like a kid who just consumed an entire liter of soda.

I pet Jason for a few minutes, then head to the fridge to take out the cake, which I ordered from a bakery in town. Setting the box on the counter, I flip back the lid. The cake looks perfect. It's a white cake with strawberry filling and gorgeous piping around the border. To go with it, I picked up a couple boxes of frozen cream puffs. Delia and I used to devour these things as kids.

I'm sure she'll get a laugh when she sees them.

Scrambling around the kitchen, I start pulling out plates and utensils. As I scour the kitchen drawers, the bathroom door in the hall suddenly pops open. Jacob walks around the corner. Our eyes meet. My heart nearly jumps out of my throat.

"Hey," he says, looking just as startled as I feel.

"Hi," I reply in a quiet voice.

We study each other for a moment, the air between us uneasy. It's the first time we've seen each other since that morning on the beach over a month ago. He texted me to RSVP for the party, but that's been the extent of our contact. I'd hoped to steer clear of him, but I suppose it was only a matter of time before we'd come face to face again, especially with the wedding stuff. Delia already asked me to be her maid of honor, and I'm pretty sure Jacob is going to be Tanner's best man.

He looks good, dressed in a simple blue button-down and slacks. His hair is soft and thick, and it makes me want to run my fingers through it. Wrap my arms around him and breathe in that Jacob smell.

It's been six weeks since I touched him, and I miss him all the time. I'm always going to miss him, I think. Jacob took a piece of me with him, and I'm never getting it back. In a strange way, I like that. The emptiness has made moving on with my life more difficult, but it reminds me we had something worth that pain.

"Delia said you planned everything," Jacob says, motioning about the room.

Nodding, I straighten the edges of the cake box. "Self-inflicted torture is good now and then. It builds character."

He chuckles slightly. "Well, everything looks great. Tanner and Delia seem really happy."

His compliment warms my insides. "Can you believe they're getting married?" My sister is going to have a husband. She's going to be someone's wife. It sounds so grown up. Yet it seems like only yesterday we were teenagers fighting over clothes and shoes and who takes more time in the bathroom.

"I'm glad Tanner finally worked up the nerve to ask her," Jacob replies.

"Hold on. You knew about this?"

"I knew about the ring. Tanner never told me when he was actually going to propose."

I clutch my chest, stunned by his betrayal. "I can't believe this." I shake my head at him like a disappointed parent. "Tanner keeping me in the dark was one thing, but you?"

"I was sworn to secrecy," he argues. "And I knew it would've eaten you alive, not being able to say anything to Delia." He's not wrong. Plus, I had plenty of secrets I was keeping from Delia already. The last thing I needed was another.

"You're officially on my list, Jacob."

His mouth forms a small smile. "What is this list for exactly?"

I match his grin with my own. "Not knowing sucks, doesn't it? I'll let you sit with that feeling. Maybe then you'll understand what it's like being left out of the loop."

Amusement plays across Jacob's face, but he doesn't try to argue with me. This is good. Us being all civil and mature. I'm proud of us.

"Do you need help with anything?" Jacob asks, glancing at the cake box.

"Not yet," I say. "But if you wouldn't mind grabbing the door in a second, that would be great. I just need to get the cream puffs..." The words stop flowing when I realize the cream puffs aren't in the spot where I left them on the counter to defrost.

My eyes scan the kitchen, the cream puff box nowhere in sight. Did I put them somewhere else? I was in a rush this morning, but I swear I stuck them on the counter. I had to put them somewhere high so Jason couldn't get—oh, *fuck*.

Jason, sitting by my feet, looks up at me with his sweet brown eyes. That innocent act might've worked on me once, but I know the deviant that lurks beneath the surface.

"Oh my god." Immediately, I'm charging through the house. Jacob must sense my distress because he follows me.

"Forrest, what—"

"Shit. Shit." The evidence is on the living room floor. Bits of the boxes that once held cream puffs are sprinkled across the carpet.

Disappointment strikes my stomach like a baseball bat. "Unbelievable. I had those on the counter. How did he even get up there? Does he have springboards for paws?"

Dropping to my knees, I frantically begin picking up scraps. Jacob is right there with me. My hands shake, and my heart races. I can't believe this. Everything was going so well. I should've known something like this would happen, shouldn't I?

Jacob puts a hand on my shoulder. "It's okay, Forrest," he says, "you still have the cake."

He's right. I shouldn't be this upset over store-bought cream puffs, especially when there's a beautiful cake sitting in the other room, but I can't help it. I was looking forward to Delia's reaction.

"The cream puffs were supposed to be a surprise for Delia," I say. My voice is tight and watery. I sound like I'm about to cry, which I will not let myself do under any circumstances. I've shed enough tears over the past month to last a lifetime.

Jacob could tell me I'm overreacting. He doesn't know the context here. I'm having a meltdown over a frozen dessert, and he has no idea why. I'd laugh at myself if I were him.

But, of course, he doesn't do that. With understanding in his eyes, Jacob wraps his hand around my other shoulder. "It's no big deal," he says. "I'll run to the store and pick up more, okay? You'll just have to hold off on dessert for a bit."

It's all I need to settle the swirl of emotions in my stomach. Jacob's reassurance. It works like an antidote, making everything better.

I can't find my voice right away, so I nod. The two of us finish cleaning up Jason's mess, then we head back to the kitchen to throw it in the trash can. Both of us wash our hands. Then Jacob grabs the open bottle of champagne resting on the counter and tops off my glass.

"Drink this and relax," he says, handing me the champagne. "The party is amazing. Everything is fine. I'll be back in twenty minutes."

I think my heart is going to explode. "Thank you."

Jacob bobs his head once, then he's gone.

Alone, I take a sip of champagne, and then stick the cake back in the fridge. My limbs feel strange, fuzzy. It's like I exited my body for a moment, and I'm adjusting to being back in it. There's so much emotion streaming through me right now. I don't know how to process it.

How does Jacob do that? He always knows what to do when something's wrong, and then he just takes care of it. Without being asked, he's off making things better. It's who he is. The kind of person who wants to make life easier on you. Who wants you to know that he cares. That's how he shows his love. It isn't bold or flashy, but it's warm and reliable and constant. I see it everywhere, every day.

There's no one like him. If I went to Jacob tomorrow and said I wanted to become a circus clown, he wouldn't doubt me. He'd find me a list of juggling classes and then offer words of encouragement while everyone else tried to talk me out of it. That's because he sees my happiness as an objective, not a consequence.

And I'd be a total dipshit to let him slip away.

What am I doing? What is wrong with me? I've been pushing away this wonderful human being who loves me when I should be gripping onto him for dear life.

"Fuck. Fuck. Fuck." I need to talk to him. And I'm not waiting till he gets back from the store. Slamming the refrigerator shut, I bolt through the house and then out the front door. My pulse hammers as I scramble down the porch steps.

"Jake!" I exclaim. He freezes at the end of the driveway, brow furrowed, and though he clearly isn't going anywhere, I keep running, anyway. In seconds, I close the distance between us, and then I launch myself at him. There's nothing graceful about it. Just me throwing my entire body weight at him, knowing that he'll catch me.

Breathing heavily, I wrap my arms around his shoulders and legs around his waist. I bury my face against the side of his neck, inhaling the fresh laundry scent that I've missed so much. Every cell in my body is shaking. "I'm sorry," I say, my tone urgent. Irrational as it may seem, there's a part of me that feels like I might combust if I don't tell him how much I regret turning him away right now. "I'm *so* sorry, Jake."

I cling to him like a sloth to a tree. As I tighten my legs around his waist, I decide that I'm not moving. Ever. He's going to have to maneuver with me locked around his body forever. Simple as that.

Jacob's arms curve around my lower back. "Izzy." There's more he wants to say, but I interrupt him. I'm not done apologizing yet.

"I made such a mess of things," I say. "I didn't lie to you that day on the beach, but I wasn't telling the truth, either. I was scared. For the longest time, I felt like nothing more than an idea to people. Like some sort of party trick."

"You're not an idea to me, Izzy. You're the realest thing in my life."

"I know. That's why the thought of being with you terrified me so much. Because you actually see me. Not just the fun parts. The hard ones, too. No one knows me like that, Jacob. I've never opened up to someone like this. I was terrified of screwing things up and making you hate me. The one person who knows all of me."

I spent so much time denying this. Pretending not to feel what was happening. It seemed easier to ignore and deflect than to come face to face with the unnerving truth. I'd already given so much of myself to Jacob. If I gave him more, and one day he changed his mind about us, it would absolutely crush me.

"But that's the thing," I say, pressing my nose to his collar. His shirt is wet, so I'm pretty sure I'm crying, but Jacob doesn't seem to care about me getting snot on him. "I'm going to mess up again. I'm never going to have all of my shit together. But I want this. I want you. Letting you in still scares me, but what's worse is acting like this never happened. I don't want a life without you. Without us."

Needing to look at him, I pull away from his neck. Taking the sides of his jaw in my hands, I observe his handsome features. Jacob looks stunned. A sinking feeling fills the pit of my stomach when I think about all the unnecessary hurt I've caused him. So I kiss him. His cheeks. His chin. The corner of his mouth. I press tiny kisses all over his face, desperate to get my lips everywhere, hoping I'm not too late.

"Please tell me you haven't given up on us," I say, looking him square in the eye. "I love you. I love you so much. If you need time, space, whatever to process this, that's fine. As long as you haven't given—"

Jacob steals my words with a kiss. It's short and chaste, but I feel it all the way in my toes. "I told you I'd wait for you, Forrest," he says, dropping his forehead against mine. We stay like that for a moment, eyes locked as we breathe each other in. He's smiling at me. That smile. The one I claimed for myself. I never want him to stop looking at me like that.

Except I also really, really need to kiss him again.

"No more waiting," I tell him before stamping my mouth over his. And there's nothing short or chaste about it this time. Jacob's tongue tangles with mine instantly. Tightening his grip on my waist, he walks us forward until my back hits something hard and solid. I'm pretty sure we're defiling the side of someone's car, and I couldn't care less.

Jacob's lips drop to my neck, teasing me with hot, open-mouthed kisses. "Say it again," he whispers against the base of my throat.

I twist my fingers in his hair. "I love you."

"Again."

"I love you."

"Fuck, Izzy," he rasps. "I love you. You have no idea how much I love you. Whatever you need, okay? Let me give it to you." Desire rushes through my body. I run my hands over Jacob's chest and shoulders, needing to feel him everywhere.

"I need you," I tell him, and suddenly we're scrambling inside. Jacob carries me through the door and up the stairs. When we get to my room, he sets me on the edge of the bed, then locks the door behind us before pouncing on me.

Our hands and mouths move urgently, tugging at clothes and nipping each other's skin. I get lightheaded at the feel of his hard body pressing me down into the mattress.

Nothing has ever felt more right than this. I thought it would scare me, but there's no reason to be afraid. It's *Jacob*. There is nothing in this universe more solid than him.

I abruptly break the kiss. "Jake."

He looks at me, out of breath. "Yeah?"

"Nothing about us is simple."

He knows what I'm saying without me having to explain it. And after a moment, he nods, then kisses the bridge of my knuckles. "No, it isn't."

Epilogue

Jacob
Eight months later
"You're trying to give me a heart attack, aren't you?"

It's seventeen degrees tonight. The wind is vicious and bone-chilling. And Izzy Forrest is standing outside in a sleeveless red dress that cuts off at her mid-thigh.

She's beautiful. Curly hair spilling down her shoulders. Soft skin on display. She's every fantasy I've ever had come to life. But she's also terribly underdressed for the dead of winter. I'm torn between wanting to tear off her clothes and wanting to put more layers on her.

Izzy smiles at me. "Don't be such a baby, Jacob," she says as she leans back against the porch rail. "It's not even that cold."

"Your purple lips beg to differ, Forrest."

Closing the door behind me, I step onto Seaview Tavern's back porch, which is basically an ice skating rink. It doesn't seem like anyone bothered to salt out here. Probably because they assumed everyone would be inside. Most people would rather count down the new year in a warm, festive bar, not outside on a frigid night. Izzy isn't most people.

When I reach her side, her arms are covered in goosebumps. She's wearing a proud look, as if the temperature doesn't affect her, but I don't buy it. Immediately, I take off my coat and drape it over her shoulders, rubbing my palms up and down Izzy's arms in a desperate attempt to create friction.

"What are you doing?" she asks, amused.

"Trying to prevent you from getting frostbite," I mutter. She gives me a funny grin, her eyes all soft and hazy. I have no idea what's happening inside her head. "What?"

"Nothing," she says, biting her bottom lip. "You're cute."

I roll my eyes, then stop rubbing her arms. "I can't believe you actually came out here," I say, even though I should've expected it. Izzy told me she wanted to be on the porch at midnight. I thought she was joking. But five minutes before midnight, she vanished from our table. When I went to text her, there was a message already waiting for me. *Come outside or I'll kiss a stranger at midnight.*

"You came out here, too," she points out.

"I had to. I couldn't let you kiss some random guy at midnight."

"That's too bad. The bearded guy at the bar has been giving me eyes all night." Groaning, I haul her up against me so *I* can kiss her, and she laughs against my mouth. I tangle my fingers in the back of her hair, and her arms wrap around my neck.

"You're evil," I say, kissing her a second time.

She places her palms on my chest. "I had to get you out here somehow."

"And why's that?" I love being alone with Izzy, but our chances of getting hypothermia are much lower inside with our friends.

She shrugs. "We started the year here, Jacob. It seems right to end it here, too."

I twirl a strand of her hair around my finger. "It *was* a pretty great year, wasn't it?"

"It was."

It's hard to believe we've been together for eight months. In some ways, our relationship feels brand new. My heartbeat *still* quickens when Izzy laughs at something I say, and I never get tired of being around her. At the same time, it's strange to think about what my life looked like before our relationship.

We integrated our lives so quickly. Izzy sleeps at my place three nights a week, and I'm at hers another three. We alternate on Sundays, and the decision is usually based on whether Izzy plans to wash her hair. She says my shower is better than hers.

Our routine is pretty domestic. Most nights, we make dinner at home. We walk the dogs and play *Galactic Rush* or watch TV. Izzy has in-person classes for her teaching program on Tuesdays and Thursdays. On those nights, we order takeout and eat on the couch, Izzy's legs sprawled across my lap. She has a habit of falling asleep on me and then waking me up in the middle of the night with her mouth and hands.

I find pieces of her everywhere. Tubes of red lipstick scattered across my bathroom counter. Floral perfume on my sheets and pillows. Sketchbooks in my car and a wild dog that now lives with me part time. Evidence of our blended life.

I love it. I spent so much time fantasizing about this, but nothing could've prepared me for the privilege of being with Izzy. I can't believe I almost let her slip away. Just thinking about it makes me want to kick myself. I won't make that mistake again. I know how lucky I am to live this life, and I'm never going to let myself forget it.

Izzy pokes my side. "If you're done lecturing me," she says, "then we can start celebrating." Breaking away from me, she turns and grabs a chocolate cupcake and a lighter off the railing. She lights the blue striped candle, then holds the cupcake out to me. Candlelight flickers over her face. "Happy birthday."

My lips twitch in amusement. "You gonna sing for me, Forrest?"

"I would give you my rendition of *Happy Birthday, Mr. President,* but you've had a lot to say about my impressions in the past," Izzy says. "Now, make a wish. And if you say something like 'oh, everything I've ever wanted is standing right in front of me,' I *will* smash this in your face."

"You know, I've never been threatened on my birthday before."

"I can wait here all day, Jacob. My legs are only getting more numb."

While I'd rather not have cake smashed in my face, I can't think of anything to wish for. I wake up every morning with *this* woman pressed against my side. My life has never been better. What more could I possibly want?

After a moment, I wish for more of this, of us, and then I blow out the candle. Izzy immediately pulls it out of the cupcake, licking the chocolate frosting off the end. Her sweet tooth is insatiable. She's always craving chocolate when we go somewhere. I've started keeping a candy stash in my car.

Watching Izzy, I can't help but smile. She looks so perfect like this, carefree and relaxed. She's completely altered my brain chemistry. It's amazing how much happiness a little smile from her can bring me.

"What?" she says, sucking frosting off her thumb.

I wrap my arm around her waist, tugging her against me. "You're cute."

She offers me the cupcake, and I take a bite from the top, getting frosting all over my upper lip. Izzy is there to kiss it off. We break apart after several seconds, her chin resting on my chest. It would be the perfect moment…if Izzy weren't dressed for summer.

"Forrest?"

"Hmm."

"I'm still thinking about your legs. Can we go inside?"

She pulls back, her eyes meeting mine. "You have to open your present first." Sliding her hand over mine, she places a folded sheet of paper in my palm. Surprise washes over me. I try to read her face for hints, but Izzy's expression is painfully neutral.

Curious, I unfold the paper. It's a screenshot of a set of dog bowls from the website where Izzy buys Jason's food. "These look great, Forrest," I say. "Thank you." It's a random gift from Izzy, who usually buys presents based on inside jokes. For Christmas, she got me a gift certificate to Off the Vine and a tie with model trains on it. I replay our recent conversations in my head, but I can't remember anything involving dog bowls.

Izzy seems to pick up on my confusion. "It's more of a gift for Lulu," she explains. "I figured I owed her since she's getting a demon for a roommate. I was thinking this weekend we could move the rest of my stuff to your place."

"You want to move in?" I can't fight the smile growing across my face.

She nods. "Yeah. I mean, as long as you're good with it."

What a ridiculous question. "Forrest, I'm more than good with it." I told her months ago that she could set the pace. The ideas I once had about meeting a specific timeline for marriage and kids don't mean anything to me anymore.

There's no doubt in my mind that Izzy is the woman I'm going to be with for the rest of my life. We want the same things, and we'll get there eventually. I want her to feel comfortable with every step.

"Are you sure?" she asks. "Because you know I never remember to put the cap back on the toothpaste, and I listen to music very loudly when I'm cooking." There's vulnerability in her voice, despite her playful words.

"I've never been more sure of anything," I assure her, threading my fingers through hers. If only she could feel the elation threatening to burst through my chest right now. Izzy and I. Living together. Nothing sounds better.

This is the love I always wanted. Messy. Joyful. Real. It makes every bad date worth it.

"I love you," Izzy says.

"I love you, too," I say.

As our lips meet, the party inside lets out a collective cheer.

It must be midnight.

But out here, time doesn't seem to exist.

***

Izzy

Ten years later

"You're moving too much. Both of you."

The leaf pile rustles, and Emmy pops out from beneath it. "It's not *my* fault, Mommy," she says in frustration. "Blake keeps bumping me."

Her little brother pokes his head out, dark orange leaves clinging to his messy curls. The two of them are practically on top of each other. The leaf pile is small, even for two tiny children. When I came up with this idea, I thought we'd have a lot more leaves in the backyard to work with. Jacob

380

must've raked when he got home last night. Annoying, thoughtful husband. Didn't he realize I wanted to use those leaves to help our children scare the shit out of him?

"It's gonna be a tight fit, Em," I say. "We don't have a ton of leaves." I'm already second-guessing whether this can work. Emmy's legs are sticking out. She's tall for her age. Blake is, too. Jacob's genes clearly won the height battle.

Unfortunately, there's not enough time for me to scrounge up more leaves from the front yard. Jacob is going to be home any minute, so the kids need to be ready. "Do you remember the code word?" I ask.

"Grapefruit," Emmy replies. Blake is only three, so I doubt he's going to remember it, but he can follow her lead.

I clap my hands. "Perfect. So, as soon as I say grapefruit, both of you jump up and scream. Got it?"

Blake nods, looking thrilled. Emmy seems less certain. "Mommy, can we do that?" she asks. My girl is a rule follower. She started kindergarten in August. During conferences last week, Emmy's teacher told me and Jacob that she's never had a student as polite and disciplined as Emmy. How I managed to produce a child who gets compliments from her teacher instead of criticism is beyond me.

I have a feeling Blake will take after me. As a baby, he snuck out of his crib all the time. Recently, he picked up the habit of drawing on the kitchen table with markers. Blake has that troublemaking gleam in his eye, but he's also adorable, with his wide blue eyes and chubby ankles. It's hard to be mad at him.

"I'm positive," I assure Emmy. "We're doing this with Daddy because he'll think it's funny. We wouldn't do this with someone else because that would be mean."

We play a lot of games in our house. I'm constantly encouraging the kids to get creative. I never want them to feel stifled. Childhood is about having fun and believing in magic and learning who you are. Emmy and Blake deserve to soak up every second of it.

"Okay," Emmy says. She still looks nervous, but she's excited, too. It might seem strange that I'm encouraging my obedient child to do something mischievous, but I want her to understand that not everything is so black and white. It's good to break the rules sometimes. I always stress the difference between playing games and being cruel.

"Both of you lie back down," I say, grabbing a handful of leaves so I can cover them up again. "Try to be as still as possible. This won't work if Daddy sees—"

"Forrest, are you burying the children?" Jacob shouts from the back porch.

I'm caught, red-handed. *Dammit.* How did I not hear him? I blame Jason and Lulu. They're both old and lazy. They barely bark at anything nowadays, content with napping by the front door.

Instead of admitting defeat, I toss the leaves on top of the pile. "I don't know what you're talking about," I say, turning to face him as he comes down the porch steps. He's smirking at me, the obnoxious prick. He doesn't know exactly what I had planned, but it's obvious he interrupted something, and he's delighted by it. "I'm just doing some yardwork."

Jacob raises his brows. "You talk to all your leaf piles?"

"Only the ones that can't follow instructions." The leaves are shaking again. Emmy and Blake are cracking up. It's impossible not to hear their high-pitched laughter. Jacob glances briefly at the leaf pile before returning his attention to me.

"So, where are the children?" he asks.

"I don't remember having any children."

"Brown hair. Small. Loud mouths."

"Not ringing any bells, I'm afraid."

Blake shoots up, screeching at the top of his lungs. He charges at Jacob, wrapping himself around his dad's leg. Seconds later, Emmy emerges from the leaves, looking annoyed at her brother. "Mommy didn't say the code word!" she exclaims.

Amusement flashes in Jacob's eyes. "Code word? Are you trying to turn the children against me, Forrest?"

"What happens when you're not home is none of your concern," I tell him.

Blake makes grabby hands at Jacob, who lifts him into his arms. "Come here, Em," he tells our daughter. She brushes the leaves off her jeans and scrambles to give her dad a hug. Seeing the three of them together warms my insides like a space heater.

Jacob is so good at this. He's a natural caretaker, so, of course, he took to parenting right away. It was different for me. The first few weeks after I had Emmy were overwhelming. They brought back a lot of my old insecurities. Could I really do this? Be responsible for a tiny, helpless human? But Jacob was there, constant and supportive. He reminded me that we were in it together. That we would figure things out as we go.

His reassurance gave me confidence. When Blake was born, there weren't any doubts in my mind. I *knew* we could handle it.

Emmy and Blake stare at Jacob with pure adoration in their eyes. There's something about the way he is with them—patient, protective, and confident—that I find so attractive. I love knowing he's mine. Knowing *this* is mine. We've created a beautiful little life together. How lucky am I to experience it all with my best friend?

My life isn't perfect. I mess up all the time. On Monday, I was late dropping Emmy off at dance class. Yesterday, I spilled coffee all over the inside of my car. Blake's birthday party is this weekend, and I haven't ordered a cake yet. There's a miles-long to-do list sitting on the kitchen counter that has gone virtually untouched for days.

I still screw things up. The difference is, I give myself the freedom to do it. Shit is going to hit the fan every now and then, but that doesn't make me a bad wife or mom. There's always a way to fix it. Plus, Jacob is there to catch me when I need him.

After a moment, Jacob sets Blake back on his feet. "Daddy, watch me go down the slide!" he shouts before taking off toward the playset in the back of the yard.

Emmy trails after him, shouting for Blake to slow down.

"Are we sure she isn't a thirty-year-old woman?" I ask, glancing at Jacob. "This could be a *Freaky Friday* situation. Maybe she switched bodies with one of the nurses at the hospital."

Chuckling, Jacob wraps his arm around my waist. "She could just have really good parents," he says, pulling my body against his. I brace my palms on his chest, feeling the warmth beneath his shirt.

"She reminded *me* to put on a jacket before we left this morning, Jake. What's next? Is she going to ask for a 401k for Christmas?"

"Is that why you were burying her under a pile of leaves?"

"I want her to have fun," I say, shrugging. Emmy is so different from me as a kid. I love how sweet and responsible she is, but I don't want her to miss out on any important childhood experiences. Mischief is a part of growing up, isn't it?

"I don't think you have to worry about that," Jacob replies, nudging me toward the playset. Sure enough, Emmy is coming down the slide with Blake, a big smile on her face.

Jacob brushes his lips over my temple. "Your protective side is hot, though," he whispers before planting a quick kiss on the corner of my mouth. I turn so I can meet him fully, running my hands down the sleeves of his crisp white button-down.

"How was your day?" he asks.

"Well, a kindergartener sneezed in my face this morning, so I'm pretty sure I'll have the flu by the weekend." Working in an elementary school for the past eight years has given me a fairly strong immune system, but I still get sick once or twice every year. "Luckily, I can use you as my personal butler."

"You can use me however you like, Forrest," Jacob says. "I can ask my parents to take Em and Blake for the weekend if you're worried about getting sick."

I shake my head. "I already talked to my mom. She said we can drop them off any time." Mom moved to Seaview a few years back. She was lonely in Boston, so she sold her house and bought a condo a few blocks away. Having her here has been great for Blake and Emmy. The kids love spending time with her. Probably because she plies them with candy every time she sees them.

Having Mom here has been great for me, too. Our relationship has changed a lot over the years. It took time, but things have gotten better with us. We don't see eye-to-eye on everything, but Mom doesn't force her opinions on me anymore. She lets me make decisions for myself. The weight of her judgment is off my shoulders, and it feels incredibly freeing.

I twist Jacob's tie around my fist. "So, how was *your* day?" I ask.

He grins, then tucks a strand of hair behind my ear. "Good now."

My heart flips. We've been married for seven years, and Jacob is still so thoughtful. Every day, he finds different ways to show me how much he loves me. Scraping the frost off my car windshield in the morning. Bringing me chocolates when I have cramps. Planning monthly nights out for us so we get time away from the kids. Jacob's love is fierce and consistent. Being with him fills me with so much happiness.

"I can get started on dinner if you want to stay with them," I tell him.

Jacob laces his fingers through mine. "Let's order pizza tonight," he says as he drags us toward the playset. "It's a nice day. We should eat on the porch." It's a great idea. Maybe the best he's ever had. I could kiss him for it.

So I do.

Thank you

Thank you so much for reading *Blue Waters*!

Want more of Jacob and Izzy? Sign up for my newsletter to receive a bonus scene. https://dl.bookfunnel.com/342pn5o6kt

The Seaview Series will conclude with Morgan's story.

Have you read *High Tide*? Check out Delia and Tanner's story to see where it all began.

Discussion Questions

1. Izzy conceals her feelings because she believes that's what is expected of her. Have you ever felt pressured to act a certain way because of other people's expectations?
2. Self-doubt is a major theme throughout the story. What are some things that help you feel confident?
3. It takes a while for Jacob to realize how his breakup with Maggie affected the way he approaches relationships. How do our past experiences shape our decision-making?
4. On the surface, Izzy and Jacob seem like opposites. What qualities do you think are most important for people to share in relationships?
5. Izzy wonders if it's too late for her to make a career change. What societal pressures do we put on people to have everything figured out at a young age?

About the Author

Paige Marie is an Ohio-based author who has been writing stories since she was nine years old. She loves romance novels, white wine, and long walks outdoors. You can find her on Instagram @paigebwrites and TikTok @paigemariewrites.

Content warning

This book contains sexual content and alcohol use. The epilogue features children.

www.ingramcontent.com/pod-product-compliance
Lightning Source LLC
Chambersburg PA
CBHW071739110726
47908CB00006B/1637